3 9082 13971 7768

P9-CCU-522

5/31/16

THE
VALLEY
OF THE
DRY
BONES

AUBURN HILLS PUBLIC LIBRARY 50
3400 EAST SEYBURN DRIVE
AUBURN HILLS, MI 48326
(248) 370-9466

A NOVEL

THE VALLEY OF THE DRY BONES

JERRY B. JENKINS

AUBURN HILLS PUBLIC LIBRARY 50
3400 EAST SEYBURN DRIVE
AUBURN HILLS, MI 48326
(248) 370-9466

WORTHYS

Copyright © 2016 by Jerry B. Jenkins

Published by Worthy Books, an imprint of Worthy Publishing Group, a division of Worthy Media, Inc., One Franklin Park, 6100 Tower Circle, Suite 210, Franklin, TN 37067.

WORTHY is a registered trademark of Worthy Media, Inc.

HELPING PEOPLE EXPERIENCE THE HEART OF GOD

eBook available wherever digital books are sold.

Library of Congress Cataloging-in-Publication Data

Names: Jenkins, Jerry B., author.
Title: The valley of the dry bones : a novel / Jerry B. Jenkins.
Description: Franklin, TN : Worthy Publishing, [2016]
Identifiers: LCCN 2016011300 | ISBN 9781617950087 (softcover)
Subjects: LCSH: Droughts--California--Fiction. | Culture conflict--Fiction. |
  End of the world--Fiction. | GSAFD: Christian fiction.
Classification: LCC PS3560.E485 V35 2016 | DDC 813/.54--dc23 LC
record available at http://lccn.loc.gov/2016011300

All rights reserved. No portion of this book may be reproduced, stored in a retrieval system, or transmitted in any form or by any means—electronic, mechanical, photocopy, recording, scanning, or other—except for brief quotations in critical reviews or articles, without the prior written permission of the publisher.

For foreign and subsidiary rights, contact rights@worthypublishing.com

ISBN: 978-1-61795-008-7

Cover Design: Jeff Miller | Faceout
Cover Images: Shutterstock.com

Printed in the United States of America
16 17 18 19 20 LBM 8 7 6 5 4 3 2 1

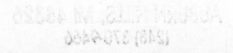

To Ray Bentley.

I thank my God upon every remembrance of you.

PART 1

REQUIEM

PROLOGUE
SEVEN YEARS INTO THE DROUGHT

Torrance, California

KATASHI AKI BACKED the beastly sanitation truck through the same gate of the same parking lot of the same building of the same industrial park he and his partner had served for more than three years. But he was running half an hour late because Raoul was taking a sick day and couldn't leap out to guide him to the bins or shoo away the kids who even now were scrambling over the chain-link fence to climb the truck.

Though he was on flat ground, Katashi set the emergency brake and took the keys when he went back to check his angle and distance. Half a dozen children, all clearly under ten, had formed a half circle behind the truck, eyes dancing.

"Keep your distance!" he barked, and noticing that a few looked like him, he repeated it in Japanese. They giggled. Who knew if they understood their native tongue, and if they did, which dialect?

"I have to come back another couple feet, so stay away," he said as the building's rear exit swung open and employees headed for their cars. He was in the way and had to hurry.

As soon as Katashi was again behind the wheel, he heard kids atop his truck. He started the engine, lowered his window, reached out, and banged on the door. "C'mon!" he bellowed, throwing the gearshift into Reverse to trigger the high-pitched beep. "Get off of there now!" Watching both mirrors as the kids leapt down, he gently pressed the accelerator, then remembered the emergency brake.

When he released it and the sixty-thousand-pound behemoth began to roll, Katashi immediately felt the dual tires on the opposite rear roll over something. He jumped on the brake pedal with both feet and slammed the shift into Park.

Screams, honks, bangs on the truck.

"Call nine-one-one!"

Strength drained from Katashi's body. He managed to open the door but his knee buckled on the step and he slid to the asphalt in a heap. *Tell me it was a ball, a rock, anything!*

He forced himself to peer beneath the massive chassis where a tiny American boy lay on his back directly in front of the right rear duallys, his feet under the truck. The tires had caught him at his midsection.

Katashi dragged himself underneath and out the other side where a tall, slender woman of about fifty knelt cupping the boy's face, his dark eyes wide. A crowd pressed behind her, most on their phones.

She cooed, "I'm Elaine and I used to be a nurse. What's your name and how old are you?"

"Junior," the boy whined. "I'm seven. Am I gonna die?"

"Do you mind if I touch you, Junior?"

He shook his head, grimacing.

Katashi struggled to his feet and squatted next to her as she gently laid her hand on the boy's shirt at the waist. It was clear the truck had flattened him from below his rib cage to the tops of his thighs.

Katashi drew in a quavery breath and buried his head in his hands. Elaine put a hand on his shoulder and spoke quickly. "Nobody's blaming you, sir. Let's deal with him for now. Can you do that?"

Katashi wasn't sure, but he nodded.

Elaine turned back to the boy. "Are you in pain, Junior?"

He shook his head again. "Just thirsty."

Elaine turned to the crowd. "Anybody have any water?"

"You kiddin'?" a man said.

"When was the last time you saw a bottle of water?" another said.

"Come on," she said. "Just a swallow for the boy."

"It'd be wasted on him anyway," a woman whispered.

"Maybe the EMTs'll have a little."

Katashi would have given Junior his last drop, but he couldn't remember the last time he'd carried a bottle.

"Everything's broke in there, isn't it?" the boy said.

Elaine nodded. "I'm sorry."

"So I am gonna die."

"I'm afraid so, son," she said. "Do you know you can go to heaven and be with God?"

"Um-hm."

"You do?"

"Yeah. Because of Jesus." His breathing had become shallow. "But I'm scared. And my mom and dad are gonna be mad, 'cause I'm not s'pose to climb the truck."

"It's okay to be scared, Junior. But it won't be for long. And let me tell you something. Mom and Dad aren't going to be mad. They'll just be sad because they'll miss you. I'm a mom, so I know. Okay?"

"Okay."

His face was ashen now. Elaine pressed her fingers against his neck and glanced at Katashi. "What's your real name, Junior? You're named after your dad, right?"

He nodded, eyelids fluttering. "Zeke," he said, sighing. "Ezeki—"

"Can you tell me your last name? We need to get hold of your—"

But he was gone.

FOUR YEARS LATER

AFTER A DEVASTATING SERIES of cataclysmic earthquakes that leveled the whole of Southern California, the president of the United States announced that with no end to the drought in sight, "Environmentalists have concluded that recovery is beyond the point of no return. My beloved home state, once one of the most beautiful and vibrant destinations on earth, now lies fallow, a cavernous wasteland bearing witness to eleven years of exposure to a pitiless sphere of roiling plasma ninety-three million miles away.

"More than two hundred twenty times the diameter of our planet, the sun could swallow more than one point three million earths. We learned as schoolchildren that it accounts for ninety-nine percent of the mass of our entire solar system. Astronomers tell me that because of its nearness, it is an astounding thirteen billion times brighter than the second brightest star in our galaxy. We depend on its power for our very existence, yet unabated by the normal balance of nature, see what it has wrought.

"It has become my sad duty to inform you that your federal government has finally, officially, been forced to declare the entire state of California a disaster area. Due to the impossibility of rebuilding her great cities on unstable ground under the unrelenting onslaught of the sun, we have sadly deemed it, 'Uninhabitable, irreparable, and verboten to citizens.'"

He said the wildfires—many ablaze for years—would be fought only if they posed a threat to bordering states.

"From this day forward, we will maintain only a military presence in California to ensure that no one within its borders on other than official government business will be entitled to the benefits, privileges, or protection of the United States. American civilians, remain or enter at your own risk. Foreign encroachers shall be considered enemies of this republic and treated as such."

The eleven Pacific Ocean ports on the California coast had also been destroyed, resulting in the exodus of tens of thousands of personnel to Oregon and Washington, and the obliteration of the international airports in Los Angeles, San Francisco, and San Diego alone had changed the economic landscape of the entire airline industry. What little remained of the infrastructure of interstate highways lay in rubble, and routes that once led into the great state now ended at the border.

From the air, California looked like a vast abandoned sand box. What hadn't been flattened and strewn by seismic activity and wildfire was either still ablaze or lay baking in the sun.

The president also announced the establishment of California memorials and museums in Oregon, Nevada, Arizona, and the Mexican state of Baja, California, where treasured antiques and artifacts had already been moved.

SIX YEARS LATER

THE DROUGHT UNABATED, a new president, Derrick Scott, has inherited an entire West Coast in chaos. Class-action suits flood federal courts demanding that remains from cemeteries be moved out of California. The Bureau of Indian Affairs is overwhelmed with the demands of more than 115 Native American tribes, with most but not all relocating. Bordering states are trying to cope with nearly forty million former California residents.

But the otherwise abandoned California republic was sparsely dotted with fewer than four hundred thousand squatters, approximately 1 percent of the original population who chose to remain . . .

THE TORRANCE HOLDOUTS

Katashi Aki, 43

Rev. Robert Gill, 64

Genevieve (Jennie) Gill, 62

Raoul Gutierrez, 39

Benita Gutierrez, 36

Elaine Meeks, 60

Danley Muscadin, 24

Cristelle Muscadin, 25

Mahir Sy, 38

Ezekiel Thorppe Sr., 41

Alexis Thorppe, 40

Alexandra (Sasha) Thorppe, 13

Dr. Adam Xavier, 36

Gabrielle Xavier, 38

Caleb Xavier, 10

Kayla Xavier, 8

THE VOICE

1

THE RAGGEDY BAND had shrunk to sixteen. Late on Sunday mornings they would break into clusters of no more than six or no fewer than three and ride separately eight miles west from their underground desert compound. Today they left three dirt bikes, a four-door pickup, a Jeep, and an SUV a quarter to a half mile from each other and walked the rest of the way to the basement of what had once been a tattoo parlor just off what had once been Ocean Boulevard, the main drag of Long Beach, California, south of Los Angeles. It had become, for an hour each week, their makeshift church.

Worshiping at their own complex would have been safer, of course. But Zeke Thorppe liked the idea of a separate sanctuary, just the prescription for cabin fever.

As always, just before the pastor and his wife arrived, Zeke peeled two inches of tar paper from an east-facing window, allowing a beam of sunlight to pierce the room. It would have to do. Though nearby LA had actually become the last capital after Sacramento had been lost to an 8.9 quake and forest fires eight years before, the power grid—like the state—was but a memory now.

All the group needed was enough light to make out the passages in the Bibles Zeke's wife of twenty years had scavenged from their abandoned

Torrance church. Their daughter, who had just turned thirteen, was handing them to the others as they arrived.

No one spoke above a whisper, and even their singing would rise to little more than humming. Young Sasha Thorppe would sound a plaintive note on an ancient chromatic pitch pipe, and the others would join her softly in a quiet worship song or an old hymn or two.

This morning, on the tenth anniversary of the ghastly tragedy that united roughly half their number, Zeke's wife had a macabre chore. As he set out the dusty metal folding chairs, he kept an eye on Alexis and noticed his daughter Sasha doing the same. How sad that a young teen had to grow up so fast.

Not wanting Alexis to see how concerned he was about her, he settled in his usual spot facing the door, trying to look nonchalant with his Glock 21 .45 automatic tucked under his shirt in a holster at the small of his back. He still found it hard, a trained hydrologist, packing anything but an iPad. But it had been how many years?

He stretched his long legs and crossed his boots at the ankles, mentally taking the roll as the rest arrived. How he had become the de facto leader he still wasn't sure. Being the one who knew the science behind the drought had somehow morphed into a sort of assumption of authority.

Zeke didn't really have to watch the door. Knowing who was there and who wasn't was intuitive. His attention was on Alexis, as it had been for two decades. He had never tired of looking at her. That she was only forty and looked perhaps fifty had not diminished her beauty in his eyes.

The hollowness in her cheeks was true of anyone who had—for whatever reason—stayed in California past when it had been declared uninhabitable. The vicious aridity robbed her skin and hair of luster, and bereavement had nearly suffocated her.

Yet resolve had carried her, infusing character and grace into every beautiful line in that face. Zeke believed those fathomless eyes glowed with a love for him and for Sasha that had never been snuffed out, regardless of the seemingly endless nights she endured.

Well-meaning friends repeated the old adage about how it wasn't right for a parent to outlive a child, and Zeke saw her nod and try to smile. Later, when he would enfold her, sleepless in the wee hours, she could only whimper, "My arms ache for him, Zeke! I can't breathe without him!" And all he could do was weep with her.

This morning she dug from her handmade burlap bag a framed picture of Junior, frozen in time at age seven, eyes afire, face aglow as if his whole being pulsed with "What's next?"

Alexis placed the photo on the table next to where Pastor Bob Gill spoke each week and gently draped a scarf over the top corners of the frame. When she headed back for the chair between Zeke and Sasha, he stood as she reached him and they sat together.

"Why do you always do that, Dad?" Sasha said. "Nobody else does that."

He shrugged. "You do the right thing because it's the right thing."

"It embarrasses me."

"That's my job, Sash."

"Can we just think about Junior this morning?" Alexis said.

"Sorry, Mom. I wish I remembered him."

"I love that picture," Zeke said.

Katashi was last to arrive, and he surveyed the room, clearly being sure all were accounted for before he set a heavy two-by-four plank into brackets to secure the door. He moved straight toward Zeke, but Alexis stopped him. "You'll still say a few words this morning?"

"Whatever you want, ma'am. It won't be easy, but—"

"But you will?"

He nodded and slipped past her, leaning to whisper to Zeke, "Mongers on the road."

"Big rigs?"

"Two, one medium."

"They see you?"

Katashi shook his head.

"How far from here?"

"Less than a mile."

"You rode with—"

"Mrs. Meeks and the Gutierrezes."

"And they didn't see the Mongers?"

Katashi shook his head. "I hung back to avoid drawing attention."

"What're you carrying?"

"My .380."

Alexis touched Zeke's leg and he noticed Pastor Bob peering at him from the table in front. The older man spoke quietly. "Any reason we can't get started, gentlemen?"

"Give us a minute," Zeke whispered, feeling all eyes on him now. He did his best to sound casual, but the others had to know he wouldn't allow anything trivial to delay today's service. Neither was it like him to hide from them any threat, especially this far from the safety of their base.

But he didn't know yet how serious this might be. Katashi had never been an alarmist. He saw what he saw, that's all. But if those who traded in the most precious commodity since the Gold Rush of nearly two hundred years before—H_2O—came upon Zeke and his people's vehicles, they'd stop at nothing. They'd done it before.

The Mongers had a way of knowing that people meant water. Nobody remained in this environment without it. If they found one trace of these holdouts, they would comb every inch of the area until they found them. Then whatever storehouses of water—or technology that produced water, or humans with the ability to fabricate or find water—would become the sole property of these roving bands of marauders.

That's why fourteen of the sixteen people in that tattoo parlor-cum-sanctuary were packing that morning—from the late-fifties pastor and his wife to Zeke's thirteen-year-old daughter. Only the two youngest among them were unarmed, and even they knew how to shoot if it came to that.

It had come to that for more than half the adults, Zeke included. He wasn't proud of it. He didn't dwell on it. The trauma had cost him more than three weeks of sleep. But it had been kill or be killed. A Monger had drawn down on him. Any other outcome would have meant his life and also the lives of his wife and daughter and the location of the compound.

Ironically, that shooting had earned him respect among the Mongers when he later found himself out of alternatives and forced to transact business with them. He could tell they believed he and his tiny group were part of a massive organization—as the Mongers were. They crisscrossed the state in tricked-out tanker trucks, some with capacities of more than ten thousand gallons, painted black from wheel rims to bumpers. They referred to themselves as *liquid capitalists*, claiming they bought and sold water, but no one anywhere reported ever having sold them any.

Their victims referred to them as Hydro Mongers.

"Should I tape the window back over?" Katashi said.

Zeke shook his head. "Just stand where you can see out there." He turned to the rest. "Mongers may be down the road. Nothing to be concerned about yet."

A tall, black man in his midthirties, sitting next to his wife and a young son and daughter, stood quickly. "Our vehicles, Zeke—"

"I know, Doc. But they don't know where we are, and they're not likely to want to track us this far in this heat. If they do, we'll see 'em coming."

The doctor's shaved head glistened. "And then what?"

"Are you armed?"

"Zeke! We planning a shoot-out with your daughter and my kids right here?"

"Let's not invent trouble. If they actually find us, who knows? It might be someone I've bought water from before."

The doctor sat back down, shaking his head. "Just like you to assume a best-case scenario. I'd feel better getting out of here right now."

"All due respect, Doc, but you pick the wrong time for that and you could lead 'em right to us."

Pastor Bob ran a hand through his thinning white hair. "Let's none of us do anything rash. While we're here for this purpose, this place is a sanctuary. I take seriously my role as your shepherd, but should any outside force try to invade, as always, elder Ezekiel Thorppe will take charge.

And Sasha, in light of the potential danger, I think we'll dispense with the corporate singing this morning."

She already had the pitch pipe out, and Zeke noticed her shoulders slump.

The pastor must have noticed too. He added, "Perhaps you'd simply like to sing one of the selections for us after I pray?"

That seemed to please her.

"Father," Pastor Bob began, "we're scared. We're exhausted. We're hungry. And we're always thirsty. Whatever right we believed we had to pursue happiness has been sacrificed to Your cause and the mission You've assigned us in the devastation and chaos in which we find ourselves. We believe in You, in Your love and Your grace and Your faithfulness. Most of all, we trust in Your sovereignty.

"And so we thank You and praise You for our deep sense of joy in our future, for of that we are certain. We offer this thanks and praise in the matchless name of our Lord and Redeemer, Your Son and our Savior, Jesus the Christ. Amen."

Pastor Bob nodded to Sasha, who began to sing barely above a whisper the old, familiar hymn "My Redeemer."

I will sing of my Redeemer,
And His wondrous love to me;
On the cruel cross He suffered,
From the curse to set me free.

Sasha sang with such passion that it took nearly a minute for her to get through the first verse. Zeke heard sniffles all over the room and chairs creaked as people dropped to their knees. Soon everyone followed suit, including he and Alexis and Pastor Bob and his wife, Jennie.

Sing, oh sing of my Redeemer,
With His blood He purchased me.
On the cross He sealed my pardon,
Paid the debt and made me free.

Zeke could see in his peripheral vision that Katashi was still standing, but even he was wiping his eyes. If the Hydro Mongers chose that moment to burst in, his only defense would be surprising his attackers with a posture of humility. Even Dr. Adam Xavier, his wife, Gabrielle, and their kids, Caleb and Kayla, were on their knees, tears streaming.

Pastor Bob let the silence play out as everyone remained on their knees for several minutes. Finally, when they moved back into their seats, he said, "Thank you, Sasha. God is here." He moved in front of the table and sat atop it, next to the picture of Ezekiel Jr. He glanced at his watch. "Before we begin, you're free to take a swallow of water now, if you'd like."

Most everyone quickly sipped from their daily allotment, though Zeke did not. He'd been training himself to get by on less and less. He wasn't yet sure why. It just seemed prudent, and he enjoyed the discipline and what he was learning from it, both psychologically and scientifically.

Pastor Bob continued, "First, we will remember a precious life. Several will be sharing, some of how his death brought you to us and gave you life. Second, I have a brief message from Jeremiah chapter one. And third, Jennie and I have a bit of news. Alexis, if you're ready?"

Zeke froze at the press of a hand on his shoulder and a voice in his ear. "Listen to me."

He nodded. How was it possible a Monger had slipped in and gotten behind him? The one entrance was secure. They'd been on their knees, but still.

He wanted to reach for his Glock, but surely whoever was behind him had the advantage. Pastor Bob couldn't see this man? Nor Katashi? Was he crouched? Was Zeke hallucinating? Maybe he should have had some water.

Alexis put a fluttering hand on Zeke's thigh and rose. So she knew?

The man's hand still lay on Zeke's shoulder, and he had heard him plain as day. He casually turned his head to the right to get a glimpse of the hand. Nothing. He wrenched farther and finally spun around in his seat, yanking out the .45.

No one was there.

2

"LISTEN TO ME!"

"Ezekiel?" she said, just above a whisper, a hand flying to her throat.

"Sorry, love," he said, sitting with his gun out. "Nothing."

Zeke knew Alexis was nervous enough without this distraction. It wasn't that she had a problem speaking. Or with confidence. She was an artist, after all, had been an interior decorator before the kids came along. She had taught at both El Camino College and the University of Redlands. She had pitched ideas to high-level executive teams at some of the largest corporations in Los Angeles. But now, standing before her family and the tiny cadre of brothers and sisters in the faith she lived with, she struck her husband as fragile.

And before she could even open her mouth, he had startled her—and everyone else—by lurching at what, a phantom?

Alexis gathered herself and dug a tiny folded card from her palm. Fingers shaking, she unfolded it, though Zeke knew she wasn't likely to forget a single detail.

"I still find it hard to believe Junior has been in heaven longer than he was with us," she began. "You'd expect a mother to idealize a boy who didn't live past seven, and I'm guilty. It was a year before I allowed myself to remember that he was his father's son. He was all boy—stubborn, even ornery sometimes."

That made the others chuckle.

"But he was like his daddy, too, in how he loved me. Sweet and thoughtful. Like most of you, we went to Pastor Bob's Church in Torrance. Junior loved everything about Sunday school, all the stories and songs and fun. I prayed with him to receive Jesus when he was six. That didn't make him perfect. He could still disobey. In fact that's what he was doing the day he died."

She stopped to gather herself just when Zeke again sensed someone behind him. This time it was a hand on each shoulder, and this time he didn't hesitate. He leapt to his feet and whirled, causing everyone to jump. Again seeing nothing, he quickly covered and whispered, "Katashi, sit. I'll take the window for a while."

"I'm okay, Zeke."

"No, please."

Katashi looked embarrassed by the attention, but Sasha was squinting directly at Zeke, clearly puzzled. He forced a smile, but she didn't look away.

"We had a fenced-in backyard," Alexis continued, "and he'd been punished before for leaving it. That day I made him come inside while I put Sasha down for a late afternoon nap. She had just turned three that week. I heard Junior in the kitchen while I was reading to her. And then I didn't hear him. If you're a parent, you hate that sound . . ."

Zeke was so rattled by the hallucinations—or whatever they were—that he worried they portended an attack by the Mongers. He peered out the slit in the window.

"Zeke?" Alexis said, startling him. "I'm up to where I called to tell you I couldn't find Junior."

"Right, sorry. So, Mahir here"—Zeke pointed at a French man with a dark-complexion about his age—"and I were working on a project at the California Department of Water Resources substation in Lakewood . . ."

He told of how he and Mahir had raced home, only to learn the awful news, and how Mahir watched little Sasha while Zeke and Alexis went to the hospital to identify Junior's body. "But I had so many questions," Zeke said. "All we knew was what the officer had put in his report. I was desperate to know more. Was he killed instantly? Did he say anything? Was anyone with him? That's when we met our angel."

The widow Elaine Meeks, sixty now, stared at the floor as she spoke. "I was about to get in my car when I heard all the noise and looked up just in time to see the truck lurch. I knew it had to be bad. I used to be a nurse, so before I knew it I was at your Junior's side." She paused and looked into Alexis's eyes. "I've always believed it was God's gift to me to get to be with your precious boy just before he went to heaven, and I know that's where he is, because he told me that's where he was going.

"But then I did something way out of character. Katashi was in a bad way, and I was worried what he would do."

Katashi spoke up. "The only thing that kept me from killing myself was that I didn't know what would happen to me when I died. Mrs. Meeks had told Junior he could be in heaven with God, and he said he already knew all about that. I couldn't believe it! He was scared of dying, like anybody would be, especially a child. But he believed with all his heart that he was going to heaven. After the police took my statement, Mrs. Meeks was there waiting, as if she knew I wanted to talk to her."

"I thought you might need a friend," Elaine said.

Elaine's and Katashi's stories never failed to move Zeke, and he never grew tired of hearing how Junior knew he was going to heaven. The room had begun to warm with the body heat and the peaking of the sun, and he squinted out the window down the boulevard. Ironic that he and his friends still called it that. True, a few street signs still dangled with hints of that name visible, despite unyielding irradiance from the sun since the day Ezekiel Jr. had been born.

What Zeke and his friends still called a boulevard had once been a bustling thoroughfare of commerce. Now the unrelenting heat from dawn to dusk made for billowing clouds of fine silt at any footstep or tire on former pavement. Even concrete and asphalt had given way to the ravages of nature.

Every other debilitating drought in the history of the state had been attributed to lack of precipitation. But just four years into this one—when it had already been deemed the worst in more than a millennium—it was determined to be entirely temperature-driven. Zeke, in his early twenties then, had predicted catastrophe if things didn't change, but nothing on this scale.

Suddenly the voice rang clear in his ear again, "That was My doing."

Great. He was losing his mind. Should he be surprised? It hadn't taken long for the most populous state in the union to become the least populous. Sane people? Gone. Yet here he was with a small crew of holdouts as fanatical as he. As cathartic as this meeting was, remembering how God had used such tragedy to bring them all together, all he wanted now was for it to be over so he could get Alexis alone and tell her.

But what would he say? *I'm hearing voices?* Problem was, it was more than that. What about those phantom touches? At least this time he kept from jumping and causing everyone else to panic. What would Lexi think? All she needed was a husband with his crazy on.

Zeke saw dust on the horizon and hoped it meant only a breeze. He turned back when the room fell silent. Mahir's hand was in the air. "Excuse me, Zeke," he said, a hint of French still in his tone. "You don't look so good. Want me to watch so you can sit down?"

"Yes," Doc said, leaning forward and peering at him. "You all right, Zeke?"

"Sure, I'll sit. Thanks."

As Mahir moved past him, Zeke whispered, "Keep an eye on the horizon, see?"

When Zeke sat, Sasha slid next to him and laid her head on his shoulder, which moved him. He hoped whatever was tormenting him would not be obvious. She caressed his back. "You all right, Daddy?"

He nodded, but almost immediately something forced him straight up and pressed him back in his chair. Without meaning to, he had pushed his daughter aside. Zeke tried to make it appear as if he were just shifting his weight, so he kept his eyes on Katashi and casually draped his arm around Sasha, fighting to maintain composure. The hand in his lap balled into a fist so tight his knuckles were white and his biceps quivered.

And here came the voice again.

"Listen to Me! I am that I am."

Lord! It's You?

"My mercy is from everlasting to everlasting on those who fear Me, and to those who remember My commandments. I have established My throne in heaven, and My kingdom rules over all. Listen to Me! Hear Me!"

Zeke lurched forward again, elbows on his knees, head in his hands, tears streaming, praying silently, *I hear You, Lord! I'm listening!*

"Daddy!" Sasha whispered, and Zeke heard Pastor Bob approach and lay a hand on his back.

"Let's give Zeke a minute. He's told us he's all right, but benchmark anniversaries like these are hard, and you never know how they're going to affect you. Let's pray. Father, be with our brother in a special way, we ask in the name of Your Son. Amen."

Zeke thought that might have been one of the least necessary entreaties in history. For God was saying to him even then, "And it shall come to pass in the last days that I will pour out My Spirit on all flesh. Your sons and daughters shall prophesy, your young men shall see visions, your old men shall dream dreams.

"And on My menservants and on My maidservants I will pour out My Spirit in those days; and they shall prophesy. I will show wonders in heaven and signs in the earth: blood and fire and smoke. The sun shall be turned into darkness, and the moon into blood, before the coming of the great and awesome day of the Lord.

"And it shall come to pass that whoever calls on the name of the Lord shall be saved."

3

DEATH BRINGS LIFE

EZEKIEL THORPPE WAS NOT from a tradition comfortable with outward manifestations of the Spirit of God, let alone dramatic ones. He didn't quarrel with those who went in for that sort of thing, though he suspected much of it was exaggerated. *If they were raised that way,* he thought, *fine, let's consider it a "distinctive" or a "denominational preference," certainly nothing over which to split hairs or break fellowship.* He had grown fond of saying, "I quit drawing lines in the sand when I realized how few of us were left on the beach" and felt magnanimous when he said it.

Well, terrific. Now what was he going to say? God Himself had invaded Zeke's cozy little theological cottage and spoken to him the way He had the saints of old. Zeke wasn't sure exactly what He wanted yet, but listening up was clearly a no-brainer. God had his attention all right. Either that or Zeke had a first-class, one-way ticket to Cuckooville.

Mahir seemed riveted by something outside, but Zeke knew he would say something if he feared a legitimate threat. He decided to relax. He sensed the support of his friends, even if they did assume his discomfort came from reliving the worst night of his life. How he and Alexis got through that, not to mention the next year, he still couldn't say—apart from God, of course.

He'd known supernatural grace as he'd seen others bear inconceivable trials. Any parent has imagined the worst of all tragedies, but no one could know how they'd hold up under it until it came. Zeke knew people expected him to say they had probably been in shock and might not have clearly remembered the first twenty-four to forty-eight hours after the tragedy, but that wasn't true—at least the amnesia part. He and Alexis had revisited it endlessly over the past decade, and while naturally their hearts and spirits, and yes, even their bodies, had shifted into some sort of self-preservation mode, they believed they remembered everything.

Now as Katashi and Elaine recalled the meeting at his place, it was as if Junior were suspended in time, tireless, lithe, running, jumping, climbing, smiling, eager for the next adventure. What kind of a seventeen-year-old would he have become? Rebellious and sullen? Unwilling to live in the godforsaken desert California had become? Or brilliant and task-oriented, impatient for the next challenge?

Katashi was saying, "I'll never forget Alexis telling me, 'I only want to blame you so I don't have to blame myself, or the building owner for not having enough security, or God for taking him too soon.'

"I kept telling her, 'No, no! Blame me! It's my fault! I should have waited, should have checked!'

"But she told me, 'We wouldn't have come if that's how we felt. We know you feel bad and that you will have to live with this all your life too. We just want you to know we forgive you, that we know it was an accident.'

"Who does that? I had to know! First their boy knew he was going to heaven. Then they forgave me for killing him. Truthfully, I wished they'd yelled at me, hit me, tried to kill me. That's what I deserved. That would've made me feel better, if anything could have.

"As soon as they left I called Raoul. He'd heard all about it from someone who called him from work, and he invited me over. I told him I didn't want to bother him when he was sick, but he told me he had just called in sick to get the day off. That made me mad. Everything just burst from me and I cussed him out and told him it was all his fault, that if he'd been there it wouldn't have happened. He hung up on me, and I didn't care if I ever saw him again. Now I had lost everything, including my best friend, and I *really* didn't want to live anymore."

Katashi broke down. "Bear with me," he said, holding up a hand. "I'm here, so you know this ends well."

"And I'm here too," Raoul said. "So it gets better."

"Raoul showed up within ten minutes," Katashi said. "He told me he didn't like something in the way I sounded. He said he'd heard fatalism in my voice."

"And I don't even understand Japanese people, you know," Raoul said, making the others chuckle. "I never have."

Zeke stood and switched places with Mahir at the window.

Mahir whispered, "The dust died down."

And so it had. Zeke didn't like it. If Mongers were in the area, the dust told him they were about a mile away. But no dust didn't necessarily mean they were gone. It could mean they were closer. Or coming from another direction.

Raoul continued, "I figured the best way to keep Katashi from doin' somethin' stupid was to make him tell me the whole thing again from the beginning. I told him I was sorry about calling in sick without really being sick. It wasn't like we both hadn't done that before, but we always told each other. Anyway, I ordered some food because I knew he needed to eat and I wanted to keep him away from the booze. Then I called Benita and told her I was going to sleep at his place."

"It's a good thing he did," Katashi said.

"I think so too," Raoul said, "because I was there the next day when Mrs. Meeks called and said the Thorppes wanted Katashi to come to the funeral a few days later. No way he woulda done that if I hadn't talked him into it."

"For sure," Katashi said. "And no way I would have gone if you hadn't gone with me."

"I had to drag you there, dude."

"It meant so much to us," Alexis said.

"It was the hardest thing I've ever done," Katashi said. "Everybody knew who I was. There's nothing worse than a funeral with a tiny casket, but to know you're the reason and that everyone else knows too . . . Oh, it was awful. I wanted to crawl in a hole."

It was hard for Zeke and Alexis too, of course, though Pastor Bob had preached a message on salvation, as they asked, including Junior's last words that though he was scared he knew he would soon be in heaven with God, "because of Jesus."

"That was the first time Benita and I had ever heard anything like that," Raoul said. "And we went to church a lot, you know? All our lives. In Mexico and when we moved to Angelino Heights. We believed something like that, but not that. It wasn't *because* of Jesus, but because of us— what we were trying to do for Him. We talked about it all the way home and all week, about what we would have said if we were the ones dying. We woulda said we *hoped* we were going to heaven, God, because we tried really hard."

"I was listening too," Katashi said, "because Elaine had explained it all to me, and Pastor Bob was making it clearer. But the whole time I was dreading going to the cemetery. I wanted out of that, because I would be standing shoulder to shoulder with all these people again, and I didn't know if I could take another minute of it."

Elaine said, "You asked me if I thought the Thorppes would mind if you slipped away after the service. I told you they'd forgiven you for something much more serious than that, but that they *had* asked you to be there, and didn't you think you owed them at least that much?"

"Well, that put a new spin on things. I owed them whatever they asked. I said I would stay if Raoul and Benita went with me, but that didn't stop people from just pushing past them and talking directly to me. It wouldn't have surprised me to be glared at, cussed out, even spit at. Who knows, maybe someone would take a swing at me."

"You had *no* church experience," Pastor Bob said.

"None at all. And everybody who said anything just told me how nice it was that I came, and they told me they were praying for me. For *me*! It was almost too much."

Raoul told how the company put Katashi on desk duty during his suspension while they waited to see if they would be sued. "When they let him back in the truck, he didn't never want to drive again. We used to trade off every day, but now I drove all the time. You never saw a guy so good at keeping kids away, man. But we never had no more trouble at that one building.

"Anyway, I didn't mind. I liked driving and him doin' all the work. We got to talk all day. And then we started going to church together."

"I won't lie," Alexis said. "Zeke and I went through some very dark nights of the soul. I remember days, weeks, when I only got out of bed for Sasha. At times prayer was my only lifeline and at other times I wanted nothing to do with God. Frankly, I didn't want to know or serve or love a God who was supposedly sovereign and yet would allow that to happen to Junior—to me.

"And poor Zeke couldn't win. When he couldn't match my grief, I hated him for getting past it, though in my heart of hearts I knew he was as devastated as I was. I would hear him sobbing and want to go to him because knowing he was hurting the way I was gave a hint of a lifeline to me, yet I had nothing to offer him. I know he thought I cared only about my loss, and he had to wonder if I would ever again see him—or Sasha—through loving eyes."

She sighed. "They say time heals, but I don't believe that anymore. God heals, and He heals through people. Loving people. I don't believe in closure either. There's a hole in my heart that will never close, and I don't want it to. Even now I am overwhelmed with grief and all I have to cling to is that same blessed hope my son had at the end—because of Jesus.

"At the end of myself and all my resources, He's all I have, and He is enough."

Zeke was grateful Alexis had a way with words, because he never could have gotten that out. It warmed him to remember that Elaine Meeks's church was dying back then and she switched to theirs, she said, because of what she saw in the people. And Katashi began coming and kept coming and brought Raoul and Benita, and they all eventually came to faith under Pastor Bob's preaching. That was when Zeke finally knew Junior's death was not in vain.

From death had come life. Because of Jesus.

PASSWORD!

4

"I MIGHT HAVE foregone my message, had I known how poignant that was going to be," Pastor Bob said. "But God did put something on my mind, and I want to be sensitive to His leading. Zeke, does it appear we're in the clear for a few minutes?"

"It does," Zeke said and sat with his family again. Alexis looked spent, and he wondered how—and when—he would break to her what had been happening to him. She often said she loved that he was so grounded and practical. What in the world would she make of this?

Pastor Bob asked the group to turn to Jeremiah 1. As pages rattled, Zeke again felt a hand on his shoulder and heard, "Hear Me. This is for you."

Zeke closed his eyes and hung his head, and the pastor read: "Then the word of the Lord came to me, saying: 'Before I formed you in the womb I knew you; before you were born I sanctified you; I ordained you a prophet to the nations.'

"Then said I: 'Ah, Lord God! Behold, I cannot speak, for I am a youth.'

"But the Lord said to me: 'Do not say, "I am a youth," for you shall go to all to whom I send you, and whatever I command you, you shall speak. Do not be afraid of their faces, for I am with you to deliver you,' says the Lord.

"Then the Lord put forth His hand and touched my mouth, and the Lord said to me: 'Behold, I have put My words in your mouth . . .'"

Pastor Bob closed his Bible and set it on the table. "May the Lord add His blessing to the reading of His Word."

That's it? Zeke thought.

"Now I mentioned that Jennie and I have news. I apologize that this will come as a surprise except to Doc. I have been in ministry for nearly forty years, most of them in Torrance and the last several with you all. While the sun and the fires turned to ash the beauty we once basked in, we have felt compelled to stay, doggedly determined to minister to those whom time—and America—has forgotten. I admire you and love you for that beyond what I am able to express . . ."

Zeke, for one, would never forget the service that had birthed all this, in which the usually low-key pastor perhaps unintentionally said something so profound that it initially changed the lives of about forty families. Though the church in Torrance had gone to one Saturday evening and two Sunday morning services, for some reason Pastor Bob had called for a special Sunday evening service. He billed it as an old-fashioned, revival-type, hymn-singing meeting with a message at the end.

That proved an understatement, though Zeke recalled having been embarrassed for Bob when attendance proved thin. The pastor, however, seemed to take it in stride and said something good-naturedly about "finally figuring out who's serious about getting down to business around here."

By that time the state had been decimated by the drought, hundreds of thousands of acres lost to the wildfires, the ecosystem turned upside down, endangered species wiped out, once-safe species endangered, industries failing, thousands of businesses leaving, virtually none coming in, millions of people moving away, the economy a hopeless morass—the state on life support and no hope in sight.

And that was even before the worst of the earthquakes had rendered the term *skyline* archaic and turned even the great metropolises to rubble. Once majestic monuments of progress, oases of cityscapes breaking up the

Mojave, Colorado, and Great Basin Deserts, had been lain waste. Now all of California, not just its southeast, was indistinguishable from Death Valley.

Zeke and Mahir had seen it coming for years. As hydrologists with the California Department of Water Resources, they'd been frantically attempting every emergency measure to preserve the state's most precious commodity—to no avail. Half their coworkers had been laid off, budgets had been slashed, and anyone with a brain in the department—including Zeke—was feverishly circulating his résumé.

But in the special service that night eight years before, the usually measured and almost taciturn Pastor Bob—whom his congregation loved for just that reason—was particularly animated. He wasn't loud or demonstrative but rather emotional and impassioned. He seemed to speak from the heart as never before. He told of his and his wife's calling as young people specifically to the state of California.

He talked, rather eloquently as Zeke remembered it, of the unique personalities and philosophical bents that made up the California ethos. Zeke thought back on how he had caught Alexis's eye at that point, particularly when Pastor Bob so poignantly described the typical Californian. Five-year-old Sasha had been asleep in the pew, her head in her mother's lap, and the moment somehow resonated with Zeke. He and Alexis had often talked about the fact that while many made fun of the quirkiness of the people of California, the two of them found such people fascinating—and needy.

Pastor Bob had gone on to speak of the sacredness of one's calling, the biblical basis for it, and how to know when it was genuinely of God. He concluded that evening with an earnest challenge. He said normally he would reference Isaiah's declaration from the Old Testament, "Here am I, send me," and ask, "Who will go?"

But that night, he said, in light of the rumored death sentence soon to be pronounced on the state and the mass exodus that had already begun, "rather I'm asking, 'Who will stay? Who will be here for those who cannot leave? What about the impoverished, the infirm, the disenfranchised? What about the indigenous tribes, the Native Americans, those who were here centuries before we were, those who consider this their sacred ground, the land their birthright? Who will be here for them? Who will stay?'"

Zeke recalled being so stirred, so moved, so overcome, so certain that God was urging him to stay, that he wanted to leap to his feet. His only fear was getting ahead of Alexis. Was it too much to ask of a mother who had but two years before buried her firstborn child?

But when Pastor Bob closed by simply whispering what he would later admit was meant only rhetorically, "Who will stay?" Alexis gathered Sasha into her arms, stood, and called out, "I will!"

Zeke rose and did the same.

Sasha, rousing with a start, squealed, "I will too! What're we doing?"

Several others all over the Torrance sanctuary stood to respond, clearly startling Pastor Bob.

After the service he met with forty who had expressed their commitment, and he soberly warned them of the cost. "It won't be long before we'll be on our own, ministering to the stranded and the abandoned, those here only because they have no choice."

All claimed they were willing, but two years later, when the president declared California verboten, the attrition among the committed began. By the time the church itself was abandoned, Pastor Bob's holdouts numbered just two dozen. "Now we're entirely self-sufficient, depending wholly on the Lord and the scientists among us to somehow produce everything we need."

Now, ten years since losing Junior, eight years since Zeke and Alexis had answered the call, six years since Washington, D.C. had pronounced California dead to civilians, and seventeen years into the most devastating drought the world had ever seen, Pastor Bob finished his last message to what was left of the original Torrance holdouts . . .

"Sadly, the day has come when Jennie and I must bid our farewells also and return to the land of the living. It is not by choice, as Dr. Xavier has diagnosed her with stage-four pancreatic cancer."

The expression of emotion seemed to come involuntarily as Zeke and the group moved as one to lay hands on Jennie and weep over her. "It should not surprise you that I have made this decision over Jennie's protest. Our children and grandchildren want her close and under acute care, and I have come to the painful conclusion that this is only fair. Bless her, she believed the Lord had called her to stay here to the end and was willing, but He has given me peace about the move. We will leave in three days, pulling out Wednesday night so we can make the first leg of the journey after dark.

"I trust God will anoint another leader, and we look forward to hearing who that is and what is in store for you all. Zeke, could I ask you to pray for us?"

Zeke raised a hand for the rest to bow their heads, but for a few eternal seconds he was speechless. *Lord, give me the words*, he said silently.

God reminded him, "Whatever I command you, you shall speak. Behold, I have put My words in your mouth."

The longer he waited the more Zeke became aware of the uneasy silence. All he heard from the Lord was, "Have you no faith? Open your mouth." And so he did.

"I am the Lord your God, who is and always will be. Fear not, for I am your shield and your exceedingly great reward. I have created you and formed you. I have called you by name, and you are Mine. I am God and beside Me there is no other. When you walk through the fire, you will not be burned. I am the true and living God, the everlasting King, and at My wrath the earth shall tremble.

"I made the earth by My power, established the world by My wisdom, and stretched out the heavens at My discretion. At My voice a multitude of waters in the heavens causes the vapors to ascend from the ends of the earth. I make lightning for the rain and bring the wind out of my treasuries."

God seemed to fall silent again, and thus so did Zeke. He felt a nudge and peeked up at Dr. Adam Xavier's scowl. The man's shaved head ran with sweat. "Pray for Jennie, man," he whispered, but of course everyone could hear him and Zeke felt obligated to defend himself.

"I'm trying to follow the leading of the Spirit, Brother."

"Just do what Pastor Bob asked, would you? Nobody expects you to speak for God Himself."

"Well, that's what *He* impressed upon me to—"

"Please, just pray for Jennie and thank the Lord for all she and Pastor have meant to us!"

"Gentlemen, please!" Pastor Bob said. "We've always been known for unity. Now, after one the most special times we've ever had—"

"Right," Doc said. "Sorry."

"Me too," Zeke said. "Let's pray. Father, I confess it's at times like this when it's hardest to trust You. But we do. You've proved Yourself faithful. You alone sit high above the heavens, and there is no other God like You.

"We praise You because You're a sin-forgiving God, and how we need that. In You there is neither change nor shadow of turning, and that's a good thing, because we admit we don't understand and we don't like what we've heard today. We love Jennie and if we could have our way, we would ask You to make her as good as new, healthy and whole.

"We say we want Your will, but the truth is we want *our* will and we want Yours only if that means she gets better. We can't imagine this place without her, ourselves without her, life without her. She's taught us, she's prayed with us, she's prayed for us. She's been an example to us. And what a rock she's been to our pastor!

"So, we beg for a miracle. Short of that we ask for comfort and peace. And finally, we ask for forgiveness for our own lack of faith and under-standing. Help us trust in Your sovereignty. Most of all, thank You for the gift of the years we had with Jennie, we pray in the name of Jesus. Amen."

Bob took a moment, seeming to gather himself. "Before I ask Sasha to lead us in 'Blest Be the Tie That Binds,'" he said, "let me suggest that sometime soon you elect an elder to join Zeke and Doc in place of me, and then the three of you decide who will be your new spiritual leader."

"Well," Doc said, "I've been studying and doing a good bit of teaching, and Zeke's busy with the logistics—"

"Don't get ahead of yourself," Pastor Bob said. "Let the Spirit lead, as

He always does." He nodded to Sasha, who breathed into her pitch pipe again.

> *Blest be the tie that binds*
> *Our hearts in Christian love;*
> *The fellowship of Christian minds*
> *Is like to that above . . .*

Zeke suggested they save their good-byes for an appropriate send-off a few days later. "We need to start heading for our vehicles. Keep an eye out. Save one more swallow of water for the trip back, and as soon as you get there, check your traps. Lunch is on your own, but let's have dinner together in the commons tonight. I'm tired of snake and lizard, so any kind of fowl or mammal would be nice. And pray about that third elder. We'll vote Wednesday night after we see the Gills off."

The sixteen broke quickly into the four groups in which they had arrived. Mahir Sy had come with the newest members, a young Haitian couple named Danley and Cristelle Muscadin, who had found themselves out of work when the mass exodus began. They had been scavenging for food when Mahir had come upon them, led them to faith, and brought them into the fold. They left first, and soon the high-pitched whine of their single-cylinder dirt bikes faded.

Next, the Gills and the Xaviers and their kids, Caleb and Kayla, headed off for the quarter mile or so walk to Doc's Land Rover. Zeke noticed Jennie was moving slowly, but Doc's wife hung back with her, and Gabrielle was not only packing, but she also knew her way around a weapon.

Zeke planned to wait till the six of them were out of sight before releasing Raoul and Benita Gutierrez, Elaine Meeks, and Katashi Aki. Once they were gone, he, Alexis, and Sasha would go.

He couldn't wait to get back and spend some time with Alexis. He still wasn't sure how he would broach this matter of God revealing Himself in such a dramatic fashion, but there was no way around it: Whatever it meant, she had to be in it with him all the way or it would never work. Zeke had to decide whether the diminished water intake experiment had affected his mental capability—which might motivate Alexis to take Sasha and accompany the Gills east—or that God really was calling him to some higher plane (which could just as easily have the same effect on Alexis).

Zeke certainly didn't feel qualified for some divine call, but everything he had ever learned told him that maybe that was the point—nobody God called was ever worthy, let alone qualified. Regardless of how Alexis reacted, what might Pastor Bob think?

With just the seven of them left in the room, Zeke nodded Katashi over and asked if he would take window duty and let him know when Jennie and Gabrielle were out of sight. Then he asked Elaine if he could have a moment. She followed him to the corner by the door while Alexis was getting ready to go.

"Could you find a reason to distract Sasha for an hour or so after lunch? I need to discuss something with Alexis and—"

"Of course, Zeke. Never hesitate to ask."

"Oh, no!" Katashi said. "Zeke! They're running this way! Even Jennie!"

Zeke yanked the Glock from his belt. "Raoul, what are you carrying?"

"Snub-nosed .38."

"Everybody else, fill your hands! Sasha, you up to speed on that nine-millimeter?"

"I'm a better shot than you, Dad."

"You know the rules."

"Yes, sir."

Alexis cried out, "God, help us!"

"Raoul, come with me," Zeke said. "Katashi, you know the drill. Set up a perimeter. Nobody gets in without the password."

"Got it."

Raoul swung the heavy two-by-four out of its brace, and Katashi held it as Zeke followed the Mexican out. At the slam of the door and a thump of the wood, Zeke and Raoul sprinted into the merciless midday sun toward the swirls of dust created by their compatriots running from who knew what or whom.

Raoul quickly put ten yards between himself and Zeke and met Dr. Xavier, who'd stopped before passing Jennie Gill, apparently to be sure she was okay. When he got to Zeke and Raoul, the three of them were already breathless and drenched.

"My Rover's gone," Doc said. "Had to be Mongers. Hope they haven't followed Mahir and the others."

"Or know where we are," Zeke said. "Get everybody safe. We'll check on the other vehicles and get back to you—either to pick you all up or figure out what we do next."

"If Katashi's back there and everybody's armed," Doc said, "I'm going with you."

"No, I need you there for Jennie or in case you guys get blindsided before we get back."

"What if you run into Mongers? Think you're going to sweet-talk your way out of it? Who's going to treat you if you get hurt?"

"You and I shouldn't be together, Doc. Anything happens to me, you're in charge."

"Obviously. But don't think you're going to railroad me out of being the next pastor."

Zeke shot him a double take. "That's the last thing on my mind right now, Doc. And it ought to be the last thing on yours too. Now get going."

Zeke and Raoul jogged about another half mile to where Raoul had left his four-door pickup. They found it on its top with all the tires slashed. "Glad I didn't bring the tanker truck, man," he said. "They woulda stolen that for sure."

"At least this is fixable," Zeke said.

"Yeah, but where we gonna get tires?"

"We'll figure it out. We always do. Barter, something. Let's see what's left of mine."

Another half mile away, Zeke's nine-year-old Jeep Wrangler had its windows and lights smashed, tires—including the spare—slashed, and fuel tank ruptured. It had to be Mongers. They'd been smart enough not to let much of it spill on the parched ground. Anyone else would have salvaged the vehicle. They took only the valuable commodity.

"You as hungry as I am, buddy?" Zeke said as they trudged back.

"You kiddin'?" Raoul said. "Know how long it's been since I've had my kinda food? I don't even remember. Sometimes Benita and me, we dream about sneakin' across the border and eating beans and rice and tortillas till we esplode."

"You're not helping. I even dream about Tex-Mex or Taco Bell."

"Oh, man! People in my town would shoot you for sayin' that."

Zeke laughed, which he found encouraging, considering. He couldn't imagine the others finding anything funny about this.

By the time the old tattoo parlor came into view, lizard and snake didn't sound so bad after all.

"What're we gonna do, man?" Raoul said.

Zeke shrugged. "What we always do, my friend. Once we're all together, we'll quote our password verse, we'll pray, and we'll start over."

"Start walkin', you mean."

"No, Mahir and Danley and Cristelle will come looking for us soon enough."

"Yeah, then we'll see how many of us can fit on one of their dirt bikes."

Zeke gave Raoul a high five as they reached the door, but they also had their weapons ready. It had been a relief to see no Mongers, but he wouldn't breathe easy until he was sure they hadn't been here while he'd been gone. He rapped on the door and was glad to hear Katashi: "Password!"

"Isaiah 9:6."

The wood slid up, the door swung open, and Zeke's brothers and sisters welcomed him and Raoul. After securing the door they knelt in a circle, held hands, and recited in unison: "For unto us a child is born, unto us a son is given: and the government shall be upon his shoulder: and his name shall be called Wonderful, Counselor, The mighty God, The everlasting Father, The Prince of Peace."

The rest looked up expectantly, and to no one's surprise, Doc broke the ice. "So?"

"We have a lot of work to do, friends."

PART 2

THE MANTLE

WHO'S ON FIRST?

5

"YOU'RE NOT THINKING of having us walk back in this heat . . ."

"'Course not, Doc," Zeke said. "Jennie'd never make it, and you can bet that with what they did to our vehicles the Mongers set us up for an ambush."

"I don't get it," Benita said. "Why didn't they just take 'em?"

"It was a message," Katashi said. "They don't need them."

"Okay, we're all hungry," Doc said. "Let's quit gassing about this and send a couple of men back to the compound for some vehicles."

Zeke held up both hands. "I've got this, Doctor. It's safest to stay right here until Mahir or—"

"Belowground with one exit? We're sitting ducks and you know it."

"Our people will come looking for us before long. How the Mongers missed the bikes, I don't know, but—"

"Meanwhile we sit here starving, hoping they don't attack and smoke us out and—"

"Wow, Doc, way to have faith and make the kids feel safe."

"Face facts, Zeke! For all we know, they followed our people and took out our whole installation and the rest of our vehicles."

"Dr. Xavier!" Pastor Bob said. "For the love of all things sacred . . ."

Zeke moved to a corner and waved Doc over. The black man's eyes were slits, his jaw set.

"What in the world, man?"

"I don't know, Zeke. You're running this like Amateur Night in Dixie."

"I have no idea what that means, but you're sure not helping. Listen, these people look up to you, so if you can't help me keep 'em calm, I wish you'd shut up. Can you do that?"

Doc recoiled. "What'd you say?"

"There's nothing wrong with your hearing. You know I respect you, but I need your attention and I need you with me. Are you with me?"

Doc pressed his lips together and shook his head. "Yeah, I hear you."

The more time that passed without any sign of their compatriots, the more Zeke began to wonder if Doc was right. He considered sending Katashi and Raoul out to forage for food, maybe something that not so long ago was considered endangered. Once the state was condemned, its animals were no longer protected.

Until the last few years, Zeke had never been an outdoorsman, let alone a hunter. He had since come to appreciate the circle of life and what men of nature could teach once office-bound men like him, Mahir, Doc, and Pastor Bob—not to mention their wives and even the children—about hunting their food and respecting the kill by avoiding waste. They were humane reapers: never for sport, making use of every bit of the target.

Zeke had grown to admire and learn the skills of his brothers and sisters in mixing the most unlikely herbs and spices and liquids to tenderize and make not only palatable, but even appetizing, creatures he would not have dreamt of as meals. Now he found himself actually looking forward to artfully prepared insects, even arachnids, assorted vermin, and other mammals hardy (and ugly) enough to adapt to the new climate realities. Amazing how hunger could influence the taste buds. Desert tortoise the way Elaine Meeks or Katashi Aki prepared it, or coyote backstrap with Raoul Gutierrez's special sauce became delicacies.

Even thinking of it made him hungry, but Zeke didn't dare send anyone out just now. If Mahir, Danley, or Cristelle didn't show up within the next half hour, he'd have to assume the worst. He asked Alexis for pen and paper, which she produced from the same handbag she used to magically supply Caleb, and Kayla with diversions during long meetings. Zeke set about determining who would stay and who would go if help did not arrive.

He had abandoned any vestige of sexism long ago. Benita Gutierrez was one of the best marksmen among the fourteen who shot (she and Doc taught their kids gun safety but wisely did not yet allow them to carry). Of all people, Sasha was also a crack shot who put most of the men to shame.

But if worse came to worst that afternoon, Zeke would not be sending out any of the children, nor would he separate them from their mothers. So, among those who would stay he listed Alexis, Gabrielle, and the three kids. It only made sense to add Jennie Gill to that number, along with Elaine Meeks.

He still maintained that he and Doc should be separated in the face of danger so the group would have a leader if anything happened to either of them, though this latest dustup made him question whether Doc was his most logical successor. Regardless, for now Doc needed to stay.

That meant that for a sortie into Monger territory to find their friends and—he hoped—at least a couple of operable vehicles, Zeke would take Katashi, Raoul and Benita Gutierrez, and Pastor Bob. Naturally, that last one gave him pause. If either Pastor or Jennie had a second's hesitation about it, he would defer to their judgment. But he knew Bob, remarkably spry for his age, would want to go, and that Jennie wouldn't deny him.

Zeke waited ten more minutes, then announced the plan. He was pleasantly surprised when Doc raised his hand.

"Actually, boss," he said not unkindly, "not only do I have you outnumbered, but I think my team has yours outclassed. Don't worry. Nobody will get through that door who doesn't belong."

"I have no doubt, Doc."

They divvied up ammunition and food and inventoried everyone's water supply. There wasn't much edible beyond emergency packs of dried seeds and nuts, and they were loath to exhaust those aside from literal life-and-death situations. The entire troop scavenged far and wide at dawn and dusk every other day, harvesting what meager foodstuffs the ravaged earth yielded. They meticulously compared seeds and nuts they gleaned from withering plants that grew scarcer every day against an exhaustive guide the scientists had prepared, specifying what was safe to eat.

Zeke remembered clearly that Pastor Bob had often referred to the "miracle" of God's selection process when He called the original holdouts, having impressed on the hearts of three scientists (two hydrologists and an MD) that they should be among those who would stay—and giving them the strength to persevere when others did not.

Zeke had begun rendezvousing weekly with his friend and co-worker Mahir Sy as well as Dr. Adam Xavier soon after that providential Sunday evening meeting eight years before. And that hadn't been easy for any of them. With the state already in grave condition, Zeke and Mahir were logging twelve-hour days at the Department of Water Resources. Zeke and Alexis were just seeing the light at the end of a two-year tunnel of grief and were desperate for more time with each other and five-year-old Sasha. And Adam Xavier was a twenty-eight-year-old resident at Torrance Memorial, sometimes working around the clock, his wife, Gabrielle, at home with a toddler and a newborn.

All that sacrifice and training proved invaluable now, and to Zeke just eight years before already seemed like the good old days. Doc's experience in all the areas of the hospital, especially the ER, seemed to come into play every day. And Zeke had to admit that, as with most everybody, Doc's weaknesses were also his strengths.

Zeke and Alexis had not really known the Xaviers until they joined those who answered the call that night at church so long ago. Zeke had noticed the striking black couple with the two infants, of course, and knew the young husband was a doctor.

It had been Pastor Bob's idea that the three most educated young men among the respondents should get better acquainted—"That is, if you're serious about this and it isn't just an emotional thing that'll wear off in a week or two."

Zeke had recognized the pastor's subtle way of solidifying a man's resolve, but it was clear Pastor Bob had flipped Adam Xavier's umbrage switch. "If that's what you think, you don't know me," Doc said. "Number one in my class, file full of top references, destined for big things. The brass at Memorial tells me they're already sizing me up for an executive office down the road. This state goes under, I could go anywhere and land the same kind of deal."

"Not if you stay," Pastor Bob said.

"My point exactly. You see what I'm giving up. This is no small commitment. I expect to play a leadership role in this holdout effort. Eager to prove myself worthy."

"We'll all be tested," Pastor Bob said. "I'm sure you're familiar with Mark 10:44."

"I've taught in every church I've ever attended but this one, Pastor, but remind me."

"It's where Jesus says, 'Whoever of you desires to be first shall be slave of all.'"

"Yes, sir. I'm familiar with it."

These days, Zeke couldn't deny that Doc's compulsion to be the alpha male also drove him to be on top of every detail all the time. Despite that he found Doc's personality repellant from the beginning and that it caused Mahir to retreat even further into his shell—if that were possible—Zeke also believed the trade-off was worth it. Whatever those weaknesses cost him and the team, they paid off in Zeke's knowing he could always count on Doc to perform at the highest level. That driven, overachiever side made Doc remarkably astute and analytical, and he could immediately size up a situation and see the big picture. That had proved valuable from the day he had answered Pastor Bob's call from the pulpit eight years before.

Regardless of how swamped Zeke and Mahir were back then, trying to save California from disaster, it was obvious Doc was the busiest of the three. Yet he had been able to carve out an hour a week for the three of them to meet. And if ever Zeke and Mahir announced that meeting the next week would be impossible due to some undeniable schedule conflict, Doc would find a way to accommodate them.

He was also the first to recognize the magnitude of the task before them. He began compiling lists of what they would need. Zeke finally determined that Doc lacked only two things that would have made him the complete Renaissance man: self-awareness—that ability to see how he came across to others—and a sense of humor. That was borne out when Zeke tried to pay him a compliment. Doc had proved prescient in predicting that when the California economy would collapse, the eco-system would be obliterated beyond repair, and the US president would announce the government's official abandonment of the state. Zeke said, "You were all over those from day one, man. How do you do it?"

Without a hint of irony—or humility—Doc said, "I'm brilliant."

Without Doc, however, they never would have been ready. Among the three of them meeting weekly and including Pastor Bob about every six weeks, they fashioned an exhaustive plan that filled several megabytes of data backed by hard copies that filled multiple, thick, three-ring binders for each of the holdouts, most keyboarded by Jennie Gill. The plan outlined everything the group would need to survive and to minister in a worst-case scenario.

It began with a financial strategy based on what had been announced by the federal government, which would be working with the remnants of the California treasury in an attempt to compensate homeowners and mortgage holders as they relocated to other states. The holdouts, natu-rally, would have this money to invest in survival necessities. But of course that wouldn't prove nearly enough in the long run. Doc's idea was that Pastor Bob should prevail upon the consciences of those in the congrega-tion who had not answered the call and persuade them that they could still play a role in this significant ministry by donating.

It was difficult to estimate the enormous cost to build a compound to house the holdouts, let alone to sustain them and provide what they needed in order to minister to the people they had been called to serve. They would need food, clothing, medical supplies, water, vehicles, fuel, power, and they would also need to make clandestine supply runs to the closest state—Arizona.

This proved the perfect opportunity, in Doc's opinion, for Pastor Bob to audition him as an alternate speaker/teacher. So Rev. Gill had Dr. Xavier make the pitch for the project in a morning service via a ten-minute devotional before the offering was taken. No surprise, Doc proved effective and helped raise a massive amount. And he became a frequent substitute speaker for Pastor Bob.

Most stimulating to Zeke about the weekly planning meetings was that Doc had a knack for asking the right questions. He mined Zeke and Mahir's brains for everything about surviving in desert-like conditions. Then they matched their needs and their budget to the available funds, scouted locations, and found the perfect spot: The navy had abandoned a former site at Seal Beach that had housed weapons bunkers. The installation sat in a dense suburban housing complex of adjoining communities that had been annihilated by a one-two punch of an earthquake-ignited wildfire.

The massive tremors had left cul-de-sacs and parched lawns mere repositories for debris, then the conflagrations swept through. That left nothing for the earthmoving equipment assigned to cart away the rubble, the area now endless square miles of ash that either drifted into the Pacific or served as a powdery base for a cadaverous wilderness.

Even vultures detoured around it.

But where Washington had bid adieu, Zeke's colleagues saw opportunity, particularly in the Seal Beach Naval Weapons Station. They rented earthmoving equipment and hired subcontractors to construct an entirely self-contained underground complex for up to forty people.

Why not more? Because atop everything they hoped to provide those they felt called to serve, God had simply not put on their hearts to shelter up to four hundred thousand people. Few would have chosen to remain unless they had somewhere to stay, especially with the federal government offering alternatives in bordering states.

The holdouts' priorities were to offer people the message of the Bible while ministering to their physical needs. They would trade with them, teach them to sustain themselves, and try to keep them healthy.

The holdouts themselves would learn through study and experience how people had survived in deserts for centuries. Their needs would be simple and basic, but not easy to meet. Their compound had to have room to store food, water, clothing, and vehicles, and it had to provide shelter, sanitation, and space to artificially produce what nature would no longer provide. In addition, it had to be sustainable, and no one knew for how long. The resulting facility—which took a year to build—was a hidden marvel.

Where naval personnel had looked out over miles of suburban houses, the holdouts' periscopes in each corner allowed unobstructed views seemingly all the way to the horizon. Inside was where the magic lay. Eight years into the experiment, Zeke still marveled at the design that somehow overcame claustrophobia.

Generators for power, light, and ventilation had been non-negotiables, as had strength and security against natural and man-made calamity. But the genius was in the sheer size and sense of space. Every room was larger than those in a normal house. Corridors were wider. Ceilings were taller. Every surface—floor, wall, and ceiling—consisted of easily washable white synthetic.

The massive floor plan flowed from a central Commons—a multi-purpose area used for eating, meeting, learning, and recreation—that fed into wings containing residence quarters (with living and dining rooms, bedrooms, private baths, and kitchens), one with a fully stocked medical facility (with lab and infirmary), one with laboratories for growing food and producing synthetic fuels and even water, and another with a community kitchen and food storage area.

The largest single area was a garage that could house a dozen vehicles and accommodate miscellaneous storage, and which led to a hidden incline to the surface. Zeke and Doc and Mahir knew the single greatest threat would be desperate people wanting to live with them—which space forced them to limit. Attrition had seen them shrink to fourteen. The Muscadins had brought them back to sixteen.

Though they had room for up to forty, the more they allowed in, the more difficult it would be to protect their hidden location. Danger from the Mongers alone could end their mission.

That could not happen.

It was time to move out. Zeke's team was to find Mahir and Danley and Cristelle Muscadin, get back to the compound even if they had to walk the eight miles, pick up at least two vehicles and some food, and determine what the Mongers were up to while steering clear of them. Doc's team was to lie low, stay safe, and protect the sanctuary. Worst-case scenario: The former tattoo parlor basement might become their new home.

Worst-case was right, Zeke thought. The best thing about their base was that fewer than half the number it was designed for actually lived there. After all he and Mahir and Doc had gone through to cover all the bases in the EOTWAWKI (End of the World as We Know It) literature and design the best underground bunker possible, the last thing he wanted was to abandon it.

If they really had to relocate to the Long Beach ghost town of crumbling office buildings and retail shop shells, they wouldn't survive long, let alone be able to help anyone else. Where else but in their own bunker could they control the climate, conduct their experiments, tend their own gardens, grow their own fish?

They had been able to plan strategic forays into settlements of Native American tribes where, because they had taught the people how to survive under the new reality without government assistance, the tribes were also open to hearing about Christ. The holdouts had also been able to minister and share the gospel with indigents, impoverished people without the means to relocate, regardless of how badly they wanted to.

Beyond sharing their faith and teaching people the Bible when they allowed it, the holdouts also taught the tribes better ways to survive and subsist off the land—which became more difficult by the day. Progress had been slow and not without suspicion and danger, but Zeke knew if their own compound were compromised they might never recover.

"Let's pace ourselves," Zeke said as he, Katashi, Raoul, Benita, and Pastor Bob ventured out. He positioned the Gutierrezes at the rear, facing backward, as the five stayed tightly bunched and moved steadily. The plan was to follow the tracks of Mahir, Danley, and Cristelle's dirt bikes to see if they reached the base, or how close they got.

"You know I served in the military, right?" Pastor Bob said.

"You've mentioned that," Zeke said.

"I mean, I didn't see combat or anything . . ."

"Something you want to say, Pastor?"

"I just have to ask. You've known Mahir a long time, but Danley and Cristelle . . ."

"They've been with us what, six months or so, right?" Katashi said. "You don't trust them?"

"I sure want to. I've heard their testimonies, but there just aren't that many Haitians who come to California. They weren't even here before the drought. But they said they got here when most people were leaving."

Zeke shrugged. "And we stayed when most were leaving. People have their reasons."

Pastor Bob nodded. "But you have to agree it's strange that all our vehicles were trashed but theirs."

"What're you saying?" Benita said, her back still to the others. "They tip off the Mongers where we are, but for what? What do they get out of it? And is Mahir in on it?"

"No way," Zeke said. "If there's anything to this, Mahir's a victim—and in big trouble."

"That's my fear," Pastor Bob said.

Zeke didn't give it any credence, but he realized he had unintentionally picked up the pace. When they reached where the three had parked their dirt bikes, the tracks were easy to follow on the cracked ground. Zeke and the others followed them east for several miles in a virtual straight line—three tracks for when they had come from the compound, and three for when they returned. That meant they hadn't been followed or didn't think they had, so they had no reason to try to mislead anyone by taking another route back.

Zeke had learned a lot living in the desert that LA had become, including that it wasn't smart to be out in the sun at this time of day. Normally he'd have ridden back in his Jeep and spent the hottest part of the day underground. Now he felt vulnerable, and not only to the heat and radiation. As carefully as he and his companions walked, there was no avoiding kicking up swirls of dust. Neither was there anywhere to hide. Even if a Hydro Monger contingent was limited to the one big rig and two mediums Katashi had seen a couple of hours before, Zeke's quintet would be hard-pressed to defend themselves in the open with only their sidearms.

"I'm no military strategist, Zeke," Pastor Bob said, "but Doc said we were sitting ducks back there. Truthfully, I'd trade places with them right about now. It's as if we've got targets on our backs here."

"I'm with you," Katashi said.

"Speak for Me now."

"What's that, Raoul?" Zeke said.

"I didn't say nothin', man."

"Speak for Me now."

"Say what?" Zeke said.

"I said I didn't say nothing," Raoul said.

"Hearing things?" Pastor Bob said with a smile.

"Matter of fact, I am."

"If I *was* gonna say anything," Raoul said, "I was gonna say I'm scared too."

"I'll give you the words."

"Okay, Lord," Zeke said.

Pastor Bob chuckled. "Who's on first?"

"What're you crazy gringos talkin' about?" Benita said.

"It's an old Ameri—" Zeke began. Then, "The Lord of hosts, Him you shall hallow. Let Him be your fear, and let Him be your dread."

"Isaiah," Pastor Bob said. "Nice."

"That's heavy, man," Raoul said. "What's it mean?"

"It means we don't have to be afraid," Pastor Bob said. "Worship God and He will take over."

"Well, He better," Benita said. "Look here."

Zeke turned with the others and saw a cloud on the horizon much too large for walkers or even three dirt bikes to produce.

"Weapons out, boss?" Katashi said.

"Not yet. We don't know who it is, but let's not provoke. Just be ready. Pray for me, Pastor."

"Lord, give him holy boldness. And me too. Amen."

Dark hulks morphed into black tanker trucks through the shimmering heat waves. Billowing dust clouds twenty and thirty feet high trailed them as they raced over the hard-packed ground.

"They're not gonna run us down, are they?" Benita said.

"I can't imagine," Zeke said. "There's no point."

As the tankers drew closer he could tell from how they bounced and swayed that they carried full loads. They appeared to be traveling at least sixty miles per hour and would need a lot of stopping distance. Zeke wondered if they planned to just hurtle on by, but then he heard the roar of the engines abate. "Give 'em some room, people."

They stepped aside as the drivers appeared to rhythmically pump their brakes. The lead driver calculated perfectly and drifted to a stop right next to Zeke, the other two trucks in tandem. The lead driver emerged and clambered down, a tall man with shaggy blond hair and wearing a sleeveless black vest. He appeared unarmed.

"Afternoon!" he said with a grin. "Wicked day to be walkin'. Need a lift? Got room fer all y'all."

"Appreciate it," Zeke said. "But no, we're all right, thanks."

"C'mon, no secret ya lost yer rides."

"That so?"

"All's I know is we come up on a pickum-up truck, a Jeeper, and a Rover yonder what all been wasted, and we know who done it."

"Yeah? Who?"

"Three foreigners on rice rockets."

"Uh-huh."

"Don't b'lieve me, suit yerself."

"You saw them do this?"

"Saw 'em hightailin' away's all I know."

"Thanks for the info."

"Ride offer's still open."

"Answer's still no, thanks."

"Don't wanna insult me, do ya?"

"I know who you are," Zeke said. "I've bought from you before."

The man squinted. "Then ya know m' name?"

"I know you go by WatDoc."

"Right! Get it? Water Doctor?"

"I get it."

"An' ya don't wanna ride with a man you done bid'ness with?"

"Have a good day, WatDoc."

"You too then, man. What's yer name?"

"You don't need to know my name."

"How come?"

"You just don't."

"I'll jes' call you Spokesman, then."

"That'll work."

"A'ight then."

To Zeke's relief, the Mongers crossed the dirt bike tracks and raced away. He still held out hope they hadn't followed Mahir, Danley, and Cristelle back to base.

"We didn't see no bike tracks around our vehicles, did we, Zeke?" Raoul said.

"We sure didn't. WatDoc and his crew did that damage."

"I don't want to think about what they might have done to our people," Pastor Bob said.

"I don't either," Zeke said. "But finding them is our only job now."

6

RUN DOWN

"Everybody take a sip," Zeke said, "and Raoul and Benita face forward. I'm not worried about anything behind us anymore, and we've got to start making time. We're about three miles from base and we've got to find our people. Jogging wouldn't be smart, but let's hurry."

"Yeah," Katashi said, "let's not be rash. WatDoc was trying to tell us something. We know he and his guys have seen Mahir and the Muscadins. What did they do with them?"

"Or to them?" Benita said.

Half an hour later, Zeke and the others were panting. He stopped short when he noticed the dirt bike tracks had deviated. The men seemed to turn as one toward Benita, who had proved herself over and over an innate tracker—at least of animals. "How are you with tire tracks?" Zeke said.

She stepped forward and squatted to examine the ground.

"Watch this," Raoul said. "Go, *cariño.*"

Benita said the three tire tracks on the left had come from their compound. "See?" she said, pointing. "The small part o' the nubs face west. These over here? The other way."

"Tol' you, man," Raoul said.

Zeke shook his head. "So on their way back, they veer off to the right here and split up. Why?"

"Not only that," Benita said, jogging ahead and kneeling again, "but they sped up. Look at this."

As the rest joined her, she pointed out that the tracks were shallower and less distinct, the sandy surface more scattered. "They were tryin' to get away from something. Look far enough ahead and I bet we're gonna see it."

Zeke knew they shouldn't be jogging in the heat, but he couldn't stop himself either. He and Katashi followed the tracks that went left while the others followed the one that went right. Soon they all saw the heavy treads of truck tires. "Benita!" he called out, "make sense of this for me!"

"C'mere!" she hollered, but as he hurried over, all four guys had trouble keeping up as she raced from spot to spot, crouching to study the patterns of circling and crossing truck tires and dirt bike tracks. She stopped, hands on her knees, breathing deeply.

"Take your time," Zeke said. "Let's get it right."

Benita straightened and rested her hands on her hips. "Pretty sure it was those same three tanker trucks," she said. "All three have duallys on the back, and even as fast as they're goin', they're leavin' flat, broad marks like they're carrying heavy loads. I'm guessin' Mahir and them saw the trucks and tried to dodge 'em, and the truck started circling them. This one here tried to make a break for it."

"Think whoever it was got away?"

Benita shrugged. "Gotta follow the tracks till we find out."

Pastor Bob shook his head. "Hope they kept the scoundrels from finding the compound."

"Let's go!" Katashi said.

"Slow down," Zeke said. "We really have to conserve our strength. We don't know what we're going to find, and we have to be ready for anything."

"Come on!" Katashi said. "These are our friends."

Zeke put a hand on his shoulder. "I just want us all at our strongest."

"Oh, no," Raoul said, pointing. "What's that?"

A little more than a quarter mile away lay a crumpled wreck. There would be no stopping his friends now. Zeke had to run too.

It took a couple of minutes to reach the mangled dirt bike, but that wasn't the worst of it. Its fenders and spokes were blood splattered. Unfortunately, the three bikes owned by the troop were identical, so it was impossible to know who had been riding and might have been injured, captured, or killed.

Again, Benita immediately went to work, striding about, surveying the area, kneeling here and there. "There's good news, boss," she said. "Least I think there is."

"Tell me."

"I don't think nobody got shot. I think the blood came from when whoever was riding got knocked off, and then the bike got ran over after that."

"How can you tell?"

"I don't wanna be too graphic, but if the rider got ran over too, there'd be more than blood, you know what I mean? Like flesh and bone maybe. But there's more good news too."

"I'm listening."

"Looks like the trucks all left together, and look over here," she said. Benita moved to where the ground was disturbed and bloody. "The other two bikes come over here too. Then one goes off toward base and the other goes back toward town, but look at this."

She slowly followed the trail of the bike heading back toward base. "The tracks are wider and flatter, see? And look close on that side. Those are drops of blood, man. The bike goin' back to base has two people on it, and one of 'em's bleeding."

"And the one heading back to town is looking for Doc," Zeke said.

"Why didn't they both go home, and one of 'em get a vehicle to go get Doc and more people?" Raoul said.

"Probably because whoever needs Doc can't wait," Pastor Bob said.

"Let's get going," Katashi said. "See if we can help, and make sure the compound hasn't been compromised."

"Wait!" Raoul said. "Someone's coming!"

Zeke instinctively reached for his weapon just when he heard the high-pitched whine of a dirt bike. The five jumped and waved, and the rider, who turned out to be Doc—his majestic head crammed into Mahir's iridescent purple helmet—raced up and skidded to a stop. "I've got to get going," he said. "Cristelle's been injured. Mahir's taken over for me."

"Take Pastor Bob with you," Zeke said, "so he and Danley can come back and pick up the others and us."

An hour later, Zeke sensed he was looking into the eyes of a somber, grateful, ravenous group who finally gathered again as one in their own underground compound. They crowded around Cristelle Muscadin's bed in the infirmary down the opposite corridor from where Mahir and Zeke distilled salt water for drinking and experimented with various formulas to produce alternative fuels. Katashi beckoned him into the hall with a nod.

"You've seen Cristelle ride, right?" Katashi said.

"Sure, why?"

"She knows her way around a bike. She ought to be able to outmaneuver a tanker. Danley's been looking daggers at Mahir ever since he got back here."

"What're you saying? Did he say anything?"

Katashi leaned closer. "Only thing Danley told me was that it sure took Doc a long time to get here. You don't think Doc's prejud—"

"C'mon, you know better'n that. For one thing, she's almost as dark as he is. And when we saw Doc, he was hurrying."

Katashi squinted. "Any reason Mahir would have been slow getting to Doc?"

"I can't imagine. I'd better get back in there."

Cristelle, at twenty-five, was a year older than her husband, Danley, who sat on the edge of her bed holding her hand. The young woman appeared barely able to keep her eyes open. Doc said he had sedated her and injected heavy painkillers into her right leg below the knee. He said it appeared the front tire of one of the trucks had crushed her shin and obliterated much of the flesh and calf muscle. She would be immobile and suffering for a long time.

Mahir said the Hydro Mongers had overtaken and harassed the three of them and, he was sure, intended to kill them.

"That makes no sense," Zeke said. "They had you outnumbered, but you should have been more nimble."

"They picked on our weakest link," Mahir said. "Cristelle's still pretty new on the bike."

"She is not!" Danley said in his Haitian lilt. "I know you didn't mean to, but you forced her right in front of that truck!"

"I was trying to distract the driver, Danley!"

"I want to kill that guy," Danley said.

"I'm sure we all do," Zeke said. "But we don't need a war, and vengeance is not who we are. Those guys are part of a huge network. They'd just as soon rub us out as have us in the way. They think we're competition."

"They don't need our business," Katashi said. "They want our brain trust and our technology."

"Well," Alexis said, "that's not for sale."

Doc, who had been glowering since clarifying Cristelle's injuries, held up a hand. "You realize how close we came to being fully exposed here, right? Today could've been the end of this place, and for all we know, they *do* know where we are. Some reason no one's manning the periscopes, Zeke?"

"You handle your responsibilities and I'll handle mine," Zeke said. "We'll scan the area in a few minutes. Nobody can get close before sundown without kicking up a lot of dust."

"I don't suppose this is a good time to be out hunting," Doc said, "but we need to eat, and everybody needs to hydrate. I hope the ration everybody took with them this morning is long gone by now and you're each able to get another gallon into you by dinnertime. Be smart."

"Doc's right about that, of course," Zeke said. "Drink up, everybody."

He led everyone out to the Commons and asked Elaine what food was available.

"You announced lunch on your own, remember? We were all going to get back together for dinner."

"I did, didn't I?"

"Just tell everybody I'm opening the pantry to tide them over till dinner. If it's safe to eat out under the awning after sundown, Katashi and I can come up with a nice barbecue. I think we deserve it after today, don't you?"

"Sounds perfect, Elaine. And are you still available?"

"Of course. Send Sasha my way in an hour, but an hour after that I'll need to start working with Katashi on dinner."

It was just as well Zeke, Mahir, and Doc had never devised a way to override the government's scramble of the airwaves to get a TV picture into the compound. Audio was the best they could manage, and it was enough. Movies and TV shows might have been just enough diversion to lend some sanity to such an existence, but Zeke was certain the entertainment would have become an addiction that would have softened them all.

As it was he'd made an executive decision and restricted recreational listening to the audio feed of most of the drivel. News and documentaries and some movies were fine. People tired of most of it without being able to see the visuals, but he at least had to know what was going on in the world every day.

Though he was ravenous, he devoured twenty-five minutes of headline news before he, Alexis, and Sasha sat munching dried hollyleaf cherries and juniper berries along with salted strips of gecko jerky. Zeke felt edgy after such a harrowing day, but he tried to head off Alexis's concern by saying how well he thought the memorial service had gone. She wasn't biting.

"It was nice," she said, "no thanks to you."

"Mom!"

"I'm not scolding him, Sasha," Alexis said. "I'm just saying he seemed less focused than I might have wished."

"Yeah, Dad, what was up with that?"

"Katashi saw Mongers on his way in, that's all. Put me on alert. But I thought you were great, hon. And Sash, that opening song—I gotta tell ya—how'd you come up with that anyway?"

"It just hit me that slow would be interesting. I didn't expect it to come out so special."

"It moved everybody," he said. "Me especially. Hey, by the way, Mrs. Meeks would like you to drop by for an hour or so. Can you do that?"

Sasha squinted at him. "Really?"

"Yeah, that all right?"

"Sure, but that's what she wants? It was her idea?"

"Well, I—uh, truth is . . ."

"Dad! You don't have to make up stories to get rid of me."

"No! I—"

"Just tell me. It's okay."

"Forgive me, sweetie. You're right."

"Right now?"

"Please. If you don't mind."

"On my way."

"Thanks, and again, sorry."

"It's okay, Dad. I like when you owe me."

She left with a smile, but Alexis looked bemused. "What is going on?" she said.

"We just have to talk, that's all."

"I had a feeling," Alexis said.

7

THE TALK

THIS WAS WORSE than being sent to the principal's office. And Zeke couldn't understand why his mouth was so dry. Why should it be hard to share something personal, something meaningful, with the person closest to him in life? If she couldn't understand, couldn't empathize, didn't have counsel or input or advice, who would?

He would talk to Pastor Bob too, but this conversation with Alexis was the one that would make or break his future—confirm that something significant was going on or that he was simply off his nut.

Here sat the most beautiful person in the world to him, inside or out—clichéd as that might sound—all her depth and character and personality in one precious package. And she gazed at him with what appeared to be wonder, expectancy, trust, and yet also puzzlement and perhaps a hint of fear.

They had been through so much together. Alexis had stood by him, believed in him, supported him, and—especially over these last several years—proved the ferocity of her most sacred wedding vows by virtually and literally giving up everything to join him on the most radical mission a couple could undertake. And now he was going to tell her what?

"I know this is going to sound strange to you . . ."

She raised her brows. "That ship sailed a long time ago, love."

"Yeah, but Lexi, you're going to find this bizarre even for me."

She grinned. "I can hardly wait."

"I'm trying to be serious here."

She reached across the table and took his hand in both of hers. "I see that, but I've had enough pathos for one day, don't you think? I was filled to the brim with all the reminiscing about Junior. It was as if he was there. How special that Katashi, Raoul, Benita, and Elaine are all with us now because of him. Wait!" she said, dropping his hand, eyes dancing. "I know what it is! It's you and the widow Meeks. She's finally stolen you from me. She's breaking it to Sasha now."

Zeke sat back. "Yep, you guessed it. You stole my thunder. Don't s'pose you want all the lurid details."

"Oh, do tell! You couldn't resist her charms!"

"'Course not. How could I? You had to know I'd grow bored with you eventually and look for an older woman."

But Zeke's chuckle quickly died and his smile faded. She fell silent too, and he felt her eyes bore into him. "You know this is how I deal with stress, Z. I could tell you were on edge, threatened by that WatDoc guy, believed the compound might have been compromised. But like every-body else here, I believe in you. I count on you to rise to every challenge. And you know I'm here when you need me. You can tell me anything. Nothing's gonna be too strange or bizarre for me. If I wasn't here for the long haul, I'd have been gone a long time ago. So I'm all ears. Spit it out, big guy."

"You sure?"

"You kiddin'?" she said. "Don't know where that speech came from, but it's the best I've got."

"Okay, here goes." He sighed. "God's been speaking to me."

"Yeah? What's He been saying?"

"Audibly." He waited. "So, did you speak too soon when you said nothing could be too strange or bizarre for you?"

Alexis seemed to study him again. She hadn't bolted, so that was in his favor. "Let's back up," she said, pressing both palms on the table. "You're serious, right? You're not pranking me, getting back at me for something I've forgotten about—anything like that?"

"I wouldn't kid about something like this."

"Just making sure. All right. Now that we know what we're dealing with . . ." She stood, quiet again. He searched her eyes, but she wouldn't look at him. Finally she said, "Tell me everything. When did this start? What form did it take? Exactly what did you hear, and what makes you think it was God?"

Alexis looked relieved when he told her it had started only that morning. He assumed she would say it was stress-related, perhaps water deprivation—or that maybe it had something to do with the anniversary of Junior's death.

He tried to recount the first couple of incidents humorously, how at first he didn't recognize the voice or the touch as God's and thought a Monger had actually slipped in and gotten the drop on him. But that didn't elicit so much as a smile from her. If he had hoped she would take this seriously, he got his wish. Alexis was clearly alarmed.

"Did you find it as bizarre as Doc did when Pastor Bob asked me to pray for Jennie and I wound up spouting a passage of Scripture?"

"Come to think of it, I did," she said. "But I'd just learned of Jennie's diagnosis, and then I was actually impressed by those verses. I didn't know you had them memorized."

"That's just it, babe. I suppose I've heard them before, probably a couple of times, but I have never, ever tried to memorize them."

"Then how—"

"I told you. God said He would give me utterance. He told me to just open my mouth and He would give me the words."

"Ezekiel, please! That's—"

"Say it, Lexi! I know you want to. It's crazy, I know. So then explain it. How did I do that? And that Scripture had nothing to do with Jennie, did it?"

"Not really."

"Then what is God doing? What's He saying to me?"

Alexis looked seriously concerned. "Can you quote the passage now? For me?"

"Let me think—no. I can't. I'm not even sure where it's from. Clearly it's Old Testament, but I couldn't tell you the reference or the context. All I remember is that Bob asked me to pray—"

"For Jennie," Alexis said.

"Right, and like you, I was shocked by what we had just been told about her. And so I prayed silently that the Lord would give me the words. He impressed on me that He had already told me that whatever He commanded me I should speak, and He said something about 'Behold, I have put My words in your mouth.'"

"Oh, Zeke!"

"I know, right? What was I supposed to think? I just stood there waiting."

"There *was* a long pause," she said.

"That's the thing—I was waiting for words from God, and He had told me to open my mouth. I remember Him sort of scolding me about having faith and that I should open my mouth. So I opened my mouth and that's what came out."

"You realize how that sounds?"

"Who are you telling? I told you this was gonna make me sound nuts."

"I should've listened."

Zeke snorted. "I knew I could count on you, Lexi. I wonder what the widow Meeks is doing tonight."

Alexis roared. She rushed around the table and fell into Zeke's arms, pulling his head down so they were nose to nose. "Nuts it is," she said. "You're certifiable. Crazy." She affected an exaggerated Jimmy Stewart impression and quoted George Bailey from *It's a Wonderful Life*: "'You're screwy, and you're drivin' me crazy too! I'm seein' things.' You're a crazy holy man, Zeke. But you're *my* crazy holy man."

She kissed him, made him sit, then sat in his lap.

"Can I be serious again for a minute?" he said.

"I think you'd better."

"I gotta tell ya, I'm scared."

She pushed back and held his face in both hands. "You're never scared of anything."

"If you only knew, Lexi."

"Tell me."

"First, you know this isn't us, either of us. God impresses stuff on us, sure. I mean, look where we are. The rest of the world had enough sense to get out of Dodge when the Drought Gang came ridin' in, six guns blazing. But Pastor Bob preached his Marshal Dillon/Wyatt Earp/Gary Cooper/ *High Noon* sermon one night, and that was all it took for us to leave caution to the wind. I didn't know if I dared ask you to dive into this with me, but if you remember, you committed before I did. And you had our only daughter in your arms at the time."

"That's what I mean, Z. You're fearless, and I'm with you. So what's the problem?"

He drew her close and she laid her head on his chest. "It's just that up to now, hard as this has been, up till today I've actually found it kind of fun. I've been in my sweet spot. God has used almost everything I've ever known or been taught. I've been stretched and challenged and used in ways I never could have dreamed."

"And you've become a leader too."

"I know, and I didn't expect that either. But today, hearing God out loud . . . That's not something I bargained for, not something I'm comfortable with."

"You want to know what I think?"

He gave her a look. "What do you think I'm doing here?"

"Trying to break the news to me about you and the widow Meeks?"

"Hilarious."

"Sorry. Let me ask you this: Do you feel like this is something new— well, obviously it's new—but I mean a new normal?"

"That's just it. I guess I'm hoping it's not. I liked things the way they were."

"Lots of people would give anything to hear directly from God, Zeke. They'd consider it a privilege. More than that. A sacred honor. A huge responsibility."

"Would *you*?"

She paused. "Good question. I don't know."

"I already have a huge responsibility," he said. "Do I really want more?"

"God wouldn't choose you unless He thought you were up to it. And He certainly wouldn't give you more than you could handle. Mostly He wouldn't leave you alone, would He?"

They were quiet a moment. Finally, Zeke said, "My leg's falling asleep."

Alexis slipped off his lap and sat next to him. "It wouldn't be like Him to force this on you if you're unwilling. But you might find yourself miserable if you miss a calling."

Zeke sniffed. "Funny, I'm just relieved you're not packing a bag and trying to sneak Sasha out of here."

Alexis chuckled. "Ezekiel, you're stuck with me. You know what I'd leave you over, and this isn't it. I've seen you in public and I've seen you in private. I've seen you at the height of success and I've seen you in the pit of despair. I know you're the same man of God when people are watching and when they are not. If the Lord has something more for you, for whatever reason—whether I understand it or I'm comfortable with it or even whether you understand it or are comfortable with it—you have to know this: Not only will I not stand in the way of it, but I will stand with you in it to the end. Any questions?"

"No, ma'am."

THE DISCOVERY

8

AFTER A DINNER of tilapia and squash from an elaborate aquaponics system designed by Zeke, Doc, and Mahir, Zeke announced plans for the retrieval of the three damaged vehicles after sundown the next day. He hoped the recitation of logistics would get everyone's minds off the near-tragedy they'd suffered. As soon as possible, he wanted everyone who was able to get back to their daily routine of seeking out stragglers to minister to—sometimes these were as random as wandering alcoholics or the mentally ill, some of whom had never figured out where everybody had gone—and also helping sustain the compound.

He explained that their one water tanker—much smaller than WatDoc's monster and slightly smaller than the two medium-sized trucks they had encountered that afternoon—would be rigged with an electric winch, allowing them to upright the damaged vehicles, mount them on a dolly, and tow them back. "It has to be after dark," Zeke said, "because we'll produce so much dust we'd give away our location."

Little surprise, Doc questioned the strategy. "The Mongers will be able to see your lights for miles."

Sasha piped up, "Just like the Israelites! It's either the cloud by day or a pillar of fire by night." When this brought chuckles all around, except from Doc, Sasha immediately said, "I'm sorry, Dr. Xavier. I didn't mean to be disrespectful."

"Oh, I know," Doc said. "No offense taken, and you're right. There's no good time to be engaging in that much activity out in the open. Let's face it, that's why the Mongers didn't take those vehicles. They've got us right where they want us. They aim to find this place, and this is how they're going to do it."

"You got a suggestion, Doc," Raoul said, "or you just criticizin'?"

"Of course I've got an idea, but you're not going to like it."

People murmured, "Go ahead, what?"

Zeke leaned close and whispered to Alexis, "He loves to be begged."

"We leave the wrecks right where they are and replace those vehicles," Doc said.

"That's a lot of money," Katashi said.

"What's your option?" Doc said. "Stir dust in the daytime or beam lights in the night: Either way you're sending the Mongers engraved invitations to our front door."

"He's right."

"I know it," Zeke said, much as he hated to admit it. Several turned to look at him, including Alexis, and he realized he had responded to a comment no one else had heard. *Terrific. Here we go again.* "Uh, yeah, I mean, that's a good word, Doc, and you're right. As far as the budget goes, Alexis and I can make do without replacing the Wrangler. We'll use whatever else is available. How about you, Raoul? You need to replace the pickup?"

"Me and Benita can make anything work, man. But she's the best shot here too. Just give me something that gets us where we need to go for good hunting."

"How 'bout a good used one?"

"*Bueno.*"

"Doc, the same? A good used car big enough for your family?"

"No, sir."

"Sorry?"

"I need the Land Rover replaced, same condition or better."

"Let's be reasonable . . ."

"Okay, first, there's no reason to have Sunday morning worship any-where but right here. I'm on record opposing that from the start. That dumpy old place has nothing to recommend it, and we leave our vehi-cles exposed not only to the elements, but also to Monger thugs—not to mention that we also have to then walk the rest of the way. What did we expect? We're lucky this didn't happen before. It wasn't my fault my Rover got trashed, and I expect it to be replaced. Naturally my insurance doesn't extend to California. I'm here at my own risk."

"As we all are. Let's be sure we consider everybody's well-being—"

"That's all I ever do," Doc said.

Zeke made the rounds of the underground compound every night. That evening he asked Pastor Bob to accompany him as he checked on those manning the periscopes in each corner of the complex. This was something anyone of any age could handle, once they were trained what to watch for—even eight-year-old Kayla Xavier and sixty-two-year-old Jennie Gill.

Gabrielle Xavier was taking her turn at the northeast post, which involved slowly scanning the horizon one minute of every five when a quiet beeper sounded. During the off minutes the assignee could read or doze or do whatever they wished. Gabrielle was a tall, trim, handsome woman who, like Alexis, had a way of making survival attire look classy.

When the men approached, she was affixed to the lens, slowing turn-ing in her chair, hands guiding the scope. "Be right with you," she said pleasantly, "whoever you are." She had a throaty, melodic tone.

"Only Pastor and me, Gabrielle," Zeke said. "No rush."

"Oh," she said, and he detected a hint of suspicion. "What's up?"

"Just making the rounds. No agenda."

When she reached the end of the arc she folded the handles and rolled her chair back. "To what do I owe the honor?" she said, smiling, but still, Zeke thought, sounding guarded.

"Like I said, just strolling through. You doing all right?"

"Always," she said. "Do I need to apologize for my husband?"

The question caught Zeke off guard, but apparently Pastor was ready. "Oh, no. We wouldn't know what to think if Doc wasn't being Doc."

"Well, he was a little rigid even for me this evening," she said. "He even asked me if I thought so. I told him yes."

Zeke shrugged. "That's good."

"Maybe," she said, "but he's not likely to admit that to you."

"It's enough to know he's aware of it. Is it still going to cost the treasury a Land Rover?"

"You do what you think is best for everybody, and he'll just have to live with it. You know he's all bark—"

"I hope so."

"Listen," she said, "I'm glad you're both here. I need to tell you something I haven't even told Adam."

"Oh?" Pastor Bob said. "I'm not sure that's wise."

"I'll tell him soon enough. I just became aware of it, and after the day he's had, I didn't want to add anything more to his plate. He's beyond stressed and exhausted, and he's going to be up late with Cristelle—probably till midnight. This can wait till tomorrow for Adam, but you need to know."

"Very well," Pastor Bob said.

"My kids like to explore, as you know."

"Of course," Pastor said. "I think they've been into every nook and cranny of this place. Especially Caleb."

"Kayla too," she said. "They compete to see who can get into the most mischief. Anyway, they were running around in the motor pool today when I was helping Elaine and Katashi get dinner prepared. They wanted to see the motorcycle or whatever it was that their father rode back here on—"

"Dirt bike," Pastor Bob said.

"Right. So they were climbing around in there, and Caleb got into all that obsolete computer stuff. I'm not even sure what it all is."

Zeke nodded. "Obsolete is right. That would have been some pretty cheery stuff if the government hadn't blocked all the Internet signals except their own when they condemned the state. That's why we're dead in the water—bad choice of words—when it comes to Wi-Fi, Internet, anything but walkie-talkies, which are useless unless we want the Mongers hearing us as well as we can hear them. So if the kids were playing with that stuff, I doubt they could have hurt anything."

"It's not that, Ezekiel," Gabrielle said. "Caleb got into all the user manuals and warranties, those kinds of things. They were in plastic sleeves and packed between the hardware and in cable boxes."

Zeke shrugged. "It should probably all be kept together on the outside chance we'll figure out how to get online someday, but we can reorganize it if we need to. No real harm done."

"Zeke. Listen to me. The kids found more than hardware and software manuals in there."

"Yeah? What?"

"About sixty pages of material in an Arabic language."

"What?" Zeke said.

"And these were where?" Pastor Bob said.

"Right in with those computer manuals."

"Where are they now?"

"Right back where Caleb found them. He brought them to me, and they scared the devil out of me. The only thing I recognized were numbers, and several of the pages included this year. I made him put them back. I don't know anyone here who could translate from Farsi or Urdu or whatever it is, and even using those terms makes me sound more knowledgeable than I am. All I remember from college is that there are dozens and dozens of variations of Arabic languages and dialects, and I know none of them. I couldn't translate one character."

"What did you tell the kids?" Zeke said.

"I just said it was someone's personal property and that Caleb was to put it back where he found it and leave it alone."

"Perfect. And he did?"

"I made sure."

"Good thinking, Gabrielle," Zeke said.

"Say," she said, "have you looked in on Adam already or—?"

"No, he and Cristelle are last on our route."

"Well, I was going to spell him for half an hour when my shift is over, but that's not for ninety minutes, and he needs a shower."

"Oh, let us sit with Cristelle," Pastor Bob said. "We can, can't we, Zeke?"

"Sure. One of us can. Don't give it another thought."

Zeke made their next stop the garage, the broadest single area in the compound, where they housed rolling stock—the two remaining dirt bikes, the water tanker, and several other vehicles they'd had since the beginning. "Sure seems like something here would suit Doc," Pastor Bob said as they headed past the heating and cooling system, ventilation and sanitation treatment utilities, and a bank of generators humming in one corner.

"Maybe he'll come around," Zeke said.

"You *do* believe in miracles," the pastor said.

They headed to the massive shelving unit laden with the computer hardware Gabrielle had mentioned. "This inventory gives me a gut-ache every time I think of it," Zeke said. "How were we supposed to know the feds would be so determined to keep everybody out that they would scramble all the signals? Do you think if they knew we were helping people . . . ?"

"Nah," Pastor Bob said, digging between boxes and hardware. "Lots of manuals here. What'd she say, sixty pages?"

The computer-related documentation was mostly in English, Spanish, and Japanese. And that was all in stapled booklets or folded brochures. The pages in question were copy machine–generated and either stapled or loose, and as Gabrielle had said, plainly in an Arabic script.

"I don't even want to think what this means," Zeke said.

"Don't be too quick to—"

"C'mon, Pastor! You don't think we have an interloper?"

"Let's just think this through."

"Be my guest. Give me one credible alternative explanation. Just one that makes sense. Somebody heard that some militant faction is planning to set up a command post in California, so they want to familiarize themselves with the potential threat?"

"Maybe," Pastor Bob said.

"Doesn't hold water. First, where would they have heard about this?"

"On a trip for supplies."

"Then why not tell us, get us all involved? And how do they know the language? Who among us reads Arabic? And why hide it out here? We've got a traitor, Pastor."

"It's not like you to overreact, Zeke. Slow down."

"I so want to be wrong! Give me one scenario I can believe in."

"All right, here's one. Hear me out. A lot of this equipment, most of it probably, originated from the Far East, right?"

"Okay . . ."

"A sympathizer, maybe even a radical, works in one of the manufacturing plants or distribution centers. He's reading his propaganda on his break or lunch hour, it gets mixed in with the manuals, someone else packs it with the merchandise, it winds up getting shipped out. That makes more sense than thinking that somebody we know and love and eat with and work with every day is a closet terrorist. Really."

"I don't know. I'm tempted to set up a hidden camera and see who comes after this."

"I hate that idea—spying on our own people."

"You have a better idea?"

"No, but Zeke, think about it. Give me one suspect."

"You were questioning the Muscadins yourself today!"

"I was just posing a question. Could they have somehow been in cahoots with the Hydro Mongers? Then Cristelle's almost killed by them. That answered that question. We know everyone else too well. Anyway, do we have a video camera?"

"No."

"Well, there you go."

"I'll get one, next time I go to Parker."

"You don't go on five-hundred-mile-round-trip drives," Pastor Bob said. "That would be bad stewardship of your time. If this stuff belongs to one of our people—and for the wrong reasons—it'll come to light soon enough."

As they replaced everything, Zeke sighed. "In all the excitement I forgot to tell you my ulterior motive for asking you to join me tonight."

"I wondered."

"Any chance Jennie would be up to joining Lexi and me for a little while after we spell Doc? I'm going through something I need your counsel on."

"Let's ask her," Pastor Bob said. They headed down a short hallway and he knocked softly on the door of their quarters. Hearing nothing, he quietly opened it and peeked in to find the lights off. "Give me a minute, Zeke," he whispered. A moment later he returned. "She's fine, but down for the count, I'm afraid."

"You need to stay with her?"

"She urged me to go actually."

THE CALLING

9

DOC WAS SUSPICIOUS of Zeke and Pastor Bob's willingness to relieve him so he could get a shower. "That ought to be Danley's job anyway, shouldn't it?" he said.

"He's on periscope duty," Zeke said. "You know we don't make exceptions or the whole fabric of this little society falls ap—"

"Then why make an exception for me?"

"Because you're starting to smell, Doc. Now get out of here, but hurry back before we change our minds."

"Well, she's sedated enough to sleep through the night, but come and get me if there's a crisis."

"Go!"

Doc left and returned in fewer than twenty minutes without a word of thanks or appreciation. "You're welcome," Zeke muttered as they left.

Doc said, "Since she didn't rouse, you weren't really necessary."

Back at the Thorppes', when Pastor Bob learned what Zeke wanted to talk about, he said, "Is Sasha asleep yet?"

"No," Alexis said. "Just reading. Why?"

"This portends to be significant, Ezekiel," Pastor Bob said. "Of course it's your call, but think about including Sasha in this conversation."

"Seriously?" Alexis said.

"I know she just turned thirteen, but she's had to grow up awfully fast, and she's unusually mature—especially spiritually. If you think this is going to deeply impact you, imagine the effect it's going to have on her. You owe it to her to keep her informed."

Zeke sat back. "I'm not sure. I'm wondering what it all means. Is God going to just tell me what to say once in a while, or does He have some big task in mind? Shouldn't I get a handle on that before I get Sasha all worked up over this?"

"I don't know, Zeke," Alexis said. "I don't want to put words in your mouth, Pastor, but are you saying Sasha might have some insight on this herself?"

"Exactly."

Zeke shrugged. "All right then. Out of the mouths of babes, eh? Invite her in, Lexi."

Sasha appeared in a floor-length terry-cloth robe, carrying a thick paperback book. She looked surprised to see the pastor. "Did I do something wrong?"

Zeke quickly filled her in.

Sasha's eyes grew wide. "Well, that sure explains a lot. This morning I thought you were losin' it."

"That makes two of us," he said.

"Hey, wait a minute!" she said. "Did the same thing happen after dinner? Seems like you answered a question nobody asked."

"I caught that too," Pastor Bob said. "Did you, Zeke?"

"Matter of fact, I did."

"Weird," Sasha said. "And did God have you say all those strange verses when you were s'pose to be praying for Pastor's wife this morning?"

"Excellent question," Zeke said. "Fact is, I can't even remember what I quoted or where it's from. Pastor, you recognized that I said something from Isaiah just before WatDoc showed up this afternoon. Do you remember what I was quoting when you asked me to pray for Jennie?"

"I don't, but I do remember there was a distinct promise in it. At first I thought it was for me, that even though I was having to leave this ministry and these people that I love so much, I might still have a mission or a calling somewhere. I just filed that away to think about later."

Zeke stood and paced. "That's what frustrates me. If I can't even remember what I said, what's the profit in it?"

"Well, Daddy, if it's really from God, won't He bring it back to you when you need it—I mean at just the right time?"

"One would hope."

With that a chill came over Zeke he could not explain. It scared and embarrassed him and made him wish Sasha was not in the room. He knew God was about to speak to him. He desperately searched Pastor Bob's eyes. "It's happening again," he said and dropped to his knees.

The pastor and Alexis also knelt.

"Mom?" Sasha said plaintively.

"Take my hand, sweetie," Alexis said.

"Let the Lord have His way, Zeke," Pastor Bob whispered.

Zeke shuddered. "He's reminding me what He told me this morning. It's coming back."

"Speak through Your servant, Lord," the pastor said.

Suddenly, all Zeke could think was, *I'm not worthy, I'm not worthy, I'm not worthy.*

"What's going on, Daddy?" Sasha said.

He didn't want to frighten her but Zeke couldn't speak, and that made him wish Pastor Bob had not suggested she be part of this.

When his voice finally returned, he found himself suddenly hoarse. "It was this morning, when I was listening to Katashi's story. I was kind of daydreaming, you know? It was just something inconsequential, really. I was peeking out the window, looking out over Ocean Boulevard and remembering what it once was—"

"Daddy, we wanted to know what you meant when—"

Alexis shushed Sasha and said, "Just let him speak, honey."

Zeke continued, "I was just sort of in my own world, remembering how I had told Mahir way back when I was like twenty-four and he would've been, what, twenty-one, I guess, that this drought was unlike anything we'd ever seen before."

Zeke fell silent struggling to remember. Pastor Bob laid a hand gently on his back. "Yes?"

"The drought was in its infancy then, and I remember Mahir was fascinated by my take on it and wanted me to unpack it a little more for him. That was one of his favorite buzzwords back then—*unpack*. You know what I'm talking about, Lexi. In fact you got tired of hearing me talk about it—all that business about how all the other California droughts happened because of lack of moisture and precipitation but—"

"That this one's totally about the heat and all that, yeah," she said. "I'm not even a hydrologist but I could probably give my own lecture on that by now."

"Right, this drought is entirely temperature-driven, and I predicted almost from the beginning that if it wasn't extremely short-term it could be catastrophic. I didn't think of anything like this, of course, but that's what I was thinking about while Katashi was talking this morning and I was looking out the window."

Sasha sighed as if she'd been hoping for more and was already bored with this.

"That's when God spoke clearly to me, out loud, even though I didn't realize at first that it was Him."

"So, what did God say to you?" Sasha said.

"He said, 'This was My doing.'"

"Wow," Pastor Bob said.

"Sorry, Dad, but you didn't know that was God? Who else would it have been?"

"Sasha!"

"Sorry, Mom, but—"

"No, I know," Zeke said. "I should've known, but I was so shaken by it, I thought I was losing my mind. Plus remember, somebody was also touching me at the same time, so not only was I trying to figure out how to break this to your mother, I was also seriously considering asking Dr. Xavier if there was a prescription for stuff like that."

Pastor Bob said, "It was during Katashi's story that you looked so upset that we paused and I came back and prayed for you."

"Yes! That was when I finally figured out it was God. He told me to listen to Him and said, 'I am that I am.'"

"Doesn't get much clearer than that," Alexis said.

"It sure doesn't, and He told me His mercy was from everlasting if I would fear Him and remember His commandments. He said He had established Himself in heaven and that His kingdom rules. Then He said, 'Listen to Me! Hear Me!' That's what made me lurch forward and burst into tears. I was assuring him that I heard Him and I would listen, but I didn't say that out loud, did I?"

"No," Sasha said, "but you were crying, and that scared me."

Zeke chuckled. "Pastor, that's when you came back and asked the Lord to be with me in a special way. Had you only known—"

"You know," Pastor Bob said, "that wasn't the first time I've laid hands on you and prayed, but I have to say, I've never felt such tension in a man, let alone you. Was God speaking to you right then?"

"He was. And I remember now what He said. It was that passage about the last days when He will pour out His Spirit on all flesh and 'your sons and daughters will prophesy, your young men shall see visions, your old men shall dream dreams.'"

"Aah," Pastor Bob said, "Joel 2 and Acts 2."

"That's a thrilling passage," Alexis said. "But I don't get the context for Zeke. What's the Lord trying to tell him?"

"Yeah," Sasha said. "Caleb and Kayla and I have been learning about the end times, and one of our teachers read us that passage—something about the sun going dark and the moon turning to blood."

"That's right," Pastor Bob said. "I wonder if the Lord is preparing you to replace me and is giving you an idea of what your emphasis should be."

"For us," Alexis said, "or for the people we're trying to reach?"

"Why not both?" Pastor Bob said.

"Hold on a second," Zeke said. "There's more. First I have to ask you, Pastor, why your message was just a chapter from Jeremiah, and why that chapter?"

"It's just what He gave me, that's all I can say. I asked the same question myself. I assumed it was a message for whoever was to replace me. I figured that whoever was chosen might be hesitant and need the encouragement of Jeremiah's example of being exhorted by the Lord. You know,

Jeremiah thought he was too young and the Lord told him He would go before him and give him the words to speak. So he needn't be afraid of anyone because God would command him and would deliver him."

Zeke nodded. "Yeah, well, I happen to know that the message was intended for me."

"Easy there, cowboy," Pastor Bob said, smiling. "Even before the elders replace me and then they follow a logical, biblical pattern of selecting a new pastor? You know how badly Doc wants the role."

"Who doesn't?" Sasha said. "Caleb and Kayla are already campaigning for him."

"You're kidding," Alexis said. "That's inappropriate."

"I'm not talking about that," Zeke said, "And I don't even care—"

"Well, I hope you care," Pastor Bob said. "This may be a very small congregation, but it's one with what I believe is a God-ordained mission, and—"

"No, no, don't get me wrong, Pastor. I'm just saying I don't care about Doc's angling for the pastorate, because I sincerely believe God's hand will be in the selection. I don't care whether it's me or not, because if it is, I'll give it my all, and if it isn't, I'll give my full support to whoever it is."

"Even if it's Doc?" Sasha said.

Zeke smiled. "The fact is, if Doc were God's choice, yes, he would have my full support. Candidly, I don't believe he will be the one, for the very reason that he wants it so badly. I think such a position requires a person who would view it with fear and trembling."

Alexis held up a hand. "Rewind, Z," she said. "You said you happened to know that Pastor's message from Jeremiah was meant for you. How do you know that, and if it doesn't mean you're supposed to be the new pastor, what does it mean?"

"All right," Zeke said. "Here it is: The Lord kept telling me, in essence, to listen up and be ready, that He was speaking to me. And when Pastor Bob asked us to turn to Jeremiah 1, again I felt a hand on my shoulder and God spoke clearly. He said, 'Hear Me. This is for you.' As I sit here now, that's what really scares me. Just think about what that passage says. Before I was in the womb, God knew me, sanctified me—"

"Ordained you as a prophet to the nations," Pastor Bob recited, just above a whisper.

"Uh-oh," Alexis said. "Is he supposed to take that literally?"

The four of them sat in silence, alternately glancing at each other. Pastor Bob finally broke the stillness. "Let me just pose this for your consideration: We've established that this whole business of God speaking directly and audibly to one of us is outside our normal course, outside our comfort level. But it's happening. We're taking it seriously. Given that, how would you assess the manner in which God speaks directly to one of His children? Figuratively? Symbolically? Or literally?"

Zeke said, "When He said to Jeremiah, 'I ordained you a prophet to the nations,' He meant it literally. This morning people were turning the pages of their Bibles, looking at the passage you told them to turn to, and God told me, 'This is for you.' Then I hear, 'I sanctified you; I ordained you a prophet to the nations . . . You shall go to all to whom I send you, and whatever I command you, you shall speak. Do not be afraid of their faces, for I am with you to deliver you . . . Behold, I have put My words in your mouth.'

"Now, Pastor Bob, I didn't ask for this, I don't want it, I'm not looking for anything. But does this sound to you like an appointment to be the next pastor of the holdouts?"

"No sir, it does not," the pastor said. "If this is real, and I have no reason to doubt that it is, you may very well be being called to a fearful role. And the fact that He impressed upon you that prophetic message from Joel could also mean that you are to foretell the beginning of the end."

"But tell who?" Sasha said. "I'm proud of what Dad and Mom do here—what we all do—but we may be the only missionaries in the whole state of California. That's okay. I mean, we're here because we're supposed to be here, but if Dad's being called to deliver some big message, where's he gonna do that from?"

"We'll just have to see, won't we, Zeke?" Alexis said. "One thing I know: You'll be up to it, right? You know this is of God, so we just plunge ahead."

"I wish I could say I was that unequivocal from the beginning," Zeke said. "But there's a reason we're all sitting here right now. I needed this input. I shouldn't have, because it's just come back to me what the Lord gave me when you asked me to pray for Jennie, Bob."

"Yeah, Dad, what *was* that?"

"He told me He had made the earth by His power and had established the world by His wisdom and had stretched out the heavens at His discretion."

"Grab me a Bible real quick, would you, Sasha?" Pastor Bob said. "I'm pretty sure that's from Jeremiah also."

When she returned with it, Pastor Bob quickly leafed through it and said, "Here it is in chapter 10: 'He has made the earth by His power, He has established the world by His wisdom, and has stretched out the heavens at His discretion. When He utters His voice, there is a multitude of waters in the heavens: And He causes the vapors to ascend from the ends of the earth. He makes lightning for the rain, He brings the wind out of His treasuries.'"

"That's what He told me," Zeke said.

"I don't know what more you need than that, love," Alexis said.

"I don't either, Dad, and I don't even understand all that."

"One thing I feel certain about, but I don't know if it's of God or just personal preference," Zeke said.

"This is no time for secrets," Alexis said.

"That's just it," Zeke said. "What I feel so strongly about is that I'd like to keep this calling just between us, unless the Lord tells me otherwise. Of course, Pastor, you can tell Jennie."

"What?" Sasha said. "My dad's called to be a prophet to the nations and I can't tell anybody?"

Pastor Bob smiled at her. "Welcome to responsibility, young lady."

PART 3

THE THREAT

10

THE HUMBLING

ALEXIS TOLD SASHA to say her good-nights, and when Pastor Bob rose to give her a hug, he said, "I'd better be going too."

Zeke said, "Could you possibly stay a little longer?"

The pastor nodded. "I suppose. I won't be getting many more of these times with you."

"You sure Jennie's okay?" Alexis said, rising to leave with Sasha.

Pastor Bob chuckled and reached into his pocket, producing a plastic box. "Remember the ancient beepers?"

"Vaguely," Alexis said, "from the Dark Ages."

"Jennie found 'em in a box of junk, and Raoul somehow got them working again. They don't reach far, but Jennie can get me if she needs me."

"Lexi," Zeke said, "let me put Sasha down tonight."

Zeke and Alexis had been able to carve out a modicum of privacy for Sasha, though there was little room for anything in her space but a single bed, a chest of drawers, and a rod jutting from the wall that served as a closet. They were intentional about spending time with their daughter every day, knowing that otherwise the sheer busyness of survivalist living could cost them any hint of normalcy. One of them spent at least a half hour with her at bedtime every night talking, singing, praying, or helping her memorize Scripture.

The older Sasha got, Zeke realized, fewer would be the nights left for this. For now, she liked having her long-legged dad lying on his back next to her in the darkness, hands behind his head, nearly crowding her off her pillow. He knew the day would come when a teenager wouldn't want that anymore.

That night she lay on her side, facing him. "Does all the stuff scare you, Dad?"

"I was about to ask you the same thing."

"It kinda does. Mostly I just wonder what it's gonna be like. Pastor makes it sound like you're going to have some big audience, but I don't see how."

"I don't either," Zeke said. "Biggest group I've ever spoken to has been about fifty in that tribe up by Santa Cruz. And I didn't need any supernatural courage. They welcomed us, remember?"

"Yeah."

"We'll have to see what God has in mind. I just want to make sure you're all right with all of it."

"What if I wasn't?"

"Well, you are our top priority, you know that."

"I better not be, Dad. What if I was totally against this? What then? Say God's telling you to do it and I'm telling you not to. Would I still be your top priority?"

"Hmm . . ."

"See? Gotcha."

"What would you have me do in that case, Sash?"

"You'd have no choice. You'd have to tell me to take a hike and do what God tells you to do."

"Wow. You must've been raised well."

"Yep."

"You know Mom and I are proud of you and love you, don't you?"

"Uh-huh."

"But we feel guilty."

"How come?"

"'Cause it's not like you had a choice. We drag you out here to the middle of nowhere before you're old enough to know what's going on, and we make our mission your life. I know you get the magazines and the letters and all that from your cousins and you know what you're missing: TV, movies, Internet, fashions, parties, friends your own age—"

"They think I'm brainwashed."

"They do, eh?"

"I mean, they're Christians and everything, go to church and stuff, but they say not everything can be about God. 'You gotta live,' they say."

Zeke was glad Sasha couldn't see his face in the darkness. This was what he and Alexis agonized about. Should they expose Sasha to the real world, let her make up her own mind, come to her own conclusions about how she wanted to live, what she believed? He could identify with people in cults, communes, extreme denominations. How must Amish parents feel when they allow their kids a year of freedom, wondering if they will ever return to the fold, to the faith?

"What do *you* say?"

Sasha didn't respond right away, which both thrilled and scared him. He liked that she was a thinker, not impulsive. But what was she thinking? Finally she said, "There's lotsa stuff I'm curious about. They seem to have fun. But how much fun can you have? Who do they help? Seems like as long as there are people who need stuff, you ought to be looking for them every day. Okay, have a party, go to a movie, have a good time. But if someone's hungry or poor or needs anything—and I can't believe you have to come to California to find people like that—it seems like there'd be somebody to help every day. I don't think I'd feel too good about myself if I went a whole day without trying to help somebody, even if it just meant telling them about God."

"That's some pretty good thinking, sweetheart," Zeke said, trying to hide the emotion in his voice. He sat up. "I'd better get back to our guest. Should we be thinking about letting you spend a few months with your cousins sometime?"

"What? Months? No!"

"No?"

"I don't think so, Dad. Don't you need me here?"

"Well, sure, but—"

"And with this new thing happening to you? Mom's gonna need me. Plus, I wanna see what it's all about. Anyway, my cousins are kinda shallow, you know? All they talk about is their own stuff, never about anybody else. It's just not how I think I wanna be."

"You getting too old to hug your old man?"

"Sorry that took so long," Zeke said as he emerged, but he stopped short when he noticed Pastor Bob wiping his eyes.

"Oh, I'm all right," he said. "Just one long Sunday, I guess. Lots of stress."

"No worries," Zeke said. "Don't feel obligated to stay. We can talk anoth—"

"No, Zeke," Alexis said. "He needs to tell you what he told me. Or I can tell him, Pastor." At that, Bob Gill broke down again and gestured that Alexis should go ahead. She said, "I was just telling him how much he and Jennie meant to us and how much we'd miss them, and I think the enormity of everything just got to him."

"I sure get that," Zeke said.

"They've been married as long as we've been alive. And it's starting to hit him that he won't be in ministry for the first time since graduating from seminary."

"That's a long, long time, Zeke," Pastor Bob said. "I'm prepared to care for Jennie around the clock. Fact is, I'm looking forward to it. That in-sickness-and-health vow is one I've really never had the privilege of fulfilling until now—she's been that healthy all these years. But being out of the ministry scares me. I don't know what I'm going to do with myself. Jennie will be my full-time ministry, I hope for a long time, but after that I'll be looking for work. And I'm a realist. There won't be much for a guy my age."

"There'll always be work here."

"Well, thanks, but who knows where you'll be by then? It's obvious God has bigger things planned for you."

"That's really why I asked you to stay longer. You up to talking about it?"

"Absolutely."

"I'm slowly getting used to the idea that God is calling me to something, but what? He's told me I should be bold, should trust in Him, and should be ready to speak to people in authority. I'm willing, but I need a mentor, even long-distance. If I promise to respect your time and especially Jennie as your immediate priority—"

"Yes. Say no more. I'd be honored."

"Then we start right now. What's my next step? What do I do?"

Pastor Bob leaned forward and held up both hands.

After a moment, Zeke said, "Am I supposed to know what that means?"

Pastor Bob raised a brow and merely gestured slightly with his up-raised hands, as if to indicate that Zeke should be quiet, say nothing, do nothing.

Zeke nodded.

The pastor glanced at Alexis and pointed to the Bible Sasha had brought him, which lay on the table. Alexis handed it to him and he leafed through it. He said quietly, "Galatians 1:10 says, 'For do I now persuade men, or God? Or do I seek to please men? For if I still pleased men, I would not be a bondservant of Christ.'"

Zeke covered his face with both hands. "Yes. Let me be a bondservant of Christ." He heard pages turning.

Pastor Bob said, "From Deuteronomy 8: 'You should know in your heart that as a man chastens his son, so the Lord your God chastens you. Therefore you shall keep the commandments of the Lord your God, to walk in His ways and to fear Him. For the Lord your God is bringing you into a good land . . . When you have eaten and are full, then you shall bless the Lord your God for the good land which He has given you.

"'Beware that you do not forget the Lord your God by not keeping

His commandments, His judgments, and His statutes which I command you today, lest—when you have eaten and are full, and have built beautiful houses and dwell in them; and when your herds and your flocks multiply, and your silver and your gold are multiplied, and all that you have is multiplied; when your heart is lifted up, and you forget the Lord your God who . . . led you through that great and terrible wilderness, in which were fiery serpents and scorpions and thirsty land where there was no water; . . . who fed you in the wilderness with manna, which your fathers did not know, that He might humble you and that He might test you, to do you good in the end.'"

"God is speaking to me," Zeke said.

"What's He saying?" Alexis said.

Zeke shuddered and waited. She moved next to him and took his hand. He remained silent until God finally gave him the words:

"Be clothed with humility, for I resist the proud but give grace to the humble. Therefore humble yourself under My mighty hand, that I may exalt you in due time, casting all your care upon Me, for I care for you.

"Be sober, be vigilant, because your adversary the devil walks about like a roaring lion, seeking whom he may devour. Resist him, steadfast in the faith."

Zeke felt as if he had run a marathon. "I need sleep."

"I'll bet you do," Pastor Bob said, rising. "But we should tell Alexis about the discovery, shouldn't we?"

Zeke stood but hesitated.

"Well, you have to now," she said, following them to the door.

"Sorry, Zeke," the pastor said. "Had you not planned to?"

Zeke shrugged. "It's going to get around. You know Gabrielle is going to tell Doc. It won't be beyond him to start interrogating people."

"We need an elders' meeting tomorrow. That's when we can urge him not to do that."

"What, what?" Alexis said.

Zeke told her of the Xavier kids' discovery.

"You don't think—you're not saying . . . That's all we need."

"We don't know what to think," Pastor Bob said.

"How can you select a new elder if there might be a traitor among us?"

"Well, look at the logical elder candidates," Zeke said. "Katashi, Raoul, and Mahir. Do you really suspect any one of them?"

"Oh. My. Word." Alexis said. "We all just thought of the same person at the same time, didn't we?"

"Who?" Zeke said.

"Don't do that," Alexis said. "I don't want to influence either of you, and I don't want you to influence me. But you each thought of one among those three, didn't you? You're not sure, you're not accusing him, but there's one you're not sure of, one you wouldn't want to unhesitatingly make an elder. Am I right?"

Zeke nodded as did Pastor Bob.

Alexis grabbed a sheet of paper and tore it into three pieces. "Let's each write the one name that gave us pause. Fold 'em and hand 'em to me and we'll all look at the same time."

Alexis unfolded the three facedown on the table, then flipped them over. It was unanimous.

"See?" she said. "We've known him forever. We love him. Sweet guy. But you can't say he hasn't been quiet and moody lately. He doesn't seem engaged, has lost the joy. Broods, can't be amused. We're not saying it's him, not saying it isn't. But we'd better make sure he doesn't get nominated for elder, don't you think?"

"I can't vote, because I'm not going to be here," Pastor Bob said. "And your two votes can't block anything. How many votes will there be without Jennie and me? Adults only, of course."

Alexis made hash marks on another scrap of paper as she squinted at the ceiling and recited, "Us two, Doc and Gabi, the Muscadins, Mahir, Elaine, the Gutierrezes, and Katashi. Eleven. You're right. We can't stop anything."

"You may have to do a little politicking," Pastor Bob said. "Talk with the Xaviers and Mrs. Meeks—one more gives you a majority."

"Seriously?" Zeke said. "I've got God speaking audibly to me and I can't depend on Him to make an elder vote go the way He wants it?"

"Well, there is that," the pastor said. "You might want to rethink me as your spiritual mentor."

"One thing's sure. We can talk about this at our elders' meeting anyway, because Gabrielle will have told Doc by then. We don't have to tell him we have a suspect."

"'Suspect' is a little strong," Pastor Bob said. "Wouldn't you say?"

"Maybe so, but you know Doc will have an opinion."

Alexis clucked. "He'll have someone charged and convicted. It'll be interesting to find out who. When's the meeting?"

"After lunch," Zeke said. "We've got a meeting with the Nuwuwu Tribe in the morning, and we're sending Raoul and Danley to Parker for supplies and the mail."

"Is Danley going to want to leave Cristelle?" Alexis said.

Zeke shrugged. "I'll check with Doc, but unless she's critical, I don't want to start making exceptions. We're too small for that. Too many dominos could start to fall."

11

THE QUESTION

ZEKE ROSE BEFORE dawn Monday, but of course that was impossible to know underground except by his digital clock, which read 5:00.

He sat on the edge of his bed, mapping the day—distracted, edgy, wondering when or if the voice of God might invade his mind. If yesterday was only a test, it would be counter to everything he knew about Him. The One he served would never make a promise and not fulfill it.

Zeke was grateful the Lord hadn't begun this day with some dramatic, audible proclamation. He had always been a quick starter, eager to get rolling, and had to remind himself to move stealthily and keep lights low so Alexis could sleep while he showered, shaved, and dressed head to toe in black, loose-fitting, breathable garb. Yes, black. Even his wide-brimmed hat. Zeke knew wearing black in the sun in temperatures that hovered in the 120-degree range and often reached 130 flew in the face of conventional wisdom—and persuading his teammates of the same had been no small task.

He had learned the trick by researching why so many sheiks and Bedouins in the deserts of Saudi Arabia dressed that way. Though it is true that white reflects light, it can also divert body heat directly back at you. While black absorbs sunlight, it also absorbs heat from the body. Zeke experimented with both and found that on a 120-degree day, wearing white cooled him by about ten degrees, while wearing black cooled him almost twice as much.

Ever the contrarian, Doc Xavier stuck with all white "because one, I don't want to look like a villain, two, doctors wear white, and three, when it's that hot, what difference does ten degrees make?"

As a rule, other than those on periscope duty, Doc would be the only other person up at that time of the morning. So as Zeke headed to the shower, he planned on dropping in on Doc first. Xavier would be tending to Cristelle Muscadin, as her progress during the first twenty-four hours after her injury would be the most telling. Zeke hoped Doc would have her treatment well in hand so the two men could talk. There was much to discuss, so Zeke would make a short list in a few minutes while he consumed the same breakfast he had enjoyed—in a manner of speaking—for the last several years.

Ever since he, Doc, and Mahir had perfected the aquaponics food growing and sustainability system, Zeke had begun his day—after praying in the shower—by sitting down to four ounces of protein jerky made of some variety of desert meat, a piece of fruit or vegetable (today's would be a sweetened carrot), and coffee, one delicacy the holdouts afforded themselves from the monthly supply runs to Parker, Arizona.

The group had agreed that all other treats or gifts sent from friends, relatives, and supporters would be pooled and parceled out to the people to whom they had been called to minister. This had been a prayerful choice ostensibly designed to prevent materialism, distraction, and even the petty jealousies that could arise from some having relatives or friends able to send them nicer things than others received.

The agreement didn't stop some from suspecting that others were somehow skirting the rule, of course, but for the most part, it seemed to be working. The Native American tribes and several impoverished individuals enjoyed things they wouldn't have otherwise. Personal items, like Sasha's teen magazines, had to be shared with the Xavier kids, but beyond that, elaborate toys were gifted to outsiders.

At breakfast Zeke also either read from his Bible or a devotional.

This month he was reading through *The Valley of Vision: A Collection of Puritan Prayers & Devotions*. He enjoyed that quiet time alone, but as he prayed in the shower for what was shaping up to be a busy and potentially contentious day, he thought he heard noises close by and hoped he hadn't wakened Alexis. One drawback of the efficient, space-saving design of the complex was that not one inch of space was wasted, so the bathroom was no bigger than that of one in a stateroom on a cruise ship, and even the sound of a water-saving shower was impossible to muffle.

As Zeke shaved and dressed in the tiny chamber, he smelled coffee and knew he had failed in his effort not to disturb. He emerged to find not Alexis but Sasha in her robe at the tiny table that also served as countertop, dining table, homework space, and whatever else was needed, depending on the time of day.

"So sorry, sweetie," Zeke whispered. "Didn't mean to wake you."

"You didn't," she said. "Just wanted to talk to you, but I'll wait. I know you've got your ritual."

He cocked his head and grinned. He gestured toward his plate, which bore his usual fare. "How did you know?"

"Easy. What does Mom call you? A something of something—"

"A creature of—"

"Habit, yeah. Eat, drink, do your thing so we can talk before you go."

Zeke scribbled on a notepad: *Doc, Cristelle, Nuwuwus, Danley, elder meeting, car.*

Then he read a page in his devotional while he ate though distracted, aware Sasha was waiting. "Okay," he said finally, "shoot."

"What's in that book anyway? Would I like it?"

"Probably not. Mostly prayers from hundreds of years ago. Lots of *thees* and *thous,* that kind of thing."

"Eew. Why do you like it?"

"The Puritans really knew how to pray. And the archaic language forces me to slow down and think. Sometimes when I read modern stuff, I fly past important parts."

Sasha nodded. "What I want to talk to you about, I mean, what I really wanna ask you and I shoulda last night but I forgot—well, I just didn't know how to say it, I guess . . ."

"Sasha, you gonna land this plane sometime soon? I really have to get going. Don't worry about wording it right."

"I'm just wondering if you're thankful."

"Sorry?"

"Thankful for this—this new thing, whatever it is."

Zeke sat back. "Hmph. That is a really good question. I'm scared, I know that. I'm puzzled. Really curious. Feel unworthy. I guess you know all that. I'm wondering what God is up to. Pastor Bob kind of walked me through getting humbled by it—really humbled. And your mom—you know she is a wise woman—helped me see that I'm not *supposed* to feel qualified, you know what I mean?"

"Uh-huh."

"So, this whole thing isn't even twenty-four hours old yet and I'm trying to get used to it, not knowing what shape it's going to take. I get the feeling something's coming and I'm not sure what. So it's scary and exciting and only the four of us know about it—us and Pastor Bob—and I'm not answering your question, am I?"

"Nope."

"Am I thankful for it?"

"Yep."

Zeke sat staring at her. "I'm guessing you think I should be."

She nodded.

He folded his arms and studied the ceiling. "I'm thankful for a lot of things. Salvation. You. Mom. My health. A purpose. A calling. A mission. The people we work with. But this? I don't know, to be honest. Maybe because I don't really know what it is yet."

"But we're s'posed to be thankful in everything, right?"

"Sure. And I'm thankful generally. But that's not what you asked. You asked if I was thankful for *this*."

"Yeah. That's what I want to know."

"Let me ask you, Sash. Why do you want to know? Are *you* thankful for it? Even though we don't know how it's going to play out, it could be very weird. If I'm supposed to emerge as some voice, some person who speaks boldly to leaders, maybe even leaders of nations, what would that look like? Do you think people are going to admire and respect that? I could look like a real jerk.

"Now I'm already humbled and willing to do whatever God wants me to do, for whatever reason. But will *you* be thankful if your dad becomes, I'll just say it, famous for looking like an idiot? I believe I can handle that, but can you?"

Zeke thought he was shedding some new light on the whole thing for Sasha until she sat there with a knowing look, smiling at him and nodding.

"What are you saying?" he said. "You could deal with that? You could be thankful for that?"

"I could, and I already am."

"Whoo. All right, I'm listening. Explain."

"It's just that it hit me last night while we were talking. Hardly anybody knows we're here. Just the people from our church and our relatives, and most of them, even if they're praying for us or sending money or other stuff, or even if they admire what we're doing, you know down deep they think we've got to be a little crazy. I mean really, admit it."

"I'm sure that's true."

"I know it's true, Dad. I don't show you everything I get from my cousins. Emily told me her mom thinks you havin' me out here is a crime. I mean, I know she's exaggerating, but that's Aunt Lynette, your own sister! And she's a Christian!"

Zeke smiled. "She said that?"

"Don't say anything, Dad! Promise me!"

"Don't worry. I'm not surprised, Sash. But you're making my point. If my own sister thinks I'm crazy now, what do you think she'll say if it gets out that I'm worse than one of those guys who walks around city streets carrying a sign that says 'The end is near'?"

"What?"

"Trust me, there are guys who do that. Some really believe it, and some are just nuts."

"God's not gonna ask you to do that, is He?"

Zeke laughed. "Let's hope not."

"Well, this morning I sat straight up in bed thinking how lucky I was and how thankful I should be. Of all the people in the world, God chose my dad for a really special important job. And then you included me when you talked about it last night."

"That was Pastor Bob's idea, you know, including you."

"Really?"

Zeke nodded.

"Well, anyway, it just made me thankful. I mean, Mom and I think you're great—and I don't mean to insult you, but you're not a preacher or anything and I don't know if you're even s'pose to replace Pastor Bob or anything, so I wouldn't have thought of this. Would you?"

"Thought of me being chosen by God, you mean? No! You know that!"

"So be thankful! That's all I mean. It must say something. God chose you for some reason. If it's not because you're anybody special, it must mean He either wants to do something big with you or for you."

"Or both. I have to think that no matter what happens, I'm going to grow and be blessed."

Sasha shrugged. "That's something to be thankful for."

"It sure is."

"So are you thankful?"

"I am now. Especially for you. Where do you come up with this stuff?"

Zeke found Doc in the infirmary, leafing through a notebook. A small plate of food that looked largely untouched lay before Cristelle, and she looked exhausted.

"How's our girl this morning?" Zeke said.

Doc just gave him a look. Cristelle appeared to try to smile but merely shook her head.

"Doc, if we go somewhere to talk, does someone need to sit with her?"

"Yes, and Danley was here most of the night, so he's sleeping."

"Sasha is up. Can she do it?"

Doc shrugged. "Just need someone who has the maturity to know when to push the call button, right there on the wall, if—and only if—there's a crisis. It triggers a buzzer on my belt, and I drop everything and come running."

"You'll clarify that for her?"

"Like I do with everyone else."

Zeke jogged back to his quarters, told Sasha, and left a note for Alexis as Sasha changed.

Zeke checked his duty log and decided to give Benita Gutierrez a break from periscope duty in the southeast corner so he and Doc could talk there. At dawn the periscopes were lowered and one guard could patrol outside.

"*Bueno*," she said. "I can get Raoul breakfast before he leaves for Arizona. Is Danley still goin' with him?"

"That was on my list to ask you, Doc. Any reason why we can't stick with the normal schedule?"

"Cristelle's not critical, if that's what you're asking," Doc said. "He's not the only person who can fill in for me when I need a break, as you just proved."

"Good."

"When I gotta be back?" Benita said.

"Give us half an hour."

"*Gracias.*"

"So what's up, Zeke?" Doc said. "I do something wrong? I know you like pretending to supervise me."

"It's nothing like that, but there is a chain of command, and things work better when we all acknowledge that."

"Oh, believe me, I know. Sir."

"C'mon, Doc, I've never asked you to refer to me that way."

"Get on with your agenda."

"I just wanted to go over today's itinerary."

"I have no itinerary. I know I was scheduled to go with you all to see the Nuwuwus, and the council of elders wanted me to see some of the kids, but I'd rather not leave my patient that long."

Benita's timer beeped. Zeke peered into the periscope and began the broad sweep of the horizon. "How is she?" he said.

"It's an acute injury," Doc said. "The cleanup was the worst of it. And then I had to operate. I used more anesthetic on her than I've used total since we've been here. She had sand, rock, chrome, clothing fibers, and galvanized rubber embedded into her flesh and bone. I had to scrape all that away before I could even attempt to salvage healthy muscle, fat, ligaments, and tendons. It'll be weeks before I have any idea whether she'll regain use of that leg. Under normal circumstances I'd have had help, she probably would have been medevacked to an ER, and her leg might have been amputated below the knee."

Zeke folded the handles and turned back, resetting the timer. "Did you say chrome?"

"I figure her leg was crushed into the bike's spokes."

"You have enough pain meds to see her through?"

"Till tomorrow. I'm sending a script for more with Raoul and Danley today."

Zeke peeked at his paper. "Just two more things, then whatever you have."

"This is your show."

"I'd like an elder meeting at one today to talk about who's replacing Pastor Bob. It'll be an important choice, because the new pastor will come from among the three of us."

For the first time since Zeke had known him, Doc lost eye contact and became inarticulate. "Yeah, uh, listen, who all's going with you this morning to see the tribe?"

"Let's see: Katashi, Pastor Bob, Mrs. Meeks, Mahir, and your wife."

Doc's eyes darted. "Uh-huh. Um, okay."

Zeke studied him, waiting.

Doc said, "Why is Pastor going, everything considered?"

"To say good-bye, of course. These people have come to mean a lot to him, and him to them, I'm sure."

Doc nodded. "And you say there's one other thing on your list?"

"Yes, but the elder meeting?"

"Oh, yeah, sure. One o'clock's good. Just need someone to sit with Cristelle."

"I'll check the duty log. The kids will be in class."

"Mine are too young anyway."

"I'll find someone. My last item was about your car. You still adamant about—"

"No, as a matter of fact, I'm not."

"No?"

Doc had suddenly regained his composure and stared into Zeke's eyes, brows raised. "Do I need to repeat myself?"

"Uh, no, great. Very helpful, thanks! If it's all right with you, I'll ask Raoul to find something adequate for your famil—"

"I don't need details, Zeke. I talked it over with Gabrielle, and we're fine with whatever you decide."

"Well, thanks again, Doc. I really apprec—"

"I'll tell you what I'd appreciate: Quit making such a big deal out of it. You act like I don't know how to be a team player."

"Sorry," Zeke said as the timer beeped. "You want a turn at the scope?"

"I'm not *that* much of a team player, Zeke. You really want your staff doctor—"

"You're right," Zeke said.

"Come on, man," Doc said. "Can't you tell when a man is playing you? Get out of the way."

He lowered the handles and hunched over, looking through the lenses. "It has been a long time." Doc slowly pivoted, and about halfway through his arc he slowed, then stopped, then reversed a few degrees and stopped again. "I shouldn't see anything on the horizon, should I? Just shimmering heat waves, right?"

"You see something else?"

"Hold on a second." Doc slowly rotated the scope about an inch each way.

"Depending on how far you're looking," Zeke said, "every inch represents several hundred yards."

"Um-hm," Doc said. "You'd better take a look."

They traded places. A massive dust cloud loomed far enough away that Zeke could not make out the source. "Not an immediate threat to us," he said. "But maybe to the tribe. We can stand them up again and explain later, though I hate to do that. The council has been warm to us."

"Not the leader's daughter-in-law," Doc said. "I don't trust her."

"She'll come around."

"Don't be naïve."

"You'll see, Doc."

"I'm afraid you'll see otherwise."

Zeke took one more look. "We're not going to want whoever it is getting any closer to us."

"Or interfering with our guys headed east," Doc said.

"That either."

"But Cristelle's prescription can't wait, Zeke."

"I hear you."

Zeke reset the timer to every three minutes. "When Benita gets back I'll let the other monitors know what we've seen here."

Doc nodded. "There's also something I need to confide in you."

"Oh?"

"It's about Jennie Gill."

"When you say confide—"

"I've told no one else."

"Not even Bob?"

"No one."

"Why?"

"Call me a coward, but I had already dumped enough on them all at once. I couldn't do it. I didn't expect them to up and leave a few days later. I thought I had time to work up to it, and now things have gotten out of hand."

"Do I want to know this?"

"You need to know it."

Zeke sighed. "Pastor already told everybody she's terminal. What could be worse than that?"

"How quickly she's terminal. Zeke, I couldn't guarantee a week, and I can't in good conscience advise Bob to expose her to the drive he has in mind the night after tomorrow. He's talking hundreds of miles."

"Really, Doc? She doesn't seem in that much pain."

"I've made sure of that. But they didn't come to me until very late. This is as advanced a case of stage four as I've ever seen. In fact it's so far beyond, 'stage four' doesn't begin to define it."

"What if someone traveled with her?"

Doc shook his head. "It'd be malpractice for me to even suggest it. The end is not going to be pretty, even here in a controlled environment. The best I can do is try to make her comfortable. I'm trying to plan for it, figure out where, scheduling Cristelle's care at the same time, all that."

"Doc, this is awful. Bob's talking about packing after the elder meeting today."

"That's when we have to tell him then."

Zeke nodded. "Then we can decide what we're going to do about the elder board, telling the whole group, a funeral, all that."

Zeke and Doc checked the periscope several more times before Benita returned.

She was chipper as usual. "You guys look like you los' your best friend, no?"

"Well," Zeke said, "Doc did see something on the horizon."

"What?" she said, grabbing the periscope. "Oh no! *Qué en el mundo?*"

"That's 'What in the world?'" Doc said.

"I reset your timer, Benita," Zeke said. "Just keep an eye on it and keep me posted."

"Got it," she said. "But don't be sending *mi esposo* that way until we know what we're dealin' with, okay?"

"You know I won't."

12

THE REMNANT

EVERYTHING IN ZEKE told him to cancel the trip to the Nuwuwu Tribe—or what was left of it. Only about thirty remained in California of the indigenous Great Basin group, the rest of whom (totaling fewer than a thousand) had relocated to the Chemehuevi lands of the Paiute, mostly in Arizona. The remnant, according to tribal leader ("Don't call me Chief") Kaga, an eighty-year-old widower, were "too old, infirm, or stubborn to move."

They weren't all too old, that was certain. Kaga's son and heir apparent, Yuma, and his wife, Kineks, were in their fifties and had a six-year-old granddaughter whose parents had apparently left her as a newborn when they moved east with the others. Little Zaltana was a dark-eyed, black-haired beauty with a gleaming smile with whom everyone from Zeke's team—and the Nuwuwu—seemed enamored.

Zaltana had leapt giggling into Zeke's lap at a tribal council meeting the last time he'd visited and said, "We're the Nuwuwu! *I'm* a Nuwu. And Granddad and Grandmom and Great-Granddad and Great-Great-Grandmaw, all of us"—and here she dramatically spread her arms wide and rolled her head to indicate the whole settlement—"we're the Nuwuwu!"

Zeke shot her an exaggerated double take. "Is that true?"

She nodded grandly and pointed to herself. "Nuwu."

"Thank you, honey," Grandmom Kineks, a severe-looking woman as husky as her husband, said, "but we have business now, so you run along."

Zaltana jumped down, but Zeke said, "Oh, let me ask you before you go. Who's Great-Great-Grandmaw?"

"You don't know Gaho?"

"We really must finish our business," Kineks said, "please."

"She's—"

"Zaltana!" Yuma barked. "Obey your grandmom!"

Zeke was eager to get back that Monday. He had come to love these people after slowly, slowly earning their trust, mostly by trading with them and showing them charity without condescension. He and Mahir—with whom they had not seemed to connect or particularly care for—had even helped them set up their own aquaponics system. The Nuwuwu were taken with Katashi, whose ethnicity made him more similar to them in skin and hair color, so Zeke took him under his wing and taught him the system so he could help them maximize it.

The women, particularly Elaine and Jennie, had endeared themselves to the Nuwuwu and developed an arrangement in which the tribe was not just the recipient of free warm clothing for cool desert nights but traded their unique crafts.

However, everything that day seemed to war against the idea of Zeke venturing the approximately twelve miles to the Nuwuwu settlement with five comrades. With Cristelle not out of the woods, Jennie near death, the crucial elders' meeting looming, the mystery of the Arabic document indicating a potential terrorist among them, Raoul and Danley about to make a vital all-day supply run, and the threatening dust cloud on the horizon—it simply made no sense. What more did he need to abort the mission?

He was with Doc, so he would tell him first, then Pastor Bob. Then he'd tell the others who had planned to join him for the tribal visit and have Sasha stay with Cristelle another hour so he could call the elder meeting for fifteen minutes later. They'd hold it in the aquaponics lab after he mapped a route for Raoul and Danley that should skirt the Hydro

Mongers or whoever had been kicking up the dust on the horizon.

Zeke was in his element, feeling as if he'd been born to this. He knew his people were in trouble on many fronts, but this kind of thing motivated him. It was the way his mind worked. He liked having lots of plates spinning at once. If people would listen and cooperate, he'd get a handle on this and they'd get things accomplished.

"Doc," he said, "here's what we're going to do . . ."

"Don't cancel."

Zeke stopped cold. That had been God.

"What?" Doc said.

"Sorry," Zeke said. "Give me a second."

Doc looked frustrated. "Well, when a man says, 'Here's what we're going—'"

"Please, Doc! I asked for a second."

Doc shook his head. "This is like yesterday. Amateur Night in—"

"Will you stop with the 'Amateur Night in Dixie,' whatever that means. If you can't give me a minute, just go back to Cristelle."

"You said a second."

"Go!"

Doc stalked off and Zeke leaned against the wall, eyes closed. *I'm listening.*

"You have a schedule. And I have a message for a leader."

Kaga leads thirty people in the middle of nowhere.

Immediately he felt chastised, realizing that when Bob and Jennie were gone, he'd lead half that number, and where was he if not in the middle of nowhere?

Forgive me, Lord. I'm on my way.

Zeke would drive the yellow tanker truck, about half-full of water, with Pastor Bob and Katashi crowded in with him. Elaine Meeks and Gabrielle Xavier would follow in a white van, loaded with foodstuffs and clothing, Mahir driving.

"Stay close," Zeke told Mahir. "I sent Raoul and Danley way south before they'll come back up to what used to be the 10 to get into Parker. If we get accosted by Mongers, let's make sure we're together."

Mahir nodded.

"Everybody have enough ammo?"

"You know I do," Gabrielle said.

"Not enthusiastically," Mrs. Meeks said. "But yes."

"You'd better shoot enthusiastically, if necessary," Mahir said.

She looked surprised. "You know I'd do what I have to, Mahir."

"Do I?"

"Would you rather I ride with the others?"

"Where would they put you, on top? Just be ready."

"Always, of course."

Zeke stepped in. "We all have each others' backs, right? . . . That demands a response, people."

"Right," everyone said.

Virtually nothing that could be mistaken for a street, road, or highway remained between the holdouts' compound and the Nuwuwu settlement, so the going was slow. Zeke didn't feel confident with the tanker at more than thirty miles per hour, given the state of the struts and shock absorbers, and though Mahir seemed occasionally to tailgate him, the van was older and in even rougher shape, so there was no sense taxing it either.

"How was Mrs. Gill this morning?" Katashi said.

"Thanks for asking," Pastor Bob said, one hand braced on the dashboard as they bounced along. "To be honest, I'm concerned. Very weak, very pale. No appetite. I made her eat, but she couldn't keep anything down. I was alarmed."

"I don't blame you," Katashi said. "If you hadn't said anything yesterday, I wouldn't have known she was even sick, let alone seriously ill. She looked great. She always does."

The pastor nodded. "Everyone was saying that. But you wouldn't say that today. She had trouble sleeping last night and could barely sit up this morning. She hardly had the energy to talk."

"No kidding?"

"She had to force me to leave her. Said I might not get another chance to tell these people good-bye for her. She loves them so much. I told her I wouldn't unless Doc assured me she would be all right."

"What'd he say?" Zeke said.

"That he would put someone with her and it was okay to let her sleep if she wanted to, and he would put her on a drip so she wouldn't get dehydrated. I guess this type of cancer really takes a toll on your immune system and you can forget your water intake. You get a lot of your hydration from food, and if you have no appetite, you have to compensate."

"Who's with her?" Zeke said.

"Alexis and Sasha both. Didn't she tell you?"

"I didn't even see Lexi this morning. Been on the go."

Zeke heard a honk and checked his side mirror to find Mahir flashing his lights. He let the tanker drift to a stop. Mahir hopped out and came to his window. "Big dust cloud behind us closing fast. Might as well just wait for 'em and not look like we're trying to get away."

"Yup, or lead 'em to the Nuwuwu." Zeke turned to Bob and Katashi. "You guys stay here unless Mahir and I are outnumbered." He climbed out and stood next to Mahir, leaning back against the tanker, arms folded. "If they pass, they pass. Anybody stops, I'll do the talking."

Mahir laughed. "Like you need to tell me that."

It soon became obvious that only one vehicle was causing the dust cloud, a big Monger rig. It shambled to a stop across from them, WatDoc at the wheel. He leaned over and rolled down the passenger-side window. "Whatcha all doin'?"

"Minding our own business, WatDoc," Zeke said. "What're you doing?"

"Well, it's just li'l ol' me, so nothin' to be afraid of."

"Do I look afraid?"

"No cause to be rude, Spokesman."

"You can keep moving."

"You don't need nothin'?"

"No, sir. Thank you."

"Sorry 'bout yer girl gettin' hurt yesterday."

"What's that?"

"Reckon you heard me."

"What do you know about that?"

"Word gits around."

"Not from us it doesn't," Zeke said. "Maybe you had something to do with it."

"Don't pin that on us."

"Then maybe you know who did."

"Huh-uh."

"Maybe you saw something."

"Oh, no."

"Then how do you know?"

"Like I say, stuff gits around."

"You'd better keep moving, WatDoc."

"And you better watch yerself, Spokesman."

"If you think I'm afraid of you—"

But WatDoc raced off, the colossal truck spewing dirt and dust.

"We're going to sit right here for at least ten minutes," Zeke said. "I don't want to move while we can still see him. He doesn't need even a clue which direction we're headed. Kaga told me he wants to be the only water supplier to the Nuwuwu. He doesn't need to know how tight we are with them."

When the tiny caravan rumbled into the settlement, half a dozen Nuwuwu kids came running, led as always by Zaltana and her gleaming smile. She embraced Elaine and Gabrielle, begging for a story, which the women promised after they unloaded the clothes and food.

Yuma, the tribal leader's son, connected Mahir and Katashi with the men running the compound's aquaponics unit, then joined Zeke at the water tank, where he had already begun the transfer from the truck. "My wife and my father are waiting for you and Pastor Bob in the council hut. He wants to show off the shoes you brought last time."

"They fit?"

"They're a little big, but do not tell him that!"

"I can see if we can get smaller ones," Zeke said.

"No! These are fine. You will see."

When Zeke and Pastor Bob finally reached the tribal council hut, where they met approximately every other time the holdouts visited, Zeke sensed tension, especially on the part of Yuma's wife, Kineks, that he had felt since the beginning of the association with the tribe. Things had been smooth for a few years, except with her. He worried about a setback and hoped he had done or said nothing to cause it.

Kaga seemed as warm and humorous—and self-deprecating—as ever. As soon as he saw the two he approached, marching in the brightly colored athletic shoes they had brought him the visit before. Everyone laughed at the contrast between the shoes and his traditional native garb, typically more ornate on council meeting days.

Kaga, as usual, insisted that Pastor Bob sit next to him as they settled around a low wood table and, as if it were the first time, commented about Bob's white thinning hair "that proves we are brothers." Kineks poured the bitterroot tea Zeke knew he would never develop a taste for, but which he sipped as a courtesy.

Seated on the other side of Pastor Bob, Zeke found the octogenarian tribal leader remarkably articulate and thoughtful. Sensing the man was about to get down to business, he said, "Sir, before we begin, if I may—"

"Oh, these young people today, Pastor Bob!" Kaga said. "Hopeless! What are we to do about them?"

Everyone laughed, and the pastor said, "All we can do is surrender and let them speak."

"Well, okay then," the old man said. "Let the child speak, and then we will have our meeting."

"Thank you, sir. Actually, I was going to ask Pastor Bob to bring you greetings from his lovely wife."

"Oh, I assumed Miss Jennie was with the children."

"No," the pastor said. "I'm sorry to say she has fallen ill, and quite seriously so."

"Oh, no!"

"In fact, I am taking her back to our home so she can be near our children and grandchildren before she dies."

"Oh, Pastor Bob," the chief said, his voice quavering. "I remember when I lost my wife. I am so sorry. And she could not even come to say good-bye."

"Sadly, no. I came to bid farewell for her."

"This is indeed a sad day. But thank you for coming and for telling us. We will pray that the heart of Jesus will be with you."

"Well, thank you, Kaga, I—I'm sorry, what did you say?"

"I said we would pray that the heart of Jesus will be with you."

"You pray to Jesus?"

"Don't you?" Kaga said.

"Well, yes, but—"

"You didn't know we knew Him?"

"No, I—"

"You didn't know He knew us!"

"I—I—"

"Did you not think we figured out what you were doing here?"

"I'm speechless," Pastor Bob said.

"I can see that," Kaga said, laughing.

Zeke wished God would give him just the right words right then. He didn't want Pastor Bob to have to bear this embarrassment alone. "You must admit you vigorously resisted us at the beginning."

"We did," Yuma said. "You must realize who we are, who we come from, who we represent. We don't dare trust anyone. Why should we? How could we?"

"But you're Christians!" Zeke said. "How long did it take for you to realize we were too?"

"Not long," Kineks said, less kindly than her husband and father-in-law. "But we are not only Christians. We come from a long tradition, a rich tapestry that incorporates a variety of religious traditions."

"Aah," Pastor Bob said. "I see. Such as?"

"Well," she said, "I'm afraid you're talking to the wrong person. I am probably the least religious person here. I accept all of it but take none of it seriously."

"Then let me ask you, Kaga," Pastor Bob said. "You said you pray to Jesus and that you would pray His heart would be with me. Where is that from?"

"My mother raised me in the Native American Church. Some call it Peyotism. It includes a lot of our ritual and the Bible."

"What does peyote have to do with it?"

"I remember we used the Peyote Rattle. It was made out of a gourd, which was a symbol of the world, and the rattle represented our prayers. It was decorated with Jesus' crown of thorns. On the handle it said, 'The heart of Jesus is with me.'"

It hit Zeke. "Your mother," he said. "That's Zaltana's Great-Great-Grandmaw?"

Silence. Everyone seemed to look at each other.

Finally Yuma spoke. "Yes, that's my grandmother."

Zeke was afraid to ask, because clearly these people did not want to admit it for some reason. He forced himself. "Zaltana asked me if I knew Gaho. Is she still alive?"

Again the silence and the looks. How old must she be?

"Is she here? May we meet her?"

Kaga and his son, Yuma, looked at the floor. Kineks spoke softly. "Enough. I want these people gone."

"I apologize," Zeke said. "I meant no offense."

When Kaga did not respond, Kineks looked sharply at him. "End the meeting, Father-in-Law."

Kaga held up a hand. "Fetch your granddaughter."

"I will not," Kineks said. "Let's be done with this—"

"Just do it," Yuma said. "Do it or I will."

Kineks rose and rushed out. She soon returned with the girl whose ubiquitous smile had faded. "What's wrong?" she said.

"Come to me," Kaga said.

She climbed into his lap and pressed her head against his chest.

"Go and see if Great-Great-Grandmaw Gaho will see us."

She sat up. "All of us?"

"Yes."

Zaltana scrambled down and ran out. When she returned, her smile was back. "She wanted to know who, and when I told her, she made me tell her how many was that. I had to count! Seven of us! She said she hadn't seen that many people at once for a long, long time."

"What did she say, little one?"

"She said yes!"

13

THE GIFT

LITTLE ZALTANA LED the others to the last hut at the end of the compound, a cone-shaped dwelling that reminded Zeke of a thimble made with dried grasses. A hole in the center of the top emitted a plume of thin, dark smoke. Inside sat a stove with a chimney that ran to that hole. Zeke also saw four mats where he assumed Zaltana, her grandparents, and their grandmother slept.

The seven were barely able to fit inside the stifling hut, and when Zeke's eyes adjusted to the light, he was able to follow Zaltana as she moved to the other side of the stove and extremely delicately settled onto an ancient woman's lap. The woman sat cross-legged about four feet from the stove, facing the fire with the metal door open.

Zeke and Pastor Bob sat beside the stove in front of Gaho, while Yuma and Kineks stood on either side of the entrance. Kaga sat next to the woman, draped his arm around her shoulder, and kissed her cheek. She giggled and squeaked something in her native tongue, which made all the Nuwuwu laugh, even Kineks, who was clearly not happy with this meeting.

"English, Mother," Kaga said. "So our guests can understand."

"Oh! I said I have never seen such moccasins!"

"This is my beloved mother, and may I tell them your age?"

"Have you told them yours?"

"They know I am eighty."

"Do they know you are not my oldest child? That I had two older than you and three younger, but that you are the only one left?"

"I am the only one left here, Mother. I have two younger sisters in Arizona."

She turned her head away. "They are dead to me. They have abandoned me. Anyway, I am 101 years old. Welcome to my home."

"We are deeply honored to meet you," Pastor Bob said.

"Yes," Zeke said.

"These men have traded with us for the past four years. They have helped us and become trusted friends."

She nodded and smiled.

"They have questions about our religion."

Her smile faded and Zeke felt her dark eyes bear into his. "Religion is private," she said. "Why would you question Nuwuwu religion?"

"We don't question it or you," Pastor Bob said. "We just wonder about it."

"Why?"

"Because we are interested. We are people of faith ourselves, and we care about your family. So we are curious."

She continued to stare as if thinking. "It is good that we are all people of religion. That should be enough. We do not have to be the same. I am not curious about yours. You do not have to be curious about mine."

"I didn't say we were people of religion," Pastor Bob said. "Our faith is not in religion. It is in God and Jesus."

Gaho looked at her son, then back at Pastor Bob. "That *is* religion," she said. "You speak in riddles."

"With respect, may I try to explain the difference?"

"Enough of this nonsense!" Kineks said, causing Gaho to look up sharply.

"I can speak for myself, child," she said. "This man is talking to me. Now I want to hear his explanation."

"Thank you, ma'am," Pastor Bob said. "May I ask you first what you mean by 'religion'?"

"What we do to please God, to worship God."

"Like you taught your son."

"Yes!"

"Which was what?"

"Our rituals and the Bible."

"Now," God said clearly to Zeke who, though startled, pressed a knee against Pastor Bob, who fell silent.

"Your son told us you used the Peyote Rattle as part of your ritual," Zeke said.

"Oh, I'm speaking to you now?" the old woman said.

"If that's all right."

"Yes, we used that, and because of our heritage we used parts of traditional tribal religion, the Sun Dance, the Ghost Dance, and Christianity."

"All for the purpose of what?"

"Pleasing God. Worshiping God. Just as you do, if you say you are people of religion."

"As the pastor said, we are people of faith but not religion."

"And you are going to tell me the difference."

"We see religion—rituals and the like—as efforts to reach God or please Him."

"Yes, so do I."

"We see Jesus as God's effort to reach us."

"You see?" Kineks said. "This is craziness!"

"Quiet!" Gaho said. "Do I have to ask my grandson to take you out?"

"No! I'll leave on my own!"

"Good!"

"Grandmother!" Yuma said.

"Let her go," Gaho said, "and go with her if you wish. I am finding this interesting. At least I'm beginning to see the difference, even if I don't understand it yet. Does not God want us to reach Him, to worship Him, to please Him?"

"He wants us to want to," Zeke said. "But we are not able."

"Then what is the point?"

"The point is that God has made a way for us through Jesus. In ourselves we cannot please God. We cannot save ourselves."

"This is profound," she said. "Is it why I have never felt worthy?"

"It very well could be."

"But I do not understand. Make me understand."

Lord, help me. Give me the words.

"The words are there. Just speak them to her."

What words?

"Open your mouth."

Yes, Lord.

"There is none righteous, no, not one, for all have sinned and fall short of the glory of God. The wages of sin is death, but the gift of God is eternal life in Christ Jesus our Lord. But God demonstrates His own love toward us, in that while we were still sinners, Christ died for us.

"If you confess with your mouth the Lord Jesus and believe in your heart that God has raised Him from the dead, you will be saved. For with the heart one believes unto righteousness, and with the mouth confession is made unto salvation. For the Scripture says, 'Whoever believes in Him will not be put to shame . . . Whoever calls on the name of the Lord shall be saved.'"

Gaho cocked her head and looked into Zeke's eyes.

"Say nothing," the Lord told him.

She maintained eye contact as she reached for her son's meaty hand and lifted it off her shoulder, then clasped her hands around her great-great-granddaughter's waist and pulled her close. She lowered her cheek to the top of Zaltana's head and rested it there. "Thank you," she said.

Zeke started to thank her but God reminded him, "Say nothing," so he just nodded.

She closed her eyes, and Zeke was aware of footsteps behind him. He turned to see that Kineks had returned. "What now?" she said, and the others shushed her.

After a minute, Zaltana whispered, "Great-Granddad, she's sleeping."

Kaga leaned close to listen and with one hand steadied her while with the other extracting Zaltana. He laid his mother down and gently pulled her shawl to her neck. They all tiptoed out and back to the tribal council hut, Zaltana peeling off to join the other children.

"What a fascinating woman," Pastor Bob said.

"I'm proud of her," Kaga said. "I think she's remarkable for her age."

"For any age," the pastor said. "If I'm not rude for asking, why had we not been introduced to her before?"

"That was her choice. She's embarrassed about her age."

"She didn't seem to be."

"The last outsiders were government officials who wanted to make an example of her, use her to prove how wonderfully we were being treated if she could live so long. She hated that and said no more. After that she refused to meet anyone."

"I understand."

"Let us finish our business," Kaga said, and he had Yuma quickly tally the day's trade of crafts for water and food.

"Now," the Lord told Zeke.

There's more?

Zeke had already learned that God was not in the habit of repeating Himself. "Kaga, may I leave you with a message?"

"Certainly. We would be honored, and of course, Pastor Bob, we wish to send back to your wife the message of our prayers."

"Thank you," the pastor said.

Zeke said, "The heavens and the earth are reserved for fire until the day of judgment of ungodly men. But, beloved, do not forget this one thing, that the Lord is longsuffering toward us, not willing that any should perish but that all should come to repentance. The day of the Lord will come as a thief in the night, in which the heavens will pass away with a great noise, and the elements will melt with fervent heat; both the earth and the works that are in it will be burned up.

"Therefore, looking forward to these things, be diligent to be found by Him in peace, without spot and blameless; and consider that the long-suffering of our Lord is salvation.

"To Him be glory both now and forever. Amen."

Kaga cleared his throat. "Thank you, Zeke."

"'Thank you, Zeke'?" Kineks said. "I say that's why I'm not religious! What kind of foolishness was that? What did that even mean? Do *you* even know what it means, Zeke? I knew from the first time these people came here, pretending to befriend us, that all they wanted to do was change us, fix us, change our culture. We should have fled to Arizona with our brothers and sisters!"

"I did not mean to offend you, Kineks," Zeke said. "It was just a message I felt led to—"

"Don't apologize to me! Apologize to the sainted matriarch of this tribe who does not need her religion, her beliefs, and her heritage insulted and challenged after a century! We are the people who owned this land. We are the ones who were brutalized and cast aside, pushed into reservations and left with nothing. And now you come with your attempts to make us just like you. Well, it's not going to work, so you can stop trying."

Again she rose as if to stomp out, glaring at Yuma as if demanding he go with her. Zeke thought he looked embarrassed and frustrated as he gestured for her to sit back down. Just then their granddaughter bounded in with a grin.

Kineks said, "Oh, Zaltana, not now—"

But the girl raced past her. "You won't leave without saying good-bye, will you?"

"Of course not!" Pastor Bob said, scooping her up.

"Are you crying?" she said, cupping his face in her hands.

"Maybe a little bit."

"Why?"

When he struggled for words, Zeke said, "Pastor Bob's wife is very sick, so they might not be able to come back here again. They're going to miss all of you."

"Miss Jennie's sick?"

Pastor Bob nodded.

"I want to see her."

"She wished she could see you too," he managed. "She told me to tell you good-bye and to keep smiling."

"Wait!" she said, squirming free. "Don't go yet." And she ran off.

"What a delightful child," Pastor Bob said, wiping his face. "You've done a wonderful job with her, Yuma and Kineks."

Yuma thanked him. Kineks looked away. When again she stood as if to leave, Kaga said solemnly, "This council is still in session."

His daughter-in-law slowly sank back down. "What business is still before us?"

"The business of silence."

Kineks folded her arms and sighed.

After a moment Zeke felt compelled to dispel the awkwardness and said, "Jesus loved children and bid them come to—"

Kaga glanced at him quickly and put a finger to his own lips, and the Lord impressed upon Zeke, "Even the right word is not fitly spoken at the wrong time."

Zaltana returned and strode directly to Pastor Bob, clutching a tiny stick-figure doll with a twine head and burlap dress. "Can you give this to Miss Jennie for me?"

"Oh, sweetheart, she'll cherish it!"

"No, no!" Kineks said. "I made that for you! You will not give it away!"

Zaltana burst into tears. "I want to!"

"But it's your favorite!"

"That's why I want Miss Jennie to have it! To remember me!"

"You take it to bed with you every night!"

"Now *she* can!"

"I made it for you, not for her!"

Pastor Bob said, "Zaltana, Miss Jennie could never forget you, don't you worry."

"But I want her to have it. Grandmom, you taught me we give to people we love. Isn't that why you gave it to me, because you love me?"

"Kineks," Yuma said, "listen to her. You taught her this. You made her this way."

Kineks looked stricken, trapped. "But-but, I—"

"Is the doll not hers?" Kaga said.

Kineks closed her eyes and nodded. "It's hers."

"Then let her do with it as she wants."

"Is it all right, Grandmom?"

Kineks opened her eyes and nodded again.

Zaltana gave the doll to Pastor Bob. He hugged the girl and clearly could not speak.

Zaltana went to her grandmother and climbed into her lap, and the woman rocked her until Kaga ended the meeting.

14

SUSPICION

BACK AT THE COMPOUND late Monday morning, Zeke and Mahir opened their respective hoods to check water levels as the others headed inside. "See you at one," Zeke reminded Pastor Bob, who still clutched the tiny primitive doll.

"Mine was starting to overheat," he told Mahir. "Yours?"

"A little. S'pose you saw WatDoc."

Zeke shot him a look. "What do you mean? 'Course I saw him. We all saw him."

"On the way back, I mean."

"What're you talking about? I saw nothing on the way back. Why didn't you alert me?"

Mahir shrugged. "He wasn't moving, so you wouldn't have seen dust."

Zeke slammed shut the hood of the tanker and faced his old friend. Mahir busied himself with the van engine. "Mahir, we've got to talk, man. What were you gonna do, let me lead him back here?"

"Of course not," he said, sounding bored. "If he'd have followed us, you'd have seen him or I would have flagged you down like I did on the way."

"Mahir! Look at me. Where was this?"

He straightened and turned. "'Bout a half mile outside the tribe settlement. It's not like he doesn't know where they are, Zeke. You know he does business with them."

"He doesn't know *we* know where they are!"

Mahir shrugged. "Probably does now, I guess."

"You say that like it's no big deal."

"So tell me why it's a big deal."

"I don't believe this," Zeke said. "We're the only people I know who have stood up to the Mongers without getting people killed—and we almost lost Cristelle. I love the tribe, and they're a lot more savvy than we gave them credit for at first. But who knows if they can stand up to the Mongers? Will he bully them, make them sell him the water we trade them? Some of that we bought from him!"

"So? You don't believe in the free enterprise system?"

"You can't be that naïve! You think WatDoc has the Nuwuwu's best interest at heart?"

"Probably not. Why would he?"

Zeke shook his head. "Do you, Mahir?"

"I don't know anymore."

"What are you saying?"

Mahir shut the hood of the van and wiped his hands. "It just seems like such a waste. We've been out here so long, and what have we accomplished?"

"Come on, man. You're one of the smartest people I've ever known. You know better than to be results-oriented. We do the right thing because it's the right thing. Whether it works or not is seldom up to us, is it? Is that how it works in science?"

"You say that, but where has it gotten us, Zeke? You and I worked our tails off on the drought thing for years, and our own government finally just gave up."

"Could you blame 'em? What was the option?"

"There was none! God won this one. But here we are, still shaking our fists in His face. What chance do we have? Everybody else is back in paradise, where they have wells and springs and city systems that give them all the water they want. Meanwhile you and I have to rely on every trick in our bag and come up with a contraption to keep our little band of friends alive. And for what?"

"Mahir, is that what you really think? That we're out here fighting God, shaking our fists at Him when He's made it clear He wants us off this ground He's cursed?"

Mahir looked away and shook his head. "I don't know what else to think."

"You've always been quiet, but is this why you've been so moody lately?"

"Have I?"

"Yeah, you have. The way you talked to Elaine this morning?"

"Zeke! I was just trying to motivate her."

"She didn't deserve that. She's one of the sweetest, most selfless people I've ever met."

"That's a nice sentiment, but sentiment'll get you killed. When someone draws down on me, I don't want sweet and selfless, I want cold and ready. So I guess I have been a little moody lately."

"When did you forget why we're here, why we're keeping our little band fed and hydrated and supplied?"

"I don't know. Are we done here, Zeke? I'm hungry and have stuff to do, and I know you do too."

Zeke stared at his friend. "We can be done if you want to be, but I worry about you."

"Don't."

"Why wouldn't I? We've worked together a long time, and I need you. I can't imagine carrying on without you, and you're making noises like you're not long for this place. We both know you could find work—good, challenging, lucrative work—just about anywhere. Is that what you're going to do? Leave me out here by myself?"

"You'd hardly be alone."

"But you are, huh? Planning to go?"

"Actually no. I have no plans."

"But you're not happy here, so I shouldn't assume you'll be here for the long haul."

"I don't know."

"Why'd you come in the first place?"

"Seemed like an adventure, I guess."

"An adventure. Wow."

"Well, why'd you come, Zeke?"

"I thought it was clear why we all came. I thought Pastor Bob made it plain as day that this was no small decision. If you didn't see it as a call of God on your life, you shouldn't have committed to it."

"You want the truth?"

"Of course!"

"I came because of you."

Zeke suddenly felt exhausted. He hung his head and rubbed his eyes. "That is the last thing I wanted to hear. And that is about the dumbest reason you could have told me. But I'll bite. You said you thought it was an adventure. What did I have to do with it?"

"I always liked working with you and for you. I liked the way you think, the way you made me think, the way you challenged me and brought out the best in me."

"Well, I appreciate that, and I felt the same way about you. But you have to know that's not enough, not for something like this. It's too hard. We're never going to see enough success, enough results. We didn't even at the waterworks! How could you think this would be any better? If we're not doing this for a higher purpose, if we're not doing it for God, because He wants us to, because He's called us to it, it's never going to work, right?"

"I guess."

"You guess? What are you going to do about it, Mahir?"

He shook his head. "I don't know yet."

Zeke sighed. "You'd better figure it out soon, don't you think? For the sake of everybody else here?"

Knowing what was coming, Zeke felt the better part of wisdom was to let Pastor Bob start the one o'clock elder meeting the usual way, leading it and opening in prayer. He thanked God for the time the team had spent with the Nuwuwu and prayed for Raoul and Danley's safety on their supply run. He also prayed for Doc as he cared for Jennie and Cristelle and asked the Lord to give the three of them wisdom as they sought his replacement as an elder.

When he finished, he pulled a crisply folded sheet from his pocket and spread it open before him. "Now then, Zeke," he said, "I'd like you to account for everyone on this roster, which I have listed in alphabetical order—aren't you going to miss me when I'm gone? Then we can chat through the likely candidates for my replacement and see how the Lord leads."

Zeke gave Doc a knowing look, and Doc cleared his throat.

"What?" Pastor Bob said.

"No, that's all right," Zeke said. "I can do that. Let's see. Katashi Aki is on lookout duty outside. Rev. Robert Gill is present and accounted for. Genevieve Gill is resting in her quarters, and I did check in on her on my way here and I must say, Pastor, like Katashi, I was alarmed at the difference I saw in her even since yesterday at this time."

"Yes, I mentioned that I attribute that to a difficult night's sleep. I think she's very anxious about leaving you all."

Zeke and Doc locked eyes again, but Zeke carried on. "Weak as she was, she seemed quite taken with little Zaltana's gift."

"Yes," Pastor Bob said. "So precious."

"Continuing, Raoul Gutierrez is on the road. Benita Gutierrez is teaching. Elaine Meeks, food prep. Danley Muscadin, on the road with Raoul. Cristelle Muscadin in the infirmary—"

"Update on her condition, Doc?" Pastor Bob said.

"I'm having trouble ameliorating her pain, to put it plainly. I've increased the dosage and more meds are coming."

"Mahir Sy, aquaponics lab. Zeke Thorppe, yours truly. Alexis Thorppe is sitting with Jennie. Alexandra Thorppe, that's Sasha, she's in class.

Adam Xavier is right here. Gabrielle Xavier is monitoring Cristelle. Caleb and Kayla Xavier are in class."

"Thank you, Zeke. Now from among that list, you'll notice that I have put check marks beside the names of four men who are of age and who would be eligible to serve as elder. They are—"

"Excuse me, Pastor," Zeke said. "I'm sorry to interrupt, but I wonder if Doc and I may discuss an important matter with you. I wouldn't ask if we both didn't feel it was crucial."

"Please," Doc said. "Trust him on this."

"Certainly," Pastor Bob said. "I yield the floor."

"Doc has something very important he needs to tell you," Zeke said, putting a hand on the pastor's shoulder.

Doc put his hand on Bob's other shoulder, causing the pastor to say, "Oh, my."

"Pastor," the doctor began, "it's only because of my deep love for both you and Jennie that I waited until now to tell you this. But you need to know, and I need to be straightforward."

Zeke felt Pastor Bob shudder.

"Jennie's cancer is much more advanced than I indicated, and I can't in good conscience recommend that she travel Wednesday ev—"

"I know it's terminal, Doc. You told us—"

Doc held up a hand. "If you'll recall, Jennie asked if she would have time to see the kids and grandchildren, and I asked her how soon she could do that."

"You said six months."

"I'm not trying to split hairs here, Pastor, but she asked if she had six months and I said she might not want to wait that long."

"That made us think—"

"I know, and I apologize if I left the impression she had more time than she did, but in my judgment you had both taken in as much as you could handle. You immediately decided that you would announce your resignation the following Sunday—yesterday—which I thought was wise. But Pastor, I need to tell you now, and you need to hear me, I double-checked my analysis of the workups I did on her a week ago today. Not only does her deterioration just within the last twenty-four hours not surprise me, I'm a little surprised it didn't happen sooner."

"So if she wants to see the kids and the gr—"

"Bob, she can't travel."

"Oh! How much time does—"

"We need to make her comfortable."

"You're saying it's a day-to-day situation."

"That's what I'm saying. I'm sorry."

Pastor Bob rested his head in his hands. When Doc inhaled as if to continue, Zeke signaled for him to wait. They just sat with their hands on his shoulders.

After several minutes, the pastor said quietly, "Would you gentlemen mind terribly if we moved the rest of this meeting to my place so I could be with Jennie?"

"Oh, Bob," Zeke said, "this meeting can be over. There's nothing pressing here, nothing as important as your being with her."

"No, really. She's sleeping, and I need to occupy myself. I'm serious. I feel strongly that I want to help you get this thing done, but of course I also want to be with her."

"Are you sure?"

"Positive. Really."

"Let me peek in on Gabi and my patient at the infirmary," Doc said, "and I can pick up some meds for Jennie too."

When they stopped, however, Zeke was surprised to hear Doc say, "What are you doing here? Where's my wife?"

"She came and got me," Mahir said.

"She left the patient?" Doc said.

"Just for a minute. Asked me to trade places with her. Said she was getting light-headed from the alcohol smell or something. I don't mind. I was done in the lab anyway."

"Mahir, listen," Zeke said, "don't you have more important things you could be doing?"

"Always. The fuel conversion regul—"

"I don't need to know. I'll send Alexis to replace you in a few minutes so you can get back to that."

"Whatever you want."

When the men moved on, it was obvious Doc was simmering. "Alcohol smell?" he said. "Gabi's been in hospitals all our married life. Never heard her complain once. And she knows better than to leave Cristelle even for a second. She could have let me know. Give me a minute to find out what this is all about."

He went off toward his quarters while Zeke and the pastor headed toward the Gills' room. When they tiptoed in, Alexis whispered, "She's finally asleep. She's so weak, but she wanted to show me what she got from Zaltana and tell me all about her last message and then the trip."

Jennie lay on the couch on the far side of the room, the tiny toy still clutched in her hand, the IV drip running from a pole behind her.

"Message?" Zeke said, following Pastor Bob to the kitchen and settling in at the table.

Bob nodded. "You know how shy she is about speaking. Well, she asked if she could talk to everybody before we pulled out Wednesday night. I told her I was sure everyone would love that."

"Of course we would," Alexis said. "She might not want me telling you this, but she told me that if the trip was tonight, she wasn't sure she'd be up to going. She said she didn't even feel like sitting up. But I'm sure when the time comes and she starts looking forward to seeing the—"

"We're not going," Pastor Bob whispered.

"What?" Alexis mouthed.

He beckoned her with a nod and she moved to the kitchen. Within seconds she was in tears.

Doc arrived with a small vial of meds, a bottle of water, and a bag of saline solution for Jennie's IV. "Rest is best," he said quickly, but it was obvious he was distracted and more than exercised. Zeke noticed his eyes darted as he spoke and he treated Alexis like a lackie, dumping the stuff into her hands and speaking in a quick monotone. "Hydration is next, so if she rouses, get some water in her too. Discomfort, here's pain meds—but that's it till the guys get back from Arizona. Zeke, we've got to go. Gabi says Mahir taking over for her wasn't her idea at all. It was his."

Zeke shot up from his chair. "You're saying he lied?"

"She says he showed up and asked her if she liked the smell of the infirmary. She told him she was used to it. He said he was hoping she needed a break 'cause he was done in the lab and bored out of his mind. She said babysitting a sleeping patient wasn't exciting, and he said at least he could read without smelling fish."

"Lexi, come with us," Zeke said. "I'll need you to sit with Cristelle. Bob will stay here with Jennie."

"What in the world is going on with Mahir?" Alexis said, as the three of them hurried off.

"We'll know soon enough."

"Listen," she said, "if Jennie's as bad as Bob says, you're gonna let her speak to everyone soon, right?"

"'Course, but right now we've got a bigger problem."

When they drew within sight of the infirmary, Zeke was surprised to see the door closed. Finding it locked, Doc rapped on it.

"Busy!" Mahir called out.

"What do you mean, 'busy'? This is Dr. Xavier! Open this door!"

The door swept open to reveal Mahir with a paperback book tucked under his arm. "Glad you're here!" he said over the high-pitched ring of one of the machines. "I was just about to hit the call button."

Doc elbowed him out of the way and rushed to Cristelle. "What's going on? What have you done?"

"I just noticed she looked funny, so I—"

"Looked funny!" Doc said, ripping the cannula tube from her nose, grabbing an oxygen bottle, covering her face with the mask, and slipping an elastic band around her head. "She's not breathing, man!" He spun the flow control valve on the tank while pressing the thumb and forefinger of his free hand on her carotid arteries. "She's got a pulse but zero respiration. How long has this machine been off?"

Mahir shrugged.

"C'mon! When did it start ringing?"

"I was reading."

"You can't read through that racket! How long?"

"It just started, I guess."

"You guess! Minutes count! We're talking potential brain damage, Mahir."

"I don't think it's been long. As soon as I heard it, I checked on her and was about to call you when you knocked."

Doc turned the oxygen machine back on. "I'm going to switch her back to the tube as soon as her color returns," he said. "How'd that machine get turned off?"

"Don't ask me."

"Who'm I supposed to ask, Mahir? You see anyone else in here? I've got her so sedated she's not even dreaming, let alone moving, and you think she turned off her own air?"

"Well, your wife was in here before I was."

"Will you stop? She knows better than to turn off a person's oxygen. Anyway, the alarm immediately comes on."

"She sure looks better now," Mahir said.

"No thanks to you."

"Can I get to the lab?"

"You're not going anywhere," Zeke said.

Mahir shrugged again, sat, and opened his book.

Doc pulled the mask away, used his stethoscope to check Cristelle's pulse and respiration, shined a flashlight into her eyes, cupped her face in his hands—Zeke assumed to feel the warmth of her face—and put the cannula tube back in her nose. He told Alexis he thought Cristelle would be all right but to call him if anything seemed amiss.

"Mahir," Zeke said, "you need to come with us."

"To?"

"Your quarters."

They walked in silence until Mahir said lightly, "So, what's up, guys?"

"What are you, serious?" Doc said.

"Let's hold off till we're inside," Zeke said.

Mahir unlocked his door and, no surprise to Zeke, the place was immaculate. Since the day they'd met when Mahir was hired on as Zeke's summer intern at the California Department of Water Resources more than two decades before—and soon became his assistant—the young man of French descent had been nothing if not shipshape. From day one, everything had a place and everything was in its place. Zeke had never been a slouch, but Mahir had even tidied him up—and his office.

His quarters could have passed muster with any drill sergeant.

Mahir pointed to the couch and began, "May I offer you gentlemen—" but Zeke cut him off as they sat.

"Give me your weapon, Mahir."

"Seriously?"

"Just hand it over and give me your backups too."

Mahir pulled a Colt .45 from a shoulder holster inside his shirt. "Have I done something—"

"You've never known me to do anything but lay my cards on the table," Zeke said, "and I'm not going to start doing anything other than that now. You've got two snubnoses, too, right? A .22 and a .38?"

"In the bedroom."

"Doc will go with you."

When Doc rose, Mahir said, "You're afraid I'll come out shooting?"

"How do we know?" Zeke said. "What you did today makes me wish we had a jail here, somewhere I could lock you till we figure out if we can ever trust you again."

"I'm finding this hard to bel—"

"Just go get the guns. And are there any more?"

"No!"

When they returned, Doc with the weapons in hand, Mahir said, "Now you'd better tell me what I've done that's caused you of all people—"

"Oh, stop with the histrionics, Mahir. You start the day with a bad attitude, insulting the sweetest woman in the group. Then we get back here and you tell me you saw WatDoc and never alerted me. You admit you've pretty much forgotten what we're doing out here."

"Yeah, I have."

"We can live with that, Mahir. Everybody goes through slumps. We're a small band. We pick each other up, we move on. But there's only sixteen of us. We can't have a liar among us, a manipulator, or worse."

"What are you saying, Zeke?"

"You lied."

"Who did I lie to?"

Zeke looked away and shook his head. "You're just making it worse, man. I thought I knew you. We worked side by side for years. You gonna make me say it, make me tell you, when you're the one who did it? You just did it!"

Mahir sat staring, then turned to Doc as if thoroughly confused.

"You lied to me, Mahir," Doc said. "You think I don't know my own wife? You told me she left the patient, told me she asked you to take over, said she couldn't take the smell. You think that was gonna fly, the wife of a doctor violating protocol or not being able to take the smells?"

"Yeah, okay, so I fibbed. Sorry."

"You fibbed, so you're sorry?" Zeke said. "If you were done in the lab and wanted to read, you come back here and read! What'd you think, I'd fire you for that? You lock yourself in with Cristelle, her oxygen machine is turned off, the alarm is sounding, she's not breathing, and if we don't show up, she's dead. How were you gonna explain that?"

"I was trying to help her and was going to call you!"

"It doesn't add up, Mahir. None of it makes any sense. It looks like you tried to kill her!"

"*That's* what you believe? *That's* why you took my guns?"

"That's why I can't trust you anymore. How can I? I can't have you among the group, man. I need your keys."

Mahir tossed them to him. "You're going to lock me in my own place?"

"I have no choice."

"For how long?"

"The elders will decide. Or you'll come clean and tell me what's really going on."

"How will I eat?"

"We'll see that you have enough."

"I'll go crazy in here."

"I don't plan to torture you, Mahir."

"How about I just leave? You'll never see me again."

"We believe you tried to kill someone. We'd have to report you."

"Then I want a lawyer."

"Maybe, when the time comes. But remember, you're not entitled to the same privileges as you are when you're living outside California."

"You're holding me against my will."

"Mahir, we have an implicit code of conduct. We can't risk you giving away our position. Plus we want to give you every opportunity to remedy this."

"How? Wouldn't I say anything, agree to anything, just to be free?"

"We'll see. I need to ask you one more thing, Mahir. Do you understand Arabic?"

Mahir looked stricken. He cocked his head. "Why would you ask me that?"

"Just curious. I've known you a long time and never knew of it, if it's true."

"Could you repeat the question?"

"Do I need to?"

Mahir shook his head. "It's just so out of the blue, out of context."

"I hope so. You going to answer?"

"No."

"You don't know Arabic, or you're not going to answer?"

"The latter. I'm being treated unfairly. I want a lawyer and I want out of here."

Back at the Gills', with Alexis gone and Jennie sleeping, Zeke filled in Pastor Bob. "We can postpone this meeting."

"Isn't this a day for great news," Bob said, sighing. "No. Thanks for being straight with me about Jennie. That had to be hard. We're going to have to talk about what I'm to do when the time comes, getting her home, dealing with the authorities, not exposing the rest of you, all that. Of course the family will want a service. But let's finish our business."

"Then I yield the meeting back to you," Zeke said.

Pastor Bob spread his roster of names on the kitchen table. "Katashi, Raoul, Danley, and Mahir," he said. "Well, that last one's moot. How are you going to manage him as a prisoner, Zeke? I can hardly fathom it."

"What choice do I have?"

"Interesting," Doc said, chuckling. "No matter who we choose from this list, I'll no longer be the minority elder, Zeke. You will."

Zeke focused on the list. "Seriously? That's what's on your mind right now?"

"Had you seen yourself that way, Doc?" Pastor Bob said. "Did you feel treated that way?"

"It just is what it is."

"Something we need to learn?" Zeke said.

Doc shook his head. "Can't, don't, won't ever. Don't worry about it."

"Even if we want to?" Zeke said. "Are open to?"

"I shouldn't have brought it up. Let it go."

Doc jumped when the beeper on Jennie's IV sounded. As he changed out the bag, Pastor Bob crept over and took the doll from Jennie and studied it, smiling. He slipped it back in her hand, fetched a small blanket, and draped it over her.

When they returned to the table, Pastor Bob said, "As I see it, our options have been cut in half. Mahir's out, and do you agree Danley is too young and too new to the faith? I mean, *elder* self-defines."

"Not to mention," Zeke said, "his spiritual father, his mentor, was Mahir. So it's down to Katashi and Raoul."

"I love both those men," the pastor said. "And they both came to Christ around the same time. Ironic that they came to us as friends, coworkers."

Zeke chuckled. "Garbagemen."

Pastor Bob sat back and crossed his arms, seeming to study Zeke. "I have to tell you something, my friend," he said, his voice thick with emotion. "This is remarkable, you sitting here seeking the Lord about elevating to the position of elder the man responsible for the death of your firstborn child."

Zeke let that sink in. "Hadn't crossed my mind."

The pastor nodded. "That's the grace of God."

PART 4

THE
OPPOSITION

THE DECISION

15

DOC AGREED THAT Danley was too young, both in age and in the faith, so the choice for elder came down to Katashi Aki or Raoul Gutierrez. "But Pastor Bob," Doc said, lowering his voice, "should Jennie pass as soon as I believe she will, are you sure you need to be replaced?"

"I was wondering the same," Zeke said, trying not to be indelicate. "Would you consider just a leave of absence, letting one of us fill in for you—"

"Yes," Doc said quickly, leaning in. "I'd be happy to do what I used to do back in Torrance."

Pastor Bob shook his head. "I know it's only been a week since the diagnosis, and I've worried what I'll do with myself without a ministry. But choosing a new leader feels right, especially if you're correct. I'm just not prepared for her to be gone in less than a month."

"Pastor, I hope you know how deeply it pains me to say it," Doc said, "but you don't want her to survive even seven more days with this. I'm sorry, but you'll be praying for the mercy of her passing before that."

Pastor Bob grimaced. "Even with you keeping her pain-free?"

Doc nodded.

"I see. Then no. I will in no way be equipped to still be pastor. I'm sorry."

"Believe me," Zeke said, "we understand."

"Thirsty."

The three turned as one at Jennie's voice, and Doc rose. Pastor Bob put a hand on his arm. "Let me."

"Of course. Water first, remember."

The pastor grabbed the bottle and the medicine from near the door and knelt by her side.

"So tired," she rasped.

"I know," he said, twisting off the cap. "Are we disturbing you?"

"Hmm?"

He slipped his hand behind her head and lifted. "Just sip." She took a couple of swallows. "More?" She shook her head.

He peeked at Doc. "It's up to her," Doc mouthed.

"Who's here?" she said.

"Doc and Zeke. Would you rather be alone?"

She shook her head. "'s okay. Sleepy."

"You hurting anywhere?"

"Um-hm."

"You are?"

She nodded. He looked to Doc again. "Give her a tablet if she'll take it."

She opened her mouth and he put it on her tongue. "Bitter," she mumbled.

"Here's more water."

She shook her head.

Bob looked at Doc, who shrugged. "It'll work that way too if she can stand it. That's an awful-tasting med."

Jennie's breathing grew even and deep.

"I think she's out," the pastor said.

"Just as well," Doc said. "Good that she got a little water down, and if she can sleep in spite of that taste, she must really be hurting. She should be comfortable for a good hour."

Pastor Bob set down the bottle and the medicine and placed one hand on her head and the other on her shoulder. Zeke saw Bob's tears. Doc looked as if he were about to go to him. Zeke whispered, "Let's give him a minute."

But it became more than a minute. The couple had been married a long time, had grown kids and grandkids they had virtually sacrificed for this life. Jennie had been the quintessential ministry wife, by Bob's side, supporting him from the beginning.

Presently he rose and wiped his eyes, grabbed his Bible from a shelf, and rejoined Doc and Zeke. "So grateful she can just rest. Funny the value of small things now." He opened his Bible. "Anyway, let me just say I'm ready to step down. We'll need to talk about logistics when Jennie's time comes. Our family will want a memorial service. I'll want to go home, I don't know for how long, and determine my future. If I ever come back, I don't need or want to be an elder. I know you'd put me to work and I'd be of some use. Now then, let's do things in order. Replace me as elder, then replace me as pastor."

"Okay, let's get on with it," Doc said. "Who votes for Raoul?"

"Slow down," Zeke said.

"Yes," Pastor Bob said. "Let me share a bit from the Scripture, then a little of what I know of both candidates, and I'll officially step away."

"One more thing," Doc said. "I am willing to be the new pastor."

"You've made that clear," Pastor Bob said. "But it isn't a role you volunteer for, claim, or even apply for. The new elder board is to select the man as the Lord leads."

"We should decide next Sunday then," Doc said, "and I would like to bring a message first—one the Lord has laid on my heart. That should dispel any misgivings on the parts of the other two elders."

Zeke was ready to burst. By then he hardly cared if Doc replaced Pastor Bob if he wanted it so badly.

"That," Pastor Bob said, sighing, "will be up to you and Zeke and whoever you select as the new elder. For now, let me read this from 1 Timothy. Consider this carefully in light of the two men under consideration, not to mention yourselves and your own roles:

"If a man desires the position of a bishop, he desires a good work. A bishop then must be blameless, the husband of one wife, temperate, sober-minded, of good behavior, hospitable, able to teach; not given to wine, not violent, not greedy for money, but gentle, not quarrelsome, not covetous; one who rules his own house well, having his children in submission with all reverence (for if a man does not know how to rule his own house, how will he take care of the church of God?); not a novice, lest being puffed up with pride he fall into the same condemnation as the devil. Moreover he must have a good testimony among those who are outside, lest he fall into reproach and the snare of the devil."

Bob looked up. "Now, neither of your candidates has children, and only one of them is married. Does that disqualify them? I think not. The principle here is that a man should not be an adulterer and that if he is a father, he should be a faithful and disciplined one. The three of us have known both these men for about the same length of time, and I have served as their pastor that entire time. Spiritually I see them on a virtually equal plane. I believe they are both men of character and principle who love God and are committed to serving Him. They are here for the right reasons. There are two distinct differences between them that I would like you to point out if they also strike you."

"I think they're obvious," Doc said.

"So do I," Zeke said.

"Well then each of you take one. Doc, you first."

"I think Katashi is more intelligent than Raoul, not that Raoul is ignorant. Raoul has gifts that Katashi doesn't, but I'm guessing Katashi has a higher IQ, is more of an academic."

"I agree," Zeke said, "but Raoul might be brighter than Katashi in some others areas. Street smarts maybe. The other major difference? Raoul is far more gregarious. More of a people person, outgoing, passionate, humorous, dramatic."

"Exactly," Pastor Bob said. "Does that make your decision easier or harder?"

"Harder," Doc said. "I'd like to have a hybrid of them both."

"Just what I was going to say," Zeke said.

Pastor Bob tore a sheet of paper in half. "Pray while I sit with Jennie a few minutes. When you're ready for a secret ballot, I'll come back."

Zeke felt smug. Part of him worried that because Doc was prideful and so badly wanted the pastorate, he might hold out for whichever of the two he thought he could most easily influence and pick him for that role. But the other part of him knew that God had chosen to speak audibly to him, so he needn't worry about trying to decide for himself. All he had to do was ask, and God would tell him. And who was Doc to stand in the way of God's will?

Yet smugness did not sit well with Zeke. What kind of an attitude was that? He was an elder among a body of believers, which meant he was Doc's elder too. Should he not be concerned about Doc's spiritual life? What was he doing for Doc? What could he do to nurture Doc? In an instant Zeke turned from smug to shame-faced. So when he went to prayer, it was not a request for wisdom but forgiveness.

I'm sorry, Lord. Forgive me and make me useful, that's all I ask.

"I'm ready," Doc said.

I'm not!

"I'll give you a word for him," God said.

I'm not being asked for a word for Doc. I'm being asked for a choice for elder.

Pastor Bob returned to the table and gave a half sheet of paper to each man. "Just write a K or an R and slide it back to me. If your selections agree, that will confirm that the Lord is in it."

Doc slid his sheet to Pastor Bob.

"I'm sorry, Zeke," the pastor said. "Were you not ready?"

"Not quite."

"I apologize. I just assumed."

Lord, please.

"I have given you a word for him," God said.

But who is Your choice?

"Use your own judgment."

Zeke felt short of breath. He quickly wrote a *K* on the back of his sheet and pushed it to Pastor Bob.

Bob peeked under both sheets and said, "Thank you, Lord, Katashi it is."

"That was easy," Doc said, holding up a fist for Zeke to bump.

If you only knew, Zeke thought.

"Now," the Lord said.

Now?

Zeke knew he needed to stop asking that question. He opened his mouth. "The elders among you I exhort, I a fellow elder and a witness of the sufferings of Christ, and also a partaker of the glory that will be revealed: Shepherd the flock of God among you, serving as overseers, not by compulsion but willingly, not for dishonest gain but eagerly; nor as being lords over those entrusted to you, but being examples to the flock; and when the Chief Shepherd appears, you will receive the crown of glory that does not fade away. Be submissive, clothed with humility, for God gives grace to the humble."

16

THE ADMONITION

Doc squinted at Zeke. "I'm all for Scripture, brother, but what was that all about?"

"I'll leave the application to you," Zeke said. "One of us ought to go find Katashi."

"Why don't you?" Bob said. "I'll stay here with Jennie while Doc checks in on Cristelle. You said Katashi was on lookout duty. You have someone who can sub for him?"

Zeke glanced at his watch. "I had been thinking Mahir, but I'll steal Sasha out of class. They're almost done, and she's proven herself before. All she's got to do is let me know if she sees anything the periscopes wouldn't pick up."

Doc looked up. "Hey, ask Benita if she can keep an eye on my kids after class till Gabi is free. I don't want them running around in the garage again."

Zeke stopped by his quarters to get Sasha's nine-millimeter on his way to the Commons, where Benita was teaching the kids.

He told her he needed Sasha, and she pulled him aside and asked if he had a minute first.

"About a minute, sure."

"Kayla said something and Caleb tried to tell her to be quiet, you know, but Sasha heard enough to make her very curious, so she kept asking for more information. Finally Kayla told her and that made Caleb mad."

"Uh-huh. What was it all about?"

"Something Caleb found in the garage, some papers he showed his *madre*. She made him put them back, but they were in a foreign language. I just wanted the kids to stop arguing about it, you know, because it didn't sound like nothing important to me, but they wouldn't stop. Sasha agreed with me and she said, 'What's the big deal?' and somehow it came out that these papers were in Arabic. I thought I should tell you."

"Thank you, Benita."

"Doesn't that scare you?"

"Does it scare you?"

"*Sí!* If it was Spanish it could have been something Raoul and I were reading, or if it was Asian, maybe computer instructions or something with the parts for the systems that you guys use for the water and the plants. But Arabic? Nobody here reads that, do they?"

"Not that I know of."

"Me neither, but with what is happening everywhere with the terror and the killings—"

"Let's not worry until we know what we're dealing with, Benita. I'll handle Sasha and deal with the Xaviers. I won't say you can't discuss it with Raoul, but—"

"We won't say nothing to no one else."

"Thank you."

Zeke gave Sasha her gun and took her outside to replace Katashi, and she was happy to be pressed into service. "Don't be a hero," he reminded her.

"Don't worry, Dad. I know what to do if I see anything."

"You need me for what?" Katashi said, as they headed inside and down the hall.

"A meeting at Pastor Bob's."

"Okay," he said, more as a question.

"I don't mean to be mysterious. It'll become clear."

"How's Jennie doing?"

"Not well, actually. Sleeping mostly."

"We won't bother her?"

"We've been meeting ten feet from her and she hardly knows we're there."

"Who's *we*?"

"The elders."

Katashi slowed. "Am I in trouble?"

Zeke chuckled. "I wouldn't ambush you. But it does depend on your definition of *trouble*. And *ambush*."

When they got there, Katashi looked hesitantly at Jennie on the couch, and Pastor Bob said, "We're just careful to keep our voices down, that's all. Welcome." He pointed to chairs and they all sat. "Katashi, you'll recall the elders needed a replacement for me, and they feel the Lord has led them to you as the new elder."

Katashi closed his eyes, shook his head, and opened them again. "Did not see that coming. Me as an elder?"

"Well," Bob said, "we believe the Lord is in this. So are you open to it? Willing? Will you accept the appointment?"

"I'm not as consistent as I'd like to be spiritually, but I strive to be. Am I a dirty, rotten sinner without hope other than the blood Jesus shed for me on the cross? Yes, that's me."

Zeke pressed a hand over his mouth, then pulled it away. "That affirms my vote," he whispered.

"Mine too," Doc said.

"I no longer have a vote," Bob said, "but I concur."

"I wouldn't have thought of me," Katashi said.

Bob smiled. "That's sort of a prerequisite too."

"I have a word for him," God told Zeke.

The Lord never ceased to amaze him. Zeke hesitated, then immediately recognized the folly of his own reasoning. The man was seeking God, and God had given Zeke a word for him.

Zeke said, "He who acknowledges the Son has the Father also. Therefore you will abide in the Son and in the Father. And He has promised us eternal life. The anointing you have received from Him abides in you, and you do not need anyone to teach you that; you will abide in Him."

Katashi looked up. "I'm honored and I accept."

Bob put a hand on Katashi's shoulder. "May God our heavenly Father, who has called you to this sacred office, guide you by His Word, equip you with His Spirit, and so prosper your ministries that His body may increase and His name be praised. 'Now to Him who is able to keep you from stumbling, and to present you faultless before the presence of His glory with exceeding joy, to God our Savior, who alone is wise, be glory and majesty, dominion and power, both now and forever. Amen.'"

Bob rose. "Now, if you gentlemen will excuse me, I'll be right over here with my wife. And Katashi, my advice is to do more listening than talking at first, but with such a small board don't hesitate to weigh in on important matters."

Doc immediately told Katashi what had happened with Mahir and that he was virtually a prisoner in his own quarters until further notice.

Katashi shook his head. "And not just lying but actually might have tried to harm Cristelle? Wow, I feel like I've been thrown into the deep end of the pool."

"That's not the half of it," Zeke said. "You need to know what else is going on."

"You sure?" Doc said.

"We've never kept secrets among us elders, and we're not going to start now," Zeke said. "Your own daughter just spilled the beans to Sasha and Benita. How long before everybody knows?"

"Fair enough," Doc said. "Katashi, my son found evidence in the garage that we have a Middle Eastern terrorist among us."

"Whoa!" Zeke whispered. "We don't know what it means." He told Katashi what Caleb had found.

"That *is* scary," Katashi said. "What else *could* it mean?"

"That's what I'm saying," Doc said. "I think it all points to Mahir."

Katashi recoiled. "Is he going to become your scapegoat for everything now? You think he's trying to kill us all?"

"You have a better theory?" Doc said.

"Uh, yeah," Katashi said. "I might not have been so quick to accept this appointment if I thought it was about witch hunts."

"That's what you think this is?" Doc said.

"Let's just say I expected more, especially from you."

Zeke was impressed. He had worried Katashi might be intimidated by Doc, maybe even unduly influenced.

"Maybe when you gain a little more experience," Doc said, "or if you'd had more formal education—"

"All right," Zeke said, "let's not make this personal. We're all on the same side here."

"Pardon me, Zeke," Doc said, "but last I knew, your authority doesn't extend to the elder board. Unless you're chosen to be the next pastor—which isn't likely—don't act like you're leading us now."

"Well," Katashi said, "someone has to if we're going to tell the others what we've done with Mahir."

"I agree," Doc said, "and because I used to fill in for Pastor Bob at the church, I'm the logical choice, and—"

"Oh, I wouldn't say that," Katashi said.

"*You* wouldn't say that?" Doc said. "What do you have to say about it?"

Zeke stared at Doc. "Is this the style of leadership we should expect from you? You'd decide who has the right to speak and when?"

"He's brand new, Zeke!"

"And he's a member of the board!"

"Very well, Katashi," Doc said, exaggerating his cadence. "Explain why *you*, as the nine-minute-old member of this body, say I'm *not* the logical choice as the next elder board chairman-slash-pastor."

"Easy," Katashi said. "With all due respect: You intimidate people. If I hadn't just been encouraged to 'not hesitate to weigh in on important matters,' I would be intimidated. But I *will* weigh in on it.

"You have many talents, Doc. You're as smart as anybody I've ever met, and I would entrust you with my life. But in all the years I've known him, Pastor Bob never intimidated anybody, though he exhorted us to live godly lives. Zeke never intimidates anybody, though he inspires us to do what we might not want to do. That's the kind of leader we want: someone who leads by example. Not someone we're afraid of."

"Finished?"

"Not till I tell you I love you, Doc."

"You have a strange way of showing it."

Katashi sighed. "I still say we need an elder chairman before deciding on a pastor."

"I agree," Doc said. "But that person would also become the pastor. I also agree with Zeke that we should have no secrets, so we should put it to an open vote. I nominate myself."

"I nominate Zeke," Katashi said.

"And I," Zeke said, "am abstaining from voting."

"Well then," Doc said, "we're stalemated at one to one with one abstention. Might either of you be open to changing your mind if you knew the Lord has given me a message for Sunday on humility and teamwork?"

Zeke said, "I might change my mind about abstaining and vote for myself if you assumed the pulpit without authority from this board."

Doc turned away. "We're getting nowhere."

"Excuse me, gentlemen," Bob said, next to Jennie on the couch. She was sitting up. "Jennie has something she wants to say, but you're going to have to bring your chairs over so she doesn't have to raise her voice."

As they settled before her, mumbling how sorry they were for bothering her, she sipped her water and shook her head. "No need to apologize. If I needed you gone, you'd be gone. Whatever Doc gave me did the trick, so thanks. You know I think you've been a godsend, Doc, and nothing's ever going to change that."

"Thank you, ma'am."

"And Katashi, welcome. You're a good choice."

"Appreciate it, Mrs. Gill."

"Zeke, you don't need more bouquets. You know what I think of you."

"I do, Jennie. Thanks."

"Now I'm old school, maybe out of step, but I've always liked being in a support role and not a talking one. But this is my house, and you boys are gonna listen. Let me tell you—what I've been hearing, God's not in it.

"I've been alongside this man here almost my whole life, and I'm not gonna tell you he's perfect—nobody knows that better'n I do. But the God he serves is a God of order, and I haven't heard order since Bob left that table. Doc, you're after a job that ought not to be sought. If it comes your way, accept it with fear and trembling, knowing you can do it only under the power of God."

"Oh, I know. I would—"

"Hush now. It's my turn to talk. Katashi, you nominated the right man, and Zeke, you're showing your true character by abstaining. There's only one way past this stalemate. You put it to the body. Katashi tells the people there are two candidates, it's not a popularity contest, so no politicking or campaigning, just a secret ballot so no hurt feelings. People should just prayerfully vote and trust the Lord's will to be done. That's all I've got to say."

The three sat in silence until Katashi said, "Did you hear our discussion about Mahir?"

"I did. Doc, you don't have to raise your hand to talk to me. What do you want?"

"If I promise you more of those pain meds, can I count on your vote?"

Jennie laughed. "First joke out of you since I've know you, and it's actually funny. No, Bob and I won't be voting."

17

THE VISIT

ZEKE'S ANNOUNCEMENT of the turn of events with Mahir created a stir at dinner Monday. He asked that everyone bear with the elders as they prayed and worked through what to do. He also said Jennie would still give a brief farewell message Wednesday evening, though the Gills' drive had been postponed. Then he introduced the new elder, and Katashi explained that the secret ballot election of the new pastor would follow Jennie's talk. He added that Bob and Jennie would not vote but that all other adults were eligible to. Katashi then closed with a prayer for Raoul and Danley's safe return—expected at around midnight.

When Katashi had mentioned their estimated time of arrival in his prayer, Zeke felt a check in his spirit. He had sent Raoul far out of his way to the south, being perhaps twice as cautious as necessary to avoid danger. He had even urged Raoul and Danley to hide rather than try to elude potential pursuers. In retrospect Zeke was glad he'd mentioned that, especially after what Mahir had said about having seen WatDoc near the Nuwuwu settlement. Where might his cohorts be? If evidence of one of them appeared in Raoul's rearview mirror, Zeke would rather see Raoul disappear than try to engage.

Regardless, it was highly unlikely Raoul and Danley would get to Arizona anywhere near the usual time, meaning their return would be delayed by that much longer too. Well into the wee hours of Tuesday was more likely.

Later Monday evening Zeke and Alexis were surprised by a knock at their door. "I can't stay long, friends," Gabrielle Xavier said when they invited her in. "I need to give Adam a break from Cristelle in a few minutes. I just wanted to suggest something. Alexis, what would you think of you and me abstaining from the vote Wednesday evening? If we each vote for our husbands, we'll just cancel each other's ballots anyway."

"I'm okay with that," Alexis said, glancing at Zeke. "Same difference either way, right?"

Gabrielle turned to Zeke. "You and Adam should do the same."

He chuckled. "Doc didn't tell you?"

"Tell me what?"

"Why we're voting in the first place. He nominated himself. Katashi nominated me. And I abstained. Had I voted for myself, it would've been two to one, the elder board would have named the new pastor, and there would have been no at-large vote."

Gabrielle looked crestfallen. "I need to sit down."

They all sat at the kitchen table. Gabrielle put a hand over her mouth and closed her eyes. Finally she looked sheepishly at Zeke. "You're serious. You're not toying with me."

"I wouldn't, Gabi. And I'm sorry. I wouldn't have said anything if I thought Doc hadn't told you. You have to know how badly he wants this."

"Well sure, but I thought he might like knowing Alexis and I were abstaining, since we would just be trading votes anyway. I mean, it's just a gesture, but it would be just like him to ask me to renege and vote for him now."

"Oh, surely not," Alexis said.

"Don't abstain," the Lord told Zeke. "Tell her you're going to vote for him."

"Gabrielle," Zeke said.

"Hmm?"

"I, uh—"

"You okay, Zeke?" Gabrielle said.

"Say it," God said. "The result is in My hand."

"Um, if you feel you need to vote for your husband, you should."

"That's not what I told you to say," the Lord said.

"What are you saying?" Gabrielle said.

"I will vote for him too," Zeke said.

"Z!" Alexis said. "I just promised to abstain! I'm not going to—"

"And you should keep that promise, Lexi," Zeke said, looking knowingly into her eyes.

"Oh, no!" Gabrielle moaned. "What am I supposed to do now? Alexis, you have to know I didn't come here to try to trick you into abstaining so I could—"

"Of course, Gabi! I know you better than that."

"And Zeke," Gabrielle said, "I don't understand. How could you abstain, cause this election, and now vote for Adam?"

Zeke shrugged. "I just feel led, that's all. Let's trust the Lord in this. What's supposed to happen will happen, right?"

"Well, sure, I guess, but my idea was that Alexis and I would abstain just for friendship's sake."

"Nothing will come between us, Gabi," Alexis said. "I'm abstaining, unless Rasputin here gets it in his head that I'm supposed to vote for Doc too. You vote your conscience—really, do what you feel you ought to and don't feel obligated even to tell me. Okay? Promise?"

Gabrielle nodded, rising, and as soon as she was gone, Zeke told Alexis what had happened.

"Well, I figured it had to be God, but good grief, Z, why don't you just hand Doc the job?"

He smiled. "'Rasputin,' really?"

"You like that one? I was proud of it. Hey, do you trust her?"

"I do. But I don't know her the way you do. She's your friend. Don't you trust her?"

Alexis nodded. "She wasn't faking it. She was really conflicted. But you have to admit, if that had been Doc, he would have tried to get me to abstain, just like you, and promised that he and she would do the same—for the sake of friendship, right?"

"Right," Zeke said, "then they would both vote for him and basically see a four-vote swing."

"You don't think he talked her into—"

Zeke shook his head. "But even if he did, God assured me the result is in His hands. I want only what He wants, don't you?"

"Absolutely. As long as it's not Pastor Doc."

"You *are* a rascal."

"You already know what I think you are," she said. "But I promise not to call you that in front of anybody."

"I don't," Sasha said, making Zeke jump.

"Oh, great. How much of that did you hear?"

"Let me think, Rasputin."

"Terrific. Do we need to remind you . . . ?"

Sasha pantomimed pulling a zipper across her mouth. "Actually, I was on my way out here when Miss Gabi knocked."

"So you heard all of it."

She nodded.

"Sash! You know better than to eavesdrop! You should have—"

"I know. Sorry. But sometimes adult stuff is so, I don't know—I just wish I could vote."

"Dare I ask who you'd vote for?" Zeke said.

"You kiddin'?" she said. "I could vote for Doc, Mom could vote for Doc, Doc and Miss Gabi and even Rasputin could vote for Doc, and those would be all the votes he'd get."

Zeke had trouble keeping a straight face, even when Alexis waxed serious. "Okay, Sasha, fun's over. Got it?"

"Yes, ma'am."

"You know you were wrong to keep listening."

"I do."

"To prove it, you're going to show your maturity by never mentioning one word of this conversation again, ever. You know what that means?"

"I think so."

"Tell me."

"We won't talk about it, that's all."

"Specifically, not even in jest," Alexis said. "Tell me what I'm saying."

"Oh, Mom!"

"Tell me."

"I can't call Dad Rasp—"

"Not even joking."

"Aw, c'mon!"

"Unless you want consequences."

"Yes, ma'am."

"Thank you."

Sasha muttered something.

"What was that, young lady?"

"I said at least I got one in before the gag order."

"Lucky you."

Zeke went to bed at ten and set his alarm for 12:01 a.m. Tuesday, asking to be awakened only if Cristelle or Jennie took a turn for the worse or Raoul and Danley returned earlier than expected.

He slept the slumber of the sleep-deprived and found it difficult to fully rouse himself when his alarm sounded. He hadn't planned on showering, but having heard nothing of Raoul and Danley, he rushed through a cold one to ensure he would be fully engaged. A change of clothes would refresh him too, but Zeke was surprised when he didn't feel right about slipping into his usual loose-fitting attire for padding about the compound after midnight.

Pawing through his closet and drawers, he kept feeling drawn to his outside getup, the black outfit from boots to hat. It made no sense, but he didn't feel comfortable even considering anything else.

He was pleased to find Elaine Meeks on northeast scope duty, the direction from which the supply runners would come. If he could count on anything from her, it was encouragement.

"Nothing yet?"

"No," she said, "but they should return in separate vehicles if all went well. I'll be eager to see what they come back with for Dr. Xavier's family. Well, look at you. Going somewhere?"

"Ah, never know." He checked his watch. "I would have expected some sign of them by now, wouldn't you?"

"Want the next look?" she said, switching places.

They traded off this way for the next thirty minutes until he grew deeply worried. He didn't hide that from Mrs. Meeks, but when Benita showed up looking for news of Raoul, he quickly affected nonchalance. She was clearly on the verge of tears.

"It's almost one, Zeke. They have never been this late before. What's going on?"

"Oh, no, Benita, look, I wouldn't be surprised if they're not back till three or even a little after."

"Katashi said midnight!"

"I know, but he shouldn't have. He forgot they got away a little late, had to take a longer route, and all they've got to do this time. You should try to sleep, because—"

"Sleep! There'll be no sleeping! I been prayin', and there was clouds on the horizon this morning, and—"

"Oh, we would have heard if that had come to anything. Don't worry about that. No, remember, Doc is looking for some different medicine for both Cristelle and Jennie, and they had to shop for another vehicle. Then they're driving back separately but they want to stay close enough to keep track of each other without attracting attention, all that. It's way too early to be concerned, okay?"

"What're you doin' down here then?"

"Just keeping an old lady company," Elaine said. "You know how boring this can get this time of night."

"Go back and get some rest," Zeke said. "If I don't have him to you by three, come and check on me again, okay? I don't really expect it will be before that. This is a much more complicated run. That's why I chose Raoul as my main man for it."

"Now you're just teasing me."

"Come on, Benita! You know what I think of him! Now go."

Usually nothing appeared blacker than drought-stricken California looking east in the wee hours of the morning with zero traffic. At least this Tuesday morning there was a quarter moon and the stars shone bright. Headlights would be visible from two miles, and the longer Zeke waited and the more he strained to see something, anything, the more he fidgeted.

Ninety minutes later, all Zeke could think of was how many things could have gone wrong. Doc ordered his prescriptions through a medical group with an address in Lake Havasu City, and the holdouts' vehicles were titled and licensed in Arizona to avoid attracting attention. The partners in the medical practice supported the mission and kept Doc informed of technological advancements, sent him the latest literature, and even let him know when he had to be in Arizona to keep his board certifications up-to-date. But still, every time supply runners picked up prescriptions, Zeke felt as if they were under scrutiny.

With Jennie Gill as ill as she was, Zeke knew Doc was prescribing heavy-duty drugs, but he couldn't imagine they were beyond the norm for a bustling Arizona practice serving an aging clientele.

Could Raoul or Danley have run into a problem buying a vehicle? Sure, the holdouts paid the bulk of their auto purchases in cash, but car dealerships preferred that. They never borrowed, covering balances with cashiers' checks issued through reputable institutions.

Zeke was glad to have the pleasant Elaine to chat with, but he found he had to be on guard to keep from getting into too much behind-the-scenes stuff. She was a trusting soul who believed the best about every-one, and he had no interest in bursting her bubble. She wasn't oblivious to Doc's abrasive personality, but even when she brought up something concerning him, she proved circumspect.

"I assume you realize the vote for pastor is a foregone conclusion," she said. "I'm glad Katashi announced the secret ballot so Doc won't be embarrassed. Losing alone will be enough of a blow."

"I never assume anything, Elaine."

"You know everyone loves you, Zeke."

"Well, I appreciate that, but Doc is a gifted man who has served every-one well when we needed it most."

"Sure, but—"

"I'll accept either outcome as God's will."

"That is why it will be you," she said, hidden behind the lenses of the periscope.

Zeke glanced at his watch. It was pushing 2:50 a.m. The last thing he wanted was Benita taking him up on his offer to check back with him at three. Maybe if he quit obsessing and just continued the conversation with Elaine. "I have plenty on my plate already."

"Like most bosses, God seems to choose busy people to—oh, Zeke, come look. I'm detecting something. But only one set of lights."

Zeke nearly knocked her over. "Sorry!"

"I'm fine. Am I right? Just one car?"

"Looks like it. And advancing fast. Hope it's one of ours. I've forgot-ten now what they left in. Check the log there, would you, Elaine?"

He heard pages turning. She read off, "AWD C300."

"Oh yeah, the all-wheel-drive Chrysler 300."

It was the smallest vehicle in the fleet but had good power and ma-neuverability. Mahir had outfitted it with a fuel-injection converter that ran it efficiently on an economical hybrid blend that also allowed it to really fly when necessary. Whoever was behind the wheel apparently felt it necessary now. The car was zigzagging from the usual route this close to the compound.

"Elaine, get down to the garage and open the door, but make sure the inside lights stay off. Don't make him wait to get within range to open it himself."

"Shouldn't you go while I keep an eye on him from here?"

"No, because I'll be able to tell if it's not the 300 and will give you two clicks on the walkie-talkie if you need to abort. You know what to do then."

"Shut the door and hit the rally button."

"Exactly."

That would keep an intruder out, wake the adults, and bring them running, armed, to prearranged posts.

"You're ready, right, Elaine?"

"Of course. And despite anyone else's misgivings, you know I'll do whatever I have to do to defend myself or any of my brothers or sisters. Even Mahir. What do you do about him if we're breached?"

That gave Zeke pause. "If I thought he was behind the breach, I'd leave him right where he is. Otherwise, I'd let him out, toss him a weapon, and take my chances."

18

THE RETURN

"It's the 300, Elaine," Zeke barked into the walkie-talkie. "Hurry back here so I can get down there."

As soon as he saw her, Zeke sprinted past Elaine to the garage. He called over his shoulder, "If it's Raoul, I'll click twice and you can let Benita know we're on our way!"

Raoul and Danley had had several errands to run, including picking up the meds at the pharmacy and shopping for a car for Doc, and then Zeke assumed Raoul would drive the Chrysler back and Danley whatever they bought. But he also figured they would return together, so he couldn't be certain who was behind the wheel.

The Chrysler came sliding in, tires screeching, headlamps illuminating Zeke as he stood by the overhead door control. As soon as the back end cleared, he hit the button, and when the door hit the floor, he switched on the lights and saw Raoul emerge. Zeke clicked his walkie-talkie twice as the Mexican slammed the car door and rushed to embrace him.

"Danley?"

"I don't know, man. I lost him about twenty miles back, but we had a signal—"

"Twenty miles? We never leave a man—"

"Hear me out, amigo. First I gotta see Benita, and then I'll tell you everything."

"She knows we're coming."

Raoul popped the trunk and they each stacked three post office–style cartons filled with books, magazines, snacks, and pharmaceuticals to lug into the compound. When they reached the Commons, Benita came running and grabbed Raoul's boxes, slinging them on the table while jabbering at him in Spanish. She showered him with kisses and wrapped herself around him head to toe.

"Thanks for the help, Benita," Zeke muttered.

She peeled herself away from Raoul and pointed at Zeke, smiling through tears. "You're on your own, gringo."

"Enough welcoming, Mexicali Rose," Zeke said. "Let me debrief him."

"I put some food on," she said. "Hungry?"

"*Sí!*" Raoul said. "I ain't eat since about two."

"The *yanqui* won't like it," she said, leading them down the hall. "But I got enough anyway."

Zeke walkie-talkied Elaine Meeks and told her to let him know as soon as she saw any sign of Danley. "Hey, Raoul, what's he driving?"

"You won't believe it, man. A Land Rover."

"Tell me it's not as nice as the one Doc had."

"Almost."

As soon as Raoul returned from the bathroom and dropped onto the couch, Zeke said, "So what happened? Do I need a search party?"

Raoul kicked off his boots. "If he's not here soon. And I'll go with you."

"You kidding? You have to be exhausted."

"But like you said, we don't leave people. He flash me three times about twenty miles back, our signal that he pick up a tail and he gonna shake 'em."

"By going which way?"

"South. And he's a good driver. No way he lead 'em here. Still, I don't like leavin' him. I almost go back."

"You did the right thing, Raoul. We can't have you both out there, not knowing where you are. When do you think he should be here?"

"No more'n twenty minutes."

"Did you really not get there till two?"

"It took us forever, man, like almost three hours longer than usual."

"But you still wanted your reward."

"'Course! Makes that loco drive almost worth it, you know?"

Raoul was talking about the privilege supply runners got for their five-hundred-mile round trip: a sit-down meal of their choice, even if it meant a different restaurant for each man.

"You didn't go all the way up to that place on the Colorado?"

"*Lo siento.*"

"You're sorry. Raoul!"

"But it was the only place we went. We couldn't find one Haitian place anywhere, so Danley agree he try *Mexicano*. And Rio Cantino is—"

"The best, I know."

"*El más auténtico!*"

"Yeah, but Parker Dam is so far, and—"

"But right on the river, man, and Danley loved it. It was worth it."

"You still think so? Even now?"

Raoul shrugged as Benita set plates before them. "*This* is authentic," she said. "Even if the meat is reptile."

"*Gracias, novia,*" Raoul said, then turned to Zeke. "Rio Cantino make us only a little more late. We eat fast and drive straight back to Parker, where we had left the prescriptions. But something wasn't right, man. The pills, they weren't ready."

"How long since you'd left them?"

Raoul made a face. "More than an hour. Maybe two. Okay, more than two hours."

"Somebody new in there?"

"No, but the guy was actin' strange. He wouldn't look at me. He say it was bigger order than usual and some different medicines. 'Course I knew that, but I didn't let on, you know?"

"Good. Did he say he had to order them from somewhere else or anything? What was the holdup?"

"No, he just say it gonna be a little longer. So while me and Danley are pickin' up supplies, an Indian comes in from one of the tribes we work with, only I don't remember which one."

"What? We don't work with any tribes there."

"Right there in the drugstore, but from one of the tribes here."

"No. How'd he get there?"

"That's what I'm sayin'. I don't know. That's all."

"I'm not following. Somebody from one of the California tribes, there in Parker? You're sure?"

"That's just it, Zeke. It make no sense to me. I didn't want to talk to him, but every time I glance at him, he look like he watchin' me and he look away. I told Danley to go around the other way and see what he think, but . . ." Raoul shook his head.

"What? He didn't recognize him?"

"Sorta."

"Meaning?"

"Well, he say think he kinda look like someone we might know from one of the tribes, but—"

"But what, Raoul?"

"See, this guy was wearin' pants and a shirt and a hat kinda like you wear, and he had long hair like mine."

"So?"

"And he was stocky, strong-looking, like about Katashi size."

"Okay."

"I thought Danley was bein' *loco*."

"Why, about what?"

"He thought it might be a woman."

"What? Well, it either was or it wasn't, Raoul."

"You know the *Luiseños* we had all that trouble with last spring?"

"In La Jolla, sure. They let us tell stories to their children and they traded us vegetables for water, but then they told us not to come back."

"They had some ugly women," Raoul said.

"Well, was it one of them or not?"

Raoul shook his head. "I don't think so, man. Anyway, they was so poor, how would any of them ever get that far from La Jolla? They didn't have no cars even."

"So are you sure it was someone you've seen before? Or maybe it just reminded you of someone."

"Yeah, maybe. I don't know."

"Raoul, there are a *lot* of Indians in Arizona! In fact, tens of thousands displaced from California, lots of 'em related to the tribes we worked with here. Man or woman, this could easily have been a relative to someone we've seen here. It doesn't have to mean anything."

"Well, hold on. That's not the last time we saw him, or her, or whatever."

"Really?"

"Yeah, but listen to this. There's two guys wearin' suits in the drug-store too, just standin' around watchin'."

"Watching what? You?"

"I think so."

"Were they watching anyone else?"

"Maybe, but they were still there when we got back from the car dealership, and they made us late. Just like two other guys at the car place."

"Okay, wait. You need to tell me this in order. The prescriptions still weren't ready?"

"Right. So we go to gas up the 300 and to look at cars."

"So by now this is what time?"

"Late afternoon. And I remind Danley what we're lookin' for and that we don't wanna take a lotta time. In fact, I tell him we don't even gotta come back with nothin' if we don't find what we want."

"Good."

"I think we were followed."

"To the dealership? Why?"

"I didn't see nobody behind us while we drive over there, but as soon as we get there and a salesman comes out, a government car pull up and two guys get out and pretend to look at cars too. I tell the salesman I'm gonna look on my own and Danley is the guy to work with, so I circle around and pretend I'm lookin' at cars near the *federales*."

"How'd you know they were government?"

"I can read English, you know."

"Yeah, I know."

"I memorize it. On the front window, a little sticker. It's got a eagle and it say 1824 and Department of the Interior, Bureau of Indian Affairs."

"Can't be clearer than that. And they were watching you?"

"They weren't shoppin' for no cars, I know that."

"How do you know?"

"No salesman. We get there, salesman come out. They get there, no. Like they knew they were comin'."

"Hmm."

"And you know how fast we can usually buy a car, Zeke?"

"Sure. Pretty fast with cash and a cashier's check."

"Danley find a Land Rover a couple years older than Doc's, good shape, take a test-drive, say we want it. Take 'em *two hours* to get the deal done! Then they want to prep it. We say no, and they still stall."

"What was going on?"

"I don't know. I finally tell 'em we're leavin' in five minutes with our money or that car, and if they think I'm kiddin' they'll find out. Five minutes later we stand up and start movin', and that guy hand Danley the papers and the keys. You ready for this, Zeke?"

"I don't know, am I?"

"We get back to the pharmacy, the Indian still there and those two other guys in suits."

"What was the Indian doing?"

"Sittin' by the cashier, like waitin' for a prescription. All that time? I don't think so."

"And the guys in suits?"

"They show us IDs from DEA and say they got questions about our prescriptions. I told 'em they weren't for us, that we're just drivers, couriers for doctors."

"Good."

"One of 'em say, 'So you don't even know what you're ordering?' I say, 'No, sir. I can't even read his handwriting.'"

"That was good thinking, Raoul."

"Good thinkin'? It's true! I don't know what Doc orders and I don't care. And you seen his handwriting? Can *you* read it?"

"Ha! No."

"English is my second language, man! Anyway, this guy ask me if I knew the doctor I worked for was also a mortician. I say I don't even really know what that is, and he say I was probably lyin'. I said, 'Well, I can guess it has somethin' to do with funerals, but I don't like to think about stuff like that and like I said, we don't really work for him as much as we just run to the drugstore to pick up prescriptions for him.'"

"What do you think he was talking about, Raoul?"

"No idea. Maybe Doc order somethin' for Jennie you get only for people just before they die, I don't know."

"That's such a strange question," Zeke said. "I'll have to ask Doc."

"But then, you know, when we finally leave there it's already late and we got that long drive ahead of us, and I see that same car that was at the car dealer's and I just know it gonna follow us. I don't know how these guys connect. I mean, DEA and Indian Affairs, and then that Indian—man or woman, whatever—it just don't make no sense, man.

"So I tell Danley to drive around while I make the grocery store run and see which one of us is followed. Then I gonna drive west of town and wait where I can see him from maybe a half mile away. I tell him to flash me once if he alone and not bein' followed, and we head back here but still stay far enough apart to keep from kickin' up too much dust. Then if he ever pick up a tail and have to shake 'em, give me three flashes and I know that's what he doin'.'"

"So that's what happened?"

"It work perfect at first. I see him comin' and he flash me, and I take off. It's late, you know, way after dark, but we makin' pretty good time.

You can't go fast but you keep it steady, and that's what we doin' most of the night till all of a sudden he flash me, like I said."

Zeke looked at his watch. "We should go looking for him."

"I wanna go," Benita said.

"No!" Raoul said.

"I can shoot better than you!" she said.

"I know! But what're you gonna do? Shoot *los federales*?"

"Before I let them find this place or take one of us, yeah!"

"We're not going out looking to shoot anyone," Zeke said. "If Danley's doing what he's supposed to, he's just making sure no one finds us."

"Zeke, come in, please, over."

"Go ahead, Elaine."

"Lights on the horizon, looks like two sets of headlamps."

"Say again, two?"

"Roger that."

"On my way."

"Comin' with you," Raoul said, pulling on his boots.

Benita grabbed her holster and sidearm from a hook by the door. "Me too."

"Keep up!" Zeke said, sprinting.

19

ACCOSTED

"REMEMBER OUR PROTOCOLS," Zeke told Raoul and Benita. "Don't draw unless you intend to shoot. Don't shoot unless you intend to kill, so—"

"Don't draw 'cept for life or death," Benita said.

Zeke outfitted the couple with walkie-talkies and told them to wait inside the garage. "Obviously Danley's safety is your top priority. Second is keeping our location from whoever is following him. Go!"

As they jogged off, he slipped into Elaine's chair at the periscope. If the lead car was the new Land Rover, it was clear Danley was doing all he could to elude whoever was trailing him. He had gotten far enough ahead that he was now creating a colossal cloud of dust in a massive arc by spinning in circles so he could shut off his lights and make a straight dash through the blur to the compound.

"Get on the squawk box, Elaine, and repeat what I'm saying."

"Ready."

Zeke watched and dictated: "Danley's executing the shroud-and-elude maneuver so, Benita, be ready to open the door on my command. Raoul, gas up one of the dirt bikes and have it running next to the utility door for me. When his lights go off we've got less than a minute, and with him coming in blind we've got to get this right. Make sure he's in and I'm out and both doors are shut before you turn on the garage light. If whoever's following him sees anything, it's got to be me on the bike."

"Copy," Raoul crackled. "How about me on the other bike too?"

"Negative!"

"Roger," Raoul said, disappointment in his voice.

"Danley's lights just went off!" Zeke said. "We're going dark! Get that door up and my bike ready!"

He lowered the scope, told Elaine to tell the other monitors to lower theirs, and ran toward the garage—already regretting denying Raoul's request. Having dirt bikes flying in different directions would be perfect. But Raoul had already driven five hundred miles over rough terrain in one day. That was a blueprint for failure.

The dirt bike stood *brr-acking* in the darkness as Zeke leapt aboard and guided it outside on his toes. He pulled the braided leather cord from the wide brim of his hat and tucked it snug under his chin. As the Land Rover roared ever closer, it sounded as if it were coming down the decline straight at him. At the last instant Danley jerked it sideways and it slid into the garage as the big overhead door descended.

Raoul slammed the utility door behind Zeke, who revved the high-pitched engine just as the headlights of a sedan emerged from the roiling cloud. Zeke let off the clutch, cranked the throttle, and the drive wheel tore into the parched floor of the California Basin, sending a rooster tail of dirt and powder flying. As the front of the bike lifted Zeke flipped on the headlamp, and as soon as the tire touched down again he spun in tight circles, amusing himself with what the feds had to be wondering. The Land Rover they had followed for hours had suddenly disappeared into a dust storm, only to reappear as a dirt bike?

And now the sedan was bearing down on him.

It would have been easy to elude, probably for as long as he cared to. The point was to lead it as far from the compound as he could and keep it there. His delicious secret was that with all four periscopes down, there was zero visible evidence of the compound, and a natural rock outcropping hid the decline to the subterranean garage. The rest was as flat as the desert floor and virtually undetectable without heat sensors or metal detectors.

After letting the sedan futilely chase him about the landscape in loops and circles for twenty minutes, Zeke slowed to thirty-five miles an hour and headed east, back toward where the feds had come from. They fell in behind him, flashing their lights and honking, as he led them in a straight line for thirty miles before finally stopping, setting his kickstand, stepping off, and leaning back against the seat, arms folded.

The sedan stopped behind him, engine idling, lights lit. The driver and the passenger, dark-haired men in their late thirties, stepped out and approached. The driver was tall and thin with short-cropped dark hair, the passenger stocky and bald. The driver did the talking.

"Good evening, sir."

"Good morning."

"Duly noted. Are you armed?"

"I am," Zeke said. "May I ask who's asking?"

In the light of the car Zeke saw the man pull a snub-nosed revolver from a holster on his belt. "Show me your hands, please."

Zeke complied, then folded his arms again. "I carry a Glock 21 in back."

"Aah, the forty-five automatic," the second officer said.

Zeke nodded. "And if you'll reholster yours, and answer my question, I'll leave mine where it is."

"Billy Fritz," the first said, putting his gun away and producing his identification. He introduced his partner, but Zeke paid no attention. "We're police officers with the US Department of the Interior, Bureau of Indian Affairs. I am obligated to inform you that I am memorializing this conversation on a digital recorder located in my breast pocket, and I shouldn't have to tell you that drawing down on a federal agent would be a felony, not to mention would likely cost you your life."

"No, you don't have to tell me that. And I shouldn't have to tell you that giving a law-abiding US citizen with a concealed carry permit a reason to do that would be royally stupid, so why don't we stop the posturing?"

"May I see some ID?"

"To what end?"

"So that I may know who you are and what you're doing in territory declared verboten to US citizens."

"It's my understanding that I am breaking no laws as long as I stipulate that I waive all protections afforded me under the laws of the US as long as I'm here."

"True, but we also have a duty to determine that you are not a foreign agent or any threat to the United States."

"May I reach into my pocket?"

"Slowly."

Zeke produced his driver's license, and Officer Fritz read aloud, "Ezekiel Thorppe Sr." and his mailing address in Arizona. "Occupation?"

"Hydrologist."

"Not much for you to do here, is there?" said Fritz, handing it back.

"Not much."

"So what are you doing, so far from home?"

"Minding my own business. How about you?"

"Our work is self-explanatory. You sure you want to be recorded showing disrespect to federal agents?"

"I mean no disrespect. I believe I have a right to do whatever I wish here, as long as I break no laws."

"Do you interact with Indian tribes, Mr. Thorppe?"

"At times, yes."

"In what way?"

"I minister to them. Trade with them. Teach them. Share with them."

"Are you a medical practitioner?"

Zeke hesitated. What was going on? "No."

"Are you aware of any Native Americans who have recently died?"

"No."

"Do others work with you as you interact with Native Americans, Mr. Thorppe?"

"I don't care to speak for or about anyone else."

"Anything else you'd care to share with us?"

Zeke was about to say no and consider himself fortunate that this had gone only as far as it had, but he found himself saying instead, "Yes" and was as surprised as Officer Fritz appeared to be.

"Oh, you do? And what is that?"

Yes, what is that?

"I, uh, I'd just like to say that, um, in the last days perilous times will come."

"Perilous times? That right?"

"Yes, sir. Men will be lovers of themselves, lovers of money, boasters, proud, blasphemers, disobedient to parents, unthankful, unholy, unloving, unforgiving, slanderers, without self-control, brutal, despisers of good, traitors, headstrong, haughty, lovers of pleasure rather than lovers of God, having a form of godliness but denying its power."

Officer Billy Fritz cleared his throat and looked at his partner. "Is that so?"

"Yes, and from such people you should turn away."

"Should we?"

Zeke nodded, feeling bold but also foolish. "Yes. This sort are those who creep into houses and make captives of gullible women loaded down with sins, led away by various lusts, always learning but never grasping the truth. Others also resist the truth: corrupt men, but they won't get far, for their folly will be obvious to all."

"Will it?" the officer said, peeking at his partner again.

Zeke nodded. "It will."

"If I have more questions, where might I find you?"

"I don't know. You might find me here. You might not."

"You trying to be smart again, Mr. Thorppe?"

"No. I'm just not sure where I'll be and I don't feel obligated to tell you. No matter where I am, I receive mail at the address I gave you."

"That where you're going now?"

"I'm going wherever I want to now."

"You've been heading east."

"I go where I want, which is my right."

"I don't understand why you want to be uncooperative, Mr. Thorppe."

"What is it you want me to say?"

"Whatever you want to tell us."

"I've told you all I care to. And now I am leaving."

184 | JERRY B. JENKINS

"You are not free to go."

"You have no cause to detain me."

"I can detain you for suspicion of criminal activity."

"Good-bye, Officers."

"I said you are not free to go."

"Then inform me of my crime and arrest me for it."

"Harassment of Native Americans, exploitation, and intolerance of their religion, a hate crime."

Zeke mounted the bike.

"Do not make the mistake of adding flight from prosecution, Mr. Thorppe."

"Do you have a warrant for my arrest?"

"Easy enough to obtain."

"You didn't even know who I was, let alone have cause to stop me. And now you would unlawfully detain me?" Zeke kick-started the bike.

"Wait one moment!"

"No, sir! Not without cause!"

And Zeke raced off into the night, bent low and flying from zero to nearly seventy in seconds, praying he wouldn't hear the crack of gunfire.

This time he made sure they had little chance to follow. Peeking back to see the car had just begun to move, he lost them by slowing, darting around cacti and rock outcroppings, and then putting as many miles as he could between him and them. Dousing the headlamp, he carefully logged a couple of dozen more miles before realizing he was in territory he didn't recognize.

Zeke slowed and stopped, hoping his dust trail would soon dissipate. It had been years since he'd made the supply run, and while he may have made a mission trip or two in this area in the past few years, it had never been after dark without a compass.

The agents, if they were determined to locate him, would have an endless expanse to explore, and without a light or cloud of dust to focus on, they would have to be remarkably lucky to choose the right one from the dozens of tracks he had left. There was no way they could see him, but he waited another half hour for safety's sake, watching for any sign of their lights or dust. Finally he began to worry about causing concern to his mates back at the compound.

And now he felt dumb. How was he supposed to find his way back? Leading the agents on a wild-goose chase had been all well and good, and hadn't he brilliantly exposed their buffoonery? But Zeke hadn't thought to leave bread crumbs in his wake.

Straddling the rattling machine, he assessed his assets. He had the right gear, all black from boots to hat. Raoul had filled the tank, so that would last a few hundred miles—not that he needed that much. He had his fully loaded Glock, slightly more than half a bottle of water, and a switched-off walkie-talkie with good batteries that he'd learned the hard way was easily intercepted by interlopers when used outside the compound.

It would reach inside only when he was close anyway, and he had no idea how far away he might be by now. Dawn would come in three hours, so maybe in the meantime he could use the stars to help him keep moving west. But being off by ten feet here could make him miss by miles rock formations he knew on the other end.

Stupid. Stupid. Stupid. He was supposed to be the leader of this brave little band of missionaries. Only he and his family and his former pastor knew Zeke had been chosen of God, set apart for some lofty role.

Well, if he'd entertained the idea that he had somehow brought an iota of value to the equation, he was disabused of that notion now. He who had just held forth for the Creator Himself to two agents of the United States federal government (who had to think he had just punched his ticket on the Disorient Express) was—there was no way to sugarcoat it . . .

Lost.

Zeke, not entirely sure what he was looking for, searched the heavens. "Okay, Lord," he said aloud, "I admit it. I'm a doofus. I blew it. Pride, overconfidence, conceit, you name it, I confess it. Forgive me, but here I am—wherever this is. I don't really know what to do or where to go. That way looks west to me. I don't want my friends or loved ones to worry about me, and I don't want to give anyone else a reason to follow me and put my people in danger. So I'm going to leave my light off, open my throttle, and head that way till I think I'm close. Then I'll risk turning my light on and see if I recognize our area. I'll turn on the walkie-talkie just long enough to tell somebody to open the door. If You can make all that work and get me there safely, I'll never do something as dumb as this again as long as I live. Amen."

Still frustrated with himself but satisfied that he at least had a plan, Zeke rotated his head, stretched, checked the brake and throttle, took a sip of water, and resecured the bottle. He felt deeply grateful for the meal he'd enjoyed at the Gutierrezes', though at the time he hadn't felt he'd needed it and was eating only to be polite. He shut down the bike and listened intently as he did a 360-degree scan of the horizon. Seeing and hearing nothing, he chose to believe the agents had given up not only on him, but also on Danley and Raoul, at least for now. He fired up the bike and lit out, heading west, that quarter moon and the starry canopy offering just enough luminosity to make each sporadic cacti or rocky outcropping appear as a hulking silhouette easily avoided.

Zeke felt confident enough to accelerate to fifty, the rushing wind cooling him as he flew along over the desiccated earth. Here and there, where the surface waxed rough, he rose off the seat and supported his weight on his haunches, letting the bike bounce and rumble beneath him. Fortunately he was in that posture when the front tire struck the boulder he never saw and launched him thirty feet over the handlebars, catapulting him into a somersault that seemed would never end.

Zeke had the strangest experience in the air. He'd heard of such things but had never endured one. It was as if time slowed and he was able to do more than think normally. His brain seemed suddenly able to process multiple thoughts simultaneously.

It was idiotic to have been going that fast.

Though I could see cacti and rock outcroppings, I couldn't see the ground. Why didn't I expect obstacles on the ground?

I've seen things like this on TV. I'm that guy, flying through the air, hurtling end over end.

The bike was so loud. This is so quiet.

When was the last time I wore a helmet? I'm going to wish I'd worn one now.

I don't think this will kill me. God has important things for me to do. But it's going to hurt bad.

Does this mean He didn't forgive me for being stupid?

I was still being stupid.

Here comes the ground. I hope I hit flush and don't land on a rock like the bike did.

Wonder how bad the bike is?

Ugh!

Zeke bounced twice and landed on his back, the Glock driving into his spine. One boot and sock slid half-off despite both boots having been fully laced. His wrists hurt, as did the back of his head. Had he lost consciousness? He wasn't sure. He lay there a moment, curling and uncurling toes and fingers, rolling ankles, flexing knees and ankles, rolling shoulders. Nothing broken? *Thank You, Lord.*

Blood anywhere? Zeke couldn't see but quickly realized his hat covered his face. He fumbled with the cord at his neck, pulled it free, gingerly sat up. His back ached and he felt liquid. He patted himself everywhere, and when he found the source of the liquid, he put his palm to his mouth and nose, sniffing and licking. Just water. He felt around on the ground and snatched up the sloshing bottle. Still about a quarter full.

The bike's engine still rattled quietly. He crawled about, following the sound, and yanked the bike up, killing the throttle. The front tire was gone, the rim obliterated. Zeke lifted the bike to examine the fork. Not good. How was he going to walk the thing back? He had no idea how much farther he had to go, and he had to conserve his strength and his water. Trouble was, he didn't have the luxury of time. He had to keep moving, to get as close to home as possible. He'd have to abandon what was left of the bike. How many damaged vehicles could the group just leave behind?

Zeke sat and took off his boots and socks, checking his feet—his lifeline now. He had to avoid blisters and ironically, both moisture and dryness. He used his hat to fan them, turned his socks inside out and back again, shook them out thoroughly, made sure they were dry, put them back on, then snugged and smoothed them all around. Then he put his boots back on and laced them evenly, stood and assessed his joints again. He would be sore all over the next day, but he felt good to go. As if he had a choice. He'd have crawled all the way if he had to.

Gazing skyward again, he guessed at the best direction and set off, striding resolutely. He would cover as much ground as he could without overexerting or perspiring too much. That proved a delicate balance.

Two hours later, when the desert floor began to change colors, Zeke knew the enemy would soon rise and peek over the horizon behind him. His water bottle bore a final inch, and his gait had grown less steady. He had no idea how far off course he might be. Just when something began to appear familiar everything looked foreign again, and he wondered if a search party had yet been dispatched. They would be watching and listening for the bike, not a solitary staggering figure.

Zeke knew it was asking too much, but he'd hoped the Lord might cut him some slack and at least salve his spirit with some balm from Scripture. But the only verse that played at his mind proved torture: "Pride goes before destruction, and a haughty spirit before a fall."

I know, and I'm sorry. Forgive me.

It seemed that was all he said for miles.

When it seemed he could go no further, Zeke looked for shade. He moved behind a tall stone formation and slid to the ground, pulling his walkie-talkie from a zippered compartment. He switched it on, relieved by the glow of the red light and the crackle of static. He mashed the button twice. He didn't dare say a word.

He waited two minutes and repeated the action every two minutes five times.

Finally the contraption came to life, making him jump. He pressed it to his ear, desperate.

"Who's clickin' their talkie?"

It took everything in Zeke not to speak. He clicked the button twice more.

"C'mon, tell me who ya are. Ya need help?"

He clicked again.

"Can't help ya if I don't know where ya are, at least. This here's WatDoc, standin' by. I got water an' I got wheels. If yer just clickin' to be a idiot, git yer rear end off the air. But if ya need me and can hear me, I gotta be within half a mile, maybe closer."

Zeke swallowed the last of his water and sighed.

How close might WatDoc be to the compound? Could they hear him too? Not likely. They never heard anything unless it was right outside. If anybody on the team heard his clicks *and* WatDoc, would they know enough to just click back?

He waited another three minutes. The ground beyond the shadow brightened by the second with the growing intensity of the sun.

Lord, what should I do?

"I have created all for Myself, yes, even the wicked for the day of doom."

Did that mean even WatDoc was under God's control? Well, of course he was.

Zeke struggled to his feet and clicked his walkie-talkie twice more.

"Now yer just toyin' with me," WatDoc said. "Lemme help ya. C'mon now. Come out, come out, wherever ya are."

Zeke squinted as he emerged into the harsh light and scanned the area. Far to his left at about ten o'clock he saw the telltale dust kicked up by the Hydro Mongers and their tanker trucks.

He held the walkie-talkie to his lips and depressed the button. "WatDoc, this is the Spokesman."

20

THE NEWS

"WELL, HOW-DEE-DOO!" WatDoc crackled back. "What ya need, friend?"

"A little water and a ride."

"Git out where I kin see ya!"

"I'm at about four o'clock."

"Got ya! On my way."

Zeke turned his back and checked his firearm. Glock was among the best in the world, but no one recommended dropping your full weight on it from a story and a half above the desert floor.

The slide still moved without a hitch, the clip dropped out and snapped back in smoothly, and a peek down the sight looked true as ever. Zeke returned it to its holster in the small of his back as he casually turned around, shaded his eyes, and beat the dust from his hat. Exhausted and sore, he was still thirsty despite that last swallow.

Zeke was furious with himself for what he was putting Alexis and Sasha through, not to mention the rest of the team. What had he been thinking, going solo? Showing off? God had put him in his place twice for it already—allowing him both to get lost and to come within inches of killing or making an invalid of himself.

This was the final straw: WatDoc as his white knight, lifesaving answer to prayer?

Okay, I'm at the end of myself, if that's what You wanted. Apparently I needed more humbling. I didn't ask for this assignment, wasn't looking for it, didn't want it. But I'm still willing. I can't promise I won't take out my frustration on WatDoc—the one character who knows how to push my buttons. If he—

"Behold, I send you out as sheep in the midst of wolves."

Oh, I know. I'm ready for this wolf, and I won't let him near the compound. I have a plan to keep him—

"Silence."

Yes?

"Therefore be wise as a serpent and harmless as a dove."

I'm on guard.

"Harmless as a dove."

Surely You don't want me to expose my people, to give him any idea where—

"Harmless as a dove."

I want Your will. But what if he—

"Is he your enemy?"

Yes! He's dishonest, exploits, overcharges—

"Is he your enemy?"

He threatens us! He or his people ran down Cristelle, tried to kill her!

The big tanker wheeled up, black smoke pouring from the exhaust. The two smaller rigs stopped behind it.

"Wait."

Wait?

"Love your enemy."

What?

Again Zeke wanted to kick himself for entertaining the idea that God should have to repeat Himself.

WatDoc gestured as if to ask what he was doing just standing there. Zeke held up a hand as if to ask for a moment, but the man wrenched open his door and lifted himself above the top of the cab. "Comin' er not? Ain't got all day."

"Need a minute, sorry." *Lord, what am I to do?*

"Look like a pile a dung. What'sa matter with you?"

"Bless those who curse you, do good to those who hate you, and pray for those who spitefully use you."

Bless this scoundrel?

"Is he your enemy?"

"WatDoc?"

"Let's go, man! Git yer tail in here!"

"Just need to say something first."

"So say it! I'm burnin' up here!"

"Thanks for stopping. I really appreciate it."

WatDoc cocked his head. "Well, sure, okay. Now kin we go?"

"Offer to pray for him."

Lord—

"Is he your—"

"WatDoc, can I pray for you?"

"What the—what? What'd you say?"

"Is there anything I can pray for you about?"

"*Pray* for me? Naw, man, come on! You sound like my aunt now." He cursed and hopped down, scuffing around the front of the truck past Zeke to the four-inch black hose attached to the side of the tank. A .357 Magnum rested in a holster strapped to his leg. "I lef' that stuff a long time an' a lotta miles ago. Looks like you need more'n a drink. Git over here."

The Lord said, "Myrtle" and a shiver ran up Zeke's spine.

WatDoc grabbed a crank near the end of the hose. "Git rid o' the hat." Zeke pulled it off, WatDoc turned the knob, and the water flooded him from the top of his head. Two seconds' worth drenched him, and WatDoc turned it on himself before cutting the flow. He waved at the other two drivers, who scrambled out and hurried over for their turns. When they returned to their trucks, WatDoc reduced the feed to a trickle and filled Zeke's bottle. "Now hop in, an' tell me where to."

Zeke was surprised at the tidiness of the cab. "Could we sit here a minute?"

"I tol' you, man. I'm doin' you a favor, but I got stuff I gotta do, an'—"

"Yeah, but God's telling me to pray for you and—"

"Now you gotta quit with that too, Spokesman."

"You can call me Zeke, because you're going to get to know me. I'm not kidding when I say God's telling me to pray for you, because He also wants me to pray for your aunt Myrtle. Can I do that?"

WatDoc's hand immediately went to his pistol.

"You've got no need for that," Zeke said. "I'm not pulling mine."

The man's face was ashen. He pressed an index finger hard into Zeke's chest and rasped, "You tell me who tol' you 'bout Myrt or I swear to God I'll blow yer brains out."

A peace came over Zeke he could not explain. "I already told you," he said.

"I been in California more'n ten years, and in all 'at time I only tol' one person 'bout Aunt Myrt, an' that was a girl I was gonna marry 'cept she got killed in a wreck. I ain't mentioned her name or my aunt's since."

Zeke nodded. "If I thought you were really gonna blow my brains out, I'd have to come up with something better than that God told me—unless it was true."

"Yer tryin' to tell me that's the God's honest truth?"

Zeke nodded. "And there's more. She's been praying for you every day since you left."

WatDoc turned away and stared out the window, his jaw set. Zeke saw his pulse hammering in his neck.

"Ever been to Pigeon Forge?"

"No, sir."

"You don't know nothin' 'bout me or my people. Don't know my ma died when I's a baby, my daddy threw me out 'fore he drank hisself to death. Myrt raised me when she didn't hafta. I give her nothin' but trouble. Way too late to pray fer me, bruh."

"It's never too late," Zeke said.

WatDoc snorted. "Ever'body else I ever done wrong deserved it or prob'ly did. She didn't."

"I could pray about that."

"Stop sayin' that! I'm tellin' you I don't want you prayin'!"

"Sorry."

"A'ight, we done with this. You don't be sayin' nothin' about Myrt. You don't know her. We gotta git goin'. Now where to?"

"You deal with the Nuwuwu, right?"

"Yup. Fact, I jes' come from there."

"Take me there. My people will eventually find me there. And if you see any of them looking for me first—"

"I kin tell 'em where ya are. But them Injuns ain't gonna be happy to see ya jes' now, gittin' ready fer their funeral an' all."

"Funeral?"

"Yeah, well, they got a different name for it. The chief's ma—she was over a hunnert. I never met her, but she's dead. They're plannin' some kinda ceremony er somethin'. You still wanna go there? We're 'bout a hour away."

"Yes, I do."

WatDoc drove in silence for several minutes, then banged Zeke on the knee with his fist. "Hey, since you tol' me yer name, you might's well call me Willard. Long as ya don't shorten it. No Will or Willie or nothin' like that. My aunt wouldn't call me nothin' but Willard, but she liked to be called Myrt. Never could figger that out."

Zeke was about to respond, but God prompted him to wait.

Finally Willard said, "Ya know, she don't even know where I am. Or even if I'm alive. All she done for me and you won't believe what I done to her."

"Don't ask," the Lord said.

The question nearly burst from Zeke. He knew Willard wanted him to ask. But he just stared.

"I knew where she kep' her cash. She didn't have much, but I took it all. An' all she had was a rattletrap car what wouldn't git me far, but I took that too. I was so horrible, see?"

"Don't answer."

How Zeke wanted to.

"It only got me to the state line, where I copped the plates offa one car and popped 'em on another an' jes' kep' doin' that all the way out here. Couldn't believe how easy it was. Found odd jobs, got a new ID, met my girl, was act'lly goin' straight till she got killed. Drought thing kep' gittin' worse, I figgered out the water scheme, an' life's never been better."

Zeke had the perfect line on the tip of his tongue, something about an unpaid bill, a loose end that needed to be tied, someone Willard had done wrong despite her loving him unconditionally. But again he felt no freedom from God to say a word.

"Somehow I gotta least let Aunt Myrt know I'm alive."

"And that you're sorry?"

"If you knew her, you'd know she already knows that."

"She sounds like one special woman."

"I jes' hope she's still alive. It'd kill me if she wasn't."

"There are ways of finding out."

"How?"

"We make supply runs to Arizona and we send and receive mail out of Parker."

"You kiddin'? I was there yesterday!"

Zeke prayed for every ounce of reserve he had to stay calm. "Really? What were you doing there?"

"Oh, the daughter-'n-law of the chief needed to git word to some o' her Arizona relations 'bout Meemaw or whoever's funeral. She needed to get there so fast, I used a small rig what was empty, and I bet we got there in record time. An' she needed to talk to the Indian Affairs guys 'bout somethin' too. I know those guys, so—"

"You do? I figured you'd steer clear of federal agents."

"Ha! You'd think that, wouldn't ya! Normally I would, but it helps to have one er two of 'em in yer pocket in my bid'ness, if ya know what I mean, an' I bet ya do."

"You've got a BIA guy on the take?"

"More'n one, but ya didn't hear that from me."

"Wow."

"Yer not gonna rat me out now, are ya?"

"To who? Sounds like they know all about you!"

Willard laughed. "Now ya know why I'm way past prayin' for!"

"Don't respond."

Yes, Lord.

"So, did you bring the tribal leader's daughter-in-law back yesterday too?"

"Naw. I jes' dropped her off in Parker. She's comin' back with her relations that come for the funeral."

"And when is that?"

"Not long 'fore I heard ya on the squawk box, I told them Injuns she and them s'posed to git in tonight. They said the funeral's tomorrow night, only they don't call it a funeral. Somthin' else. 'Cryin' service,' that's it. They made it purty plain I ain't invited."

"They may not want me there either. Hopefully my people will come and get me before then."

When they finally rumbled to within sight of the tiny Nuwuwu settlement, Willard parked at least a hundred paces from it. "Good luck. I'll be on the lookout fer yer people, and you'll lemme know how to get word to Aunt Myrt, 'kay?"

"It's a deal. You want to meet here at noon on Saturday?"

"I kin do that."

Willard thrust out his hand and Zeke shook it, deciding it was the most unlikely outcome of an encounter he'd had in years.

As the tankers rolled away, Zeke realized he had already been spotted and was being approached by Yuma and his granddaughter, Zaltana. She seemed to be trying to pull her grandfather along faster, but she didn't have her usual grin. When they drew within twenty feet of him she broke away and ran into his arms.

She wrapped her arms around his neck and said, "Mr. Zeke, did you know my great-great-grandmaw Gaho died?"

"I heard that, sweetheart, and I'm so sorry!"

"Did you come for the Crying Service?"

As Yuma joined them, Zeke said, "Zaltana, I came to see you and your grandparents and your great-granddad. The service might be private."

"Come here, child," Yuma said, pulling her away and setting her down. "Zeke, my father is in mourning, as we all are. But he will want to see you, and we have much to discuss."

PART 5

THE PURIFYING

21

THE VERSE

Yuma led Zeke to tribal leader Kaga's hut and told Zaltana to stay outside. They entered to find the eighty-year-old seated cross-legged, barefoot, wearing only a loincloth and a thin ragged shawl draped over his head. His hands were clasped in his lap with a small folded square of paper visible between his thick fingers. His chin was tucked to his chest and his breathing appeared even and deep.

"I don't want to wake him," Zeke said.

"I am neither deaf nor sleeping, Ezekiel," he said, raising his head. "Thank you for coming. Please sit."

"You have my deepest condolences, Kaga," Zeke said, leaving Yuma standing just inside the entrance to sit next to the old man and take his outstretched hand in both of his. "I am so grateful I got a chance to meet your mother."

"Thank you. How did you hear?"

"WatDoc told—"

Kaga shook his head and turned away. "Villain," he said. "And yet he has done us a favor. Yuma's wife, Kineks, you know her—"

"Of course."

"She needed to get to some of our people with the news."

"He told me."

"He has a loose tongue. I warned her."

"My wife is not easily warned," Yuma said. "Especially when her mind is made up."

Kaga said, "She had just better not bring back your daughter and son-in-law, who—"

"Abandoned Zaltana?" Yuma said. "I'm more worried she'll kill them on sight. No, she will bring back people who cared about Gaho."

Kaga groaned. "The people who cared about my mother never left. Anyway, if they hear Kineks is in Arizona, they wouldn't dare show their faces to her."

"Offer to pray for him."

Yes, Lord.

"Kaga, may I pray for you?"

"Please. Yuma, join us."

"Father, I'd rather not."

"Do not deny me in my hour of grief. You loved your grandmother."

Yuma sighed and plodded over. He sat heavily on Zeke's other side, putting Zeke between father and son. He reached an open palm to each. Kaga immediately offered a firm grip. Yuma hesitated but Zeke waited until the man finally offered a limp hand.

Just as Zeke bowed his head, Zaltana appeared at the entrance. "May I sit with you too?" she said.

"No!" Yuma snarled just as his father was saying, "Yes, child, come in."

The little girl's face contorted as she clearly fought tears.

"Yuma, let her," Kaga whispered. "What's the harm? She so loved her Gaho."

"We all did. But her grandmother will be livid."

"I won't tell her."

"Zaltana will! She tells her everything! And Kineks doesn't want the child's head filled with all this—"

"With all this what?" Kaga said. "Does Kineks believe in nothing? Not even in prayer?"

Yuma looked away. "Kineks does not pray, no."

"Invite the child in, son. Say I insisted. I was honoring our guest. Tell me, Ezekiel, what would Jesus say about a child?"

Zeke couldn't suppress a smile. This was like a batting practice pitch. "Oh, Jesus said, 'Let the little children come to Me . . . for of such is the kingdom of heaven.'"

Kaga leaned forward to peer past Zeke at his son. Yuma muttered, "Come in, Granddaughter."

She leapt into Zeke's lap, her legs dangling over her grandfather. She put her hands on the men's.

"Father," Zeke said, "I pray for my friends as they grieve the loss of their precious Gaho. Thank You for her century of life and what she meant to them. And thank You for Your Word, which tells us that You see the oppression of Your people, that You hear their cries, and that You know their sorrows.

"May You give them the peace and courage of the psalmist who said that though he walked through the valley of the shadow of death, he feared no evil because You were with him. Your rod and Your staff comforted him. For You have not despised their affliction or hidden Your face from them, but when they cry to You, You will hear.

"Turn to them, I pray, and have mercy on them, for we know that weeping may endure for a night, but joy comes in the morning."

Yuma suddenly tightened his grip, and Zeke could tell from his breathing that he was deeply moved. Zeke continued, "Lord, we know You are near to those with broken hearts and save those who have contrite spirits. Be their refuge and strength, their very present help in this time of trouble. I pray my friends will believe Your promise that if they will in all their ways acknowledge You, You will direct their paths.

"I trust You to turn their mourning to joy, to comfort them, and to make them rejoice rather than sorrow. Your own Son said, 'Blessed are they who mourn, for they shall be comforted.' And we know that He was moved to tears at the death of His friend, He bore our griefs and carried our sorrows, and He tells us, 'Let not your heart be troubled.'"

At this, Zeke felt Yuma's tears on his arm.

"Father, Your Son promised He would not leave us orphans but would come to us, and we know He heals the brokenhearted and binds up their wounds. So now blessed be the God and Father of our Lord Jesus Christ, the Father of mercies and God of all comfort, who comforts us in all our tribulation, that we may be able to comfort those who are in any trouble, with the comfort with which we ourselves are comforted by God.

"I pray this in the name of Jesus, the Christ, the Son of the living God. Amen."

Yuma gave Zeke's hand a final squeeze, then covered his face with both hands, wiping his tears. "Thank you," he managed. "That reminded me of my childhood."

"It did?" Zeke said. "What do you mean?"

"My grandmother used to read the Bible to me."

"I had no idea."

"She told you, Zeke," Kaga said. "She said she had raised me in a religion that mixed many of our traditions with the Bible."

"Yes, but I assumed—"

"You assumed it was an oral tradition, even the Bible."

"I confess I did."

"My mother was the only woman of her generation who read in our native tongue."

"You had the Bible in—"

"In Paiute. Yes, we did. I do not recall where it came from, who translated it, or anything else about it. But like Yuma, I remember her reading to me as a child. A mission or missionaries, someone taught her to read, and then she taught me and I taught Yuma. But somehow over the years, we got away from it. That Bible does not still exist. For a long time we were a nomadic tribe, and somewhere along the way, it was lost. She recited some of it, but the younger generations, they were not so interested. Especially as they got older."

"I wasn't," Yuma said. "And Kineks was not at all. But your prayer was so much like what Gaho used to read to me and recite to me. And then what she had in her hands when we found her . . ."

"Sorry?"

"After you left her the other day, Zaltana said Gaho was writing. She didn't write much, and it took her a long time. She wrote in Paiute, and she shaped each character just so. Very proud to make it just right. But then she would show no one. When one of the women found her and thought she was sleeping, she saw the writing clutched in her hand. But Gaho's hand was frozen in a fist of death and only Kaga was able to remove it."

"It was not easy for me," the tribal leader said. "I was so sad. I had seen her asleep many times, but to know that I would never see her awake again, it was so painful. But I also knew that whatever was so important for her to write had to be very special to me. I did not want to defile her, and I did not want to damage the paper. I was weeping when I finally pulled it free. Would you like to see it?"

Zeke wanted nothing more. "Only if you care to show me," he said.

"You will need to see it in the light," Kaga said, rising and moving toward the entrance.

Zaltana moved from Zeke's lap to Yuma's and said, "Are you all right, Great-Granddad?"

Zeke followed Kaga, and then he took the square of paper, carefully unfolding it.

Te Naa no'oko numu ka teepu-koobatu besa soobedyana, tu besa dooa tamme-koobatoo nemawuni. Tooe haga tooe nu-kwi tunaka'oedyukudu gi ya'ekwu ooosapa gwetzoinnummekwu.

"That is amazing penmanship for a woman her age," Zeke said. "Can you translate it for me?"

The old man tilted the page so the sun caught it flush, and though it shook in his hand, he slowly interpreted it word by word. "For God so loved the world that He gave His only begotten Son, that whoever believes in Him should not perish but have everlasting life."

"You know that's the essence of the Scriptures, Kaga," Zeke said, his voice thick. "How meaningful that must have been to your mother. Don't you think it would please her to have it read at her burial service?"

"You would honor her and me if you would do that, Ezekiel."

"It would be *my* honor, Kaga, but I don't know whether it would be appropriate for—"

"I would like many of you to join us, and I don't care what Kineks—"

"Forgive me for interrupting you, Kaga, but I need to tell you that I am here by accident." He told him the story of how he had heard of Gaho's death and how he got to the settlement.

"First we must feed you. Then we must see about getting you home. Only then can you invite others to the Crying Service and the burial."

"Oh, Kaga, I don't want you to have to worry about me. WatDoc will see someone looking for me or I'll walk back."

"Do not trust him. You do not want him finding your dwelling. I wish he had never found ours. Let us at least feed you and then we can talk about what to do."

Sitting at a hot meal at dusk, Zeke felt fatigue and soreness wash over him and he wondered what a guest cot at the Nuwuwu Hilton would feel like. He decided it wouldn't bother him much longer than he could keep his eyes open.

The biggest problem, of course, was how long he dared let Alexis and Sasha needlessly worry about him while keeping the rest of the holdouts in crisis mode. Did he really have the luxury of spending the night here? While Kaga had a point about the danger of WatDoc's following him right to his door, if he waited till dark, he was talking about a twelve-mile hike. It wouldn't have been Zeke's first choice, but he'd endured worse. He'd be home long before midnight, would be able to fully recover by the next day, could indeed bring a contingent back for the burial service, and it would turn into a win-win.

The downside, of course, was that he knew something Kaga and Yuma didn't. Kineks had clearly gotten to the feds and was the reason for the questions he'd been asked the night before. The DEA and the BIA had put two and two together and gotten five. They believed they had a contingent of missionary types pushing their religion on the Indian tribes, confirmed by some kook on a dirt bike spouting doomsday prophecies in the desert in the wee hours of Tuesday morning. And they had prescriptions for last resort–type meds that appeared to be headed for verboten California.

If Kineks had gone to Arizona, not to round up shirtsleeve relatives of her husband's recently departed grandmother but rather to sic the feds on tribe interlopers, the last place Zeke needed to be found was sharing John 3:16 at the burial.

Naturally he couldn't tell Kaga and Yuma the whole truth. For now it would be enough for them to expect him to return the following evening with several of their friends. He presented the plan. Both men looked grave.

Finally Kaga spoke. "You make sense, of course. But I worry. You have to be weary, and you may have been hurt worse than you know."

Zeke started to respond but fell silent when Kaga held up a hand and turned to his son. "Yuma, what would you think of going with him?"

"Oh," Zeke said, "I couldn't ask him to do that."

"You aren't asking him," Kaga said. "I am. Yuma?"

The younger man, still more than fifteen years Zeke's senior, folded his hands under his chin. "Do you trust me? Would I be welcome at your dwelling?"

"I do and you would, but—"

"But still it would mean revealing your location to us."

"Right, but—"

"It might be worth it to you," Yuma said. "My problem is Kineks. She left angry. She will return angry. If anything prevented me from returning tomorrow . . ."

"You don't need that," Zeke said.

"No," Kaga said. "He does not. Neither do I. You do what you feel you must do."

"I'll leave at total darkness," Zeke said. "Alone."

22

FLIGHT

LESS THAN AN HOUR into his walk toward the compound, Zeke became less vigilant about scanning the horizon. His gait had been steady and strong despite pain and fatigue, but that was no surprise. No destination was more magnetic than home, and home was wherever his girls were. Alexis and Sasha's faces drew his every step, and though he knew he had a lot of explaining and apologizing to do—and not to them alone—just being back with his people would set everything right again.

He concentrated on his own body weight, the footfall of his boots on the hard-packed desert floor, the sweat, the stillness of the night, and the miles ahead. Whatever God had allowed him to endure, and for whatever reason, he accepted it as part of the process, the price, the preparation.

But for what, Lord? I offer myself afresh.

"Remain vigilant."

I will.

"Hear Me."

I'm listening.

"A message."

Silence. Zeke kept moving, unsure what to do. Should he stop? Had he lost the ability to hear God? Had he only imagined the Lord was still speaking to him? Was he to kneel, show reverence, respect? He estimated that in the ninety-degree heat and the way he was pushing himself to maintain a pace of about three-and-a-half miles an hour, he would reach the compound around eleven o'clock

He had enough water, but he dared not stop. Surely a search party was out. They couldn't have, wouldn't have given up on him yet. And while base camp would still be largely dark to keep threats away, they would have walkie-talkies on, listening for any sign of him—and they would raise the scopes intermittently at least to watch for him or to ensure they weren't taken by surprise.

Yet Zeke was willing to stop, if that was what God wanted.

"Share My message."

My only mission is to serve You, Lord.

"Tell him."

I will.

The question was, to whom should he be telling? Zeke no longer questioned that God would give him both the words and the courage to say them, regardless of the cost.

"Tell the one who believes he is unworthy."

That could be anyone. Zeke himself had felt that way not so long ago.

"Tell the one who believes he is beyond My reach."

I will.

The gospel? The message of salvation?

"I will raise a Branch of righteousness, a King who shall reign and prosper and execute judgment and righteousness on the earth. He will be called The Lord Our Righteousness."

Zeke felt, as always when God spoke to him, as if he were being filled. Temporal things seemed to disappear, and he became cognizant only of the Spirit alive within, sharpening his mind and heart and soul. Questions were answered before he could pose them. It was as if God allowed him to process pure truth simultaneously rather than linearly, in the same way his brain had functioned between the time he flew off the bike and when he landed.

He knew the Branch of Righteousness was Jesus, and he even understood that this was what God meant when He had inspired Paul to write to the Corinthian church that if anyone is in Christ, he is a new creation, that old things have passed away and all things have become new.

So the one who believes he is unworthy, the one who believes he is beyond the reach of God's love does not *have* to be righteous or worthy!

"Be vigilant."

Yes, Lord.

"Now."

Zeke stopped, ending the rustle of his clothing with his stride and the soft crunch of his boots. No wind. No animal sounds. On the horizon a pinprick of light.

Thank You, Lord.

At least two miles away, Zeke couldn't even tell yet whether the light was coming from one source or two. But it was moving. A cycle? Car? Truck? Whatever it was, it wouldn't likely leave this unpaved but well-worn route. Zeke estimated it would be upon him within four minutes. Wearing all black was in his favor in the meantime, but he'd have to find a secluded spot fast. If it was a vehicle he recognized from the compound, he'd have time to reveal himself. Otherwise, he could remain hidden.

About four hundred yards ahead to his left, a hulking silhouette reminded him of a rock formation surrounded by scrub he had seen only from inside a vehicle, but if memory served, it could work. In fact, if he hurried he could scatter enough obstacles in the vehicle's path to force it to slow and pick its way through, making it briefly face the outcropping. That should reflect the headlights into the windshield and give him a brief look at whoever was inside. It was a long shot worth the risk.

Zeke had to get there fast enough to accomplish the task and find a secluded spot with a view before the headlights were close enough to expose him. He broke into a trot, reminded afresh of everything that hurt. About ninety seconds later he reached the area, and the approaching light had defined itself as two and to be a sedan. The rock formation proved to be the one he remembered, and its pale red face would serve his purpose.

He yanked at the edges of the brush, finding it hardier and sharper than he expected and his wrists still tender from his accident. *No time to wimp out.* With an expanse of scraggly brush about eight feet wide and two feet high in the path, Zeke knew that if the driver didn't see it till the last instant and didn't swerve, the car could blast through it with no problem. He had to be sure.

A quick peek told him he had fewer than thirty seconds to move a boulder of about 150 pounds into position where the car would have to weave its way to the right, between it and the outcropping. And Zeke didn't dare injure himself in the process if he had any hope of making it back to the compound in the next two hours.

He straddled the rock, squatted, straightened his back, breathed evenly, and lifted it just enough to lessen the friction between it and the ground. He duckwalked as quickly as he could and thudded it into place, then dove off the road and settled into the rest of the brush at the side of the outcropping.

Zeke was mostly hidden provided the headlights didn't catch his face as he peeked through the thicket, but he had not accounted for the thorns that dug through to his skin. He wondered what damage he might do to himself if he had to make a break for it. The car was close enough to hear now, so he was stuck in more ways than one. At least the lights wouldn't hit him head-on. Because the prickly branches pressed into his haunches, Zeke dared not rest his weight on the foliage so he squatted again, straining the same muscles and joints and ligaments he had just used to move the boulder to now support his own weight—causing him to shake.

Lord, You caused a bush to burn. You can keep this one from shaking.

He prayed all this work had been needless and that this car would carry his own search party from the compound. *Just let them see the boulder in time not to wreck. Wouldn't that be ironic? I crash my own rescue team.* Couldn't he have one thing go his way after twenty hours of reminders that he wasn't in charge?

As the low-slung sedan drew into view, it was clearly the same make and model as the one that had chased him fewer than twelve hours before. That didn't mean it had to be the Bureau of Indian Affairs. It could have been the Drug Enforcement Administration for all he knew.

The car suddenly slowed and nearly stopped when the driver apparently noticed the obstacles. Zeke held his breath at the soft crunch of tires over the rocky soil as the car turned right and snaked its way around the boulder and the brush. The headlights illuminated the foliage in which Zeke was suspended, desperately trying not to shake, then swept left to reflect off the tall rock formation.

Which allowed Zeke to clearly see three passengers.

Officer Billy Fritz was behind the wheel, talking.

The man next to him, however, was not his partner from the night before. He was pale and blond, wearing a tie and jacket.

Yuma's wife, Kineks, sat in the backseat directly behind the blond, her profile plain as they passed, and she seemed thoroughly engaged, as if listening to Fritz.

Things quickly became clear to Zeke. If Kineks had gone to Parker to inform relatives of her husband's grandmother's demise, they had refused to return with her for the burial. More likely she had not gone for that purpose at all. Rather she had used that as a cover for her real mission: to rid her people of Zeke and Pastor Bob and Doc and their ilk—anyone who threatened the tribe and its way of life.

Though to Zeke's knowledge Doc had never met Gaho, he had treated nearly everyone else in the settlement except Kineks. And it wouldn't have taken much for her to unknowingly implicate him in Gaho's death because of his coincidental ordering of an acute treatment regimen for Jennie Gill.

If, as Zeke suspected, the other man in the car was DEA, the two agencies were working together, meaning it wouldn't be long before the holdouts would be exposed. Even if Kaga and Yuma vouched for Doc and he was cleared of malpractice in Gaho's case, Kineks would pursue the religious harassment charge against Zeke and Pastor Bob until the entire group was banished from California.

When the taillights disappeared, Zeke gingerly extricated himself from the scrub. He couldn't let Kineks succeed. That Gaho had been found with Scripture in her hand when she died meant the holdouts could be on the verge of a real spiritual breakthrough with the Nuwuwu in spite of Kineks. Kaga had invited Zeke and his friends back for the burial, and the old man and even his son, Yuma, would want that Scripture read at the Crying Service ritual.

What an impact that could have on the whole tribe!

But what would happen when Kineks showed up with officers from two federal agencies and discovered Zeke had just been there? Would she talk the agents into trying to find him before he got back to the compound? Or was she crafty enough to let the invitation stand and have them ambush Zeke and whatever friends he brought with him to the burial service the next night, Wednesday?

She didn't know he knew the agents were there, and the easy answer was to get back to the compound and not show up at the service. But that would be thumbing his nose at the invitation of the tribal leader to the burial of his own mother—and reading publicly the salvation verse that clearly meant so much to her. It would also mean sacrificing, out of fear, everything they had been working toward with the Nuwuwu. Could Zeke not trust God to protect them?

Of course he could, even if it required a bedfellow as strange as Willard the WatDoc.

"He who believes he is unworthy."

That's who You were talking about!

Kineks and her federal agents would get to the Nuwuwu settlement long before Zeke would reach his compound. Even if Kaga and Yuma were wise enough not to tell her he had just been there, could they keep Zaltana from saying anything?

Kineks was likely angry enough to invent a story about why no relatives had returned with her, and she would make up another about why the agents had come. It would probably have something to do with legally documenting Gaho's death and properly disposing of the body, though she had never trusted the United States before. Why now?

Whatever she devised, Zeke only hoped it wouldn't cause her husband and her father-in-law to let down their guard and reveal that they had invited him and others from the compound to return for the Crying

Service. But he was kidding himself. Except for how long it took them to reveal the existence of the ancient Gaho, he had never known of a kept secret in that tiny community. Everyone knew everyone else's business, and if the adults didn't say anything, the irrepressible Zaltana would.

Zeke's best-case scenario was that if the agents did learn of his plan to return with friends, they would resist the urge to come looking for him and wait to ambush him when he arrived.

Against his better judgment, Zeke guzzled half a bottle of water and broke into a trot again. He was beyond exhaustion now, but he had to be proactive. He wasn't about to wait around to see whether he had to elude agents or hope to be rescued by his own people. It was time to get home.

23

THE SCHEME

ZEKE NEARLY WEPT when he realized he was standing atop the decline that led to the garage door of the compound. In his absence Doc would be in charge, and he had apparently made the wise decision to go dark. He had also undoubtedly sent out a search party, and whoever was left inside raised the periscopes only intermittently.

Still reluctant to announce himself orally over the walkie-talkie, Zeke switched it on and clicked it twice.

Almost immediately two clicks came in response and the two east-facing periscopes rose a couple of inches. Zeke apologetically waved wearily, hoping Alexis or Sasha was monitoring one of the scopes but knowing they would be immediately informed regardless.

The garage door began to rise and he started down the decline, but just as quickly his walkie-talkie squawked to life, the scopes sank back down, and the door stopped and reversed itself.

"You gotta be kiddin' me, Zeke!" Willard's voice came over the air. "What the heck'r you doin' all the way back over'n this area! Wasn't a half hour ago I run into some o' yer people and sent 'em hightailin' where y'all tol' me ya said ya's gon' be! If ya ain't there, where ya at?"

"Oh, no, WatDoc! Where are you?"

"Jes' sittin' here havin' a smoke, man. I sent my guys home."

"You're comin' in loud and clear, so you've got to be close. Your engine running?"

"I'll turn it on an' hit the lights."

Zeke ran away from the compound, knowing they could also hear him inside and would know to stay dark. At least they knew he was safe and was protecting the place, but they had to wonder why he and WatDoc sounded so chummy.

"You need to pick me up," he said, "and we need to catch my people before they get there. Who was it?"

"I don't know 'em, man. Three foreigners in a Rover. They was all with ya the other day. Oriental guy and the Mexican couple. Purty suspicious o' me, I kin tell ya that. Can't blame 'em, but I tol' 'em what you said to tell 'em."

"I hear your engine, I don't see you. Flash your lights or something."

"I'll cut a cookie."

"There you are. I'm at six o'clock."

"I'm comin'."

Zeke jumped aboard and Willard raced off toward the Nuwuwu.

"If you saw them half an hour ago, they've got to be there by now."

"Maybe not. I seen 'em quite a ways east."

"That's good."

"So, what's with the change o' plans?"

Zeke shrugged. "Didn't think it all the way through."

"So you live back there somewheres, eh?"

Zeke hesitated but knew he was going to have to start trusting Willard if he ever expected the same in return. "Yeah."

"Yer secret's safe with me, man. I won't do ya no harm."

"I hope not. A lot of people depend on me."

"Lemme tell ya somethin', Zeke. You can have worse guys on yer side. You got no idea how much help I kin be."

"Good to know." Over the next several minutes, as Willard guided the big tanker over the rough terrain, Zeke brought him up to speed.

"Oh, man!" Willard said. "You know who that blond guy is?"

"How would I?"

"He's the guy who's in my pocket. Least I got that on him. I heard o' Fritz but never met 'im. None of them Injuns like me, but the one yer talkin' 'bout, she owes me 'cause I run her over to Parker yesterday. Anyways, we got to get yer people outta there and keep them feds from even seein' you, right?"

"That possible?"

"Ever'thing's possible, Zeke. First, I don't want nobody knowin' we're even there. I'll kill the lights 'fore I get near the place, then I'll roll up short an' see where they're parked. Then we'll stash you someplace where yer people kin pick you up on their way back."

"How're you going to get them free of the feds? They might have already arrested them."

"What they gonna charge 'em with, that religious stuff? Where they gonna put 'em out here in the middle o' nowhere? More likely they want you and that doctor, so they'll be tryin' to force yer people to give up you and yer compound."

"They won't get anywhere with that."

"'Specially not when I get through with 'em. Give me somethin' I can say or show yer people so they know I'm talkin' fer you. I'll tell 'em where to find you and I'll distract the feds till they get outta there."

"How're you gonna do that, Willard?"

"You jes' watch."

"I'm going to be where I can watch?"

"Maybe. First I'm gonna have me some fun with their car. Then I'm gonna tell 'em I was jes' with you and can lead 'em right to ya. By time they figger out an' fix what's wrong with the car and then follow me the whole wrong direction, you'll be home with yer family."

"Sounds risky."

"Risky's my middle name, man. Well, really DeWayne is, but you know what I mean. Okay, here we go."

Willard turned off his lights as they rolled to within sight of the Nuwuwu settlement, then shifted into neutral, turned off the engine, and let the rig roll about a hundred yards to about a quarter mile from the site. "There they are."

The government-issue sedan sat next to the Land Rover.

"Here's where I wish we was wearin' moccasins, am I right?" Willard said, slapping Zeke's knee.

Hilarious.

"What can I write on?" Zeke said. Willard leaned over him and pulled an order pad and pen from the glove box. "I need a little light, something that won't be seen from down there."

"Overhead's gonna come on when we jump out, but that'll only be fer a second. Lemme see." He rummaged deeper in the glove compartment and found a flashlight. "Jes' keep it pointed down."

"Okay, where am I gonna be?"

"Well, first yer gonna be with me an' we're gonna see what we can see an' hear. If they're meetin' in the tribal hut, which looks like the only one with a fire goin', see?"

Zeke leaned close to the windshield and looked across a dusty plain. "You're right."

"After I mess with their car we oughta be able to hear what's goin' on in there. Then you git down there past the last hut on the right and wait about thirty yards back in them mounds o' dirt where they was tryin' to plant last year."

"You think the Rover can get in there?"

"It kin can go past there. All's you gotta do is show yerself when they come by, and then yer gone. If I do my job, the G-men'll be lookin' under the hood by then or followin' me the wrong way."

Zeke held the flashlight between his knees and the pad near the floor-board. He printed in small, neat lettering:

Will explain later, but on the lives of Alexis and Sasha, you can trust WatDoc. Follow his lead. Look for me past the last hut to the northwest. I'll emerge from the dirt mounds when I hear you coming. Just open the left rear door. Then straight back to the compound. Z.

As they made their way across the plain toward the cars at the end of the settlement, Zeke whispered, "You need to promise me something."

"Sure."

"If this works, I want you to visit us at our compound."

"What, you serious?"

"I am."

"Knowin' who I am and what I done?"

"I think so."

"Even to yer vehicles?"

"That was pretty obvious."

"And to one o' yer people?"

"You left a lot of tracks, Willard."

"That was me, personal."

"You could've killed her."

"Thought I did at first. Didn't mean to, but I had cause."

"What's that mean?"

"You got a rat inside. More'n one."

Zeke stopped. "You trust me enough yet to tell me more?"

"Now's not the time, but I kin tell you it ain't any of the three here."

"And we'd better keep moving."

"That's what I was gonna say. There'll be time to talk. Now if we're lucky, these agents didn't think to lock they ride."

"That doesn't sound like any federal operative I've ever encountered," Zeke said.

"Me neither, but let's see," Willard said as they crept up on the sedan. "Nope." He swore. "Wish I'd brought one o' my shivs. I'd be in this thing in a second. Well, more'n one way to skin a cat." He felt around the grill and breathed more curses. "Hood release is in the car. Gotta do this from underneath. Least I got this."

He showed Zeke a Swiss Army knife he tilted toward the moon and extracted a dull, solid blade before dropping to his back and shimmying under the front of the car. Zeke heard clinks and scrapes, and Willard soon scooted back out. "Bing, bang, boom," he whispered. "Wonder how them batt'ry cables come loose anyhow. Thing jist won't start, and no-body won't know why till they have a look. Then it'll be, 'What in the Sam Hill?'"

He signaled Zeke to follow and they tiptoed to the one lit hut from which voices emanated.

"So it's settled then," Kineks was saying. "I think this is a most agree-able solution. While I might have wished more of Gaho's progeny could have joined, it will be very special to have representatives from the Bureau of Indian Affairs as well as my father-in-law's dear friends here with us for the burial service. We will make you all as comfortable as possible tonight and look forward to Ezekiel, Pastor Bob, and hopefully the doctor and some others joining us tomorrow for the occasion."

"We're just sorry we missed Ezekiel due to the breakdown in commu-nication," Katashi said. "We would be happy to try to connect with him even tonight and be sure he knows that those others are also welcome."

"No," a male voice said quickly, and Zeke was sure it was Officer Fritz. "I think it is best if we all remain here and welcome him and the others tomorrow. Should they arrive early enough that we could accompany him back to bring even more, so much the better."

Willard held out a hand for Zeke's written note and whispered, "You'll know when to git into position, right?"

Zeke nodded as Willard moved around the entrance.

"Well, hey there, ever'body! Glad I caught ya! Never guess who I jes' run into. Zeke! I was makin' a final run and let my guys go on home, and who was headin' toward his own place but yer boss! I give him a lift and tol' him I was surprised to see him 'cause I had left him here earlier in the evenin', an' he'd left me with 'structions to tell anybody lookin' fer 'im that they could find 'im here. Which is what I'd done not so long ago to you three, right?"

"Right," Katashi said, "which is why we were surprised to get here and learn he had gone home."

"Well, he asked if I wouldn't mind comin' back and tellin' you how sorry he was fer the mix-up and to give you this."

"Thank you," Katashi said.

"He figgered you'd probably stay over and he wanted you to have an idea what he wanted ever'body's part to be in the service tomorrow night, just in case any of y'all were asked to say anything. And chief, er, uh, Mr. Tribal Leader, sir, he wanted me to tell you not to feel, um, obligated er nothin' to have him er anybody else say nothin' if that wasn't 'propriate—he jes' wanted his people ready in case."

"So you say you just saw him, sir?" Fritz said.

"Yes, sir, I just come back from droppin' him off. You know he's not terrible far away. Fact, I'm sure he'd be right proud to know you're here and gonna be takin' part."

"Well, I wonder if he'd be available to meet even at this late hour."

"I cain't speak fer him, sir, but I reckon it'd be easy enough to find out. It's on my way home and I'd be happy to lead ya right back there. I parked 'bout a quarter mile across the plain so's not to bother any of y'all if y'all'd already turned in. But if ya jes' wanna follow me, it'd be no trouble."

"And we could get these folks settled," Kineks said.

"That would be fine," Katashi said. "We'll just want to get a few things from the car."

Kaga, the old leader, said, "The hour is late for me. There is much activity and there are many people, while I am still in mourning."

"Sorry, Father," Yuma said. "Let me get you to bed and I will make sure our dwelling is quiet till dawn."

Zeke started moving when he heard Willard telling the agents, "That's my tanker yonder. I'll be waitin' and when I see you comin' I'll head out an' you kin jes' follow me."

He peeked back to see Katashi and the Gutierrezes climb into the Land Rover. The blond agent said, "You're staying, right?"

"Yes," Katashi said. "I'm just going to park down by the guest hut."

When Zeke was some hundred feet from the vehicles and hidden in the dirt mounds he watched Willard in silhouette stride to his truck, saw the inside light go on and off, the headlights turn on, and the tanker maneuver into position to leave the area. And there it stood idling, as if waiting for the government sedan to approach.

Soon the Land Rover rolled slowly toward Zeke as he heard the doors of the sedan open and close, muffled conversation between the agents, and finally the slamming of the hood. The Land Rover lights went out, the back door opened, he leapt in and said, "Wait," and the four of them craned their necks to watch. The sedan backed up and turned around, then raced across the open plain toward the tanker, which led it in the opposite direction.

"Go," Zeke said.

"Oh, I'm going," Raoul said, Benita next to him staring back at Zeke.

Katashi sat next to Zeke, shaking his head. "As for you, my friend, you got some 'splainin' to do."

"Just get me home, guys," Zeke said. "I don't even know where to start. And I'm not gonna want to repeat myself. Isn't everybody going to want to hear this?"

"Probably," Katashi said. "But what in the world, man?"

"First, is everybody else okay? Cristelle? Jennie?"

"The meds have helped them both," Katashi said, "but not as much as Doc hoped."

"Speakin' of Doc," Benita said, "I'm not so sure he's gonna be as happy as everyone else to see you, you know? He was pushin' for the vote whether you got back or not."

That made everybody laugh, including Zeke.

Raoul said, "You woulda needed a absentee ballot, boss!"

"Hey, we're not really going back for that funeral, are we?" Katashi said. "I don't trust Yuma's wife, and I really don't trust those feds."

"I haven't decided yet."

"Under what possible circumstances can that make sense? Before you and WatDoc showed up—something else you're going to have to clarify, by the way—they were asking all kinds of questions about Doc, pretending to be impressed that he would be so social-minded and selfless and help people like this. But both Raoul and Danley said DEA agents detained them in Parker yesterday."

"And that blond guy was one of 'em!" Raoul said. "And I think that Fritz guy was one of the Indian Affairs guys at the car dealership. And both of 'em didn't say a word about recognizing me or ever seein' me before or nothing. I mean, you gotta be kiddin' me."

"Well," Zeke said, "the only way we would go for the service tomorrow night is if God makes it clear He wants us to. But in truth I'd hate to miss it, even with the feds there."

"Seriously? Why?"

"Because of what Gaho had tucked in her fist when she died."

24

HOME

"LET ME ASK YOU SOMETHING," Zeke said. "If the beloved matriarch of your family died with a self-written note in her hand, wouldn't you insist it be read at her burial service?"

"Depends," Katashi said.

"On what?"

"Whether it was appropriate."

"Yeah," Benita said from the front seat. "Lotsa things might not be right to be read at a funeral."

"This was from the Paiute Bible. John 3:16."

"Are you kidding me?" Raoul said. "I wanna be there myself when they all hear that, especially Yuma's wife. I don' trust her, man. You remember, right?"

"Oh, I know," Zeke said.

"Who?" Benita said.

"Danley was right about her," Raoul said. "She was tryin' to make nice an' everything tonight, but she was the Indian I thought was a man in the drugstore yesterday. I knew I had seen him before. I told you that, Zeke."

"You did. But I didn't know it was her either until Willard, er, WatDoc told me."

With that, all three of them started in on Zeke at once. He held up a hand. "I told you, save it till we get back or I'm gonna have to repeat it for everybody."

"You'd better call a meeting for the morning, Zeke," Katashi said. "Tonight you're gonna have four people on the scopes, somebody with Jennie and Cristelle, the kids in bed, everybody exhausted."

"Good call. I'll have to tell Alexis tonight anyway. I'll have Sasha stand guard outside tomorrow and we'll do it after breakfast."

"I got to wait that long?" Benita whined.

"I need my best shooter sharp tomorrow," Zeke said. "Especially if we all go back for that burial."

"You know Jennie's little talk and the vote for pastor is set for tomorrow night," Katashi said.

"Ah, that's right. Seems almost a moot point now. Think we'll even need a pastor, come next Sunday?"

"I wouldn't say that too loud," Katashi said. "Everybody's already on edge, thinking the end is near. Better give 'em some sense of normalcy."

"So I tell what happened to me, Jennie speaks, then we have the vote?"

"I would," Katashi said.

Alexis and Sasha met Zeke at the door from the garage to the rest of the compound, Alexis with a haggard look of relief and barely contained rage. The three embraced fiercely and headed to their quarters, while Katashi and the Gutierrezes passed the word about the next morning's meeting and vote.

As soon as they were behind closed doors, Alexis said, "I want every detail—Sasha, bed, now—but first, you're going to—"

"Mom! I want every detail too or I'll never sleep! Please!"

Alexis looked from Sasha to Zeke and back and threw up her hands. "All right! Listen, I need a moment with your father and then I'll come get you. Now go."

"Thanks, Mom."

"Go!"

"I'm going!"

When Sasha's door closed, Alexis pulled Zeke close and whispered desperately, "Z, I don't care if God's called you to be the next—"

"I know, Lexi, I'm sor—"

"I don't care if you know, I'm going to say this and you're going to listen. I gladly, *gladly*, gave up my whole life for you and this cause. I brought our only surviving child with me and never looked back, and I have not once *ever* criticized you or complained or even questioned you—"

"I know—"

"*Shush!* I know God has His hand on you, and now it's clear He's called you to something bigger and more important and I-don't-know-what than ever. But you are going to promise me right now that you will never again leave this compound alone. I'm not going to ask why you did or why you thought you could or should. I don't even want to know. All I want out of you right now is the promise that you will never do that again."

"Lexi, I know. I was just—"

"Did you not hear what I just said? No reasons, no excuses—"

"It was stupid. I'm sor—"

"And no apologies either! If the next thing I hear isn't the promise I'm asking for, I'm done! Nothing in Scripture tells me God calls men to go it alone. You never even see the apostle Paul by himself! You've got one more chance, Ezekiel Thorppe. Don't screw this up."

"I promise. Never again."

"Welcome home. Now kiss me."

Wednesday morning the three elders met in the Commons an hour before the meeting. "I have no problem rolling Cristelle's bed out here," Doc said. "Your wife's on record that she's abstaining from the vote, so she can keep an eye on Cristelle."

"So I suppose your wife, on the other hand, has reneged on her pledge to abstain, eh, Doc?"

"At your insistence, Zeke. Thank you very much for that and for your expression of support."

"What's this now?" Katashi said.

"I am assured of three votes," Doc said, "in case you hadn't heard. As a loyal supporter of your man here, I might expect you would follow his lead. And in that case, we could just announce that the elders are unanimous and thus there is no need for the general election."

Katashi shook his head. "It's fair to say I am thoroughly confused. Zeke, your abstaining was the whole reason for—"

"And my saying I'd vote for Doc was wholly in the spirit of good sportsmanship. Silly of me to dream he might return the favor. Gabrielle sweetly suggested our wives agree to abstain in the interest of their friendship, so—"

"How nice," Katashi said.

"That's what I thought, so I—"

"So, after Alexis promised to abstain," Doc said, "Zeke naïvely told Gabrielle he would vote for me and that she shouldn't feel bound to abstain."

"Wow," Katashi said, "that *was* naïve, wasn't it, Zeke? Why don't you just hand it—"

"That's exactly what Alexis said. But in the spirit of fairness—and in the spirit of his wife's original intent, Doc ought to—"

"Oh, no you don't," Doc said. "Don't be changing the rules of the game now that it's already begun."

"This is hardly a game, Doc," Zeke said.

"I agree," Katashi said.

"Well, you're the one who's put things in motion," Doc said, "and I am formally protesting that you have given yourself the option of speaking before the vote. My request to bring a message in advance of the election was summarily dismissed."

"It's just coincidence, Doc," Zeke said. "I thought everyone wanted to know why I was out all night."

"No one will be surprised to learn that you blundered by venturing out alone and somehow stumbled into trouble."

"Well, I wouldn't put it that way." But Zeke realized that pretty much was what had happened. "I'm not married to the idea of speaking before the vote. We can have the vote first or after Jennie, or whatever you guys think best."

"I say vote first," Doc said. "Then Jennie, because who's to say how she'll be holding up by then. She may need to get back to her quarters to lie down. Then you can tell about your caper and how you have all but given up our location to the Mongers."

"Where'd you get that idea?"

"Human nature, Zeke. People talk. That's one reason I'm eager to get the vote out of the way early. Let's just say your popularity ratings are at an all-time low. And the idea of a field trip to the Nuwuwu tonight after you attracted the feds? Good luck getting any takers for that little suicide outing. Why didn't you just invite 'em here? They could just follow your new best friend's tanker truck."

"We've got a lot to cover before the meeting," Katashi said. "Can we get back on track?"

"By all means," Doc said.

"If we're going to start with the vote," Katashi said, "why don't I open in prayer, pass out the ballots, have Mrs. Meeks collect and tally the votes, and report the result to me?"

Zeke nodded.

Doc said, "Sounds good. With the Gills on record as not voting, only adults voting, Mrs. Thorppe abstaining, and Mahir out of the picture, there will be just nine ballots. Do we agree a simple majority wins?"

"Is that right," Katashi said. "Only nine?"

It was clear Doc had been obsessing over this. "Well, yeah, there's you, the Gutierrezes, Mrs. Meeks, the Muscadins, Zeke, and Gabi and me. Right?"

"Guess so."

"So, five votes wins it, yes?"

"Yes, Doc!" Zeke snapped. "Can we move on?"

"And speaking of how people talk," Katashi said, "what were the meds you ordered that got the authorities so worked up, and what was the letter that came with the prescriptions that got *you* so worked up?"

"What're you talking about?"

Zeke had wondered how Doc knew so much already. He couldn't imagine Katashi with such a loose tongue. The question about the meds was logical, but the letter was news.

Katashi leaned in. "I was told there would be no secrets among the elders, which sounded like a good idea. Word is that when Danley finally got in, he went to check on Cristelle, which gave you time to come out here and find the box full of meds. He mentioned that you seemed pleased with everything he and Raoul had brought you until you came to an envelope, which you tore open and then started slamming stuff around."

Doc cleared his throat. "Oh, that shouldn't have come as a big surprise. For years I've written scripts for common maladies as any doctor would—antibiotics and such."

"Yeah, but this time . . ."

"This time I'm treating two people for some pretty significant stuff. Cristelle is still in serious pain and, who knows, could still lose that leg. And we all know Jennie's diagnosis. Any one of the meds I ordered for either of them could raise an eyebrow. In this case, apparently they did."

"All right, Doc," Zeke said, "I need a direct answer. You're going to hear many details of my activities in the last twenty-four hours, but let's leave the specifics for later. At one point I was questioned by a police officer with the Bureau of Indian Affairs, and while I knew better than to offer unsolicited information, he asked me if in the course of my work I associated with Indian tribes, and I saw no harm in admitting that I did."

"No harm?"

"I did not disclose our location or anyone's name but my own."

"But they could have followed you and—"

"Had they been able to stay with me, they'd be here by now. Hear me out. He asked if I was a medical practitioner and when I—"

"Oh, tell me you didn't give him my name!"

"And when I told him I was not—of course I didn't give him your name, Doc. What kind of a fool do you think I am? Anyway, he asked if I was aware of any Native Americans who had recently died. I told him no, because at that time I was not aware. But you can imagine what I thought."

Doc hesitated. "How should I know? I wasn't there."

"C'mon. I assumed he had been put on to us for working with the Indians and now end of life–level drugs had been ordered and tracked heading back into California."

"So what you're saying is, it's my fault that we have authorities snooping around now."

"I'm wondering if you ordered more than just heavy meds, Doc. I'm asking if you ordered embalming fluid, which would *really* raise a red flag. The feds may think it's for an ancient Native American woman, because general practitioners would use embalming fluid only for studying cadavers, right?"

"Correct. Well, are you going to tell me how to do my job now, Zeke? Yes, I ordered embalming fluid, and if you want to know how much, maybe you ought to weigh and measure my dying patient. Did you think we would just dig a hole in our little churchyard here next to the compound? The woman has a family, in case you didn't remember. And it's 250 slow-driving miles to the border of Arizona! Do you have any idea how quickly a cancer-ridden corpse begins to decompose in this environment, even if we wrapped her as tightly as we could in whatever materials we could find? I don't have anything remotely resembling a body bag, let alone a coffin, casket, or vault. Cremating her would require a fire hotter than we're able to generate here and would create a plume that could be released only in the dead of night and create a stench that might draw creatures you'd regret. Not to mention that cremation may not be her wish or that of her husband or the family. Any other questions?"

"Just one."

"Fire away."

"What would have been the downside of informing us of such a potentially attention-attracting action?"

"I take full responsibility."

"Well, that's real big of you, Doc. But if you want the truth, I dare say it *is* the reason we have federal authorities crawling all over us right now.

And while we're on a roll, why don't you come clean about the contents of the letter that so upset you last night?"

"It's related, that's all I'll say."

"No!" Zeke said. "That's not all you'll say. Let's put everything on the table. If nothing else comes of this day, this whole team is going to come together again with everything out in the open. I'm going to own up to, yes, the monumental mistake I made by charging out of here on my own and coming close to ruining everything we have in place. And we're going to get to the bottom of who's bringing Middle Eastern propaganda in here, wherever that leads. Now let's finish this with you. Who was the letter from and what did it say?"

Doc pulled it from his pocket and spread it on the table. It was from the consortium of doctors who claimed him as a partner and allowed him to use their address in Lake Havasu City. The managing partner expressed his appreciation for Doc's professionalism and his willingness to "serve humanity and exercise your personal faith by serving the indigenous people of the former state of California."

However, he also said that it was with regret that the rest of the partners had voted to suspend Doc's association with them, along with all the privileges it entailed, due to his having ordered "certain prescriptions that stimulated unwarranted attention to our group on the part of federal agencies which could have been avoided, had you merely followed standard protocols of preauthorization. We will be happy to revisit this suspension in six months, based on a written appeal from you."

25

THE VOTE

IN THE COMMONS, Zeke and the other two elders sat facing the tables as people began to gather. They stood as Bob Gill walked Jennie in, one arm around her waist and the other in front of her, serving as a brace she gripped with both hands. Her gait appeared steady, though slow.

Alexis followed, pushing the IV drip stand and carrying a pillow she placed on a chair at the end of a table in the front row, onto which she and Bob gently sat Jennie. Alexis also set a bottle of water and a notepad before her. Jennie looked pale and tired, but she returned the embraces, handshakes, and smiles of everyone, from each elder all the way down to both Xavier children.

Zeke had always been amazed by Doc's bedside manner, which seemed at odds with his general disposition. As it seemed he was with anyone under his care, Doc took a few extra minutes to speak quietly with Jennie and apparently make sure she was up to what she had planned to do this Wednesday morning. He also must have reminded her to stay hydrated, as he opened her water bottle and got her to take a few sips.

He seemed preoccupied when he returned to his seat next to Zeke. "I know we both agreed to wait till after the vote to speak," he whispered, "but at some point I'd better say something about my suspension from the medical group and what that will mean here."

Zeke nodded. "What *will* it mean?"

"Not much, really. On the bright side, it was private, not some official board sanction. I'll just have to change my mailing address to something independent for a while. Fortunately I stocked up on the basics, so we shouldn't run short on anything in the meantime." He looked at his watch. "I'd better go get Cristelle. This will be her first time out since Sunday."

"She up to it?"

Zeke could see from Doc's look that he had reverted to form. "You think I'd risk her health if she wasn't?"

Zeke raised his hands in surrender. "Sorry for asking. Who's with her now?"

"Her husband, but your wife agreed to sit with her so Danley can concentrate. Alexis doesn't need to, because—"

"She's not voting, Doc, I know."

Danley and Doc slowly rolled Cristelle's bed into the Commons, and Alexis followed pushing an IV drip stand. The patient was sitting up and looked alert, but as everyone seemed to rise at once and begin to approach, Doc said, "One at a time, please! And be brief. We don't want to delay the meeting. Also, I'd ask you not to touch her. There's still the risk of infection."

Cristelle smiled shyly at the attention, and when everyone returned to their seats, Alexis went back to the infirmary for a table that slid under the bed and provided a writing surface.

Raoul and Benita, looking refreshed in clean clothes, settled in next to the Gills, and the Xavier children were typically reserved and well behaved, though Zeke thought Gabrielle seemed beyond nervous. Agitated? Maybe worse. She actually looked petrified. What could she be afraid of?

The calmest presence—besides Zeke's rock, Alexis, of course—was Elaine Meeks. Since the day he had met her, one of the worst of his life, she had been the same: tall, thin, soft-spoken, and—how would he put it?—wise. Some found her naïve, others docile, but Zeke didn't. He recognized iron at her core.

When others had apparently recoiled in horror at the sight of Junior, his tiny son, crushed under the wheels of the garbage truck years before, it was she who had flown to his side, comforting him in his final moments. She was the one who rescued Katashi from himself, from believing he didn't deserve to live if Junior died due to his mistake.

Elaine, despite her unlikely physique, was among the very few to sign on for one of the most demanding missions anyone could be asked to consider. And today she was the natural, unquestioned choice to be entrusted with counting the ballots.

As he surveyed the room, however, Zeke was struck by the disparity between the feel of today's gathering and that of the one just three days before. It wasn't just the eight-mile difference, or that here they were safe in their own underground base camp. No, Sunday had begun with only a hint of danger, a potential threat. Katashi whispered of having seeing Hydro Mongers on his way in, just as Pastor Bob was ready to start the service.

Zeke sat forward and planted his elbows on his knees, rested his chin in his hands, and rehearsed all that had changed in the mere seventy-two hours since then.

God had spoken to him audibly, called him, set him apart, was preparing him to be His spokesman—for what and to whom, Zeke did not know.

Five holdouts' vehicles had been trashed—four deliberately, one through his own negligence.

They learned that one of their beloved sisters would soon die.

Their pastor had resigned.

Another of their sisters had nearly been killed and was still suffering.

A brother in Christ had been locked away, suspected of threatening another's life and treason.

They had been followed, accosted, challenged, their location jeopardized, and one of their most dangerous opponents might have become one of Zeke's most unlikely allies.

But the biggest difference between this and Sunday's gathering was that Sasha was outside—armed with a walkie-talkie for emergencies and a nine-millimeter, with which she was proficient but thankfully had never had to use.

This meeting would begin soon with Katashi's prayer, but without

Sasha's music. With contention over the vote and sharp disagreement over what should happen that evening regarding the Crying Service, Zeke felt a deep loss.

How he longed for the team spirit, the feeling of family, the sense they had so long cherished that this little band represented the body of Christ.

Lord, he prayed, his eyes filling, *don't let us lose Your Spirit.*

And once again Zeke felt that hand on his shoulder and heard, "Be still and know that I am here."

Katashi pressed a knee against Zeke's and whispered, "Jennie wants your attention."

He looked up quickly and rushed to her. "You all right?"

"Sorry to bother you," she whispered. "You know I don't want to be a complicator . . ."

"Whatever you want, Jennie."

"I wouldn't ask if I didn't feel the Lord was in this, Zeke, honestly, I wouldn't."

"Name it."

"Mahir needs to be here."

"Oh, I don't know."

"Just go talk to him."

"It's almost nine, and we were to start at the top of the hour."

"For me, Zeke. Please. If I'm wrong and he gives you any reason to hesitate . . ."

"Hesitate? Jennie, you know what he did."

"I'll trust your judgment."

Zeke tapped Raoul on the shoulder, giving him a nod to follow him out. He told Katashi, "Stall till we're back."

On the way down the hall, Zeke said, "If I bring Mahir into the meeting—"

"What?"

"Hear me out. Sit him in the back and stand behind him. Zero tolerance, you got it?"

"You sure, Zeke?"

"Don't let me down, Raoul. If he tries anything, you have full authority to do whatever you have to do."

Zeke heard Mahir approach as soon as he slipped the key into his lock. "Back away from the door," he said. "Give me some space."

"No worries!" Mahir called out. "I could use some company!"

He looked like he hadn't slept and was unshaven, but his clothes were clean and he had showered. "Let me turn this off," he said, flipping the switch on the TV network news audio feed. "I've had a lot of time to pray and cry, Zeke."

"That so?"

"You don't have to believe me. I don't expect you to. All I can tell you is I must've lost my mind. I don't even know the person I became. I still think you've got a serious problem in the ranks, but I should've just come straight to you and the elders with what I knew and not tried to take matters into my own—"

"We're having a meeting right now."

"What? Who? The elders?"

"Everybody. Voting on a new elder board chairman and pastor. Jennie's giving a farewell."

"Oh! I'd love to hear that!"

"I can't let you vote."

"I wouldn't expect to, but I'd give anything, do anything if I could be there, I swear I would."

"You'll sit in the back with Raoul, and we're still going to have to deal with . . ."

"Anything you say, Zeke. Yes. Anything. Thank you."

Zeke wasn't surprised at the wide eyes that greeted them in the Commons. He signaled Katashi to get started, but as soon as Zeke sat, Doc whispered, "I suppose Mahir's voting for you."

It was all Zeke could do to keep from saying, "That's right, and so am I and both our wives."

Katashi greeted everyone, prayed, and explained that the elders had decided the vote for pastor should precede everything else. "We have a lot to cover this morning, and if I seem ill at ease, it's because I am. As you know, I'm the newest elder, but it may come as a surprise to you that with the resignation of our former pastor, I happen to now be the oldest member of this board. I don't expect my colleagues to extend to me the respect that should elicit, because that hasn't been the case so far, but it's true nonetheless. I am two years Mr. Thorppe's senior and eight years Dr. Xavier's."

Katashi's own chuckle was the loudest. "Thus ends my attempt at comedy, so let's get right into the voting. Mrs. Meeks will handle the counting of the ballots, so please raise your hand if you are an adult, eligible, and choosing to vote. Don't be shy. I'll be first."

Katashi raised his hand, as did Raoul and Benita, Danley and Cristelle, Zeke, Doc, and Gabrielle. Elaine carried a small tin around the room from which she passed out sheets of paper and pencils, then returned to her seat with her own sheet.

"Instructions, Mrs. Meeks?" Katashi said.

"Just write either Zeke or Doc as your vote for the next pastor," she said, "then fold your paper once. I will come back around and ask you to place it in the tin. Then I will count the votes and write the results on a separate sheet for Mr. Aki."

Doc raised his hand. Katashi appeared to panic, as if he didn't want to recognize him. He leaned between Doc and Zeke and whispered, "I thought we agreed neither of you was to say anything before the vote."

"Fair enough," Doc said. "I was just going to suggest that whoever loses moves to make the vote unanimous and pledges his full support to the winner."

"Well, sure," Zeke said. "We believe God's in this regardless, so that should be a given. And Doc, just so you know I'm a man of my word . . ." He openly wrote *Doc* on his sheet and showed it to him.

"I never doubted you," Doc said, smiling, and he showed Zeke his own ballot with "DOC" on it in large block letters.

"Sorry for the delay," Katashi announced. "Carry on, and Mrs. Meeks will collect your ballots."

As Zeke sat waiting to drop his in the tin, he noticed Alexis praying while the three couples sitting with each other seemed animated. The Gills, who had not voted, were whispering. Raoul and Benita showed each other how they had voted, though Raoul kept his attention on Mahir. Danley held Cristelle's paper so she could write with her free hand.

Strangely, Zeke noticed that when Elaine reached Gabrielle, it appeared she hadn't voted yet. She was hiding her paper from Caleb and Kayla. She turned her back to them, wrote, folded it quickly, and dropped it in the tin.

Finally Elaine returned to the front, where the elders put theirs in, then she sat off to the side and carefully pulled out and unfolded each one, making hash marks on a separate sheet. She wrote on it and handed it to Katashi, who stood and said, "The will of the majority, and we believe of the Lord, is that Zeke is our new pastor. Our former pastor has agreed to come and pray for him, but before he does that, Dr. Xavier has asked to say a word."

Zeke reached to shake Doc's hand but pulled back when he noticed Doc was not looking, and he didn't want it to appear that Doc had refused. He knew Doc had to be disappointed and might even take it hard, but he had not expected to see Doc look as if he could barely move. Had he waited another two seconds, Zeke would have felt compelled to cover for him somehow.

But Doc finally rose, arms rigid at his sides, as Katashi sat. "Yes," he said quietly, unlike his usual, confident self. "Thanks. I, uh, I wanted, I had wanted, I had said that, ah, here's what I'd like to suggest. I just have a motion that I want to make, if I could just ask Elaine, or Mrs. Meeks, excuse me. Mrs. Meeks, if you could just tell me the votes, then I'll make the motion, move the motion."

"I'm sorry?" Elaine said. "What is it you want, Doc?"

"Pardon me," Doc said. "I wanted to know the number."

"Oh!" she said. "I was under the impression that we weren't going to announce—"

Zeke looked sharply at Katashi and shook his head. Katashi rose. "Yeah, Doc, ah, it was just either a tie or a majority was all we were gonna say, so apparently it was a majority, right, Elaine?"

"That's right."

"So, Doc, if you want to make a motion, like you said . . ."

"So," Doc said, gathering himself and finding his voice, "you're saying it was a simple majority, a five-to-four thing?"

Elaine looked stricken. Katashi looked helpless.

Zeke stood. "Doc, there's no need to do this."

"Yes, there is! Now I'm a grown man, and I want to know. I'm going to make my motion, but I want to know what the vote was. If it doesn't bother me, it shouldn't bother anyone else. Now, Elaine, if you don't want to tell me, just let me count them."

Elaine looked to Zeke. He shrugged. She said, "Doc, if you must know, it was a clear majority."

"Clear? What does that mean?"

"The vote was seven to two," she said.

He looked as if he might topple. "Seven to two," he said. "Seven to two, Zeke. And you and I know who the two were, don't we?"

"Don't do this, Doc."

"Well, I said I would and so I do. I pledge my full support to the *clear* winner, Mr. Ezekiel Thorppe. And I move that we make it unanimous! I hereby change my vote from Doc to Zeke and ask that all my followers— all one of you—do the same. Will you do that? Will you, Zeke?"

"Thanks for your support, Doc," Zeke said. "Everybody here loves and appreciates you. You know that."

"Oh, I do! I do! Now can I get a second to my motion so we can vote? Gabi! Honey, do *you* want to second my motion?"

"Adam, don't," she said, tears streaming.

"*You* voted for him! Second the motion!" But Gabrielle was out of her chair, pulling the children from the room. "Welcome to the pastorate, Zeke," Doc added, and staggered from the room.

Elaine, face flushed, busied herself tidying up the pencils and ballots and the tally sheet, putting everything in the tin.

Katashi sprawled in his chair as if he'd just lost a prizefight.

Alexis stared at Zeke, hands folded before her as if still willing to pray.
Zeke turned to Bob Gill, who simply appeared sympathetic.

Lord, I'm lost. This is chaos, and I'm supposed to be in charge.

"The truth shall set you free."

I don't know what that means.

"Yes, you do."

Zeke stood and felt every eye on him, as if he were to make sense of this awful embarrassment.

"My role from the beginning of this radical endeavor has been practical, largely physical. Now I've been thrust into a role not of my choosing and for which I don't feel qualified but which—with God's help—I accept as His will. I hope it's been clear that I have always been transparent. You've always known when we faced a threat or had to tighten our belts. I never sugarcoated anything or tried to cover my own mistakes. A little later I'm going to own up to some serious mistakes I made within the last twenty-four hours.

"But now my role has become a spiritual one, and in the spirit of full disclosure, you deserve to know that the truth is I don't have a clue what to do. All I know is that we are the body of Christ, brothers and sisters in the Lord, and one of our members—along with his family—is hurting. When one is in pain, we're all in pain, and until we're all healthy, none of us is healthy.

"So in my weakness, here's what I'm going to do. Our former pastor was going to pray for me in my new position, and I still want him to do that, but not just yet. I'm going to refer to you as Pastor Bob one more time and request that while we here all covenant to pray as one for our brother Doc and his family, you go minister to him. Let him know we love him and want him and his family back here with us. Tell him we'll not finish this meeting without him. Would you do that for me?"

"You bet I would," Bob said, rising.

As he left, Jennie raised a hand. "I have an idea," she said, clearing her throat. "I think it would be good if we all moved close to Cristelle to pray. Bob has a way of succeeding in situations like this—or I should say the Lord does, through him. God's going to bring Doc and his family back in here, and we're going to want to lay hands on him and forgive him and restore him, so we'll all want to be closer together to do that. If you agree, I'll need a little help moving."

"Works for me," Zeke said, as people headed that way. But what was he to do with Mahir? For now, he would leave Raoul with him in the back.

When he and the others had settled near Cristelle, Zeke put a hand on hers and said, "How are you doing? I haven't had a chance to check in on you."

"Pretty good, sir," she said shyly in her engaging lilt. "I didn't sleep so good until Danley was home, but then I worried about you."

"Yeah, sorry. I'll tell more about that later. But do you feel you're making progress?"

"I don't know. I've never been hurt this bad before. Doc's been very good to me, and I know he cares. Can I pray first?"

The question so surprised Zeke that he didn't respond immediately and noticed that even Danley looked twice at her. It struck Zeke that he had never heard her pray. "Absolutely," he said. "And then others, as you wish."

Cristelle began. "Dear God, thank You for saving me from my sins. Thank You for dying on the cross for me. Thank You for bringing me to these people, my friends. And thank You for Dr. Xavier. Please help him not feel bad or angry or hurt. He's so smart and we love him and we know You love him too. Forgive him and bring him back to us so we can tell him we forgive him too. In Jesus' name. Amen."

Zeke was stunned. Cristelle was so new in the faith, yet she seemed to understand its simplicity. How long had it been since he had enjoyed that "first love" of Christ? And what could Willard have meant when he said he had "cause" to run her down? That made Zeke wonder if Mahir had some-how changed his mind about her after having been the one who discovered the couple and brought them into the group. None of it was making sense.

Several others prayed, including Alexis, and Zeke had the sense that she was as staggered as he to realize that Gabrielle had apparently voted for him instead of her own husband. Who knew Doc would insist on knowing the count and it would be revealed that his and Zeke's were Doc's only votes? Zeke could only imagine how things were going with the family and Pastor Bob.

Elaine Meeks was praying when Zeke's walkie-talkie crackled to life and he jumped. He hurried out the nearest door, Alexis on his heels. "Sasha, that you? This is Dad, over."

"Daddy, I'm comin' in! I'm seeing something I've never seen before!"

"What is it?"

"Helicopters!"

"Zeke!" Alexis said. "Get her in here!"

"Copters, plural? How many?"

"Six, maybe more."

"Get inside!"

PART 6

OPERATION DRY BONES

26

MENACE

"SORRY TO INTERRUPT," Zeke said, returning to the Commons. "No need to be alarmed, but Sasha's spotted choppers. Unless they saw her, which is unlikely, they don't know we're here, so they should pass us by. Just wanted you to be aware that we're on it."

Naturally that changed the tone of the prayer meeting, though it still largely centered on Doc. And as soon as Sasha appeared, Zeke and Alexis pulled her into a corridor.

"Start at the top," Zeke said. "Sight or sound first?"

"Sight."

"Great. They see you?"

"Not unless they've got some crazy technology. I got to the decline and into the shadows pretty fast."

"Smart!" Alexis said.

Zeke grabbed Sasha by the shoulders and forced her to look into his eyes. She was shuddering. "Sash, you did well, but I need you to focus. This is crucial."

"Okay, so they're not flying real fast, and they're staying in formation even though they're changing direction. So unless they're searching the ground, they probably haven't seen me. I get down the decline far enough that I'm in the shadows where I can see them and they shouldn't be able to see me even if they come straight over the top. And pretty soon they're close enough I can hear 'em."

"That's when you called me?"

"Yeah. And I'm guessing there's six or eight of them. And they're big."

"This is important, Sash. Were they close enough that you could see what color they were?"

She nodded. "Green."

"Dark, olive drab?"

She nodded again.

"No kidding."

"What?" Alexis said.

"I'm guessing US military and carrying troops. But why? There's been nothing on the news about any threat to the US in California. If Doc ordering embalming fluid and us offending the religious sensibilities of the Nuwuwu are the first things to get the feds' attention in all the years we've been here, these choppers have to be lost, because they flew right over the top of us and apparently didn't know it. Lexi, let me get back in there. Why don't you and Sasha take a peek through the southeast scope, just three to six inches every ten minutes, otherwise totally dark."

"What are we looking for? More choppers?"

"And anything on the ground. Just give it a half hour. I hope to wrap up this meeting by lunchtime, then I'll monitor the news until dark before deciding if any of us should go to Gaho's burial service."

"Seriously, Z? That's still on the table?"

"Only if God gives me peace about it."

"Well, I have no peace about Sasha going, and I won't go without her."

"I understand."

Back in the Commons, Benita was praying as Zeke sat next to Jennie Gill. Jennie touched his arm and whispered, "Everyone else has prayed, so when she finishes you ought to bring everyone up to speed."

Benita was always emotional in her prayers and had a habit of finishing in Spanish. She said, "So God, we're askin' You to work in the heart of our brother to show him Your love through us, and we ask this *en el nombre de Jesús.*"

"Thank you, Benita," Zeke said. "Now if we could just get you to develop a little enthusiasm . . ."

"Don't tease me," she said.

"I just hope the Lord has translators up there."

She waved him off. "You're gonna find out Spanish is the language of heaven. What's the deal with the choppers?"

Zeke told them everything Sasha had reported, which led to more questions. "I know no more than you do," he said. "I can't imagine it has anything to do with us. If it does, it's overkill, but when we're all back together, we'll talk strategy and monitor the news feeds and see if we can determine what's got the military so interested in California."

"There must be some real threat," Katashi said. "Otherwise why bother? Half a dozen choppers alone—"

"Maybe more," Zeke said.

"That's a lot of money and manpower, especially if they're as big as you say. Where are they putting all that personnel, how are they feeding them, supplying them water, all that?"

Zeke's walkie-talkie crackled. He turned away from the group. "Zeke, go."

"Z," Alexis said, "get where you can hear me alone."

"Roger."

He jogged into the corridor. "Go, Lexi."

"I'm seeing tanks."

"You've got to be kidding me. How many?"

"A dozen. Accompanied by at least two covered trucks. Sasha confirms."

"Direction?"

"Coming from the northeast. They're going to come right past us, maybe right over us. We fortified for that?"

"Roger, but it's not ideal. How close?"

"Guessing half a mile."

"ETA?"

"Wish I knew, Z. Not a huge dust cloud, so maybe thirty miles an hour, so—"

"Maybe a minute. We're gonna feel it and hear it. I'll tell 'em here. Stay dark, send Sasha here. You run and tell Bob and the Xaviers."

"Roger."

In the Commons the news caused most to stand and mill about. Raoul, still hovering behind Mahir, said, "What's goin' on, man? They fightin' some kinda invasion? Terrorists or somebody comin' from the Pacific? What else could it be?"

"All we can do is hunker down," Katashi said.

About ninety seconds later the vibrations began, and then at least one of the monsters rumbled directly overhead. Lights flickered and ceiling tiles separated. Someone whispered a question about load-bearing capacity and others fiercely shushed them.

Alexis had arrived by then, and Zeke saw more terrified faces than he'd seen in all the time they'd been in the desert.

"Everyone sit again, please," he said.

As he sat before them he again felt every eye and knew they would have accepted anything from him just then, even a lie. If he even pretended to know this was some training exercise or a false alarm, that it was already over and the soldiers were heading home and no more were coming, the people in his charge would swear to believe him on the lives of their sainted grandparents.

Instead he turned the attention to Alexis. "Did you get to Pastor Bob and the Xaviers in time to give them a heads-up?"

"I did," she said. "And I was able to reassure them. I'm also happy to say it appears they've made some real progress. Gabi wanted me to tell you that the kids didn't really understand what happened, except that their dad lost the vote, so she'd appreciate it if no one talked to them about it. I've sent Sasha down there to keep them occupied in another room, so she's asking if we would not involve the kids in all this."

"We can do that, can't we?" Zeke said. "That sounds positive and easily accomplished—something we can do for Doc and Gabi. Should we break awhile? I don't want Jennie to speak without them here, especially without Bob."

"Good idea," Alexis said. "Cristelle, you look like you could use a nap, and—"

"No, I'm okay."

"Elaine, we could start thinking about lunch, which should be in about ninety minutes, and I could take Jennie back to her quar—oh, hold that thought!"

Pastor Bob stood at the door with Gabrielle, beckoning Alexis. She hurried over and the three of them spoke quietly. Bob left and Alexis brought an obviously shaken Gabi back to the group. She sat in the midst of them, Alexis holding her hand.

Zeke started to say something, but Jennie Gill squeezed his arm and said, "Gabrielle, you are among friends who love you."

Gabi broke down. Those within reach touched her and let her cry. Finally she wiped her face and took a breath. "I don't need to tell you Adam's qualities."

Several spoke at once: "No, you don't."

"He's brilliant."

"Smart."

"A great doctor."

"He's deeply embarrassed," she said. "Terribly sorry. Humiliated. He feels he's disqualified himself as an elder."

Many protested. "No, no. Not if he's sorry, and—"

She held up a hand. "Adam is also, I don't have to tell you, extremely proud. That's no secret. What made him the brilliant doctor he is was confidence that grew into a cocky self-assurance that makes him difficult to live with."

The protests became less enthusiastic, and Gabi said, "You can't argue. Everyone knows it, me most of all. I was taught as a child that people were supposed to be humble, to not talk about themselves, that you were supposed to let others praise you. I was an honor student just as he was, but I learned early who was the star of our home.

"I put him through school and took care of two babies by myself so he could finish his residency and make a name for himself. I never questioned his faith or his morals, but imagine having no say, no opinion, never winning an argument even when you're right. I never stopped loving him or admiring his mind or his talent, but I was jealous of the patients he treated and wondered if I had to be sick to get the attention I was starved for.

"Adam had many qualities required of an elder, but pastor? No. That's why, when I consulted my conscience, I voted for Zeke. But let me tell you the good news. Pastor Bob has been walking us—actually, Adam—through this, and Bob is not so much a peacekeeper as a truth teller. Is that fair to say, Jennie?"

Jennie smiled. "That hits the nail right on the head."

"He's been speaking some hard truth to a hard man, and I believe Adam is sorry not just for having been caught, but also because he realizes what he has become. Bob gave him both barrels and from the Scripture, a basic 'Who do you think you are? And how could you possibly think God would allow you in a servanthood role when the last thing you want is to be subservient?' By the time Bob, the Word, and the Lord were finished with Adam, I believe he had come to the end of himself."

"Had he?" Jennie said. "Or was he sorry he'd been exposed?"

"Both."

The word came from Doc himself, next to Pastor Bob in the doorway. His voice was strong and clear, the tone Zeke knew so well, but the man looked different. As he approached his wife, all but Cristelle and Jennie rose, but this was no hero's welcome, and there was no strut to his step.

Doc truly looked beaten. He sat across from Gabrielle and took both her hands in his. "She spoke the truth," he said, tears streaming. "All of it. And I am both ashamed and sorry. Ashamed of the man I became, and sorry for everything I've said and done to hurt the love of my life. All I can do is apologize to her and to all of you and beg your forgiveness. I don't expect it overnight. I know I have to prove myself to you, to humble myself and become the man God wants me to be.

"I've asked for forgiveness from my former pastor, and I ask the same from my new pastor. I also pledge you my full support, Zeke. I don't feel worthy to remain an elder, but that's up to you and Katashi, and I submit myself to your authority."

As the holdouts pressed in around Doc, Bob Gill laid a hand on his head and prayed, "All praise to God, the Father of our Lord and Savior Jesus Christ. As it is written, 'If we confess our sins, He is faithful and just to forgive us our sins and cleanse us from all unrighteousness.'"

27

EXPOSÉ

"Doc, if Jennie is up to speaking," Zeke said, "we should give her the floor."

"If she'll still have me as her doctor, I'm happy to check."

"Please do," she said, reaching to him. "But I need to tell you something in front of your brothers and sisters, and I'm going to speak to you not as my doctor—"

"After the way your husband talked to me, you can treat me like the family dog and it'll be a relief."

"Adam, I just want to say that in a lifetime of church work, you're not the first person I've seen humbled. If you want it to stick, don't go solo," she said. "These people are here for you. Submit yourself before them and before the Lord, and *He* will lift you up."

Doc teared up again. "Thank you, Jennie."

"Now, Dr. Xavier," she said, "clear me for takeoff, because I'm about to preach."

He cupped her face and lifted each eyelid, asked when she had last taken her meds, and felt her pulse. He whispered which pills she should take and urged her to take more water than was required to get the medicine down. "How long do you expect to talk?"

"Just a few minutes."

"And can you stay seated?"

"I need to."

"Then you should be fine."

Zeke said, "Can the kids join us?"

"Oh, sure," Jennie said, and Alexis hurried to get them.

When they returned, Caleb and Kayla sat on the floor at their parents' feet, Sasha sat on Zeke's lap, and Alexis sat next to him atop one of the tables.

The holdouts gathered around their second oldest member, and as her husband dug her worn Bible from a bag and opened it before her, Doc made his way to Cristelle and made her comfortable before returning to sit with Gabi and their kids.

Jennie said, "As you know, I had hoped to speak briefly this evening before Bob and I left to move back home. Since Doc tells me that's no longer feasible, I just want to share two verses and say a word about what we learned from Zeke and Alexis's son.

"When I think of Junior, it strikes me that only half of us ever met or knew him. But what a legacy he left, and what an impact he has had on this group.

"As I face the end and look forward to seeing him again—he who was so confident of heaven, he said, 'because of Jesus'—I love the Scriptures more every day. The story is told of the great Christian philosopher and apologist, Francis Schaeffer, who, near the end of his life, said he so loved his Bible that when he woke up in the morning and saw it on his bedside table, he would reach over and affectionately pat it. I can identify with that.

"I find it interesting that the verses that have been my favorites nearly all my life mean more to me today than they ever have. They come from that wonderful story in John 11 where Jesus is talking to Martha after she has scolded Him for being late to reach her and Mary when Lazarus was sick, and she tells Him that if He had gotten there sooner, Lazarus would not have died. He tells her that her brother will rise again, and she says she knows he will at the resurrection.

"And then Jesus says—and I have long believed this may be the most beautiful paragraph ever translated into English—just listen to these words and let them sink in: 'I am the resurrection and the life. He who believes in Me, though he may die, he shall live. And whoever lives and believes in Me shall never die.'"

Jennie paused, and it seemed to Zeke that no one moved or barely breathed, probably imagining as he did how poignant this was to Jennie now, already too weak to even endure a ride home to her family and not likely to survive another week.

"And then Jesus follows with the question that resounds through the ages, that I know you have all answered but I pray you will never stop asking others for as long as you have breath: 'Do you believe this?'"

Jennie closed her Bible with a sigh, and everyone sat in silence until eight-year-old Kayla Xavier stood and said, "I do!"

Sasha slid off Zeke's lap and said, "I do too."

Katashi rose. "So do I."

Elaine Meeks and the Xaviers were up at the same time, saying in unison, "I do!"

Raoul said, "Me too!" as he rose, Benita following with, "*Sí! * Yes!"

Danley Muscadin's chair scraped the floor as he stood quickly and said, "I do."

Bob Gill stood, one hand on Jennie's shoulder and the other covering his mouth as he wept and nodded.

Zeke and Alexis and little Caleb all stood at the same time, announcing their *I do's* over each other.

As people slowly sat, Mahir struggled to his feet and leaned forward, hands flat on the table before him. His arms shook and his face contorted. The room that had come alive with affirmations was suddenly still as a mausoleum. With a hard look back to Raoul, who had a hand on his sidearm, Zeke surreptitiously lifted his hand to indicate he should stay calm.

"That leaves two of us," Mahir whispered. "Zeke, I'm begging permission to speak freely."

"Just be careful."

"I promise."

"Go ahead."

"If the question is 'Do you believe this?' my answer is yes." He pushed off the table and rose to his full height, turning to face the pale young woman in the infirmary bed, IV line in her arm, heavily wrapped leg elevated, eyes red and swollen, tears flowing. "How about you, Cristelle? Do you believe this?"

She twice appeared to try to speak and finally pulled the sheet up to wipe her face. With a fragile voice she said, "Inside I am standing tall and raising both arms. I don't know why you, of all people, are asking me this, Mahir, since it is because of you that both Danley and I can say yes. In fact it was you who told us that new believers should read the Gospel of John first, and that is why I have been memorizing so much of it.

"I was so happy to hear Mrs. Gill read those verses just now, because I have been memorizing them in my devotions this week. I just memorized the next verse too, where Martha answers Jesus' question. So I will proudly say with her, 'Yes, Lord, I believe that You are the Christ, the Son of God, who is to come into the world.'"

Mahir appeared to be hyperventilating. "Cristelle, I so want to believe you."

She looked wounded. "You *can* believe me! Why wouldn't you?"

Danley said, "What are you saying, Mahir?"

"Do we really want to do this right here," Mahir said, "right now, in front of everybody?"

Zeke stood. "Yes, we do, Mahir. It's time. Let's have it out. What are we talking about?"

"You'd better be sure you want me to keep going."

"Yes!" Zeke said. "Nothing is off-limits! This body is going to be one or—"

"Zeke, the children," Bob Gill said.

He groaned. "Sasha . . ."

Her shoulders slumped. "On it, Dad. Caleb, Kayla, let's go."

As soon as they were gone, Zeke said, "Mahir, just say it."

Danley said, "Yeah, what're you talking about?"

"Please," Cristelle said, obviously terrified.

"All right," Mahir said. "Two and a half weeks ago I was on the supply run. Everybody got mail, including you, Cristelle. Next morning I was checking the levels on Zeke's Jeep, which I'd used for the drive. You didn't see me when you came in there, 'cause I'd parked in the far corner. I was about to greet you when I saw you hide something in the shelves where the computer surplus stuff is. Do you deny it?"

28

CONFESSION

CRISTELLE STARED.

"Well, do you, or am I right?"

"You're right."

"I had to know," Mahir said.

"What do you mean?" she said. "You looked at it?"

He nodded.

"Do you read Arabic?"

"I don't," he said. "But you do, don't you?"

"Yes."

"What was I supposed to think, Cristelle?"

"I don't know, Mahir. What *did* you think?"

"I thought how strange it was that Haitians had come all the way to California in the middle of the worst drought in history without much hope of finding work or being able to travel. And then I remembered how open you were to the gospel."

"We were hungry for it."

"You sure were. You came to faith like you'd been looking for Jesus all your lives."

"We had, even though we didn't know it."

"I'll bet. It was like I was the perfect evangelist, the perfect witness."

"We believed God had sent you, just for us."

"You sure treated me that way."

"Because you led us to the truth."

"Oh, stop! We've seen a lot of people come to faith since we've been out here, but we don't bring them into the family, into the compound. Why you?"

"We asked ourselves the same thing. We felt so blessed, so special. We still do. We thank God every day."

"Oh, you're good. You thank Allah, you mean."

"What are you accusing us of, Mahir?" Danley said.

"I haven't decided about you yet, Danley," Mahir said. "But her, yes."

"Her what?"

"Do you not know what's going on in the world? Terrorists are radicalizing people everywhere, infiltrating. She would say anything, pretend to believe anything, do anything to get in here."

"Mahir!" Cristelle said. "You think this because of what you saw me hide in the garage?"

"What else was I to believe?"

"I am your friend, your sister in Christ, your *daughter* in Christ! Why did you not just ask me?"

"Because you would have lied to me!"

"Mahir!" she wailed. "You are breaking my heart! Please honor me by asking me now."

"About the document?"

"That is what a friend would do," she said.

"I am not your friend!"

She burst into sobs. "That is plain." And she muttered something.

"What did you say?"

"I said I would like to still be yours."

"I'll bet you would. So I'll humor you. Go ahead. Tell me all about the document."

"I didn't ask you to humor me. I asked you to honor me, honor our friendship."

"Our friendship is over. You would jeopardize the safety of this group, this place—"

"I would never do that! That is why I hid the document, so no one would feel threatened."

"All right," Zeke said. "Enough of this. I want an explanation. You admit the document was yours?"

"That's what I said. I don't deny it."

"So what is it?"

"I had written to my mother in Carrefour, where we were raised, knowing she would be worried sick about what had become of us. The truth about how we got to California is actually silly and embarrassing. We had heard that we could find work and make money in Las Vegas, but we spent the last of our money on the wrong bus tickets and wound up in Los Angeles. We were trying to work our way to Las Vegas.

"We were stuck, barely getting by, hardly making enough to eat, and sleeping in shacks with other workers when you all were giving out clothes and food and telling people about Jesus. Danley noticed Mahir's French accent and we shared a few Creole phrases. If you remember, Mahir, we told you our religious background."

Mahir nodded. "You said you'd been raised Baha'i. Your mother was devout. And Danley's relatives—uncles?"

"Right," Danley said.

"My mother still is," Cristelle said. "You must understand. Writing my mother that I had become a Christian would be like you writing your loved ones that you had become a Buddhist or a Muslim. I had to write a long, long letter, telling her both Danley's and my whole story and why the gospel made so much sense to us. You know Jesus plays a big role in Baha'i. They believe in the unity of all religions, so He's okay with them. They revere Him, but of course they do not believe He is the only Son of God and certainly not the only way to God. By telling my mother that we, and especially I, had become a believer in Jesus as *the* Christ, *the* Son of God, I might as well have been telling her that I was turning my back on her and everything she believed in. I knew that to her that meant I was leaving the family.

"I tried to tell her I was not doing this, that I still loved her and always would, but I had no idea how she would take it. Well, that is not entirely true. I had little hope that she would be convinced or that she would respond in any way other than the way she did. What I got back from her had no personal note, nothing telling me that she got my letter, agreed with me, disagreed with me, loved me, hated me, was kicking me out of the family, or what.

"It was simply Baha'i propaganda and doctrine that I am sure she expected me to read all the way through, see how wrong I was, and come back to my true religion. But I have no interest in that. My heart was changed when I found Jesus and my sins were forgiven. And as much as it hurts me to cause pain to my mother, my mind is made up. We do not burn things here, and I did not want to risk someone seeing this document in the trash, so I made the wrong decision and thought I could put it somewhere no one would find it."

The bravado was gone from Mahir's tone. "Your story could be easily proved if anyone else here could read Arabic."

"I can," Danley said.

"Someone without bias," Mahir said. "Sorry to be so suspicious, but I'm pretty far out on a limb here and need to be sure."

"Actually, I can read a little Arabic."

All eyes turned to Jennie Gill, and even Bob looked surprised. "Really?" he said.

"I have no idea how much I'd remember," she said. "But forty years ago I took a comparative languages course and learned how many dialects there were. I might be able to decipher a few words or phrases."

Zeke said, "Cristelle, tell Danley exactly where you put the pages."

He was back in minutes and spread them before Jennie. She studied the first page, a few from the middle, and the last. Slowly following her finger from right to left, she squinted and hesitated and pressed her lips together.

Finally she looked to Mahir. "You'll be happy to know that this appears to be exactly what Cristelle says it is. Copyrighted by the Baha'i International Community."

Zeke was staggered when Mahir sagged in his chair and banged his forehead on the table. He sat back and covered his eyes with his hands, sobbing. "Oh, no!" he wailed. "Oh, God, forgive me! Cristelle and Danley, forgive me! I've been such a fool!"

"You misunderstood, Mahir," Cristelle said. "You should have just asked—"

"No!" he yelled, "You don't understand!"

"You should have assumed better about your friends," she said, "but—"

"No, no! I tried to have you killed! I don't deserve to live!"

29

INTERRUPTED

ZEKE RUSHED TO MAHIR. "What're you saying?"

The Frenchman pounded the table as Danley approached. "I knew it! You forced her into that tanker Sunday!"

"I did! I even told WatDoc she was a terrorist and to go after her!"

"Mahir!" Zeke said.

"Just kill me!"

"Take my gun or I will!" Danley said as Katashi rushed over and pulled it from his holster.

Doc and Bob Gill stood to move Cristelle back into the infirmary, and Alexis grabbed the IV stand.

"Danley!" Cristelle said, fighting to be heard, her voice evidencing how weak she was. "Leave him alone! And Doc, I don't want to go anywhere. Everyone stay right here. Mahir, you calm down, and I mean it."

Mahir sat with his head nearly to his knees, banging his thighs with his fists. "I'm such a fool, such an idiot! Somebody just shoot me!"

"Nobody's going to shoot you," Zeke said. "Just calm down now."

As Mahir sat rocking and weeping, Zeke felt a huge sense of relief. But why? Here he had just confirmed that a man he had worked with for twenty years had tried to have someone killed. But he no longer feared a terrorist among them. What was he to do about a friend who had committed a crime?

"Mahir, do you also want to tell the truth about the oxygen?"

He nodded miserably. "I lost my mind, Zeke. What if Doc hadn't gotten to her in time?"

"We can't cover up either of these incidents," Zeke said. "They're more than just personal offenses."

"I don't understand you, Mahir," Cristelle said hoarsely, "and I'm deeply hurt. But I forgive you."

"I don't," Danley said.

"Danley!"

"I'm sorry," Danley said. "You can forgive him and God can forgive him, and maybe someday God can help me forgive him. Be he tried to take you from me! And all he had to do was ask!"

"You're right," Mahir said. "I don't deserve your forgiveness. I couldn't be sorrier, but I don't blame you. And I know I need more than your forgiveness. I need help."

Zeke's walkie-talkie clicked twice and he flinched. Others with units—Alexis and Katashi and the Gutierrezes—had checked theirs too. Protocol was to not click when you were inside, and everyone was inside. He held up a hand to tell everyone to not respond. He pulled his from his belt and held it aloft, clicking twice.

Two quick clicks came in response.

"Lexi, run and see if Sasha's doing that. She'd better not be, 'cause she knows better. If it's not her, give me one click. I'll be at the southeast periscope. Katashi, Benita, come with me. Raoul, keep Mahir right here."

"Thanks for letting me come here, Zeke."

"We're gonna have to talk about WatDoc."

"I'll tell you whatever you want to know."

Zeke had a feeling it might be sooner than later, because if the walkie-talkie clicker wasn't anybody inside, it could be only one other person.

Hearing one click, Zeke raised the periscope and quickly scanned the area. He found a small water tanker nearby with one occupant slouched behind the wheel.

"Willard?"

"Gotta lemme in, bruh! Sorry!"

"Get that rig at least a quarter mile from here so you don't give us away if you haven't already, and we'll talk about it."

"You got it."

"First you're gonna tell me how you found us, and then no promises. I'd have to convince an awful lot of people, and that's not gonna be easy."

"Zeke!" Benita said, "hold up, man! What're you thinkin'? That's WatDoc, right?"

"You've got to trust me on this—"

"Whoa, Zeke!" Katashi said. "Nobody's saying we don't trust you, but what happened last night that would make you think we'd want—"

"Listen, he saved my life when I woulda been history. And I can't believe God gave me a word for him for nothing. I truly think he's—"

"Save that!" Katashi said. "You've got a room full of people in there who need you, and they don't know any of this. You can't just bring the enemy in here without explanation. Mahir's about ready to kill himself, Doc's lower than I've ever seen him, and everybody's still wondering what happened to you. Bob's waiting to pray you in as the new pastor, and this is how you want to start?"

"What'm I supposed to do? I didn't give our location away. For all I know Mahir did. But I'd rather get Willard inside before he gives us away to someone else. Who knows how far away the military is?"

"How do we know they're not with him?" Benita said.

"No way he'd do that to me, not after yesterday."

"You don't know that," Katashi said. "You've got to tell us the story."

"What do I do with him in the meantime?"

The other three looked at each other. "You tol' Alexis, right?" Benita said.

"Everything that happened, 'course."

"Then she don't gotta be there when you tell us. Make WatDoc wait outside the utility door. She can be in the garage on the other side in case he tries to get in or bring anybody else."

"I don't like it," Zeke said.

"C'mon," Katashi said, "you've got be sure everybody's on board with this before you let him in here. The Mongers have been our nightmare since we got here."

"They almost killed you once," Benita said. "And now Cristelle."

"He's gonna be here soon," Raoul said. "Make a decision, man."

Zeke returned to the periscope. "He's about two hundred yards out and he's put the truck out of sight. All right, Katashi, explain it to Alexis. Get her stationed in the garage and be sure Sasha stays in the Xavier quarters with the kids. Then get back to the Commons with the rest of us. Benita, go tell Bob I need a minute with him when I get there, and tell everybody else to take a break if they need to because in five minutes Bob's going to pray for me, and I'll talk."

Zeke raised the scope and connected with Willard on the walkie-talkie. "Come down the decline and wait at the utility door. Don't try to communicate until you hear from us. It'll be at least twenty minutes. I'll have personnel stationed on the other side of the door. If we detect anyone else in the area, you won't get in. You'll surrender your weapons when you enter. Click once if you copy and agree."

Click.

Zeke felt a sense of urgency on his way back to the Commons, but he couldn't make himself hurry. Neither could he shake the ominous feeling of a major transition. That was natural, he knew, with the retirement of his pastor of so many years and the impending loss of Jennie, who had meant so much to him and his family.

But he had personally undergone such a change in just three days that it was as if he were suffering jet lag or even whiplash. Called of God, thrust into a pastorate (small as it was), chased by federal agents, nearly killed yet hardly injured.

And now an archenemy had become an unlikely ally and someone for whom God had—he could think of no other way to put it—made him sympathetic. No one else could have accomplished that. Zeke knew the paradoxical nature of his faith, how the meek were to inherit the earth, the poor in spirit were to be comforted, to be rich you were to give, to lead you were to become a servant, to live you must die. But the real crucible for the Christian was that the true believer was called upon to love his enemy.

Well, Willard had been more than an enemy. Here was a character, a personality, a type Zeke found abhorrent—crude, rude, in-your-face. Yet now God had not only given Zeke a word for him—a name he could not have known of a relative Willard hadn't seen for more than a decade—but He had also made Zeke care about the man. And not just his soul. Sure he wanted Willard to come to faith, as any believer should want everyone to do. But this was more than that. Zeke found himself drawn to Willard as a person, a human being. He cared about him.

How could he communicate that to the rest of the holdouts? They would be wary, and he couldn't blame them.

As he moved through the underground complex, he recalled the final days of construction. When it all came together, the final pieces taped and glued and snapped to a superstructure designed to withstand enormous weight and shifting earth—the integrity of which had just been tested by the weight of a tank—he, Doc, and Mahir had brought Pastor Bob for the initial walk-through.

Their fear had been livability, of course. Could normal people, middle-class suburbanites who joked that their spiritual gifts were crea-ture comforts, maintain their sanity? Or would it have the feel of a steamy, cramped, echoing submarine from which people would long to escape every day?

That walk-through made them nervous initially, and they split up, feeling too close. But when they reunited, realizing there had been plenty of room to pass each other as each checked every corner of the place, they had to admit they believed the others would like it—not just settle for it.

They had been right. Though this would be no one's first choice, they weren't here for the luxuries of home. Many, many missionaries who lived aboveground had things much worse. The holdouts had made it work, and for many years it had served its purpose.

If Willard entered, would that mean the end? Had Zeke misread him, and was he disingenuous, paving the way for others with ill motives to finally thwart all the holdouts had accomplished? That didn't gibe with Zeke's apparent calling to become God's mouthpiece, but for all he knew it could be the way He closed one door and opened another.

As Zeke came within sight of the swinging double doors that led to the Commons, Alexis arrived with her look of determination and that purposeful stride he knew so well. She grabbed him by the shoulders. "I wish I could be in there with you," she said, "but you know you can trust me with this. You sure you want him inside?"

Zeke nodded. "In twenty minutes or so I'll give you one click. Go to either of the west periscopes to be sure no one else is in the area. By the time you get back, Raoul and Benita will be on either side of the door. Make Willard show you both hands when you let him in. If he tries anything—"

"I know."

"All three of you—"

"I know, Z."

"I have to say it, Lexi. You've got to put him down. This place, these people, are all on me. I'm letting him in because I trust him. But if I'm wrong, he's dead. He should be carrying a .357 Magnum, so have Raoul take that and bark at him to hand over the other one as if he knows for sure he's got one."

"Does he?"

"No idea, but if he does, he'll give it up. Then just bring him on in. I want to see how he responds to Mahir and Cristelle especially."

"Me too."

"But if you send Raoul to be with me, who's going to be with Mahir?"

"Let me worry about him."

30

CONSECRATED

ZEKE WAS IMPRESSED with how the Commons had been refigured. Cristelle's bed and IV stand had been moved to the center of the back row. Danley was on her far side feeding her something. She looked tired. Mahir sat at a table on her other side, and while he still looked miserable, Cristelle was close enough to speak to him, while Danley and many of the others looked wary and Raoul still stood directly behind him.

The Gutierrezes sat at a table directly ahead of them, and next to them Elaine Meeks sat with Gabrielle Xavier. Bob and Jennie Gill sat to her right, at the end of the table, Jennie dozing, her brow knitted—Zeke assumed in pain.

Three chairs faced the group, the one in the middle empty. Doc sat in the one on the right, Katashi on the left.

Bob had risen and approached when Zeke entered. Zeke summoned Benita to join them.

"You fix the room like this?" he said.

"*Sí*, with Pastor Bob."

"Perfect."

"*Gracias.*"

He told her what to do when he finished speaking. "And have Raoul join you. I'll give you a nod, and you head down there right away."

"He ain't gonna give three of us no trouble," she said.

Zeke nodded. "But don't hesitate—"

"We won't," Benita said. "But you gonna leave Mahir alone?"

Zeke shook his head. "I'm taking him with me to my quarters and we'll wait for you there."

Bob shot him a double take. "You're sure about this?"

"Still playing it by ear. If it doesn't feel right at the time, I can abort. I won't give Alexis the signal to let Willard in and I won't send Raoul and Benita down there. But if everybody here feels okay about it, it's gonna be a 'go'."

Zeke didn't like the look in Pastor Bob's eye. He asked Benita to excuse them.

"Sure," she said. "Good to go."

Zeke pulled Bob to the side. "You worried about Jennie, or about what I'm doing?"

"I don't have peace about this yet, Zeke. I'm not hearing you say God's been clear with you about this. Has He?"

"I can only tell you He was working on Willard yesterday."

Bob nodded. "Like everyone else, I want to hear all about it. I'll offer a pastoral charge–type prayer, then just give us the basics from last night."

"What happened with Mahir while I was gone?"

Bob shook his head. "She wants to forgive him and won't take no for an answer."

"What're we gonna do? We're in no-man's-land, so she couldn't press charges if she wanted to."

"And she wouldn't, Zeke! She's working on Danley to forgive him too. It's not right that Mahir tries to kill her twice in three days and yet he walks. But you're the shepherd of this flock now, and you know what that means."

Zeke nodded. "I can't look the other way, and I don't want to. I'm the gatekeeper. The safety of these people is on me. I can't believe I have to protect them from Mahir, of all people."

"We need to get started. Listen, if you do decide to bring WatDoc in here, you'd better tell these people what's been going on with you."

"God talking to me? You serious?"

"Do as God leads."

When Zeke was seated between Doc and Katashi, Bob stood behind them and the three of them laid hands on his shoulders.

"Join me," Bob said. "Father, thank You for what You have done in Zeke's life, for saving him, calling him, teaching him, and using him. Thank You for his family and that today he stands on the threshold of expanded ministry.

"Our passion, Lord, is that You use him beyond his highest expectation, keep him clean in the midst of a corrupt generation. May he shine in a dark world. May he draw deeply from the rich well of grace. Keep him learning the power of prayer.

"Give him the passion of the Savior, who commanded His disciples, 'Go therefore and make disciples.' As a Good Shepherd, go before him, keep him from sin, and humble him under Your mighty hand.

"And now, Ezekiel Thorppe, I commit you to God and to the word of His grace, which can build you up and give you an inheritance among all those who are sanctified. This we ask expectantly in the wonderful name of our Savior and Lord, Jesus Christ. Amen."

To Zeke's surprise, when he rose, the people clapped.

"Thanks, Bob. I accept this role as from God. My task now is to explain what happened when I left here in the wee hours of Tuesday morning. I intended to create a diversion to make sure Danley eluded his pursuers—which he had done well without me. Raoul offered to help, which would have kept me out of a whole lot of trouble.

"But I unwisely went rogue, endangering not only my own life, but all of yours as well. I owe you every detail, but I am going to rush, because I have a guest I'd like to invite for lunch. By now you have an idea who that is—which I also must explain and answer for."

As Zeke sped through the story, the looks of alarm were punishment enough for his errors in judgment. But when he reached the account of God providing, of all people, the holdouts' archenemy to rescue him from certain death, Zeke was reminded of what was so special about this little band of evangelists. They too seemed suddenly interested in the soul of one who had so long been a threat.

And when he told of God giving him the name of Willard's sainted aunt, he knew Bob had been right about telling them everything. Elaine held up both hands like a grade-school crossing guard. "So sorry to interrupt, but are you saying God gave you a word of knowledge?"

Zeke said, "I don't claim any special revelation or gift. All I know is that God impressed that name on me, and I just told you Willard's reaction. Here is a man who may not have been reached any other way, and he's not reached yet. But I'm sure curious about why he's here now, aren't you?"

"Very," Elaine said.

"Now let me tell you what else God has been saying to me." And Zeke told them everything from when he first heard God's voice Sunday morning through what had happened surrounding Gaho's death.

"That how you knew you could vote for me and not worry about it?" Doc said, smiling. "God told you?"

"Actually, yes. He didn't tell me the outcome, but He told me to vote for you and to tell Gabi I was going to."

"That's scary," Gabrielle said.

"It was to me too," Zeke said, "but I realized God is not in the business of scaring His children. There has to be a reason for this."

"All those verses He's giving you sound evangelistic," Katashi said. "If you're supposed to tell those to people in power, that's exciting."

Zeke nodded.

"That's why it's so important that we come back together as we once were. God is calling us to something strategic."

"You think He wants WatDoc on our side?" Mahir said.

Zeke wasn't sure how to respond. Where was Mahir coming from? He had gone to Willard behind their backs, maybe thinking he was rooting out a suspected terrorist. But who else's attention might that have brought to them?

"Where does Willard think you stand, Mahir?" Zeke said. "If he saw you and Cristelle and Danley, how would that go?"

"I'd have to straighten him out. All due respect, Zeke, but you almost gave us away—in fact, maybe you did. How else did Willard know where to find us? I never told him. Yeah, I messed up worse'n you did, but at least he knows I was trying to clean house. If he knew Cristelle forgave me, which she's got no business doing, it would turn him inside out. Where's he ever seen anything like that before?"

"Let's find out," Zeke said. He nodded to Raoul and Benita and they left. "Elaine and Katashi, start working on lunch. I'd like Bob, Danley, Mahir, Alexis, and me to meet with Willard in my quarters. Doc, check in on your patients. Gabi, if Sasha could hang with you and your kids awhile longer, I'd appreciate it. After they help Alexis deliver Willard, I'm going to have Raoul and Benita monitor the news and see if we can find out what the military is doing in California. I also have to figure out who's going with me to the burial at the Nuwuwu settlement tonight."

"You serious?" Katashi said. "That's still on?"

"Kaga has asked me to speak, and besides wanting to honor him, what an opportunity! His mother wants John 3:16 read at her service. I have a chance to share the greatest gospel verse in all the Bible, and I can say it appears to be her dying wish! How can I pass that up? I'll go if I have to go alone."

"You might have to," Katashi said. "Is Alexis going?"

"No. She's made that clear."

"Smart woman."

"I was hoping the elders would be with me, at least."

"Oh, boy," Katashi said. "I'm going to have to pray about that."

"Ah, Zeke," Gabrielle said, "Adam is in submission mode, but remember, the DEA is sniffing around *because* of the scripts he wrote. Even though he never met, let alone treated, the woman they're burying tonight, the tribal leader's daughter-in-law must be implying that Adam's prescription for embalming fluid is somehow tied to the tribe. Federal agents are going to be there, and you expect him to show up? Sounds like suicide. At least like surrender."

"Are we afraid of the truth?" Zeke said.

"No!" Gabi said. "But apparently this woman—"

"Kineks."

"Right, wouldn't know the truth if it slapped her in the face. She got the authorities to come all the way from Parker, and—"

"Gabi, listen. She can say what she wants. Her own husband and her father-in-law, head of the tribe, will give the lie to her story. They'll vouch for Doc, swear he never even met Gaho. Doc can tell them why he ordered the embalming fluid, show them Jennie's chart if they need to see it. We have nothing to hide."

"I'll go if they want me to," Doc said.

"Adam," Gabrielle said, "I don't know."

"Zeke," Bob said, "Raoul and Benita have to be in position by now."

"Right," Zeke said. "We'll all be on the same page before we do any-thing, Gabi. You have my word."

He pulled his walkie-talkie and gave Alexis a single click.

31

WILLARD

Z EKE DIDN'T KNOW till later that it was Benita who locked her walkie-talkie Send button on so he could monitor how the first-ever outsider was received into the compound.

First he heard Alexis's footsteps as she moved from the periscope to the garage and the utility door, where Raoul was to be stationed on one side, Benita on the other. Then knocking, apparently by her. "Willard, you out there?"

"Yes'm, I surely am," he said, voice muffled. "I kin hear ya in there an' on my squawker. Smart! I assume yer Zeke's wife?"

"Sir, when I open this door, I'll have a Smith & Wesson M&P compact pointed at your face. If I don't see both hands empty above your head, I'm going to put a forty-caliber bullet you'll never see or hear right between your eyes. Are we clear?"

"Woo-hoo, yes, ma'am! My kinda woman! Cain't wait to meet you, an' I *hope* yer Zeke's wife!"

Silence.

"Willard, if you think this is a joke, you're going to make a mess on my garage floor."

"I hear you, ma'am, and my hands are high."

"What are you carrying?"

"I got a .357 Magnum on m' right thigh that yer welcome to."

"My associate will be taking that."

"I b'lieve you, ma'am."

"I'm opening the door, which pulls in. Don't move."

"Well, hello, purty lady."

"Keep your hands where I can see them. Step in and stop."

"I'll take that," Raoul said.

"I seen you before."

"Where's the other one?" Raoul said. "You don' wanna surprise her, man."

"Small o' my back."

"Got it," Benita said.

"Bet the señorita b'longs to you, eh, amigo?"

"Face the wall, man," Raoul said.

"Aw, if I gotta be frisked, let one o' the ladies—"

"Quiet," Raoul said. "Zeke trusts you, I don't."

"Jes' joshin', dude. We cool."

Alexis told Benita to let Zeke know they were on their way, but Zeke cut in, "Copy. Welcome, Willard. Behave yourself."

He met them outside the Thorppes' quarters and gave Raoul and Benita their assignments.

"You know I's jes' foolin' back there, ma'am," Willard said. "Kin I know yer name?"

"I hope you were," she said. "You can call me Mrs. Thorppe."

"Well, okay then. Would you've really put one in me?"

"Without a second thought and then slept like a baby," she said, and it was all Zeke could do to keep from bursting out laughing.

When Willard saw Bob, Danley, and Mahir, he said, "Hey, I seen all y'all before. How ya doin'?" Alexis slipped into the bathroom, and Zeke heard her retching. She rejoined him as he was passing out water bottles.

"We've got about half an hour before lunch, Willard, and we'd like you to join us—"

"Really? Hey!"

"But we need to get a few things on the table first. You and I have been through a lot together, but as you can imagine, your being here is a shock to everyone else."

"Well, I—"

"We know some of what's gone on between you and Mahir—"

"Frenchy? Oh, sorry, I'll wait."

"First I want to know how you found us."

"Yer place here? Well, it wasn't Frenchy or whatever you jes' called him."

"My name's Mahir, and I didn't tell you where we were."

"No, you didn't."

"I didn't either, did I?" Zeke said.

"Not 'xactly, but you come closer. I kinda homed in on it by time I brought you close and then I sorta come over here by accident an' was havin' a smoke when you was tryin' to raise yer people an' I overheard ya. Then today I come lookin' and got lucky."

"So that's on me," Zeke said. "Anyone else know about it?"

"Don't think so."

"You're not sure?"

"Well, you seen I come in one o' the smaller rigs."

"Right to the entrance, which wasn't too bright."

"It wasn't, was it? Sorry. Anyways, the guy I traded with coulda follered, I guess, but I woulda knowed, and he had no reason. He don't know what I'm up to. I honestly don't think nobody else knows, no sir."

"So, what *are* you up to, Willard?" Bob said.

"Well, it's kinda private why I'm here, between me and Zeke."

"We have no secrets here," Bob said.

"But what if I do?"

Alexis cleared her throat. "You're going to have to get over it. It's just not how we do business. Zeke's going to tell us anyway, so you might as well. But first we want to tell you something."

"Tell me what?"

"Mahir?"

"Um, yeah, WatDoc, I made a terrible mistake, and I talked you into a terrible mistake. I believed this man's wife here was a terrorist, all because I was brainless enough to not just ask a simple question."

"What the heck was it?"

"That's not important. What's important is that I believed the worst about somebody that I know and care about, and I got it in my head she wasn't who I knew her to be. I became so sure of it that I even tried to help you kill her. If we'd succeeded, I'd never be able to forgive myself. I still don't know if I can."

Willard sat shaking his head. "Man, that's awful. You know I was jes' tryin' to help. I even told Zeke what I done 'cause he had rats in his camp. Now yer tellin' me I didn't have cause."

"We didn't," Mahir said.

"I done a lotta bad things in my life, but usually I at least had a reason. Not always a good one, but at least somethin'. That makes me feel bad as you."

"This man here, Danley, it was his wife, so he's having a tough time with it and I can't blame him. Can you?"

"'Course not. I mean, we kin tell him we're sorry till we're sick o' hearin' ourselves, but that don't change nothin'. You prob'ly like to kill us, right?"

"In a way," Danley said. "Cristelle's my whole world. You got anybody who means that much to you?"

"Used to," Willard said. "I know what it means to lose somebody like that."

"I don't want to find out," Danley said.

"She could still lose her leg," Mahir said.

"Yeah?"

"But she's forgiven me."

"She's what? I don' get that, man."

"And I'll get there," Danley said. "I'm praying about it."

"Prayin' about fergivin' us? That don't make sense. But see, now we're gettin' to what I'm doin' here."

"What do you mean?" Bob said.

"First, I didn't know I was gonna see y'all. I was hopin' to jes' talk to Zeke." He turned to Danley. "This is all a su'prise an' I'm sorry 'bout yer wife and all, and if you thought she'd see me, I'd like to tell her I'm sorry. I don't know if I've ever been fergiven of nothin' before, sir, but I'm tellin' ya the truth when I say I thought I was doin' the right thing. Frenchy tells me she's a traitor, I got no reason . . . Well, I'm not blamin' him, an' it's not like I only do the right thing. You people know better'n most that that ain't true.

"Anyway, I come here to tell Zeke to quit prayin' fer me, and don't tell me you ain't, Zeke, 'cause I kin feel it. I ain't been sleepin' since we talked and you tol' me Aunt Myrt's been prayin' fer me. I still want ya to try to let her know where I am and that I'm okay—she deserves that after all I put her through—but that's it. I'll leave y'all alone. We kin do bid'ness on water if ya want, and I'll be fairer than I ever been, but that's the end of it. Deal?"

"Sorry," Zeke said. "No deal."

"Whaddya mean?"

"Can't do it."

"Sure ya can."

"No, Willard. What kind of a deal is it when there's nothing in it for me?"

"What do you want? I know my guys and me been a pain to ya. We'll leave you be. That's a good deal."

"Yeah, but if you think you've had it rough because I've been praying for you, imagine how hard it's going to be for me if God won't leave me alone. He's the one who told me your aunt's name, remember. He's the one who's been reminding me to pray for you. He's got a message for you. If I don't give it to you, He's never going to let me hear the end of it. I can put up with the likes of you, but I don't want to cross Him."

"You're puttin' me on."

"I'm not."

"I tol' you, man. I'm too far gone, I done too much. God don't want no part o' me."

"That's a funny thing, then, because you know what He told me? He gave me a message, saying—and these are His exact words—'Tell the one who believes he is unworthy, the one who believes he is beyond My reach.'"

"Get outta here."

"Call me a liar if you want to, but that's what He said. If I were you, I'd at least hear the message."

"I don't know, man."

"God wants to tell you something and you don't want to hear it?"

"You gotta admit, that's a little scary."

"It's a lot scary, but you've been swaggering around California for ten years like you're afraid of nothing."

"Yeah, but God?"

"So you do believe in Him?"

"My aunt sure does."

"Bet she'd want you to listen."

"I reckon."

"Ready when you are, Willard."

Bob slipped to his knees.

"What y'all doin', old man?"

"Fixing to hear a message from God," Bob said. "You can sit, stand, lie on the floor, or leave if you want. It won't make any difference to Him. Just tell Zeke when you're ready, because we'd like to hear it."

"I don't know if I do."

"That's up to you."

Zeke sat with his head in his hands. *Please, Lord.*

"I am here."

I know. But does he know?

"He knows."

Zeke knelt and soon Mahir, Danley, and Alexis did too.

"I'm not gittin' on my knees," Willard said, rising and pacing.

"You don't have to," Zeke said. "God won't force His message on you."

"Where's that Mexican with my guns?"

"I can have him meet us in the garage, if you want to go. Is that what you want?"

Willard was in the kitchen now, panting. "I don't know what I want." He sat heavily. "Go ahead. What's He wanna tell me?"

"Okay, listen. God says He's going to raise a Branch of righteousness, a King who will reign and prosper and bring judgment and righteousness on the earth."

"That's fer me? I don't even know what that means."

"He says that King will be called The Lord Our Righteousness. That means the Branch of Righteousness is Jesus. The Bible says that people who believe in Jesus, like your Aunt Myrtle, become new, like they've been re-created. Old things pass away and everything about them starts fresh."

"Man, it's too late for me to start fresh—"

"God told me to tell the one who believes he is unworthy, the one who believes he is beyond the reach of His love, that he does not have to be righteous or worthy because God made Jesus become that for all of us who believe in Him. The Bible calls it a mystery, and it may be hard to understand, but get this—Jesus, who was perfect and didn't sin, *became* sin for us when He died on the cross in our place for our sins. He became sin for us, took our punishment, and became our righteousness.

"Willard, I know, we all know, what you mean when you say you're too far gone, you're not worthy, you're not good enough, you've done too much, it's too late. That's true of all of us. None of us is good enough for God. That's why we need Jesus to become our righteousness. That's what God wanted me to tell you."

The silence hung for several moments until Alex began humming, then they all sang:

Lord, I need You, oh, I need You
Every hour I need You

Willard's voice was so soft Zeke had to strain to hear him. "God knows ever'thing, right?"

"Right."

"Hard to b'lieve He knows all I done an' can do that."

"You want to know what else He says?"

"'Kay."

"He says, 'Your sins and iniquities I will remember no more.'"

"But all I've done, man. That's a lot to ferget."

"'I will be merciful, and your sins I will remember no more.'"

"I learnt the Ten Commandments. I can't 'member 'em all, but I bet I broke all of 'em and more times than—"

"'I am He who blots out your transgressions, and I will not remember your sins. Your sins and transgressions I will remember no more.'"

Willard began to weep. "Too many, too many . . ."

"'Though your sins are like scarlet, they shall be as white as snow.'"

He was sobbing now, and Zeke went to him and put an arm around his shoulder. "'Though they are red like crimson, they shall be as wool.'"

Willard fell to his face on the floor. "Oh, God, I wanna be forgiven! I wanna be clean!"

"'I have blotted out your sins like a thick cloud.'"

Willard struggled to his knees and wiped his face on his sleeve. "Man, oh, man," he said. "I feel like He done it!"

"God keeps His promises," Zeke said.

"So am I like a b'liever, like one o' y'all?"

"You tell us," Bob said, as they returned to their chairs. "Jesus came so we could have abundant life, but our sin separates us from Him. And the wages of sin is death. So where does that leave us?"

"Dead, 'cept God fergive me!"

"So that's good news."

"Sure feels like it!"

"So are you a believer like we are?"

"I think I am!"

"What do you believe?"

"Wait. Don't tell me. I b'lieve Jesus died for my sins so God fergive me."

"Did you deserve that?"

"Not on yer life!"

"The Bible says if you confess with your mouth that Jesus is the Lord and believe in your heart that God raised Him from the dead, you will be saved."

"Then I b'lieve I'm saved."

"So do I," Bob said.

"I got a lot to learn."

"You do," Zeke said.

"Am I still invited to lunch? 'Cause I'm starvin'."

"Me too," Alexis said.

They headed toward the Commons. "Do I still hafta call ya Mrs. Thorppe?"

"No, sir. I'm your sister now. You can call me Alexis."

"And I kin quit worryin' 'bout you puttin' one 'tween m' eyes?"

"If you behave yourself."

32

THE PLAN

HAVING FEARED WATDOC and the Hydro Mongers for years, the others at lunch were wary. Bob and Danley were absent, tending to their wives in the Gill quarters and the infirmary respectively. But Alexis had fetched the children, and by the time Zeke had told everyone what had just happened with Willard and they began to get to know him, Elaine suggested that Cristelle and Jennie would also probably like to meet him.

"I don't wanna push nothin'," Willard said, "but I'd like to meet them too. I'm gonna need all the friends I kin git. An' I 'specially need the one lady's fergiveness."

"Cristelle Muscadin," Elaine said. "What will you do now, Willard?"

"Don't know, 'cept I gotta git outta the water bid'ness, and I owe it to my guys to tell 'em. That's nothin' but a rip-off. I don't know how I'll make a livin', but it won't be doin' that. Maybe Zeke'll find somethin' I kin do fer him, but he don't owe me."

"You can't see Mrs. Gill for a while," Benita said, "'cause she gonna be sleepin'. But maybe you can meet Cristelle."

"Make it fast," Raoul said. "We gotta tell Zeke what we heard on the news."

"What's up, Raoul?" Zeke said.

"You're not gonna believe it, man. You're famous."

"Me?"

"I'm tellin' you, man. You and Doc? They're comin' for you. No way you want to go anywhere tonight. Huh-uh."

Zeke left the table and signaled Raoul to follow him to a corner. "This had better be major, because I'm going to that burial service, and I know who I want there with me."

"Not me, I hope."

"Actually no."

"Good."

"You scared?"

"Not usually, you know that. But tonight I would be, and I'd be scared of you or anybody else goin'."

"What in the world, man?"

"I'm tellin' you, I heard your name and Doc's name on the news and I'm not messin' around."

"All right, I'm going to see about taking Willard in to meet Cristelle. You round up Bob, Katashi, and Doc and tell 'em we're meeting with you and Benita in a few minutes in my quarters. Bob might need you to find someone to stay with Jennie."

"Those guys would be goin' with you?"

"And probably Willard."

"You changin' your rules, Zeke?"

"You mean Doc and me being together on an op?"

"Yeah. 'Cause this one is really gonna be dangerous."

"Still praying about it."

Zeke sent Benita to ask Danley if Cristelle was up to seeing Willard. Mahir asked if he could go too. Zeke turned to Doc. "What do you think?"

"Cristelle should be okay as long as you're in there to keep the peace. That *is* a lot of people." He counted on his fingers. "You, Mahir, Danley, Cristelle, Willard. I don't need to be there. Neither does Benita."

Zeke told Doc about the meeting in his quarters afterward in anticipation of the burial service. "And yes, I'm planning on violating protocol. You all right with it if I decide to bring you along tonight?"

"Hey, you're talking to the new Adam. Just here to serve, and you know I mean that. But you might have to answer to my bride."

"Got it. See you in a few."

The meeting in the infirmary was almost as thrilling as the one in Zeke's quarters had been. Willard was emotional just meeting Cristelle. "Last time I saw you, I thought I'd killed you," he said. "Sorry jes' doesn't seem enough, but I am, an' I mean it."

"I know," she said. "Danley told me what's happened to you, and I want you to know we've forgiven you. Haven't we, Danley?"

"We have. And we forgive you too, Mahir. Both of us."

Mahir looked to Danley as if to see if it were true. Danley nodded. "I'm not gonna pretend it's easy, but we either believe this stuff or we don't."

"Willard and I have a meeting to get to before he leaves," Zeke said. "Can I trust you three together?"

"Mahir's why we're here," Cristelle said. "We need to get to know him again."

"We all do, Mahir," Zeke said, pulling him into the hall. He whispered, "I'll be telling the whole team this before the end of the day. The elders are going to serve as your parole board for six months. You'll report to us. You won't be armed during that time, you won't go outside alone, and you won't leave the compound area. We'll monitor all your assignments, which will be drastically altered from what you're used to."

"I'm just grateful to still be here, Zeke."

"You realize if you were anywhere but California, you'd be behind bars."

"I do."

"We'll see how it goes."

When Zeke and Willard got back to the Thorppes' quarters, Alexis had already let in Bob, Katashi, Doc, and the Gutierrezes. "Gabi's with Jennie," she told him. "Sasha's with the kids. Elaine's on watch. I want to sit in on this if you're still planning on going tonight."

"In case you have to put a forty-caliber bullet right between my—"

"Stop it."

"You were great, Lexi."

"I almost wet myself."

"So did I."

He had everyone sit at the table in the kitchen. "Raoul and Benita have been monitoring the TV news audio feeds to see if anything's been said about the military buildup in California."

"And they've all been talkin' about it," Benita said. "The news changes and gets more *loco* all the time."

"I can hardly wait," Zeke said.

"We started listenin' right after Willard got here," Raoul said. "Man, it's the most craziest, messed-up story you ever heard. They got it all wrong, mixin' a little of this with a lot of that, and makin' up somethin' that's supposed to be bigger than Jonestown and Waco and Ruby Ridge put together. And you're like the dictator of this cult, and—"

"*I* am?" Zeke said.

"Yeah, and Doc is the mad doctor, killin' the members and committin' mass genocide on the Indian tribes."

"They're mentioning us by name?" Doc said.

"Not only that," Benita said, "they're interviewin' people who know you, like the doctor that runs that medical group you belonged to. He was sayin' they always knew you were involved in something strange and they had to part ways with you."

"What?"

"And Pastor Bob," Raoul said, "your son-in-law was on there sayin' he knew years ago that you would murder your wife. And Zeke, an Indian Affairs agent said you escaped from custody with the help of your vast network of coconspirators. But a member of the Shadow Wolves tracked you down and knows you head up—what did he call it, Benita?"

"A warren."

"Yeah, a warren of underground bunkers full of hundreds of armed combatants and, what was it? Munitions dumps."

"What are Shadow Wolves?" Alexis said.

"A really small contingent of highly specialized Native American trackers who cooperate with the government," Bob said. "The only hole in that theory is that they don't come from the tribes we work with or live anywhere near us. Makes for a good story, though. I could see Kineks wanting to be part of that, but there's only about fifteen of them representing a whole bunch of tribes, just none of them hers."

"Where do they come up with all this stuff?" Zeke said. "What possible intelligence could they be relying on to concoct all that? They fly choppers directly over our only location and roll a tank right over the top of us and don't know where we are or that this is the *only* place we are?"

"It has to be President Scott," Bob said. "The election's coming up, he needs something dramatic to get reelected. A noisy raid that heads off a 9/11 or a Paris shooting before it begins makes him a hero—as good as being a wartime president. Government agencies piece together bits of unrelated information and build a huge story they start believing themselves."

"It's just ludicrous," Zeke said. "Makes me almost wish we *were* a threat to the US government. We're so small-time, it's laughable! Aren't they gonna look like fools when it turns out we're just thirteen schlumps and three kids who live in a cave and act as a sort of poor man's Salvation Army? I mean, we help poor people and tell 'em about Jesus."

"That's the problem, Zeke," Bob said. "If they paint this thing to the public like we're some dire threat that Derrick Scott must stop at all costs, the last thing he wants is for us to turn out to be paper tigers. Even if all he's authorized so far is six or eight helicopters, a dozen tanks, and a couple of personnel transport trucks—and you know he's probably mobilized exponentially more than that—they're well into a seven-figure investment already."

"Oh, yeah," Raoul said, "they've even got a name for it: Operation Dry Bones."

"Really?" Zeke said. "They're going Old Testament on us? One of the networks, or—"

"They're all calling it that," Benita said, "so it musta come from Washington, eh?"

"Sure seems like a stretch, but whatever captures the public's imagination, I guess."

"My point," Bob said, "is that what might seem the best course for us would be the biggest embarrassment for the president."

"You mean immediately going public with the naked truth?" Zeke said.

"Sure. We've broken no laws; we've only tried to help people. We've given up normal lives, willingly sacrificed everything. There are only this many of us, no network, no warren; we're basically Christian missionaries, social workers. We don't force our beliefs on anyone. We have a few converts, we have a few detractors. We have weapons for hunting and self-protection but we've never fired at anyone. The respected tribal leader of the Nuwuwu and his successor son will testify that Doc has never met, let alone treated, the woman they're burying tonight—that his heavy medications and embalming fluids are for one of our own, end of story."

"Right," Zeke said. "You shall know the truth and the truth shall set you free."

"But in this case," Bob said, "that has a huge downside. It makes the government, particularly the sitting president, look like a buffoon."

"Truth hurts," Doc said.

"It could hurt us," Bob said. "You can see why the administration might stop at nothing to keep the truth from being revealed. If the press and the public were to find out how much time and effort went into such a meaningless operation—even if Scott could convince them he had been led to believe we were a real threat—he'd never survive the outcry. It would be considered just another politically manufactured military offensive for the sake of a president's image."

"So he needs us to be the evil menace he claims we are," Zeke said.

"We've got no one to blame but ourselves," Doc said. "I've got to take my share for those reckless prescriptions."

"I smarted off to a federal agent," Zeke said, "then showed him my ID, then spouted prophecies and raced off in the night. I sure fit the profile."

"I know I wasn't part o' yer team, but I tol' you I had a guy on the take. I was playin' the big shot and tol' him you had a terrorist in the camp."

"Well, there you go," Doc said. "And with the Nuwuwu tribal leader's daughter-in-law conspiring against us, you just know the feds will be lying in wait for us tonight."

"You can't go," Alexis said.

Everyone nodded. Except Zeke. "I'm not so sure."

"Under what possible circumstance would it make sense?" Katashi said. Zeke chuckled.

"I find nothing funny about this," Alexis said.

"Well, I don't either, really," Zeke said. "But what *has* made sense this week? I'm certainly not going to decide based on whether it makes sense. It's solely about what I believe God wants. Anyone who does not share that peace will not be required to go."

"How are you going to decide?" Bob said.

"I'm going to pray. And within two hours of sundown, I'll decide. If we go, I'd like it to be you, Bob, along with Katashi and Doc and me. Willard, you don't report to me, but I would expect to meet you there."

"I'm goin' whether y'all go or not."

"Why's that?"

"Well, b'fore it was 'cause I knew they didn't want me and I was bein' cantankerous. But now it's 'cause o' what you said was gonna happen at that service. And I wanna tell 'em 'bout what happened to me. Maybe they'll be nicer to me now if at least some of 'em and me b'lieve the same. Plus, I gotta find out if all them tanks and choppers got Special Forces in 'em and what they're up to."

"You'd better get going. Raoul, give him his weapons at the door. What're you going to do for wheels, Willard, assuming you're giving up the truck?"

"I got a little money. Maybe buy me a bike or somethin'. I'll walk if I hafta. But I'll git there. And somehow I still got to get word to Aunt Myrt. Ain't that gonna be a time!"

The Gutierrezes and Willard rose and Bob said, "Zeke, we ought to pray for our new brother before he leaves. Zeke?"

"Z," Alexis said, "Bob's talking to you."

"Sorry. Give me a minute. Willard, sit down a minute, will you? Raoul and Benita, you can go. Thanks, by the way. Good work."

Raoul said, "I still got his guns—"

"Yeah, hang on to those for now. Check on Elaine, see how things are going outside."

When they were gone, Zeke sat staring as the others waited. Willard's mention of a bike and of his aunt had triggered something he was sure was of God, and Zeke was determined to let it come together in his mind.

"Sorry, everybody," he said.

"We trust you, Zeke," Bob said. "Take your time."

"Lexi, get me pen and paper. Please."

When she brought it she asked if he was okay. He nodded.

"Willard, what's your aunt's last name?"

"Geer."

"Remember her address?"

He recited her box number and county road in Pigeon Forge, but he couldn't remember the zip.

"Phone number?"

"I'd only be guessin', but it's listed."

"The name of the BIA agent on the take."

"Clarence Cianci, but I don't know how to spell it."

"Probably just like it sounds."

"Where you going with this?" Doc said.

Zeke sat back. "Tell you in a second. Willard, you disconnected the battery on Agents Fritz and Cianci's car the other night and then led them the wrong direction when they tried to find me. How'd you talk your way out of that?"

"I tol' 'em some kids in the tribe had done that to my truck battery once too, an' I was surprised they even know how since none of 'em had cars. Then I tol' 'em you musta got a ride er somethin' 'cause you were right around there somewhere, only I couldn't find where I'd let ya off."

"They bought it?"

"They weren't happy, but they had no choice."

"You think they still trust you?"

"Cianci does. I never miss a payment, and he looks the other way."

"This all hinges on how sure you are you weren't followed here."

"I wasn't. Yer people'd know by now, wouldn't they?"

"Let us all in on this, Zeke," Bob said.

"That's what I was going to say," Doc said. "Enough mystery."

"It's still coming together," Zeke said, "and I'm going to need a lot of help this afternoon. But President Scott needs me to be the crazy leader of a huge armed cult that's a threat to the US and indigenous California tribes, right?"

Everyone nodded.

"And we believe God has called me to speak for Him to a huge audience."

No one nodded, but it was plain they were listening.

"Through Willard, I have access to a federal agent who sounds like the type who'd love to be a hero. I'm guessing Clarence Cianci would enjoy being the guy who could relay messages between me and whoever has been assigned to apprehend me tonight.

"It appears the president wants a very public success. But imagine how many emotional points he can score with the masses if in the process he honors the sacred grounds of the tribe, the burial service of a 101-year-old Native American, the wishes of her son, the tribal leader, and the public even gets to hear the rants of the crazy cult leader before he and his adherents are forced to surrender without a shot."

"And this all came to you in the last few moments?" Bob said.

"I can't claim it as my own."

"How do you intend to pull this off?" Katashi said.

"By working up through the chain of command. Willard will connect me with Clarence. Clarence will connect me with the commander in charge of Operation Dry Bones. The commander will connect me with the White House. And before the five of us show up at the burial service tonight, the loony leader of the California terrorist cult threatening the safety of North America will negotiate with the president of the United States."

"You *are* a crazy man," Alexis said.

"Aren't I?"

"You don't actually expect to speak with the president, do you?" Doc said.

"No. But with someone with the authority to speak for him."

"And what about the US policy that forbids negotiating with terrorists?"

"He can save face on that too. All he need do is insist on honoring the revered tribal leader, octogenarian Kaga. In recognition of his willingness to allow troops on his sacred land, the president will ask that a brief portion of the ceremony for his mother be broadcast live. What an altruistic thing for a president to do. I will be required to do nothing to stand in the way of that caveat. The president will get the credit for showing the ultimate respect and in some small way healing relations between the government and Native Americans.

"And with the pool network feed under presidential order not to be delayed or interrupted, I will, at Kaga's request, share the verse that was found clutched in his mother's hand at her death, as well as whatever else God gives me to say."

"To the nation," Bob said.

"And probably the world," Doc said.

33

THE CALL

ZEKE REALIZED HOW INEPT the planning had been on the part of the government when it became obvious that no traffic, military or otherwise, had been within sight of the compound since Willard had arrived. Still, in the interest of caution, he planned an elaborate scheme to put into effect the negotiations he hoped to complete well in advance of the burial service that night. A lot would have to happen in a very short time.

Zeke released Doc to check on Cristelle, and Bob to be with Jennie. Alexis went to spell Benita so she could teach the kids.

"Katashi, Willard and I need your mind on this."

"I'm not sure you wanna know what I think, Zeke. Truthfully, it's sounding nuttier by the minute."

"But doing nothing is a choice too," Zeke said. "I'd rather be proactive. We sit here and wait for them to come to us, they'll find us. We've got to act while they think we're dangerous. If they had any idea what they were really dealing with, do you think they'd have a tenth of the personnel or equipment they've sent?"

"I suppose not, but—"

"Of course they wouldn't. Now I need to communicate with Kaga. By now, just with my name and address, they have enough on me to know who I am, what I look like, everything. I don't dare leave here without guaranteed protection. And I need a means of communication beyond these toy walkie-talkies. You know the military has something I can use. Let's find a way to get our hands on it."

"I know I sound like a clod kicker," Willard said, "but I kin git this done. Git me back to my truck, give me a ride er somethin' so I'm not exposed out there too long. Then I'll go straight to the Injuns, 'cause Clarence's got to be there. You know he's the reason the cavalry showed up, 'cause o' somethin' I said about yer terrorist. I kin git him aside and do what you said 'bout makin' him a real hero. I'll make him the main man, the guy who kin deliver you, but what's he got to give you?"

"I need a satellite phone, some way to communicate with whoever's in charge of the military there. But I also need to talk to Kaga and know it's private."

"I don't see how you're going to be able to do that, Zeke," Katashi said. "You can't get to him, and Willard can't bring him to you, and you can't meet somewhere neutral without being followed. You can't talk, even if they outfit you both with sat phones, because those are easily monitored. What do you want with Kaga, anyway? You'll see him tonight if you're still determined to go."

"Oh, I'm going, especially if all this works out. But what I need him to do is to tell the military or even the White House, if I can get that far, his demands."

"His demands?" Katashi said. "You sure he wants any part of this?"

"He will! All I need is for him to insist that the service not be violated."

"Hey, Zeke," Willard said, "jes' tell me what you want him to say, and I'll tell 'im."

Zeke had to think about that.

"C'mon, man. I done caused ya 'nough grief over the years. Lemme help ya now."

"You'll remember if I tell you exactly what I need him to say?"

"Can I remember? I kept accounts in my head for a week and never fergot a nickel. Give a bid'nessman some credit."

"Tell me this," Katashi said. "If you can talk some military leader into a satellite telephone for Zeke, how're you gonna get it to him and be sure you're not followed?"

"Well, I guess I can't guarantee nothin', but you borrow me a bike and I'll do some kinda ridin' you or nobody ain't never seen b'fore. If they can track and keep up with me, y'all oughta just surrender'n' and tip yer hats to 'em."

"All right," Zeke said, "you need me to write out what you need to say to Clarence and to Kaga so you can memorize it?"

Willard laughed. "Do I look like somebody what can read? Jes' tell me and I'll have it. Then gimme my guns and I'm outta here."

Zeke leaned forward and gestured so both Katashi and Willard pulled in close too. "As a new believer, you need to know how this works. I feel like God is in this and wants me to do it. But Katashi is on the elder board with me, and I need his input to confirm that. If I'm right, God will give him peace about the decision too. If He doesn't, I have to wait. So before I just forge ahead in the heat of the moment because it sounds exciting, I'm going to ask Katashi to prayerfully think about it, and he knows there's no pressure from me. If he doesn't feel peace and freedom about it, I'm not going to push it."

"How long y'all gon' wait?"

"I'm leaving for the service at dark. If we go without a plan, we all know what will happen. If I'm the only one at peace about going, so be it."

"Like I said, I'll be there."

Katashi smiled and shook his head. "You're an idiot, Zeke."

"You're not the first who's told me that, and you won't be the last."

"And we're probably going to be arrested."

"We?"

Katashi nodded. "I've got nothing better to do tonight."

Willard looked them both full in the face. "Is that his way o' sayin' he's got peace?"

"I guess," Zeke said. "And he calls *me* an idiot. All right, so here's what I need you to say to Clarence and to Kaga . . ."

Zeke spent forty minutes listening to the TV news audio feeds about himself, Doc, and Pastor Bob, the dangerous cult, the cache of weapons, the terrorist threat, the oppression of indigenous tribes' religions, and the rumors of Native American genocide. Then he strolled the perimeter of the compound, scanning the horizon and the skies for any hint of foot, vehicular, or air traffic while praying that God would calm him and keep him focused on what He wanted Zeke to say, if indeed this was the audience the Lord had in mind.

About half an hour later a dot appeared on the horizon to the southwest, so Zeke moved quickly to the decline and descended till only his eyes cleared the ground. The high-pitched whine of the dirt bike soon reached him and the wide-arcing swerves told him it was Willard. He slipped inside the utility door to see Alexis waiting by the garage door button. He gave her a nod and she pushed it. Willard flew in and skidded to stop.

As he leapt off the bike, he pulled from his belt a phone and held it aloft. They followed Alexis down the corridor to the Thorppes' quarters. "Bob, Doc, and Katashi are waiting," she said. "Everybody else is in the Commons, praying. They're expecting dinner with you all before you leave. Jennie wants to meet Willard."

"Sounds good," Zeke said, noticing she looked near tears. He stopped outside their door and pulled her close. "You all right?"

She pressed her lips together and nodded. "This is what we signed up for, isn't it?" she said.

When the three of them entered and sat and the others saw the satellite phone, Doc clapped. "Let's hear it from the top. What happened?"

Willard set the phone in the middle of the table. It was encased in black leather with a solid rubberized antenna about six inches long. "This here's the power," he said, pointing to a button. "And this here's a speed dial that goes to—"

"Can't he start at the beginning, Zeke?" Doc said. "I'm not trying to be diffic—"

"Right," Zeke said. "Walk us through it."

"Well, I git there, and it's like they think I'm stupid er somethin', like I can't see the soldiers in the trees 'cause they're wearing camo. They got binocs pointed at me an' stuff, and I figger they got their sights on me too, ya know, so I don't worry much about field glasses. The Injun kids are playin' like nothin's goin' on, and the only car there is the agents'. They're hangin' around in their suits like it's gonna be a picnic and like I'm s'posed to think there's nothin' goin' on 'cause no other cars, right?

"So the little girl, that real friendly, smilin' one—"

"Zaltana," Alexis said.

"That's the one. She comes runnin', hollerin' somethin' about am I there for the Cryin' Service what ain't gonna start till after dark and what-not an' her ma comes out and yells at her tellin' her 'No, he is not.' So I go up to Fritz and Cianci and I say, 'So I'm not welcome, but are all the GIs invited?' and they're like, 'What? What're you talkin' about, dude?' and I'm like, 'Oh, yeah, sorry, I fergot I was blind and stupid. I don't listen to the news!'"

"Good one, Willard," Katashi said.

"So then the best thing that coulda happened happens," Willard said. "Clarence, my guy, tells Fritz, he says, 'Let me handle this,' and he pulls me aside and we start walkin' between the huts! How cool is this? He tells me, he says, 'WatDoc, you better make yourself scarce when this thing goes down tonight if you know what's good for you.'

"So I tell him I happen to know that unless he plays his cards right and does somethin' smart, the whole thing's gonna blow up in his face and he's gonna look stupid. 'Course he says what do I mean so I tell him, 'What I mean is I finally found Ezekiel Thorppe after losin' you the other night and you guys listen to the news too and unless either the coast is clear or certain promises are made, Thorppe's not comin'.'

"I thought, *He's gonna blow a gasket*. He turns white an' tells me that can't be, that Kaga invited you and you gotta come an' his repatation's on the line, the whole bit. I say too bad, there's still a way he kin be a hero but the way it stands it ain't gon' happen, and I start walkin' away."

"You're good," Katashi said.

"I know I am. I mean, I'm not braggin', I'm jes' havin' fun. But he says, 'How do we fix this, how do we make it work?' an' I say, 'My man's gotta talk to whoever's in charge.' Well, he says that's impossible so I say, 'Fine, he ain't comin',' an' we go back and forth like that and finally I say, 'If you don't send me back with a phone and don't follow me, you kin just keep lookin' for these people.' He asks me, he says, 'Hey, how many of 'em are there?' an' I say, real slow like, 'Nobody has any idea.' I wasn't lyin', 'cause I didn't count, and far as I know, nobody else knows, do they?"

"They don't," Zeke said. "Good answer."

"So anyways, he says he'll talk to somebody, and I go find Kaga. His daughter-in-law is on my tail, waggin' her finger at me and tellin' me to remember she said I wasn't welcome tonight and all that, and I told her 'I know, I won't ferget, but I need to talk to the chief.' 'Course I know that bugs her and she tells me, 'He's not the chief, he's tribal leader and he's in mournin',' but still she shows me where he is.

"I get there and he waves her off and I tell him everything you tol' me to."

"Do you know if he told anyone?"

"He did! He followed me out and when Clarence got back with that phone, Kaga told him. He said, 'Nothing stops the ceremony. Mr. Zeke and his friends are my guests, and whoever I choose to speak will speak. No one is to dishonor my mother by interrupting.'

"But then the best thing ever happened! Kineks comes marchin' over and tells him, 'Remember, you said this man was not to come tonight.' And he says, 'I remember. But I have changed my mind. He may come.' And she says, 'No!' And he says, 'As long as I am tribal leader, you do not tell me "no"!' Oh, she was mad! And I was happy!"

"Good job, Willard!"

"I thought so. I tol' you I could remember."

"You remembered everything, man," Zeke said. "So this phone direct-dials to—"

"The army guy, I guess. They said you can't even try to call anybody else."

"Did you see this man, know who he is?"

"Nope. Clarence give me the phone. Said it'll connect right to the guy. He'll be waitin'."

"Any idea whether this thing will work underground?"

"I'm guessin' it will. Clarence said somethin' about usin' them things to call Washington from overseas, so . . ."

Zeke mashed the power button, a green light came on, and the unit whined as it came to life. "I'm going to ask you all to pray for me as I talk to this man, because I sense this call is going to be just as important as whatever I say tonight."

"Let's pray," Bob said, and they all knelt as Zeke pressed the speed-dial button.

After several loud chirps, a crisp, male voice said, "I'm listening."

Zeke said, "To whom am I speaking?"

"This is United States Special Forces Alpha Team Detachment Commander Brent Kendall. Is this Ezekiel Thorppe?"

"Yes, it is."

"The phone you have been issued accommodates your request to speak with me, sir."

"Commander Kendall, I understand you intend to arrest me and certain associates of mine for reasons unclear to me. As we are innocent of any actions requiring this, we would like to avoid any confrontation."

"Avoiding confrontation is advisable, Mr. Thorppe. As I said, I'm listening."

"We have not met, have we, Commander Kendall?"

"Affirmative, although I have been issued a complete dossier on you, sir."

"Meaning you know where I was born and raised and educated, where I worked, and you have a record of my moving violations."

"Up to and including your eluding arrest as recently as the early morning hours of Tuesday."

"Is it fair to say you have no idea the size of my organization or what ties I might have with any others?"

"I prefer not to reveal the extent of our intelligence, Mr. Thorppe."

"I'll take that as another affirmative."

"May I know your intentions at 1930 hours this evening, sir?"

"Four associates and I plan to attend a burial service at the Nuwuwu settlement, where you are encamped. I have been asked to bring remarks on behalf of the tribal leader."

"Will you or your associates be armed, Mr. Thorppe?"

"Will you or yours, Commander Kendall?"

"Not only will we be armed, Mr. Thorppe, but we will have metal-detecting equipment operable from nearly half a mile away, and our weapons have a kill range of twice that distance. You do not want to engage our personnel."

"If I can be guaranteed that we will not in any way be—"

"Before you proceed, Mr. Thorppe, I must inform you that you are considered by the United States government an armed and dangerous enemy combatant, and thus a party with whom I am forbidden to negotiate."

"Allow me then to stipulate that if I can be assured that neither I nor my associates will be in any way confronted, harassed, or detained in advance of or during the service, we will arrive unarmed and will accede to publicly and peaceably surrendering to you and returning the phone you provided."

"That sounds reasonable."

"That sounds like a negotiation, Commander."

"I submit that is merely an agreement."

"I will, however, need a commitment from the White House," Zeke said.

"I'm sorry?"

"Do you really need that repeated?"

"No, but I assume you know that it is out of the question."

"Ask him if he belongs to Me."

If he belongs to You, Lord?

"You know the answer."

"Excuse me, Commander, but are you a man of faith?"

Pause.

"Mr. Thorppe, we may have a difference of opinion on what constitutes faith. I understand that you lead a group—"

"I apologize for interrupting, Commander, but you may be surprised at my definition of faith. It's not a trick question. Are you a follower of Christ?"

"It happens that I am, but I do not discuss my personal life in the course of military busi—"

"I understand. I just wanted to assure myself that we have something in common. I'm aware that I would not have access to President Scott. Despite whatever intelligence you have access to, I'm not a lunatic. But surely someone at a national security level can be given access to this line and assure me that if my associates and I show up at this sacred ceremony unarmed and in peace, willing to surrender at the end of it, we will be treated fairly and with respect and assured due process. When I receive a call from the White House with that assurance, we will arrive on that basis. Otherwise, your search for us will incur much more time and personnel and expense, and surely no one wants that. Until then, my brother in Christ, good-bye."

34

THE ARRIVAL

ZEKE, AND LIKELY everyone else in the room, thought the commander had called his bluff when twenty-five minutes passed and the phone sat silent. One by one they rose and sat with him at the table.

"Y'all really not goin' if ya don't hear from nobody?" Willard said.

"I'm going," Zeke said. "I can't ask anyone else to go."

"I'll take ya."

"Thanks. You guys wait for me in the Commons. Alexis and I will see you at dinner."

When they were gone, Alexis said, "Are you sure you should go?"

He nodded. "I won't take anyone else. They'll find they've got nothing on me, and when they come here they're going to be very disappointed at the extent of our massive terrorist organization."

"But are Bob and Doc right? Won't they have to invent a story to make you—and us—look horrible so the president looks heroic?"

"If that's the price of my getting a chance to say whatever it is God wants me to say—"

The sat phone chirped and they stared at each other.

"This is Ezekiel Thorppe."

"Will you hold for a call from the White House?"

"Yes, ma'am."

"One moment please."

"Mr. Thorppe?"

"Yes."

"My name is Lauren Pugh. I'm assistant to the president for National Security Affairs. It's my understanding that you and four associates are willing to attend the ceremonial burial service at the Nuwuwu settlement tonight unarmed and then you will surrender to Special Forces Detachment Commander Brent Kendall immediately following, provided you are allowed to speak unimpeded at the ceremony per the request of tribal leader Kaga."

"That is exactly right."

"I have been authorized by President Scott to approve that."

"Really?"

"Yes, sir. Will there be anything else?"

"Is he there, in the room?"

She chuckled. "You know I would not be at liberty to confirm that even if he were, sir. But no, he is not."

"There is one more thing I could use help with."

"There is?"

"Since you asked."

"I was just being polite, sir."

"I know, but I'll pay for it, and it might reflect well on the president."

She sighed. "I can't promise, but I'm curious now."

He told her of hoping to reunite Willard with his long-lost aunt, and he gave her Myrtle Geer's address. There was a long pause.

"Our travel office is the best in the world, but you know there are no commercial airports still operating in California."

"You flew a lot of military personnel in here today."

"You wouldn't want to pay for a flight like that."

"I'm willing."

"But you're not even sure she's still living or if she has an operable phone?"

"I'm not. But Ms. Pugh, if you find her and she wants to know what it's all about, just say Willard and John 3:16."

Another pause. "No promises, and our previous arrangement holds regardless."

"Agreed."

Alexis went to tell the others the visit was on while Zeke spent the rest of the time before dinner praying that God would give him just the right words.

The meal proved a quiet, nervous affair, where it was obvious many were worried that this night might mark the end of their ministry. "Look at it this way," Zeke said. "Maybe it will be the end of us as a secret. We'll have no more reason to hide. Everyone will know we're here and why. We might even gain support from people eager to help."

Jennie seemed intrigued with Willard. "So you're the one we have been afraid of for so long."

"That right?" he said. "Guess that was my deal. Tryin' to threaten people."

"You don't look so tough," she said, smiling. "At least not now that Jesus has got hold of you."

"Maybe I never was, huh?" he said. "Maybe it was all jes' fer show."

Before they left, Jennie asked to speak privately with Zeke. "Alexis told me what you're trying to do for this young man. It's wonderful, but how can you afford it?"

Zeke shrugged. "It's going to have to be personal funds, I know that, because I committed to this without a vote. We have some socked away, though the car and the bike things have cut into it a little. God will provide. But for all I know, Myrtle Geer's already in heaven anyway."

Jennie beckoned Zeke close and whispered. "Would you do another old lady a favor?"

"Anything for you, you know that."

"I've got a little nest egg of my own, and I want ten thousand of it to go to this."

"Oh, Jennie, no."

"What happened to anything for me? You going to deny me this blessing? I'll tell Bob so he knows when the time comes, and don't you dare stand in the way of it. Now you know if she is alive and they can get her out here by tonight, it's going to cost a lot more than that, so I don't want to hear another word about it."

Zeke was overcome. "Anything for you," he managed, embracing her.

Zeke, Katashi, Bob, and Willard rode with Doc in his new Land Rover after nightfall, and as they passed the small water tanker rig Willard had driven to the compound that morning, Zeke told him he ought to find one of his former coworkers and give him the keys. "We can talk about living arrangements," he said. "But if we do connect with your aunt, maybe you'll want to go spend a little time with her first, huh?"

"Maybe. Wouldn't that be somethin', her still bein' alive? When kin we get a letter off to her and see?"

"Maybe next week if I'm not sitting in a federal pen somewhere."

When they rolled to within site of the Nuwuwu settlement, Doc was stopped by a military vehicle, asked for identification, and they and the Rover were searched top to bottom while they waited outside. The last stretch across the plain Zeke had come to know so well was now a long, slow parade of mostly vans bearing satellite dishes on expandable poles that reached high into the night skies.

When Doc parked and they disembarked, they were soon met by the BIA agents and then by a heavily armed man in camouflage who introduced himself as Commander Kendall. Once he established which was Zeke, he pulled him aside, procured the sat phone, and said, "We've run into a snag."

"That's not what I want to hear," Zeke said. "I was assured by Ms.—"

"Sir, no one is reneging on anything. You will be allowed to speak unimpeded, but it's going to be later than any of us anticipated, and these news crews are disappointed at how long they have to wait."

"You mean they're not broadcasting the whole ceremony? That was not part of the agreem—"

"Top priority is the sanctity of the ceremony. We're to accede to the wishes of the tribal leader, and we'll do that. Kaga allowed them to set up their lighting and sound, but they can't use it until the crying portion of the ceremony is over. Were you aware of how long that was to last?"

"No, sir."

"Well, at the end of it he wants you to speak after he does. He tells me the last crying ceremony he attended was for an uncle of his, and it lasted all night."

"All night?"

"But that was when hundreds of people lived here and everyone in the tribe danced and sang what they called Salt Songs. He said something about a 142-song cycle, but don't worry, with only thirty people in this settlement, there won't be anything that extensive tonight. But during that portion he's not allowing pictures, so no broadcasting until he and you speak."

"When does he expect that to begin?"

"Close to midnight. The news people aren't happy."

"I can imagine."

"They're probably going to want to make a big deal of your arrests for their morning shows."

"We're upholding our end of the bargain," Zeke said. "So it's not going to be dramatic. You have warrants for Doc's and my arrests?"

"We have three."

"Who besides us?"

"A reverend?" He pulled a sheet from his pocket. "Robert Gill."

"What's the charge?"

"Suspicion of murdering his wife, Genevieve."

"You'll want to sit on that one, Commander. The five of us here just had dinner with Jennie Gill. She's dying of stage-four pancreatic cancer, and Dr. Xavier doesn't expect her to survive another week, but a disgruntled son-in-law saying something nasty on TV is pretty thin soup for a murder warrant—especially when the woman remains alive."

"Even if true, that doesn't change my orders. And you have to admit, you are not exactly unbiased witnesses."

"But her own physician—"

"Is being arrested in connection with the death of the woman being buried here tonight."

"Commander, do yourself a favor and talk to the dead woman's son and grandson."

"I have. Kaga and Yuma are the ones who told me about the cameras and about you speaking."

"Did you ask them whether Dr. Xavier treated Gaho?"

"Kaga's daughter-in-law made that charge."

"Do you know Dr. Xavier has never met the deceased?"

"What are you saying?"

"That it's impossible to treat a patient you haven't met, or to be guilty of malpractice on a patient you haven't treated."

"And you're telling me Kaga and his son would corroborate this."

"That's what I'm saying. Even I met the woman only once, and I've been working with these people for years."

"Then why does Kaga want you to speak at her service?"

"That's a good question in light of the warrant for my arrest. What's that about again?"

"Intolerance of the religious beliefs of indigenous Americans, intimidation of Native Americans, suspicion of sympathy for illegal aliens, suspicion of harboring radicalized terrorists."

"So the complaints about the Native Americans have come from someone whose own husband and father clearly disagree with her. The other charges will be so easily disproved that I will likely not be inconvenienced more than half a day. And by the end of my remarks tonight, anyone watching the news will discover how much it cost for the government to investigate the activities of what amounts to a tiny parachurch organization doing outreach in an impoverished area in the middle of nowhere."

35

THE PROCLAMATION

WHEN THE SINGING, dancing, lamenting, and crying finally ended and all the stories had been told about the tiny ancient body that lay wrapped tightly near a freshly dug grave, tribal leader Kaga solemnly stepped before the rest of the Nuwuwu.

It was after eleven thirty on yet another sweltering, cloudless night, and sitting in the dust before him were his son, Yuma, his scowling daughter-in-law, Kineks, and in her lap, their granddaughter—his great-granddaughter—the soundly sleeping Zaltana. Behind them sat the rest of the tribe, weary from all the reveling in the life of the aged matriarch.

Kaga nodded to Commander Kendall, who signaled to the news pool director that the lights, cameras, and sound equipment could be ignited, and the dusty patch behind the row of shabby huts blazed brighter than the noonday sun, making Kaga briefly shield his eyes.

Clearly he knew nothing of speaking into microphones, so an audio assistant darted in and out, peeking for cues from a director while adjusting and pointing and rearranging them for maximum pickup. Yet Zeke, who stood behind Kaga with Bob, Katashi, and Doc in a row and Willard looking ill at ease off to one side, thought the old leader seemed a natural with all the attention—almost as if he somehow knew millions of people might see and hear this. But how could he?

"I allowed that ceremony in honor of the traditions of my people," he said, "because many of them believe that these rituals help my mother's spirit travel from one sacred place to the next along what is called the Salt Song Trail. That is why our visitors saw men on one side and women on the other, some holding gourds or rattles and others holding pictures or other items belonging to my mother and saying nice things about her, believing they are helping her spirit journey easier to the final crossing.

"I do not have a problem with this if it makes those who cared about her feel better, but I want you to know that my mother did not believe any of this. This is called the Crying Ceremony because we are intended to release all our emotions when we sing and dance, and I admit I cried when I remembered all the wonderful things about her and think about how much I will miss her.

"But my mother did not count on rituals and dances and songs to get her from one place to the next in the afterlife. She believed in the God of the Bible and in His Son, Jesus, and that He was the way to heaven. This she taught me from childhood, and it is what my wife and I taught our son, Yuma. And though I confess I strayed from this and was not as devout as my mother, I was reminded of it later by dear people who helped and befriended us. And they are here tonight.

"They honor me and they honor my mother by being here. Doc," he said, turning and waving at him, "thank you for coming. Though you never met my mother, you have helped many here and especially me. And our friend"—he pointed at Katashi—"Zeke, help me with his name."

"Katashi."

"Yes, forgive me. It is not a name that falls well from a tongue not used to English. But this man has become our friend and has helped us with many things in our little dwelling. And over there, that man, remind me of your name, son."

"You kin call me Willard!"

"Yes, Willard, he has often supplied us with water, and only recently he took my daughter-in-law, Kineks, on a much-needed journey. Thank you. And then my dear friend Bob, who shares my lack of hair and the white color of what is left. His wife is also ill, so he will soon know the pain of loss. He has told me how he decided to stay in California when so many left. Would you tell that story to our people, my friend?"

"Oh, certainly, very quickly, Kaga," Bob said, and he recounted how he felt led of God to challenge the people of his great church in Torrance to stay when California was condemned so many years before. He talked of how a few made the hard commitment and fewer still stayed with it when things grew difficult, but sixteen were left, and that he and the others there tonight represented them.

"And now," Kaga said, "I saved till last my friend Ezekiel, because I wanted him to tell you what was found in my mother's hand when she died. It was something she copied from a Paiute copy of the Bible and which I translated for him. I want him to tell you what it says in English and then anything else he feels God wants him to. When he is finished, our memorial is finished. Our men will bury my mother in private. So I thank you all now for honoring her by coming." Kaga moved to sit next to his son, and Yuma reached to help the old man down.

Zeke moved before the lights and microphones and put his hand over his eyes to assess the extent of the masses behind the Nuwuwu who sat before him. The press milled about behind them, and in the distance he made out the silhouettes of dozens of soldiers. But at the far left, next to one of the huts and standing regally next to an officer was a woman out of place, rail-thin in a long, straight dress. She clutched a white purse in one hand and had her other over her chest.

"Kaga," Zeke began, "we are here in tribute to the memory of your mother, but it's hard for me to express the depth of our gratitude for the honor you have bestowed on us by inviting us to such a sacred occasion. We'll never forget the privilege of having been here tonight. Thank you.

"It has come to my attention that this event, not by your own choosing, has taken on an identity all its own and has even been given a name—Operation Dry Bones. Perhaps whoever came up with that thought it was a creative extrapolation from the Old Testament book that shares my name. I can only hope it proves as prophetic as the passage it refers to, because God promises His Word will never return void.

"That passage tells of the prophet Ezekiel being set in the midst of a valley full of dry bones, which couldn't have been terribly different from where we find ourselves tonight. And God asks the prophet, 'Can these bones live?' He answers, 'O Lord God, You know.' God tells him to prophesy to the bones to hear the word of the Lord and live, adding, 'Then you shall know that I am the Lord.'

"So the prophet obeys and the bones come alive and become a great army. I sense an obvious question, don't you? Are we dry bones? Can we hear the word of the Lord and live and become a great army?

"I want to be brief, but I do want to fulfill Kaga's request to quote the passage that his mother painstakingly copied from her Bible, which was found folded on a sheet and clutched in her palm upon her death. Oh, to be found clutching the very words of God when we are ushered into His presence!

"The text that meant so much to her is the most famous verse in the Bible, John 3:16, and it reads like this: For God so loved the world that He gave His only begotten Son, that whoever believes in Him should not perish but have everlasting life.

"That was the message of Gaho's life. For more than one hundred years she walked this earth, and I believe she copied those words and held tightly to them knowing she was about to go and wanting them to be her parting message to you. What will you do with Gaho's last words?

"Yes, I was one of the few who answered Pastor Bob's challenge so long ago when he sent out the call, not 'Who will go?' but rather, 'Who will stay?' My wife and I felt called to stay right here in California to share the good news of Jesus with others who either chose to stay or had no choice but to stay. We've seen people come to faith, many after years of searching, others after years of running from God.

"We have with us tonight one who just found the Lord today as an answer to more than a decade's worth of prayers on his behalf on the part of his dear aunt, who I dare say had to wonder what ever became of him."

Zeke turned to Willard. "Isn't that right? She must have prayed and prayed, not even knowing if you were still alive, wondering if her miracle would ever come."

Willard nodded, looked wholly embarrassed.

"Wouldn't you love to let her know?"

"I would. I surely would."

"Wouldn't it be something if she were here tonight, right here, right now?"

"What?"

And here came Myrtle Geer, housedress swishing, white purse swinging, church shoes kicking up dust in the tiny Nuwuwu settlement in Southern California more than 2,200 miles from Pigeon Forge, Tennessee.

Willard, mouth agape, staggered to her and grabbed her, swinging his aunt in a circle before apparently realizing that might not be appropriate just before a burial.

EPILOGUE

AUNT MYRTLE AND WILLARD were the hit of the morning TV shows, and their reunion went viral. After they spent two nights at the holdouts' compound, he spent six weeks at her home in Pigeon Forge before returning to join Zeke and the others full-time.

Zeke, Doc, and Bob were detained overnight in a mobile military lockup before Commander Kendall led a regiment on a search of the underground complex. Following his report to an inquiry board, the three were exonerated, the suspicious Arabic document identified, and Operation Dry Bones roundly vilified by the press.

Jennie Gill surprised even Doc by lingering ten more days before passing. Memorials were held in both California and Arizona, where she was buried. Bob Gill reconciled with his son-in-law and returned to the holdouts a month later.

Clarence Cianci was convicted of bribery and sentenced to federal prison.

Cristelle Muscadin's leg was spared, but she walks with a limp.

Derrick Scott lost his bid for reelection.

And Internet geeks discovered an anagram of Zeke's last name they didn't believe was coincidental.

JERRY B. JENKINS's books have sold more than seventy million copies. Twenty-one of his titles have reached the *New York Times*, *USA Today*, *Publishers Weekly*, and *Wall Street Journal* bestseller lists. The phenomenally best-selling Left Behind series inspired a movie starring Nicolas Cage. Jenkins has been featured on the cover of *Newsweek*, and his writing has appeared in *Time*, *Guideposts*, *Parade*, and dozens of other periodicals. He and his wife, Dianna, have three grown children and live in Colorado.

IF YOU ENJOYED THIS BOOK, WILL YOU CONSIDER SHARING THE MESSAGE WITH OTHERS?

Mention the book in a blog post or through Facebook, Twitter, Pinterest, or upload a picture through Instagram.

Recommend this book to those in your small group, book club, workplace, and classes.

Head over to facebook.com/jerry.b.jenkins, "LIKE" the page, and post a comment as to what you enjoyed the most.

Tweet "I recommend reading #ValleyofDryBones by @JerryBJenkins // @worthypub"

Pick up a copy for someone you know who would be challenged and encouraged by this message.

Write a book review online.

WORTHY®
PUBLISHING

Visit us at worthypublishing.com

twitter.com/worthypub

worthypub.tumblr.com

facebook.com/worthypublishing

pinterest.com/worthypub

instagram.com/worthypub

youtube.com/worthypublishing